Praise for Jason Phillip Reeser's

Lady in the Lazaretto

"The Lazaretto is more than just a place of exile, it is a state of mind. Part psychological thriller, part murder mystery, part bitter-sweet romance, the *Lady in the Lazaretto* is always science fiction at its best." — A.C. Flory, author of *Vohktah*

"The *Lady in the Lazaretto* takes readers back to the gritty moon-world that serves the space-faring universe as a quarantine station. Why do I like going there when it's so dark and unforgiving? Because I love a good mystery, I enjoy listening to two of my favorite future detectives poke at each other with classic comradely sarcasm when they aren't facing lethal dangers; and because, most of all, the Lazaretto is a unique creation. There is only one Lazaretto. Another first-class intriguing noir science fiction mystery from Jason Phillip Reeser." –S.J. Hunter, author of the *Longevity Law Enforcement* series.

Books by Jason Phillip Reeser

<u>Fiction</u>
Jury Rig

Cities of the Dead

The World that Slid Downhill

The Mistress
(Winter 2013)

<u>The Lazaretto Trilogy</u>
Book One: The Lazaretto

Book Two: Lady in the Lazaretto

Book Three: Kiss of the Lazaretto
(Spring 2014)

<u>Non-Fiction</u>
Room with Paris View

Lady in
the Lazaretto

a novel by

Jason Phillip Reeser

First Trilogy Edition, August, 2013
Copyright ©2013 by Jason Phillip Reeser
Cover Art Copyright ©2013 by Jason Phillip Reeser
First Printing August, 2013

ISBN: 978-0615796697

Rocket Fire Books
Westlake, Louisiana
rocketfirebooks.com

Acknowledgements: Writing a book can be a lonely journey. There are, however, people along the way who not only break the isolation but lend a helping hand to ensure the destination is reached. This journey would not have been possible without the keen insight and the sharp eyes of my wife Jennifer, my children Kathryn, Maxwell, and Simon, and my good friends John Z. and Paul B. Their time and attention are greatly appreciated. Their contributions have made this a better novel and a fun journey.

For John Z.
A faithful friend
in a fickle world.

"To be trusted is a greater compliment than being loved."
— George MacDonald

"Do not swear by the moon, for she changes constantly.
then your love would also change."
— William Shakespeare

"The abandoned infant's cry is rage, not fear."
— Robert Anton Wilson

The people of Earth had never given the Lazaretto system serious thought. The quarantine moon was not hidden from public view, though it did suffer from a collective ennui in society which had grown so bored with anything remotely connected to bureaucracy that all government functions were virtually ignored. Those aware of the Lazaretto took the usual, cynical view of government programs and assumed that it was either an excessive budgetary drain or inefficient and inept process worthy only of disdain and a certain macabre derision.

The inception of the Lazaretto controls had become necessary in the wake of rampant interplanetary epidemics. By the time the Lazaretto system had brought a measured control over the migration of interplanetary diseases, the great interplanetary travel age had ended. No longer did the average man seek to fulfill his wanderlust by booking a flight to the outer planets. Colonists found fewer reasons to visit the home world. Technology had stepped in where angels and tourists had feared to tread. Virtual Vacations replaced actual off-planet larks and there were even segments of the population who had rediscovered the joy of reading about far-off lands. Travel writers like Gloria Dempsey and Pete Nguyen risked the dangerous trip to the stars and wrote poetically of Phasis, Dnepr and the other exotic planets in the Euxine system. The Lazaretto came too late to save the massive travel needs of the early, heady days of space travel.

Interplanetary travel, however, was far from dead. The business of trade was far too lucrative and necessary to die from fear. Death and disease could not stop men from plying their trades in the dark recesses of the universe. The dangers only served to decrease supply and increase demand. Profits soared. The implementation of the Lazaretto built and toppled empires in a matter of months. Old bastions of finance came crashing down while enterprising young upstarts built upon their ruins.

It was this association with massive trade empires that ensured the Lazaretto's corrupt and distant reputation with the general population. And if the corrupting influences of business were not enough to keep one away, the second dominant presence in the Lazaretto was equally distasteful: the government.

The Lazaretto was a throughway for government diplomats, military leadership and personnel, and a myriad assortment of lesser members of the massive central governing institution. Although there were fewer government employees traveling through the Lazaretto than employees of the trade conglomerates, their penchant for corruption was on an equal scale.

It had been the needs of both business and government that had finally convinced the government to spend the money to establish the Lazaretto. At first, small lazarettos had been built on as many planets as possible. They were small facilities, designed for minimum traffic. There had been too many sites to build to allow for any sizable Planet Lazarettos. Before they had been built they were outdated, run down, and in dire need of upgrades. All of them were too small to handle the regular flux of travelers. It took two years of crippling logjams at the lazarettos before the central Lazaretto was given the green light.

Built in the center of the Euxine system, on the largest of Sinop's moons, the Lazaretto was a gateway. All traffic into and out of the system came through the gateway. Any traffic headed back into Earth's Solar System had to leave through the gateway. Any traffic connecting a planet to another planet within the Euxine System—Bukovina, Dnepr, Phasis, Arcobia, and Sinop—had to pass through the gateway without exception.

Once the government had issued the directive to build a central lazaretto, there was a surprising lack of conflict over where it should be based. Sinop's moon, Aegean, was an optimum choice that found nearly universal favor.

Aegean was an anomalous moon that had surprised early space explorers. Though clearly a moon of Sinop, it was found to have its own atmosphere. Moreover, nearly 98% of its surface was covered in water. Its one continent, nothing more than an island, was originally named Far Britain by its founder, British astroexplorer Sir Edward Brown. Though smaller than his homeland, Brown was astounded at how identical the weather patterns reminded him of home.

Far Britain was never settled due to the overabundance of good land available on Sinop. A gentler climate and less hostile environment made the colonists on Sinop forget all about their odd little moon. The decision to build the Lazaretto on Aegean changed all of that. Suddenly, that odd little moon was the center of attention. Despite its rainy atmosphere, it gained a population as workers descended on its wet island to build the interstellar quarantine port.

The Lazaretto was built as two separate ports: one for travelers, one for shipping. Both ports had profoundly different procedures for controlling the spread of contagions.

No human was allowed to enter the shipping port. This restriction also applied to animals, although by this time most of the planets had adopted a ban on the transshipment of livestock between planets. The entire operation was controlled and operated by machines.

As freighters arrived at the quarantine port, all crewmembers were required to disembark and transported to a ship that was leaving quarantine and destined for their planet of origin. In this way, the crew avoided quarantine.

The freighters that entered the shipping port were sprayed down with a toxic biocide that could guarantee the eradication of all known contagions. The toxin was lethal to all living beings. This toxin, once applied, remained on the freighter for twenty-four hours, after which it was deactivated with a heat wash. Nine days were set aside as a safety measure to ensure the toxin was no longer a threat. Although this method of decontamination was expensive, it had a valuable benefit: all freighters were allowed to leave quarantine after this ten day period—one-fourth the time required for humans in quarantine.

Human travelers were required to participate in a more passive quarantine system. Upon arrival at the Lazaretto, all travelers were processed and placed into one of four quadrants. Each quadrant was on a fifty-day cycle. Each quadrant was open for ten days to allow travelers to arrive. Once that quadrant shut its doors, it remained sealed for forty days. No one was allowed in or out.

The travelers who were in quarantine were not treated with any vaccinations. A careful study of the contagions known to be found on the various Euxine planets had determined that any contagion already infecting an individual would manifest itself within ten days. But travelers were forced to wait another thirty days. This was the most important precaution taken by the Lazaretto protocols to make certain that no passengers carried the Euxine Spirare.

The Euxine Spirare was an influenza strain that had once nearly wiped out one-quarter of the populations of the Euxine System and was the final factor in the decision to build the lazarettos. The Plague, so named by a fearful populace, was deadly to nearly eighty per cent of those infected with the virus. The virus had one predictable trait: it could not live beyond four weeks. IHS added two days to the four-week period and required the thirty days of quarantine.

There were no treatments used on sick travelers. IHS had recommended that treatments and vaccinations be avoided as cost-prohibitive. While shipping must be expedited, travelers could wait. The time wasted in quarantine meant nothing to IHS.

Book One

Plan

1

By the time I had heard of the Lost Platoon, everyone had heard of them. Of course, it was no surprise I was one of the last. I wasn't anybody important. I wasn't even unimportant. To those around me, I didn't exist. I was, more or less, an appliance. I had a job to do and I did it. That was all that mattered. What I thought, what I believed, who I was; these meant nothing. Not to my employer. He only cared about what I did. He only cared that I nurse his child; my sole purpose to care for the girl. And to the best of my abilities, that is what I did.

The news of the Lost Platoon had little impact on the girl's father. Kjarsta Zoltis was a hard man who had no room for empathy or compassion. What little capacity he had for such weaknesses was used up in his love for his daughter, Calla. It was our one bond, this mutual love for her, though it spawned from two widely different sources.

Zoltis loved her because she represented his name. His family. His reputation. These things were of great importance; important in ways I did not understand at first. I had judged his motives as prideful, lacking in familial tenderness. I saw myself as one who could give what he never could—love that was not bound up in my own pride. I loved her for the child that she was, not for whose child she was. I was different than her father. I wanted to make sure, as she grew, that she understood this.

Some delusions in our youth can be forgiven; others haunt us the rest of our lives.

The Lost Platoon had a great impact on me; a heartbreaking story. It wasn't the number of men involved that bothered me. Twenty-six men diagnosed with a rare respiratory infection was certainly shocking news, but in those days people were being denied exit from the Lazaretto on a daily basis. No, the real tragedy, as I saw it, was that these men had survived the fighting on Arcobia only to fall victim to one of its viruses. These were men who were expecting to go home to their loved ones; Men who had not been sure if they would live through the hellish combat of what would eventually be called the Arcobian Rebellion. Men—heroes—whom fate had sentenced to death.

But it was not empathy for these men that filled my eyes with tears. My true fears were for Calla. If fate could deal a blow to so many good men, what lay in store for this little baby in my care? How could a child raised in the middle of the Lazaretto survive? Protecting her seemed impossible. How was I to know the deck was stacked against me from the beginning?

"Della," Mr. Zoltis called to me, "come into my office."

I had just put the child to sleep and stood outside her door. His office was on the other side of the house. I could hear him calling through overhead speakers that ran throughout that great house. He knew I could hear him and did not repeat his demand.

I had no idea why he wanted me. We had little interaction during the day. We had no interaction whatsoever during the evening. He was not a social man, and the other house domestics indicated that he often retired to bed extremely early. I was curious that he had called at such a late hour.

"Come in." *He knew I was at the door, despite the fact that it was closed. He knew everything that happened in that house. The surveillance system was as necessary as the plumbing. We all knew this and never forgot that we were under constant observation.*

"Was there something you wanted, Mr. Zoltis?" *I always made an effort to be deferential, though I drew the line at obsequiousness. I was one of the few domestics who did not fear him, though I saw no reason to remind him of it.*

"Tell me about the girl. Is she well?"

"Yes, she is fine." *I understood his concern. Any parent on a normal world had similar questions. The Lazaretto, however, added a great deal of weight to such matters.* *"I've made sure she has taken her supplements. There is nothing to fear."*

He did not respond—not verbally—although it looked as if he did not believe me. I didn't like that. I knew my job. I was a good nurse. I would not allow him to question my abilities.

"Your daughter is in no particular danger, Mr. Zoltis. She is, in fact, quite healthy. Do not trouble yourself. If I may be so bold, that is what you have hired me to do. And I will take all the steps necessary to keep her safe as she grows."

"You're very confident, woman." *His tone was hard. His rebuke stung.*

"Why do you doubt me?"

"It's simple." *He stood from his desk, approaching a small table full of glass bottles.* *"I'd offer you something to drink but since you're on duty, so to speak…"*

"If you have something to say, Mr. Zoltis—"

"I'll say it." *He barked. I hated to hear him like that. He was a big man, barrel-chested and strong as a rocket booster. He could see he'd disturbed me and made a clumsy attempt to put me at ease by wagging a finger.* *"Don't go silly on me, Della. You've never been afraid of me, and there's no reason to start now. Nothing here is your fault, understand? I've gone behind your back on this. Suckered you in. I won't apologize, so don't expect me to. I needed you, and you needed a way out of that damned contract with Health Services."*

He was right about the IHS. I had been desperate to get out of my contract. I'd had no idea what I was getting into when I signed on for the Lazaretto. I'd been a foolish girl with a bright future and poor counsel. Somewhere between my desire to get into nursing and my eagerness to make a difference I became convinced that the exotic climate of the Lazaretto had been what I needed. I had no idea what Kjarsta Zoltis had actually done to break the contract for me. I only knew that work contracts with the Interplanetary Health Service were unbreakable and that Kjarsta Zoltis was one of the few men in the Lazaretto who had the power to break the unbreakable.

It had surprised me at how desperate I'd become. I still don't like to think of the lengths I had been willing to go to tap into the power of his influence.

"Sit down, Della." He picked up the drink he'd poured and drank it with one deep draught. The size of the drink and his ability to take it in without effort was alarming and I had to make an effort not to stare. "It's time you and I were perfectly honest with each other."

"I've been honest with you, Mr. Zoltis." I had been and would not allow him to think otherwise.

"I suppose you have," he laughed at me. "A damned bit more honest than I'd have liked, that's a sure bet!" He poured another drink that was as big as the first.

"You said you would never speak of that again." I stood and made a motion to leave. He waved me back to my seat.

"Oh, stop." He backed away to prove he was no threat. "I meant what I said. You're the one who started talking about your honesty. God, don't go jumping to conclusions. And don't go worrying about who's been honest and who hasn't. All I meant to say was that there needs to be a complete— whatever."

He waved his hands to fill in his loss for words and finished the gesture by downing his second drink. Some of the alcohol spilled down his chin and he made a lazy attempt to wipe it with a sleeve. Some of it glistened as it dribbled down his neck.

"What I have to say doesn't leave this house. You understand that? I'm not going to pretend like you don't have obligations to me. So I won't be gentle on that point. You owe your freedom from those government pukes to me, hey? And you pay that back by listening and holding your tongue. You hold your tongue as tightly as you hold to your virginity."

I didn't shy away from his look. He had made his point and I did not argue.

"And what is this news that I must guard?"

"Calla's sick, woman." I still remember the way he said that; a vulnerable moment that he tried to hide with a tone of impatience. "She's sick."

I'd been ready to hear an ultimatum from him, ready even to fight him off if he'd become aggressive. I hadn't been ready for such desperate news. But as soon as the words left his mouth, I hadn't needed to ask for details. Fear swept through my heart.

Sickness is a scourge that drives many parents and nurses to the edge of panic. But here in the Lazaretto, even the hint of sickness was anathema. Sickness meant exile.

I bowed my head, the news heavy on my spirit. When I looked up,

Calla's father was standing beside me with a smaller drink in his hand. He held it out and I knew he expected me to drink it. I admit quite readily that I needed it. I don't even know what kind of drink it was.

"Has she been seen by IHS?" Once the government labeled her nullus exitus *she would never get the chance to leave the despairing world of the Lazaretto.*

"She has only been seen by my private doctor. And he has already been sent away. He is well aware of the consequences of disclosure. Do not worry about him."

"You intend to conceal this?" My expression must have revealed my willingness to accept that. I was surprised at my own eagerness to do so, but he was not. I think—even knew—that he always expected me to help him. To help Calla.

"I am already concealing this, and will do so until perdition. I am told there is a chance she will live. But she will require constant care once the disease manifests itself. That's your job. You care for her and see that she comes out of this as healthy as a newborn baby. This is your obligation."

He already knew that I would comply, although I'm certain he couldn't understand that I did not do it out of obligation to him. Maybe I would have, if that had been necessary. But the truth was, I had agreed to care for Calla, and I could see that this was the only way to do it. I could not stand the thought of that little girl being trapped in the Lazaretto. I would not allow it to happen.

"I will need to see the doctor's notes. And you must supply whatever I need."

He nodded in reply, his eyes locked with mine. From that moment on, we were of one mind, co-conspirators, and I would not back out. I suspected that Kjarsta Zoltis was accustomed to breaking the law. It was what he did; it was possibly the foundation of his business. But this was new ground for me, and I knew that I had never hesitated to take a step in that direction. I told myself that I was nothing like Kjarsta Zoltis. That I was breaking the law for compassion's sake, not for my own desire and greed.

I believed myself. I had to, in order to live with myself as I cared for the child.

2

Darkness had not yet settled over the Lazaretto as Lieutenant Ed MacNally and his young partner, Menya Russell, walked across the uneven surface of a West End landfill. Shards of glass and broken sewer pipes mixed with decomposing soil to create an alien landscape that made walking both difficult and dangerous. The sun, as much as could be seen through the overcast sky, was still out. It would sink out of sight soon and already crews were assembling a large tripod topped with fiber optic lamps. They were ancient, compared to the newer models MacNally's partner had seen at the academy, but they would do the job.

"Over here, detective."   A haggard man in an ill-fitting suit waved MacNally toward a small ditch between two mounds of debris; the man's skin as pockmarked and scarred as the ditch.

MacNally found a semi-solid path that had been formed by a tracked vehicle and followed it into the ditch. The soil there was dry and crumbly. With all the recent rain, MacNally hadn't thought that was possible. Halfway down, MacNally realized it wasn't dry soil. It was plaster dust. Each step he took crushed it into a trillion little dust particles that floated a few inches from the ground and never seemed to settle back down.

Despite the freshly disturbed plaster dust, a body was visible in the deepest level of the ditch. The fiber optic lamps cast a shimmer of light now, enough so the two detectives could see what all the fuss was about. Midst the disjointed shapes of the broken soil and debris lay part of a body; the lower half of a human adult. There was little left save for the bones and most of the synthetic clothes with which the body had been covered. The legs were badly twisted; the feet buried in the soil.

"It that all?" MacNally asked the man with the scarred face.

"We thought it was. My operator stopped digging when he saw it. We did some soft digging with hand shovels after he backed the rig out. We almost gave up until we hit this."

MacNally's eyes followed the man's pointed finger. A bundle of rags lay at the far end of the ditch, fifteen meters away. MacNally made sure not to step on the lower half of the body and motioned for Russell to do the same as he traversed the ditch and stopped near the bundle of rags.

"Looks like a match," Russell said, no humor in his tone.

The little dust cloud clung to the ground as if it were afraid to float away. MacNally squatted down and fanned the plaster dust with big meaty hands to get a clearer view of the upper half of the body. It was face down, its shoulders hunched forward, hands and arms strung out in front. The rib cage, visible through the heavily torn shirt, was full of fresh soil.

"I don't guess it's gonna help to take Visuals, huh?" Russell held back a few steps and showed little interest in the skeleton.

"Doesn't matter," MacNally shook his head. "We run every Aspect. Doesn't matter that there isn't much left. There's information here. We just can't see it yet."

"I didn't mean that," Russell mumbled.

"What?" MacNally turned with exasperation. It didn't take much for the young Arcobian to get on his nerves. "If you're gonna say something say it loud enough so I can hear ya. I ain't twenty years old anymore."

"I said I didn't mean the Visuals wouldn't pick up any data. I meant we don't have a reason to investigate." Russell did not raise his voice.

"I still don't hear him," MacNally mumbled, though in fact he had. He just hadn't heard his partner make an attempt to speak louder. "I say we investigate him and that's good enough reason for you. Okay?"

Russell looked down at the rags with the same pinched expression he always wore when arguing with the Lieutenant, wrinkling his brow in a way that always made MacNally think the boy had swallowed a bug.

"Okay," he said. "I'll make sure the VTechs get a good set of shots. And a full set of tests on the soil. Do you want anything else?"

"Maybe," MacNally stood still for a few seconds, mesmerized by the remains of the man at his feet. He felt around in his coat pockets until he found a pack of cigarettes and put one between his lips. He put a silver lighter to it and his shadowed face was briefly lit.

"You think he was buried here for a long time?"

"I doubt it," MacNally pulled the cigarette out of his mouth and used it to point. "This soil looks fresh, it's only been in it for a short time. See how loose all this is?"

"Well, that ain't exactly soil," the scarred man in the bad suit spoke up. "This is debris from a building that was just torn down. I figure the guy was inside the building—basement maybe. When the rigs dug it up he was pulled out. Something like that."

"Maybe he was just some guy who died before the building was erected," Russell said, shrugging his shoulders. "Maybe he died of natural causes and was buried and no one remembered he was there."

"Russell," MacNally was almost patient in his reply, "I realize you had little warning before your transfer, but you could have bothered to learn something about this place. The IHS is very particular about people here. They keep a zero sum count of everyone here. If you arrive, you either depart, you're still here, or you die. Besides, no one gets buried in the soil here. There's too much risk of contamination. That's why the burials are up on the high slope's bedrock."

"Maybe your IHS isn't as all-knowing as you imagine."

"Speaking of IHS, they ought to be here pretty soon. Go back to the car and wait for them. Tell them we got to get Visuals." MacNally watched Russell climb the unstable embankment.

"He could be right," the scarred man offered without invitation.

MacNally glared at him until the man grew uncomfortable and

retreated to the other end of the ditch.

Once alone, MacNally knelt beside the skeletal remains, examining the outstretched hands. With a flashlight no bigger than a pencil, he illuminated the bones of the right hand.

"You stupid sonofabitch," MacNally stuck his cigarette between his lips. "I should have known you never made it out of here alive."

He brushed away enough of the dust to free the middle finger of the right hand and completely reveal a silver ring with a Cross of Lorraine on its crest. MacNally gingerly removed the ring and dropped it in his coat pocket.

A new cloud of dust appeared at his feet as he kicked at the debris surrounding the boney fingers, erasing the signs of what he'd done.

This was the worst kind of end to a day. A new investigation was about to begin, and while Ed MacNally knew the body's identity, he wasn't about to reveal it to anyone. He was, in fact, going to have to keep anyone from quickly identifying those bones.

MacNally watched Russell stumble back through the landfill with two VTechs in tow. It was about to be one helluva week.

3

The gray light of the late afternoon could not illuminate Gregor Lepov's third floor office. Even with three large, front windows, he had to switch on overhead lighting as well as the lamp that rose from the corner of his desk. The glare from the lamp outlined every scratch and scar on the surface of his deskscreen. He didn't have the money to replace it; neither did he have the desire. His own visage was scratched and scarred, why shouldn't his desksystem be?

The woman sitting across from him might have agreed, judging by the way she never looked directly at him. She had once had money enough to erase the blemishes life had dished out during her fifty-two years; a wasted effort. Lepov knew exactly how old she was even with the face of a woman in her thirties. Most people never realized that their posture gave them away. The exhausted drop of her shoulders contrasted conspicuously with her smooth skin.

The angle of her shoulder dropped even more as she read Lepov's report. It wasn't extensive, just the necessary facts. Lepov had learned long ago that clients rarely read his impressive details after reading the headline. And the woman sitting in front of him had definitely read the headline.

"Mrs. Truiit?" Lepov sat forward in his chair and adjusted the lamp. It didn't help. The glare made it almost impossible to read his copy displayed on the deskscreen. "Do you have any questions?"

She said nothing.

"Is everything okay?" What a damned stupid question, Lepov thought. But he had to ask it, had to find a way to get her to talk, to react; take that first step in what would be a long walk home.

"It is no business of yours, Mr. Lepov. Our business is finished. What do I owe you?" Her hands trembled for a heartbeat.

"Nothing."

"Excuse me?" That got a reaction. The woman rose to her full height. She wasn't a tall woman, but for that moment, she appeared to be. "I have not paid you. Now tell me what I owe you."

"You don't owe me anything. My private investigator's fee is on the door of this office." She already knew how much she owed him, but Lepov took no offense at her grandstanding. His tone softened as he pointed to the report. "As you should have seen in that report, you don't have any money, Mrs. Truiit. Your husband shot himself—just as the police said—because he'd lost everything gambling, including your exit passes. Since you can't pay my fee, I've waived it. I'm sorry about the outcome of my investigation, but that's all there is."

"This is absurd!" She shook the report at Lepov. "You wrote what those detectives told you to write. My husband never gambled, and he certainly never took his own life. Someone murdered him, Mr. Lepov. And if you can't see that, you don't deserve my money!"

It would have been easy to be angry with her. Lepov might have even laughed at her just as easily. Instead, he stood, circled the desk, and opened his office door.

"You're right, Mrs. Truiit. I don't deserve your money. I'll have to live with that. Would you like me to call you a TransitCar?"

She didn't answer, opting, instead, to stuff the report in her bag. Lepov caught a hint of her perfume, reminding him that she had once been a wealthy woman. The scent hung in the air after he closed the door. Not strong enough to kill the smell of self-pity—nothing was that strong. And maybe nothing should be. She would have to face her husband's death sooner or later.

That was the kind of thing Lilly Stewart would have told him. Sinking back into his chair, Lepov tried not to think of her. Cases like this were depressing; thinking of Lilly was usually a counterbalance to that. But not this time.

"Why haven't you come back, Lilly?" She didn't answer, and he couldn't think of an answer for her. Not one he'd believe. There was no reason at all why she hadn't come back to the Lazaretto.

Self-pity indeed.

Lepov was tempted to wallow in it for the rest of the night. He could have trailed Mrs. Truiit home and cozied up with her and a bottle of bad whiskey. *He left you, she left me, pass the damn bottle.*

The room darkened as night crawled across the city. Lepov couldn't see outside his office windows save for the white glow of street lamps. He could, however, see his reflection in the windows, lit in the pale yellow wash of his office lamp. He sat hunched forward over the desk; an old man. Even his father had never looked so old.

Lepov laughed. Maybe it was no mystery why Lilly hadn't come back. He decided even Mrs. Truiit wouldn't have him.

"That's enough of that." Lepov turned his chair from the windows and climbed to his feet. The Lazaretto was a lousy place to nurse a case of self-pity. Back home, Lepov could allow such moods to fester for hours. Whenever he was ready to get on with life he would just change gears. But not here. Not in the Lazaretto. It relentlessly dispirited the soul.

Lepov often wondered why he stayed. The answer to that question bothered him. It was something he would never admit, not even to himself. Had he honestly only stayed to test Lilly, to see if she would come back for him? True, he hadn't wanted to go back to Bukovina; there was little to go back to. He had just wanted Lilly to change her mind. But she hadn't, and he was alone. What had he been thinking? He had only met her shortly after arriving in the Lazaretto, had only known her for a short time before his futile search for Ethan Layne had ended. He should have gotten out then, as she had.

But Lepov knew that wasn't entirely true. No, he'd stayed because no matter how cold and despairing the Lazaretto could be, Lepov had found something that he had thought he would never find again: a purpose. Back home, he made no difference. Maybe things on Bukovina were too orderly, too clean—maybe Lepov's only chance to do anything worthwhile was in a world where even the smallest good deed shone like a laser on the dark side of a dead moon.

Locking the door to his office, he headed toward the stairs at the end of the hall. The elevator worked, but since his knee had been repaired, he enjoyed the climb. It was something he never would have appreciated if Lilly had not insisted he get it fixed.

It was going to be a long night. They were always long and irritating when all thoughts led to Lilly. He wondered if Lilly had similar nights. He would have bet money she didn't.

Lepov walked three blocks to his apartment. Each time he tried pushing Lilly Stewart from his mind, he ended up remembering something she'd said, or he pictured one of her smiles. As he climbed the two flights of stairs to his empty apartment, he could hear someone talking in an adjacent apartment. He always heard someone talking: above him, below him, all around him. Someone always made enough noise to underscore the fact that he was alone.

Lepov reminded himself he had always wanted to be alone, had never wanted to be with anyone. He couldn't even remember why he had agreed to his first and only failure of a marriage. There was nothing wrong with being alone, apart from the loneliness.

4

The Thief was a soldier. It was how he would forever imagine himself. No matter how many years had passed since he'd last worn the uniform, he was and always would be a soldier. It was in his blood—how many of his ancestors had carried the rifle and killed for their leaders? Twelve? Twenty-four? He couldn't remember anymore, though there had been a time when he could have named each of them. Twenty-two. Yes, there had been twenty-two generations of soldiers in his family. All good men; honorable and full of courage. How fitting, he thought. That was the kind of soldier he had been: honorable and courageous.

His father would have been proud. If there had been a way for his old man to see his acts of honor and courage on that distant planet, his father would have split in two from the sheer force of his pride.

And that was how it should be; sons splitting their fathers in two.

The Thief had no sons. What good was a son, anyway? The old kings were forever murdering their sons to protect their kingdoms. Who should have to live like that? Who wanted to keep an eye on each and every child that came along? That was no way to live. That was a formula for madness. No, the Thief would not mourn the lack of a son. Life was full of enough anxieties.

The body was an unexpected anxiety.

"Body?" asked the Thief. He'd been asleep when the Liar called. The clock beside his bed told him it was close to midnight.

"The police found a body, an old one." The Liar's voice betrayed excitement, but no trace of panic. "It was in the basement debris dragged up from the dig."

"What dig?" The Thief sat up and brushed at the filthy sheet draped across his legs. The chill air helped clear his head.

"The Roth Building. Wake up."

"I'm awake. What's it got to do with us?" Body? The Thief hadn't put any body in any basement and he said as much to the Liar.

"It wasn't in the basement. It must have been near the basement, behind the walls. Do I have to say it over an open circuit?"

"You mean—" the Thief was fully awake now, and understood the implications. "Do they know where it came from?"

"No."

"Are we compromised?"

"No." The Liar paused before adding "Not so far."

The Thief was angry. He had expected trouble when the demolition had begun—he'd been worried about structural problems. But this kind of news was worse than structural damage. The last thing they needed was Lazaretto Homicide poking around.

"How old? You said the body's old, right?"

"They aren't sure. But I understand it looked pretty bad. It might have been there for twenty, thirty, even forty years."

"That's good. That's a break." The Thief explained. "I doubt any detectives want to spend time tracking a killer from decades ago. They might not even spend time at all on it."

"We could always give them a new murder to investigate," the Liar suggested. "Lure their attention away from the old body."

"God," the Thief snorted derisively, "You're cold-hearted. I think we'll be okay. This isn't going anywhere."

"If you say so." The Liar did not sound convinced, but said nothing more and terminated the connection.

"That's a crazy one." The Thief laughed as he lay back. Not many people would suggest murder purely to mislead the police. It was something to keep in mind. You had to keep an eye on such partners. They could be useful; they were definitely dangerous.

But the Thief was a soldier, used to dangerous people and dangerous situations. More importantly, he was an old soldier. And old soldiers were cautious. They had to be, or they never lived long enough to grow old. The Liar was young. And while that made a partner even more dangerous—youth was impulsive, unpredictable, uninhibited—it also meant the Liar would never be cautious.

But he would be cautious. Despite what he'd said, the body discovered by the police would be a problem. He would have to be cautious. He should even be prepared to change his plans. But only change, not cancel. He would have to be flexible as events unfolded.

It was an old adage all soldiers knew: planning and improvisation went hand in hand. The Thief drifted back to sleep as the words repeated in his head: planning and improvisation.

5

As the shuttle doors unfolded, Major Sun Uijong stood up from her seat, unruffled by the press of passengers in the aisle. She had expected close quarters. She had, after all, waived her right to a seat on a military flight into the Lazaretto. That flight would have landed a few hours later, but she had wanted to get through Lazaretto Registration as early as possible. She knew it would take an hour or two before she was processed and settled in her hotel room and she wanted to avoid getting to bed late.

Arriving in the Lazaretto was a familiar operation for her. Sun had passed through the quarantine planet many times. Most of those times she had been with other members of the military, but she had been through on her own on two separate occasions. She had passed through the year before as she made her way back home for an extended leave of duty.

Each trip through the Lazaretto had been uneventful. There had been that incident with the young Battalion Commander from Phasis who had allowed his intoxication to get the better of him, but she was aware that the Lazaretto had played no part in that debacle. That little ass would have done the same thing on any of the planets in the Euxine system. It had been awkward for the both of them—there had been over half of the forty-day quarantine period left to serve—but the Alpha quadrant had been large enough that they had been able to avoid each other until it was over. Altogether, her experiences in quarantine had been unremarkable. She had no reason to believe this trip would be any different.

"Can I assist you?" an attendant wearing the red jacket and pants uniform of the shuttle crew stood at the base of the ramp with a ready smile. He was an older man, late fifties, with a full head of white hair.

"No, thank you." Sun smiled back at him.

The rest of the passengers moved forward with a similar familiarity of the registration process. Sun had read somewhere that travel was becoming less and less the domain of first-time tourists and more and more the domain of a select stratum of business and military types. There were rumors of new and lethal viruses loose in the Lazaretto, though IHS officials were adamant that the system was as effective as it had always been. Sun had worried about this for a short time, but in the end decided there was no need. If the Interplanetary Health Service had been aware of any real threats the public would have been duly informed. At least Sun had chosen to believe this. If she allowed herself to believe otherwise then the whole system would be in question and the possibility of infection and exile would be too great to contemplate.

As she entered the Lazaretto Registration annex, she recognized that such rumors could not be true. The stadium-sized room, while not at full capacity, was certainly filled enough to make her point. If the system had been compromised in any way, IHS or Earth's governing body would never spend the kind of money required to operate the Lazaretto.

The effort involved in sorting and quarantining thousands of travelers was far too great if it were only a smokescreen. Sun knew what kind of budget her small department demanded. And if the

Department of Veterans' Health Benefits demanded constantly larger budgets, what must an operation like the Lazaretto demand? More importantly, she knew how difficult it was to wrangle budget approvals from any government agency.

"Major Sun Uijong?" A man behind the registration desk read her name from his deskscreen before looking up. He was the perfect example of that government institution known as a bureaucrat. She tried not to stare at the flat dark hair pasted to his scalp. "You are here on government business?"

"I am." It was hard not to laugh at his overblown earnestness.

"Your military status allows a complimentary digital or cerebral guide if you wish to be issued one."

"No, thank you." She shook her head, her short black hair swinging easily with the motion.

"I assume then, *Major*, that this information is correct and you have previously been in the Lazaretto?" He seemed irritated to be dealing with her. Sun decided it must be her rank that he objected to. Men were forever disturbed by her title. Most of them were civilians who had no idea of the importance or unimportance of her rank, suspecting it was both too high and unwarranted.

"Yes, I have," she answered in an effort to be pleasant. "But you've been most helpful. Thank you for all you've done."

The man behind the desk didn't have the slightest chance of recognizing her good-natured sarcasm. He nodded at her, full of his own self-importance. He never actually said she was welcome; that would have been too polite. Instead, he only glanced in the direction she was to go and promptly forgot her.

Sun left the registrar, glad to be finished with him. She was too tired to contend with his peevish ways. It had been a long day for her, despite the fact that she had only traveled from Sinop. The Lazaretto was located on the surface of Aegean, Sinop's only moon. But in addition to the three hour shuttle flight from Seagen, a major port city on Sinop, Sun had first taken a seven hour RailTransit from Fort Mai Ling to Seagen's central hub. From there, the SubTransit delivered her to the Shuttle Launch with more than a two hour layover. In all, she'd been moving or waiting to move for more than twelve hours. The only good news had been that a shuttle flight from Sinop to Aegean did not require being placed in stasis.

That would have put her in a bad mood. Stasis wreaked havoc with her emotional state. Her last time in stasis had been her worst. It had taken four full days for her to regain any kind of emotional balance.

She'd been right to take the earlier shuttle. She was already stepping through the last of the scanners in registration. It wouldn't

13

be long before she would be in her hotel room. Then it would only be a matter of stripping off her uniform and slipping between the sheets. Her mission in the Lazaretto would start in the morning. But for that evening, she had only one intention; to sleep like the dead.

6

"Are we doing this tonight?" Menya Russell dropped his coat on the back of a chair and sat down slowly. He clearly hoped the answer was *no*.

"What?" MacNally stood over his deskscreen, poking listlessly at it. Despite his hearing's decline, the big man had clearly heard his partner. He was simply getting in the habit of making the kid repeat himself.

"Are we going to wait for the Visuals tonight? I don't see any point in it. This guy's been dead a long time. I can't see any reason to hurry."

There was little question about waiting for the results on the Visuals taken at the landfill. They wouldn't be ready for hours, and Russell was right; who cared how fast they looked into this? But MacNally would have to play the game. He would have to make Russell believe he was following procedures. The last thing he needed was to give the rookie the idea he was trying to hide anything. Russell was too new to Homicide. Too eager to follow procedure.

"There's no reason for you to stay, Russell. I'll stick around and see what the V-techs find." That should satisfy him, MacNally thought.

"You sure? I could stay if you're tired."

"What does that mean? You think this old man can't sit around the office late at night all by himself?"

"Pretty much," Russell muttered under his breath.

"Speak up, dammit." MacNally leaned forward, both hands spread in front of him on the deskscreen. Lights flashed as multiple contacts confused the system.

"I said yeah, you might be too old." Russell spoke louder and stared down his senior partner. "You're certainly too deaf to hear what the V-techs will tell you."

"I got it, okay?" MacNally pushed away from the desk and chuckled at Russell's stony glare. "Go home, Menya. I've got paperwork to do. And you clearly want to get out of here."

"You're the boss," Russell smiled. He was getting used to his partner, and he was getting pretty good at irritating him.

"Yes, I am." MacNally scratched at the bushy mustache that had more salt than pepper in it. Russell might be able to get under his skin from time to time, but MacNally didn't mind. At least they were getting to know each other. Their partnership would never reach anything resembling his relationship with his former partner Arturo Fenelli, but it was unfair to compare Russell and Fenelli. Fenelli had been with MacNally for too many years to count. As much as MacNally wished to be reunited with his deceased friend, he knew that he had to let him go. Russell needed time to mature.

By the time Russell shut down his desk system and left the Homicide office, MacNally was the only detective left in the room. He was glad of that. Since Fenelli's death, he'd found it increasingly difficult to deal with people. He made the effort to get along with Russell; he had little choice in that matter. He had been forced to find a level of interaction that facilitated their investigations. But that was nearly impossible for him with anyone else in the department.

He'd never been the most sociable cop. His quick temper and blunt demeanor gained him a reputation as *difficult*, something that he had actually been proud of when he was younger. But now, in the later years of his career, he regretted it. Not that regrets could correct a lifetime of mistakes. He knew that, and accepted it. So the regrets were pushed aside as much as possible, and his reputation remained unchanged.

Fenelli's absence compounded MacNally's problem. Fenelli had always been the one to keep MacNally out of trouble with the other detectives. If he couldn't keep MacNally out of trouble, Fenelli could at least keep him out of deep trouble. MacNally couldn't see Russell ever filling that void. He was too young and too sensitive to play that role. And he doubted if Russell cared much if MacNally got into trouble anyway.

MacNally waited a few more minutes to ensure he was alone. Captain Jenkins' office was dark. That was good. The one man he didn't want checking up on him was the Captain. He'd be able to bluff his way past anyone but the Captain, though he'd rather not have to bluff anyone if he could help it.

Leaving his desk, he moved around the perimeter of the room. A dozen desks were set in a square around a central storage of paper documents. Most of these were in old-style drawer-cabinets. The poorly maintained computer systems had been unreliable for many years. It had become necessary to back up files with paper documents — an unheard of practice on the better-funded planets like Bukovina and Sinop. But the cabinets overflowed long ago and the detectives had been forced to store files in boxes and in open stacks that combined to form a mountain of confusion and impossible data retrieval.

New detectives like Russell overlooked the stacks of files. They could not imagine trying to locate information within that mountain. Information stuck in that mess was considered irretrievable. MacNally knew otherwise.

He waded right into the paper chaos. He'd been there the day the first cabinets had been installed, and he'd actually participated in printing out many of the files and filing them in the old slide drawers. This had been when he was as new as Russell was now. As a rookie Homicide detective, he had been given the dubious honor of filing much of the paperwork.

He carefully pulled a stack of boxes away from the cabinets. MacNally intended to replace everything as it had been. No one would know he had been digging in the files. A heavy layer of dust had accumulated on the boxes, and he did his best not to disturb it. He had to lift eight boxes out of the way before he could see the cabinet for which he'd been searching. Faded, hand written labels stared out from the drawers. They might have been labels that he'd written. He couldn't remember. He did remember, however, the thoroughness he'd exhibited as a rookie detective.

Not only had the Homicide department printed out their own files, but MacNally and a few other detectives had convinced their old Captain to print out most of the other departments' files. They had assured their Captain that one day they'd be glad they did. Murder investigations often overlapped with the investigations of other departments. Keeping backups of their files was logical. You never knew when information from a theft or arson would prove invaluable to a murder case.

The top label on the seven drawer cabinet read *Alpha Quadrant Security*, followed by a set of dates. MacNally bent down and pulled out the third drawer. If his memory was correct, the file he was looking for would be near the back. He pulled out more than a dozen files, starting from the file farthest back. By the time he'd pulled out and examined the contents sheet on fifteen files he decided his memory wasn't as good as it had once been. He gently pushed the drawer closed, making sure he did not disturb any of the poorly stacked papers on top of the cabinet.

The file he was looking for was down in the fourth drawer: second file from the front. He hadn't been off by much. The events that were detailed in that file had happened one month later than he had remembered. Well, MacNally shrugged, who could blame him? He wished he could have forgotten about it altogether. Of course, it would have been better had it never happened.

Stepping away from the chaos of the paper storage, MacNally found a shuttered desksystem. He laid the file out on the black desktop, staring at the label on the tab; this was definitely his handwriting. He had made sure to be the one to handle that file, made damned sure no one in homicide caught a glimpse of what was in that dull yellow folder. He had even considered destroying it back then, but doing something that drastic had seemed too unlawful. MacNally wasn't sure whether he now wished he had destroyed it. There were good reasons to want this to go away. But even MacNally couldn't ignore his curiosity. Could a resolution to something that happened so long ago be forthcoming?

Possibly. So for now, the file had to stay, though it didn't have to stay in the cabinet. MacNally knew that although he couldn't destroy the file, he could hide it temporarily. Russell and Jenkins would probably never discover its existence. And if they did, they'd come to MacNally for help in finding it. But that needed to happen at a pace set by MacNally. He couldn't risk anyone finding this file too quickly.

MacNally replaced the stack of boxes. It took some time to ensure they were back in their original order and position. When finished, there was no way to tell that anyone had even looked toward the mountain of data.

He pressed his luck opening the file. He should have stuffed it in his shirt and left, but the temptation was too great. Under the light of a small desk lamp, MacNally read the contents page. The file had never been accessed. No one had made any amendments to it for over thirty years. That's as it should have been. As the originating officer, he would have been notified if anybody had poked around the file. But it was worth checking out all the same. Not everyone followed procedure. MacNally was living proof of that.

Paging through the first few documents to confirm that it had never been touched, he saw no reason why he should start reading it. He knew most of it by heart. Nearly everyone remembered their failures in far greater detail than their successes. MacNally was no exception.

There was no reason to stuff the file in his shirt, no reason for him to conceal it at all, for that matter. He walked straight out of the office with it in plain sight. None of the officers on night shift would notice it. Even if one of them did, they would not think to ask what was in the file. Nobody would care. MacNally counted on it.

7

I will explain how I learned about the Double, though I would rather not. I cannot, however, leave gaps in my account of what happened. Too many unanswered questions would work against my purpose. I want the truth to be told, not debated. But as I am the only witness to these events, I must do my best to logically detail everything.

Jason Phillip Reeser

Calla did not show signs of sickness until three or four days after the night Kjarsta Zoltis told me of her condition. No matter how hard and how long I watched her, my little charge appeared perfectly healthy during that time. I looked sicker than she did. I wasn't getting any sleep; pacing in her room all night long. I was a nervous wreck. I had no appetite. I was in no shape to care for a sick child. Yet, I watched over her night and day. Sleep was impossible.

I had never been the type to lie awake in bed imprisoned by insomnia. If I could not sleep, I was not going to lie in the dark and waste the hours with sleepless dreams. It was one thing to watch over Calla in the dark; it was quite another to lie awake at the stroke of midnight with only fear and anxiety for companions.

On the fourth night after the conversation in Kjarsta's office, having watched Calla for nearly two hours after she had finally given in to sleep, I sought relief from the slowness of the hours by making my way to the kitchens.

As mentioned before, I did not drink alcohol, though I did like to drink large cups of jasmine tea. The later the hour, the more I enjoyed its flavor. And the process of making the tea calmed my late-night agitations. The Zoltis house had every technological kitchen advance available for that time. But despite this, I did not like to drink the tea made by the menu-machines. I knew that every food and drink processed in the machines carried the exact taste and texture of those made by hand, but I could never convince myself of this. Besides, I did not care. I wanted to boil the water, to steep the tea leaves and strain the tea. I did not care that I was incapable of measuring out the exact amount of honey for each cup I drank. This was all part of the ritual that accompanied each cup of tea and I wanted to be a part of that ritual. It had been that kind of attitude that had perplexed and troubled my parents when I had been a child.

I remember thinking about that as I made the tea. I remember realizing I was troubled by my own child; not a child of my own flesh and blood, but mine nonetheless.

I made the tea in a small kitchen near the back of the house. This was not the main kitchen—the main kitchen was located in the center of the house and dinner could be served to three different dining rooms from its central location. The smaller kitchen I used was more like a break room for the domestic staff. It was a closed room, with no windows and only one door that led into a hallway running the length of the back wall of the house. Both ends of this hall had doors; one opened onto the back driveway and the other opened onto a walk terminating at the waste disposal system. I had only seen domestic staff use that hallway.

I had turned off the burner under the teakettle, not allowing it to whistle. Despite the remote location of the kitchen I did not want to disturb any one at that late hour. I stood at one of the counters, pouring the steaming water into a cup. As soon as I heard footsteps in the hall I knew

18

they were trying to slip through unnoticed.

I don't remember being afraid, though I wondered if someone had forced their way into the house. I was more curious than afraid. I did want to make sure that no one was entering the house with ill intent, but I am not sure how I expected to do that beyond watching them. I left the tea on the counter; it needed to steep for at least fifteen minutes before it would taste right anyway. Slipping out of the kitchen, I passed down the hall, following the sound of the stranger's footsteps.

They were not difficult to follow. The stranger did not attempt to be quiet, and obviously was not expecting to be followed. In fact, I made no effort to remain unseen. I simply followed him. He made a few turns and I had an idea where he was headed: Kjarsta's office, where I'd been summoned four nights before. Who was this man?

The man—I caught a glimpse of him as he entered the office, enough to know he was a man—did not close the door completely behind him. He was either careless, or he liked to keep his exits easily accessible. I am not a woman who is afraid to seek out answers, nor am I a woman to stand on ceremony. In a word, I eavesdropped.

I suppose I could rationalize my behavior by saying I was looking for information about Calla. And that was part of what led me to stand beside that open door and listen where I had no business listening. I do remember thinking that this might involve Calla. And I would never have passed up the chance to find out anything I could regarding her. But I will also admit I was too curious about this late-night visitor to turn and leave.

"Everything is set to go." My employer's deep voice carried easily into the hall. "You go in now, and your double arrives in thirty days. You have everything?"

"I'm ready," the visitor's assurance was overdone.

"I asked if you have everything."

"Yes." I couldn't tell which of them was more annoyed.

"Show me."

Calla's father must have seen what he wanted. He grunted in approval.

"Now you remember one thing," I could hear Kjarsta pouring himself a drink, "and don't ever forget this. You work for me. You take orders from me. You don't do a damn thing unless you know I'm the one giving the orders. My partners like to try and call the shots from time to time. But where they're concerned, you don't listen."

"Make sure they understand that. I don't want one of them thinking I'm being uncooperative." The visitor didn't have to say more. Even I knew what he meant.

"They won't do anything stupid, if that's what you're worried about. You work for me. That guarantees your safety—from the others. But only from them. I don't guarantee anything if you screw this up. Worry about me. Not them."

"You're the boss."

"Yeah, I am." There was a pause. "Is there something else?"

"I'm curious how you're going to do it. How are you going to get the double in?"

"By keeping my mouth shut. If I told you, I'd increase the chance of bashing it. Don't ever ask me a goddamned question like that again."

Mr. Zoltis barked at the visitor, angry in the blink of an eye. A chill spilled from the room into the hall. I had stayed too long. Whoever this man was, he had nothing to do with Calla. And I knew I had better have nothing to do with him. I made sure to leave without making a sound.

At that point, I had no idea what a double was. And I had no clue as to what Kjarsta Zoltis was involved in. But I had an idea that it was important, and that it could eventually threaten Calla's safety. It may have been only dumb luck that I made such an assumption, but I don't think so. It was simple logic to me. Instinct is strongest when loved ones need protecting. It is even stronger than our instinct for self-survival. I felt all sorts of pins and needles the rest of that night. I had no idea what Calla's father was doing, but I would be prepared if any of it threatened Calla.

I determined to be ready to protect the child at any cost.

8

Sun stood in front of a full length mirror and smoothed down the stiff material of her dress uniform. The black skirt stopped right below her knees. It was longer than the current fashions, but the military had little use for current fashions and rarely made adjustments to their standards. Sun had never considered shortening the hem—a few of her fellow officers had done so regardless of the possibility of a reprimand—but not for lack of sufficient nerve. In truth, her knees weren't worth the risk. They were a bit large for her slender legs; too mannish for her ego. Better to hide them behind an outdated dress code than bare them to the world for fashion's sake.

She pulled a dress jacket over her white blouse and carefully twisted each button into place. Who cared about the length of her skirt? Sun knew her olive skin looked good in her black uniform and she enjoyed the looks men gave her. A last check of her reflection confirmed everything was in place. Even her hair was behaving, despite the wet of the Lazaretto weather. She could only hope it would continue to cooperate.

As one last confirmation of her successful efforts she noticed the concierge staring at her as she stepped through the hotel's lobby. She could see him reflected in the glass of the front entrance; he was still staring as the doors rolled up and out of her way.

Sun should have worn an overcoat. Shocking cold air hit her as she reached the curb and spied a TransitCar. Thank God her skirt was lower than her knees; there was enough of a draft as it was. The morning wind funneling between the buildings on Masthead Avenue tossed her hair in several directions at once.

"Where to?" The Transit driver asked as she climbed in.

"16441 Fifth Avenue." Sun had double checked the address before she'd left her room.

"Are you serious?" The driver wrinkled his nose. "You're aware—"

"Yes, I am. Can you drive me there?" Sun looked directly at him with a pleasant yet firm stare. As he mumbled a reply, she attempted to push her hair back into place. At least it wasn't raining yet, she thought.

Sun watched the passing street scenes with only mild interest. The Lazaretto lacked the mysteriousness of her first few visits, her fears of infection conquered on subsequent stopovers. The faces of the people on the street reminded her of the Lazaretto's overriding spirit; life was dull here. Most people showed little resistance to the pervading sense of sluggishness that filled the streets. It drained the psyche knowing that one couldn't get off-world without passing a desultory forty-day stay in one of the quadrants. It rendered time pointless. Where time was often the presiding factor on planets like Sinop and Bukovina, life crackled with an electric rhythm that never seemed to slow. But the Lazaretto defied the clock and such stimulating lifestyles.

Sun had fallen victim to this listless spirit before and had determined not to let it happen again. Life was naturally stirring for Sun; always had been. She wasn't about to let this quarantine moon change her, no matter how lifeless the people on the streets appeared. Let them wade through the day as if nothing mattered. Sun had come to do a job and she eagerly anticipated completing it.

Once the TransitCar turned off Masthead, the scenes sliding by her windows transformed from the sleek modernity of the hotel district into a more shadowed and older section of the city. This alteration occurred slowly as they drove further north along Fifth Avenue. They passed more than two dozen intersections before the addresses on the brick buildings began sporting numbers in the 16000 sector. The change was more than just architecture and building materials. The morning crowds had both thinned out and dropped several classes. No longer did Sun see well-dressed bureaucrats heading to their office jobs for the day. The few traveling families bundled in heavy coats that dotted the hotel zone had gone as well. In their place Sun could see people dressed in frayed clothing that looked far too thin for the cold morning air. A large proportion of those people she saw were unnaturally thin or just as unnaturally heavy.

These neighborhoods weren't like the poor sections of her home town. There was something else at work here. The cornered and hunted looks on the faces of the people signaled that desperation held a strong grip among them; desperation that reached well beyond economic anxiety. It was disquieting. Sun had expected something akin to this, but nothing quite so tangible. Her determination to fight the listlessness of the Lazaretto might have been enough for a routine layover. But this immediately hit her in the gut.

There was sorrow here she had not anticipated. She was ashamed at her miscalculation. Had she never actually considered what she was walking into? She would have said she *had* considered it. But now, having entered this section of Center City, she knew she hadn't. She was certain the Transit driver could see the truth of this on her face. She turned her head in the direction of the window and hoped he wouldn't look at her.

To her relief, he did not make an effort to comment on the changing scenery as he came closer to their destination. Sun waited, closing her eyes as they stopped at yet another intersection. She'd seen the address over the door of a liquor store before closing her eyes: 16401. They were close now. She took in deep breaths and tried to refocus on her task.

"This is it," the driver said, a hush in his voice. "On the right."

Sun opened her eyes.

"I've heard of these people." The driver pulled to a stop in front of a small storefront. The aluminum window panes and doorframe had been freshly painted, as had the sign on the glass of the door: *The Lazaretto Benevolence Society*. "You here to make a donation?"

"No, I have something more substantial than a donation." Sun sat forward and waved her Personal Data Tag over the TransitCar's tag reader. "Can I arrange to have you pick me up later?"

"No, we don't work like that." The driver did not attempt to apologize for his answer. He was unhappy to be making this run and Sun had a feeling he would avoid coming back if possible. "Just call dispatch and they'll send whoever's closest."

"Well, thanks all the same." Sun shut the TransitCar's door and faced the Lazaretto Benevolence Society. The new paint and clean entrance encouraged her. At least it served to dispel her growing sense of depression.

She hadn't boasted to the driver. If everything went according to plan, her work there would have a far greater importance than a simple donation. More importantly, it would go a long way to right a thirty-year-old mistake. And that made every step of this trip worthwhile to Major Sun Uijong. She had assigned herself to this mission to ensure every effort was made to see it through to completion. With growing confidence she opened the Society's door and her sadness drained away.

It was going to be a glorious day.

9

The Thief had wrestled phantoms throughout the night. The image of an old, brittle carcass still cluttered the recesses of his mind as he awoke. First he had imagined the body as a crusty misshapen thing that broke when it tried to straighten itself into a sitting position. A brief image of it as a wet, slimy corpse did not last; the body had been dead far too long for that. Eventually the Thief had imagined a skeletal body with mummified clumps strung along its bony arms and legs.

Who cared what it looked like? The problem was how it would look to the cops. Was it old enough to ignore? Could health officials begin digging in inconvenient places? He would have to watch this closely.

Thief stared closely at his image in the mirror, dragging a razor across his jaw. His cheek bones were more prominent than when he had been a young soldier—when he had been a young man—so many years ago. His sallow cheeks reminded him he was sinking into himself; his body slowly digesting the man he had once been. And, after all, wasn't that what was happening? Wasn't an older, less refined organism gobbling up the strong young man of his youth? Wasn't that why he had embarked upon his plan?

Yes. His plan was an outgrowth of the basic fact that time would never pause long enough to be kind. Time was having too much fun beating at him like waves driven by the winds of an Arcobian *mahsuhl*. If the Thief did not act soon, there would be nothing left of him, no matter how successful he would be. It would be meaningless to lie, cheat, and steal his way to a fortune that he could never enjoy.

Catching the razor on a rough patch of stubble, the Thief pulled it away and probed his neck in search of a cut. He did not like the idea of scarring his face, no matter how minor the scar. Despite his fears of growing old, he was still a handsome devil. And he did not want to disfigure himself; no, the ladies would not like that. Women would always want their men to have two things: the attractive features of gods, and money. He had always been attractive. Soon he would have the money.

Over the sound of cold water running in the sink, he heard his front door open then close. He'd been expecting the Liar, but not so early. She must have found more information about that body.

Hunched over the sink, the Thief made a few last swipes with the razor at the base of his neck.

"That doesn't help, you know."

The Thief looked up into the mirror and saw a reflection of the Liar in the doorway. He smiled crookedly but did not respond to her mockery.

"You were never easy to look at," she added, baiting him more.

"You can make fun, I don't care." Putting the razor back to his throat, he scratched at one last stubborn spot. "What are you doing here at this god-awful hour? Still jittery about that dead man in the dirt?"

"Laugh, if you like." The Liar's scorn could be clearly seen in the mirror. "But you'd be an idiot to ignore this. That's not why I'm here, though. I'm here about the basement recorders. You must know they've got double coverage over the whole spread. I've been checking into it."

"You what?" The Thief spun toward her, the razor shining in his left hand.

"You heard me. I'm making sure that you're not overlooking anything. It's fine to disable a recorder momentarily — one recorder. That won't flag the most conscientious of security systems. But you'll have to take out six or eight recorders, for two or three minutes both in and out."

The Thief should have expected this. She had always been hard to control. He almost said as much but held his tongue. There would be time for recriminations later. Tossing the razor in the sink, he dried his hands on a rumpled towel and threw it on top of the straight blade.

"Overlooking something." He leaned in toward the Liar, grinning at her with eyes wide. "You've got no idea what I'm able to do. Recorders? God help me, I hadn't thought of recorders."

The Liar said nothing as the Thief waved his hands in mock dismay.

"In here." The Thief pushed the Liar into a small filthy room cluttered with mismatched furniture and a disordered bank of equipment and monitors. "You'll notice as I switch these on that I have four recorders projecting the center of the room on these monitors. You see? That's you and that's me. From all around."

"And?"

"Patience, patience. You wait right here." He leaned in, whispering in her ear. "Don't move."

The Thief backed from the room. In the adjoining room he picked up a silver, foil body suit from the floor, straightened it, and quickly slipped it on. He activated a thin plastic panel at hip level on the right side and pulled the hood over his head. Silently, he slithered into the bathroom, snatching the razor from the sink. Holding it against his body and covering it with his hand, he stole back to the front room.

The Liar stood with her back to him, watching the monitors. The Thief could see two of the monitors as he stepped behind her. Only the Liar appeared on the monitors. The Thief grew excited as he uncovered the razor from behind and it became visible on the display. Reaching over the Liar's shoulder, he dug the blunt edge of the razor into her throat.

"I heard you coming into the room." The Liar did not flinch as the steel blade pressed against her.

"You were listening for me," the Thief hissed through unseen lips. "But you couldn't see me, and neither could the filthy recorders."

He pulled away the blade and peeled off the hood. The rest of the suit came into view on the monitors as he deactivated the panel at his hip.

"This works on all recorders?" The Liar had trouble hiding her admiration and astonishment.

"Not really," the Thief admitted. He shut down the recording display. "The funny thing about this is that the better the system, the more vulnerable it is. This worked so well here because of the four viewpoints. The suit simply reads the four images and replaces the movement with filler. It's a simple script. But it can't do it unless there are multiple angles. The more angles there are, the easier it is to completely replace an object. Overlapping recorders are the key. As long as there are two or more recorders, we're in business."

"You aren't going to tell me where you got this, are you?" The Liar knew the answer to that even as she asked. The Thief did not respond. "Don't take offense at my checking up on you. I'm just trying to make sure there aren't any mistakes."

"As far as mistakes go, I hope you checked up on yourself. If anyone flags your interest in the recorders in the basement, I'm going to use that razor on you. No offense."

The Thief stared at the Liar, watching for signs of rebellion. He did not expect an outright admission of guilt, but he wasn't about to let her go without acknowledging she had been out of line.

"No flags. I was careful. Don't worry about that."

"I'll worry about whatever I want to. That's not for you to decide." She had been as apologetic as she could be. He expected nothing more.

"But you should worry about that dead man," whined the Liar. "That's going to lead to trouble."

"And I'll watch what happens. We'll adjust to whatever comes."

25

The Thief had satisfied her. He could see it in her eyes. What had she thought he would say? That he wasn't going to be careful? That he wouldn't watch developments and act accordingly? It was obvious she had forgotten he was a soldier. If she hadn't, she would have known he was ready for any contingency. That's what soldiers did; plan and improvise.

And that's what he would do. The Liar might check up on him, but no matter the outcome, the Thief would end up on top. She'd better worry about her own mistakes and realize what kind of man she was dealing with. He would win the brass ring. He would beat everyone.

Plan and improvise.

Gregor Lepov was awake and in his office by eight o'clock. There were days he couldn't drag himself there before noon, but for the most part he made sure to be at his desk when eight rolled around. When Lepov had decided on opening his office from eight in the morning to five in the evening he had laughed at the absurdity of it. He could have opened in the afternoon for all anyone cared. The rare appearance of a client inevitably came at the worst possible time—at five-thirty in the afternoon, or even twelve-thirty in the middle of the night. When most people had an urgent need for a private investigator, they rarely paid attention to the time of day.

That's what made the landlord's appearance so strange. It hadn't been Lepov's landlord. That would have been stranger still. Lepov's landlord lived on Sinop, and never paid the slightest attention to things like rent money. If Lepov paid late, his landlord either knew nothing about it or didn't care. No, the landlord that walked in his office that morning was none other than an actual client. A client that not only arrived as the sign on the door signaled the opening of the working day, but one who actually had money to offer up front.

It was the kind of auspicious beginning to a relationship that made Lepov want to run and hide. This much good up front had to indicate something awful on the back end.

"Are you Gregor Lepov?"

The man was thin. Lepov had come to believe everyone was thin in the Lazaretto; no one had an appetite in that gloomy world. But the man wasn't only thin. His head was long and cartoonishly oval with little hair save for the bushy blond mustache that dominated his mouth.

Despite the man's oddly shaped head, he was carefully dressed in a creased pair of heavy pants with a shirt that had been pressed and starched. The cloth was more in line with the uniform of a working man than an office worker, but he looked far too clean and orderly to have done much physical labor.

"Yeah, I'm Lepov." He stood and offered a hand. The early-bird client watched his hand warily and made no attempt to reach out in kind. Lepov no longer offered a handshake from habit. He knew the inhabitants of the Lazaretto minimized contact for fear of transmutable diseases, but Lepov offered his hand anyway. He learned a lot about people by the way they responded. This man was obviously not new to the Lazaretto, though he was no prima donna. He showed no offense at the offer, merely a cautious non-response. That could be a good sign.

"I would like a few minutes of your time, Mr. Lepov. I intend to hire an investigator, I can pay up front, and I would like to know a few things about you before I commit to hiring you."

"Sit down, Mr.—"

"Branithwaite. David Branithwaite." He sat and crossed one leg over the other.

"Well, let's get to know each other, Mr. Branithwaite. I've got a general questionnaire we could both fill out if you like. Nothing too elaborate, just a six page affair that asks all the embarrassing questions."

"I'd rather not!" Branithwaite seemed incensed at Lepov's suggestion.

"And neither would I," Lepov smiled to lighten the mood, "that was something a generous person might call a joke. I'll try to refrain from making any more if you like. What exactly would you like to know?"

"You are, of course, discreet in all matters, aren't you?" He leaned forward and put a hand on the edge of Lepov's desk.

"I'm terribly discreet on Mondays, not so much on—sorry, I said I'd drop the jokes. Yes, by all means, I'm as discreet as a...well, I'm discreet."

"And what is your background?"

"I was a homicide detective back on Bukovina before I went into business for myself." Lepov didn't like being questioned. "If you require more information than that you'll have to hire someone else like me to find out all the details. You see, I ask the necessary questions to solve whatever problem you have. It's not customary for the client to spend his time vetting me. Do that on your own time."

Branithwaite sat silently for a moment, deciding how to proceed.

"Maybe you'd be more comfortable with another investigator. I'd recommend someone but I don't have much detail on what few competitors are out there. Your best bet is to go to the police station and get one of the officers there to suggest someone."

The man sat still and nodded in response, never recognizing Lepov's sarcasm. "I did that. I went to the police. One of the officers there gave me your name."

"How nice." There were few detectives who would recommend Lepov. As far as Lepov knew, Lieutenant Ed MacNally was the only one. He would have to remember to thank Mac for sending him this skeptic.

"You're not too friendly with the police, I hope." The idea obviously irritated Branithwaite.

"I have no idea what that means, Mr. Branithwaite. I'm not too friendly with anyone. If fact, I've been told I'm downright unpleasant. And that was from a woman who was fairly fond of me. Pardon my rough edges, Branithwaite, but are you planning on telling me what you want or are you just window shopping?"

Lepov expected the man to stand up and leave without saying another word. As much as Lepov would have liked a paycheck for that week – the impoverished Widow Truiit came to mind – he hoped the jittery landlord would take his anxieties elsewhere. His daily rate wasn't nearly high enough to put up with difficult clients, mainly because difficult clients were quick to discover that Lepov was a difficult employee. His daily rate was definitely not low enough for them to put up with Lepov.

Branithwaite did stand, but he did not flee. Instead, he bit his lip, mustering the courage needed to speak.

"I've always been one to leave well enough alone. And a great deal of my hesitation has to do with the fact that I'm about to stick my nose into business that is not my own. Do you know what I mean?"

Lepov didn't like the sound of that. That could mean this investigation might eventually anger somebody; somebody Branithwaite wanted to avoid. "I think so. You don't want anyone to know that you're the one who initiated this. I think you'd better give me details. Your conscience notwithstanding, I may end up turning you down. So don't get so worked up yet about what might happen. Let's take this one step at a time."

"Okay." Branithwaite bit his lip once more, then let out a breath. The jitters had gone. He seemed to have accepted the fact he was going to reveal his story to Lepov. "Is this recorded?"

Lepov nodded.

"I don't mind. I just wanted to know either way."

Lepov watched him. He had decided not to speak again until the man said his piece. Every interruption seemed to unbalance him more and Lepov wanted him relaxed enough to speak coherently.

"I'm the building manager for the Chettleham Keep. It's an

apartment building down in the Bowsprit section of the city. Do you know where that is?"

Lepov held up a hand while he ran the name through his desksystem. A map display highlighted Chettleham Keep on the western edge of the Lazaretto. It was four miles from Center City and one block from the border of Alpha Quadrant, one of the four quarantine sectors where departing travelers waited out their forty-day quarantine before being allowed to exit the Lazaretto.

"Yes, that's it." Branithwaite was distracted by the map for a moment before he continued. "Chettleham is not mine. I'm only employed there. But I've worked there for over twenty years and it is important to me that I remain there. I'm in no shape to begin looking for a new job at my age.

"I've come to you because there is some—" Branithwaite had trouble with his next words, nervously shrugging his shoulders, "—suspicious activity going on in one of the ground floor apartments. I have every reason to believe that something very wrong is happening there. People have been seen going into an apartment. They do not come back out."

"What exactly does that mean?" asked Lepov.

"People are going in and they don't come out. I can show you I'm right. This data tag will back me up. The recorders clearly show these people entering the apartment, and to date, they have not come back out."

"That sounds like quite a party."

"This isn't about a weekend party. I've recorded six people who have disappeared inside that apartment over the last ten months. The only thing that has come out of there are shipping containers. Storage containers of some kind."

Lepov said nothing, though his face must have betrayed his interest in the man's story. Branithwaite leaned in with more confidence.

"You see what I'm getting at? These containers are roughly over a meter long, small enough to be wheeled out but bulky, you know?"

"Have you been in the apartment?"

"No. I've tried. The owner of the lease, a man by the name of Morvees, always manages to keep me out on some pretense. Now, Mr. Lepov, I won't go to the police about this. I can't have them raiding the rooms if there is a logical explanation. And worse, if there is criminal activity going on under my nose, my employers would instantly sack me."

"The police won't do anything with the story you've told me. They don't have the time or manpower to chase after phantom people."

"These aren't phantoms, Mr. Lepov. It doesn't take much imagination to come up with a disturbing scenario here."

"Imagination is overrated, Mr. Branithwaite." Lepov did not need this guy to start spouting theories. "Let's stick with what you know. Basically, you need to get a look inside the apartment. And you need me to check up on this leaseholder and see what he's up to. Beyond that, you don't know anything. Have you tracked the shipping containers?"

Branithwaite shook his head.

"Well, I think I can help you, if you want to hire me. More than likely there'll be a simple explanation that will leave the both of us feeling silly. Only I won't feel too silly, because you'll still have to pay me in full. But on the off chance there is criminal activity —"

"You can't go to the police." Branithwaite's mustache jumped in agitation. "You don't understand my position. I'm too old to lose this job. I've spent too many years in the Lazaretto to find work back on my home planet. And this is a good job. I like it. I won't have you crying *foul* to the police due to some moral obligation!"

"I won't have to." Lepov wished Branithwaite would calm down. "You're hiring me to look into this. When I find out what is going on, I'll give you a complete report. I'll only give it to you. I'll take my money and leave with a clear conscience. You will have the unenviable position of deciding what, if any, moral obligations you are under."

"Really?" Branithwaite seemed shocked at Lepov's attitude.

"If I'd wanted to be a crusader, I'd have stayed with the police." That was only half true, Lepov knew, but he did not feel he was obligated to point out he'd been fired from the force on Bukovina. All that mattered was that he was telling the landlord the truth. He wouldn't take this story to the police. Not officially, anyway. And if he did decide MacNally needed to know anything, he wouldn't feel guilty about misleading his client. Personally, he was disgusted with a man who cared more for his job than doing what was right. But professionally, he could live with it.

Besides, Lepov was sure this would turn out to be much ado about nothing.

"Is there something I sign?" Branithwaite asked. "I mean, to officially hire you."

"No. You don't sign anything. Simply pay me, and I'll get started."

"You need to be paid up front? I hadn't thought you would."

"I don't require it, but you did mention you were ready to pay up front. I see no reason not to take you up on that part of the offer."

"How much?"

"A three day fee should get me started. I'll let you know if I need more by the second day. By then, I expect I'll have been inside the apartment and will be able to tell you where all of this is headed. All I ask is that you go home, Mr. Branithwaite. I'll take care of this."

"Just go home?" The landlord held out his personal data tag and Lepov captured the signal on his desk system; the three-day fee would be transferred immediately. "You don't need anything else?"

"One thing." Lepov walked to the door and opened it, stepping aside for his client. "Make sure that the next time you see me you act like you've never seen me before in your life. Can you do that?"

"I guess so." Branithwaite rubbed his mustache nervously. He walked a dozen steps down the hall before he turned back. "I'm afraid I've forgotten to tell you the number of the apartment."

"Don't worry about it, Mr. Branithwaite. Leave me that tag with the recorder data and I'll take care of this."

Lepov shut the door and decided to begin by looking for information on the apartment's occupant—Morvees. It was time to drink a cup of coffee and forget about Lilly Stewart. It was time to do a little work.

Menya Russell sat at his desk with his hands in his lap. His chin was down on his chest and his eyes were closed. If MacNally's hearing had not begun to weaken, he was sure he could have heard the kid snoring. This was not a sight he enjoyed upon his arrival in the morning.

"Is this job interfering with your sleep schedule?" MacNally asked the question loudly enough that most of the officers in the room heard him.

Russell lifted a hand with one finger pointing skyward. He mouthed a word silently, but MacNally couldn't tell what it was. The older detective shook his head and went in search of any form of coffee he could find.

He hadn't slept well. And what irritated him was the suspicion that he had slept fitfully because of that file he'd removed from the cabinet. It shouldn't have bothered him at all. He was doing the right thing; he was sure about that. So why would it give him trouble sleeping? There was no reason for it. And that made him all the more cranky. It didn't help that his partner was asleep at his desk. If MacNally couldn't get any sleep, the kid shouldn't either. Worse, Russell had probably slept plenty.

MacNally tried to think of work that he could give the kid as he poured a cup of coffee. Maybe he would ask him to run downstairs and buy a newspaper. That wouldn't accomplish much; for once, the elevators were working. He'd be back in three minutes and that would only irritate MacNally more.

"Did you want something?" Russell opened his eyes and sat up. "I'm finished, now."

"With what?"

"It's a memory technique I'm trying. It seems to be working, but I can't remember the name of it." Russell stared at MacNally with an expression that made it impossible to tell if he was serious.

"You know, for once I could hear you just fine." MacNally looked down at the cup of coffee in his hand. It was old coffee and tasted bitter. "I don't think it did any good, but I could hear you. You been here long?"

"A few hours. VTechs are slow. There's no report for us yet. Unless they gave you one last night. But I couldn't find one."

"No, nothing last night." MacNally poured the coffee into his wastebasket. "I wasn't able to get the Captain to make this a priority case, so they're going to be slow. I wouldn't look for a report until tonight — maybe not even before lunch tomorrow."

"Well, I looked over the inventory." Russell made it obvious he disapproved of the wasted coffee by staring hard at the coffee-soaked trash. "There wasn't any kind of personal stuff on the body. Nothing that might identify him. You know, that was fresh coffee. I just made it."

"Damn, Russell. That was bad coffee. Was that some kind of Arcobian pesticide?" MacNally had learned early on that Russell was sensitive about his Arcobian heritage. They were easily singled out for harassment in most of the Euxine system. Theirs was a reputation of a backwards culture and education system. If MacNally were honest with himself, he'd have acknowledged Arcobians were considered to be sub-human. But men were not supposed to admit that kind of prejudice, and MacNally was no exception. He just couldn't pass up the occasional chance to put the young Arcobian in his place. He had no good reason to do it, but MacNally rarely looked for a good reason to do anything. He wasn't about to admit he was jealous of the newly trained young man from Arcobia. That would never happen.

"It's only coffee." Russell's pinched expression told MacNally he was more puzzled than offended that his partner didn't like his coffee. "I like it like that. In fact, I'll drink some more of it unless we're going somewhere. What were your plans this morning?"

"Believe it or not, Russell, I actually thought you might have had a good idea yesterday." This was not entirely true, but MacNally had felt a touch of regret when he'd seen the kid's perplexed face. There was no reason to get him emotionally upset over a rash critical remark. "You suggested that maybe this was some guy who'd been buried before the building had been built. You might have been on to something."

"But you said that was impossible. That IHS kept too close an eye on everyone for someone to be buried without the proper notifications. You seemed pretty sure about that."

"And I was right. But go back a bit, to the first days of the Lazaretto. Before the system was put in place—during the construction of the original buildings and facilities—it is possible that someone was buried there without IHS being told of it. Things were a little wild at that time."

MacNally knew that what he was saying was only technically true. But it sounded close enough to the truth that Russell would buy it. And that's all he needed. If MacNally had it right, there was nothing to be gained by following up on Russell's idea, and that was fine with MacNally. For now, he wanted to waste time and resources. And trying to get information from the first few years of the Lazaretto's operations was going to be time consuming and useless.

"So where exactly do we start?" Russell had obviously bought into MacNally's idea without hesitation. It was always the same when using other people's ideas to deceive them: flattery will get you everywhere.

"We can see if that soil, or whatever it was filling the ribcage, has been tested yet. If so, we might be able to find some kind of match. Something that tells us which building he was buried under. While I'm looking at that, you can check out any currently issued permits to see who's been doing any excavating in the city. Between us, we should be able to figure out where this old boy's been hiding all these years."

"And then?" Russell cocked his head and waited for more.

"Then what? I don't know. We'll wait and see."

"If you don't mind—" Russell hesitated, his voice low.

"Huh?" MacNally leaned forward with a pained expression. "Don't start mumbling on me, Russell."

"I don't think it will take long for me to look up the civil permits. Could I look at the soil composition with you? I don't think it will take much more time and I'd like to maybe learn a little from it."

"I suppose it's worth the extra time it'll take." Better and better.

"I'll make sure we don't waste time. I'll show you what an Arcobian can do." Russell pulled his chair closer to his desk. The idea he might slow down the investigation seemed to have motivated him. Or maybe he just liked the fact that he had something to do. At any rate, he was energized now. Before MacNally could stop him he had begun his search.

"Hey," MacNally said abruptly, "sorry about that crack about your coffee. That was uncalled for."

Russell waved off the apology.

"No, I'm serious. In fact, let me ask you something. I watched a report about Arcobia last night. No, no. It wasn't anything bad. They were discussing the rebellion. And how it's coming up on thirty years now since the Arcobian's won control of the Board of Parliament. They were suggesting that if Pan Juarez had actually made it to the referendum vote, the people would never have been able to take control. They even suggested Juarez' own people had him killed to make him a martyr. You guys on Arcobia believe that?"

"That's old stuff, MacNally." Russell stopped typing on his deskscreen and looked up. "Someone's always going to try to keep that foolishness alive. Juarez wasn't that important to the vote. The Board members who wanted to break up the Industrial's power had already made up their minds. Pan Juarez' role has always been blown out of proportion. And nobody killed him. He was a selfish bastard who ran when he got the chance. He was nothing more than a thief."

"Yeah," MacNally was glad to see Russell no longer paying attention to his deskscreen, "I know about the diamonds. I never thought that made sense, though. A patriot running off with the loot that he was collecting to buy off the voting members. He'd of had to be a real—"

"*Boutrach*." Russell spit out the word.

"A what?"

"Nothing," Russell shook his head. "It's an old Arcobian word. It's like a—well, I'll put it this way. If someone called your father a *boutrach*, you wouldn't hesitate to cut the man's eyes out."

"I'll remember that." MacNally did not press his partner for more information. He had not raised the topic of Pan Juarez randomly. But he did not want Russell to think otherwise. He would have to tread lightly in the future. As he had hoped, Russell was going to be a good source on Arcobian politics and history. But he had not expected him to be so passionate about them.

"They've got it." Russell punched at a red heading and a white document opened in the center of the deskscreen. "Soil composition. Somebody's working down there."

MacNally wasn't surprised. He should have figured the lab guys would actually get something done quickly for once. Never when he wanted them to, of course. Only when he didn't.

"Looks like the guy down at the landfill was right." MacNally read through the composition list. "That's mostly building materials. Foundational stuff. Sand. Rock."

"What's all this?" Russell pointed out several names on the list.

"That stuff is all over this city—a filler. They used it to reinforce concrete. It was a synthetic metallic fiber that was ground up and mixed in with limestone and sand. They hit it with an electrical charge once it was poured. Anyway, like I said, this stuff is everywhere under the city."

"Hadn't they ever heard of HardTack?" That was the commercial name given to a chemical that had become widely used to strengthen foundational concrete. It had revolutionized the construction industry at that time. HardTack was cheap and the chemical bond it created virtually indestructible.

"No, actually." MacNally couldn't help but laugh at the youngster's question. "HardTack hadn't been invented yet. Remember, the Lazaretto is over fifty years old. HardTack's only been around about thirty-five years."

"Well, I didn't know." Russell shrugged off his mistake. "It's not like there's a big difference between thirty-five and fifty years ago."

"There is, Menya. Believe me, there is." MacNally would have been annoyed at the kid's stupid observation if he hadn't been distracted by the realization that there was a great deal of difference between those two moments in time.

Fifty years ago, MacNally, only a child, had watched the NewsVision coverage of the building of the Lazaretto. In fifteen short years, he'd become a young policeman in that Lazaretto; green, eager, too poorly trained to handle the job. Menya Russell had no idea how much difference there could be. But he would learn. The older he became, the more he would understand. The past did not solely consist of simple dates and historical facts. The past was full of volatile memories that warped and reshaped each man's world according to his experiences. The past was a dangerous, evolving realm that should be avoided at all costs.

As soon as he'd seen that body in the ditch, MacNally had known that this particular portion of the past should never have been disturbed. But he did not have the luxury of avoiding it. The body, nothing but dried bones and bits of rags, had managed to claw its way back to the surface, a specter demanding the past be revisited. Well, MacNally promised himself, I'll be damned if I'm gonna let that ghost dictate how I reopen the past. His hand might be forced, but he was determined to keep as much control over this as he possibly could.

"Maybe we should look at those permits." Russell sat back in his chair and looked up at MacNally. "This composition list doesn't tell us much."

"Not a lot, except that this body was buried a long time ago. Your theory is holding up. Let's see who's been digging holes in the

Lazaretto." MacNally couldn't think of another excuse to delay.

There was no avoiding it. He was being forced to dig a hole in the Lazaretto's past. He hoped to God no one ended up buried in it.

12

Sun Uijong stepped into the front office of the *Lazaretto Benevolence Society*. An open floor plan allowed her to see a sitting area, two desks set apart by low railings, and a door leading toward the back of the building. There were no windows, save the large plate-glass windows on either side of the wood-framed glass door she'd just closed behind her.

The desk on her left was empty, though covered with piles of papers and a great deal of what looked like spare computer parts. The desk on her right was just as cluttered, with a young blonde woman sitting behind it. She was typing on her deskscreen as she spoke on the phone.

"Mrs. Donegal, I can assure you we're doing everything to make Stanley comfortable. There's no reason to think he's been treated like that. No, ma'am. The nurses there are very kind. I'm sure he'll be fine. No, ma'am. I'm positive that he doesn't think you've abandoned him."

Sun stood just inside the door, making an effort not to eavesdrop on the conversation. It was difficult not to. The room was small. Even if the woman had not been speaking loudly Sun would have heard everything she'd said. As it was, the woman's attempts to reassure Mrs. Donegal dominated the room. Sun examined the woman in a vain attempt to ignore what was being said.

The woman was younger than Sun; she must have been around thirty years old. Her blonde hair was short, cut like a young boy's. The more Sun looked at it, and the more the woman turned her head in the poor office light, the more Sun wondered if, in fact, the hair was red. It seemed to shift from blonde to red depending on the angle of the light. It was most red when the woman tilted her head to the side; the greater the tilt, the darker the shade of red.

The woman's face was small, with barely perceptible eyebrows and even lighter eyelashes. Her skin tone was golden bronze, as if she'd spent her life on Dnepr, the planet closest to the Euxine system's sun. Despite the fact that she was sitting down, it was obvious to Sun that the woman was short. But at the same time, the woman had long fingers that jabbed repeatedly at her deskscreen. She was a thin woman who looked as strong as a bar of steel.

"Do not even think about it, Mrs. Donegal. That is what we are here for." At this point, the woman looked up at Sun and waved her toward the desk. "I want you to stop worrying about your husband and stop worrying about us. Just make sure you take care of yourself. Can you do that? Or is there something we can do for you too?"

Sun approached the woman's desk and stood uneasily. She was tempted to turn and leave. It was obvious her timing was lousy. Perhaps she should have called ahead. Sun was trying to think of a way to leave the office without making a scene.

The woman pointed at a chair and Sun awkwardly sat as directed.

"You call me if you need anything else, okay darling?" The woman hung up the phone and looked at it for a moment, as if she were humoring a nut from her extended family. After letting out a short breath, she turned her attention to Sun.

"That's the job, right there. Holding their hands and patting their heads. I'm Chitti Sienté. Can I help you?"

"I hope I can help you." Sun reached into a pocket and withdrew a small plastic card. "I'm Major Sun Uijong from the Department of Veterans' Health Benefits. Is the Director in?"

The woman turned and looked at the door in the back wall. A small plastic sign with the word *Director* hung crookedly in the center of it.

"That's my office, but it's a bit too small. And since no one else is currently volunteering out here, I like to use this desk as much as possible. To be more clear; I'm the Director of the Society. You must be the representative that I was informed about three weeks ago. I was beginning to think you wouldn't show up."

Chitti's manner was straightforward. She did not hesitate to look Sun in the eye. Neither did she hesitate to examine the ID card and compare the picture on it to Sun's image. She did not explain or justify her behavior in any way. Instead, she ran a search for Sun's data on her deskscreen and sat silently until she was satisfied with the results.

"Okay, Major Uijong, what can the Lazaretto Benevolence Society do for you? I was not able to get much information out of your people when they first contacted me."

It was difficult to make an immediate judgment, but Sun had the feeling that Chitti Sienté was suspicious before she was friendly. Her reserved formal manner was nothing like her interactions that Sun had overheard on the phone.

"Miss Sienté, I'd like to explain everything as plainly as I can. However, I have to proceed cautiously. I hope you understand. I have traveled here to work with your society on a face-to-face basis. This is a sensitive issue that we—Veterans' Health Benefits, that is—wish to keep out of the NewsVision for now. I can assure you that the

Jason Phillip Reeser

lower we keep this on the radar, the easier and more properly it can be handled."

Chitti reached out with one hand and cleared the deskscreen, leaving it black. After nodding a few times, and with visible exasperation, she stood. She was shorter than Sun, as she had speculated, but not by much.

"Major, that's all mysterious, and fascinating. But I hope you can cut out the government legalese and just tell me why you're here."

If Chitti had expected Sun to put up a fight, she had completely misunderstood Sun's purpose. Sun had not intended to be mysterious. She simply did not want to hit the young director of the Society with too much at one time. But as she was quickly learning, this young woman was no weak vessel. She was, in fact, a tough lady in a tough job. There was no reason to beat around the bush.

"I'll do that. I'm sure you are quite familiar with the Lost Platoon?"

"More than anyone else in the Lazaretto. And far more than anyone else outside the Lazaretto. What does this have to do with them?" Concern clouded Chitti's face.

"My department has authorized me to examine the records of the Lost Platoon members and make recommendations for appropriate compensation. Under the terms of a rider that was attached to a budgetary provisions bill, Veterans' Health Benefits will assess the current needs of the remaining members of the Lost Platoon and dispense funds to meet those needs. Each dispensation will be awarded individually as per those assessments. This should answer any questions you have."

Sun held out a data tag and waited until Chitti's deskscreen logged the signal and captured the document. It appeared in the center of the deskscreen: a three page document with the seal of the Veterans' Health Benefits at the top of the first page.

Chitti said nothing, enlarged the document for easier reading, and read through the entire text twice. Only after she had taken a moment to consider what she had read did she make a comment.

"This is authentic. This is not a joke."

"I didn't travel this far for a laugh." Sun meant that to sound funny but she could see that Chitti glanced at her as if she were off-balanced.

"I realize that. I'm just having trouble getting around the fact that you're serious. Despite the fact that you guys are thirty years late, I think I can accurately say that you're going to be welcome here. I look forward to making sure you have everything you need to complete your assessment. You have no idea how much good this will do."

"I'm glad to hear it," Sun said, relief in her voice. "I was beginning to think you were going to work against me."

"That's my fault, Major." Chitti's manner loosened up a little. "I take a proprietary interest in the men and women who receive aid from this charity. The Lost Platoon is something of a personal crusade for me. I'm highly protective of them. I did not mean to offend."

"No offence taken. And please, I work for the military, but you don't. Don't call me Major. It would be fine if you called me Sun."

"Okay, Sun. I think we're going to get along just fine." Chitti came out from behind the desk. "Let's find you a seat, something to drink, and then have a long talk. How does that sound?"

It sounded good to Sun. She had been a little unnerved by the scenes she had passed in the TransitCar. Making her way into the heart of the Lazaretto, she had begun to wonder just how difficult it would be to accomplish her mission. But now, as Chitti poured her a cup of tea, she began to believe that everything would be all right. The aged veterans of the Lost Platoon were going to get some much needed attention, and somewhere along the way, Sun was going to feel like she had actually done some good. It had been a long time since she had felt that way about anything.

13

That next morning after the late night visitor met with Kjarsta, I went in to see Calla and found her exhibiting the first symptoms of her sickness. As a trained nurse, I was not daunted in the least with the task before me. I had been prepared for it; I had been able to read the doctor's notes on Calla's diagnosis and his recommendations for treatment. I'm not sure which fact I found more shocking; that the doctor had refused to care for her or that Kjarsta had allowed him to leave without harming him. At any rate, I was there. And I was able to care for her.

Calla had become infected with a virus that had been around since the first ships from Earth had settled the Euxine system. The virus had a mild effect on animals that were indigenous to the Euxine planets. But its effects on humans had been alarming to the early colonists. After a dormant period, the virus attacked the sinus cavities. The infected sinuses always reacted in the same manner; flooding of the sinus cavities occurred in an attempt to flush out the virus. The resultant mucus could actually cause suffocation in the patient as the cavities drained into the lungs. If the patient could be kept from suffocating, the more serious side-effect was the buildup of scar tissue in the nasal passages as the body fought to remove the entrenched virus.

Neither of these complications was life-threatening if the patient received basic but constant care. The greatest problem came in the guise of its timetable. The virus was undetectable during its dormant period. This dormant period could last up to four weeks. Once the virus began to attack the sinuses, it could take two or three weeks for the body to finally eradicate

Jason Phillip Reeser

the virus. This meant that anyone attempting to leave the Lazaretto would never make it through the quarantine period if they had the virus. And since the virus had been the cause of many deaths, it was listed as a deadly virus that could not be allowed out of quarantine.

Most importantly, anyone who had once fought this virus — the scar tissue in the nasal passages was easy to detect — was never allowed to leave the Lazaretto. It mattered little to the bureaucrats that the virus was everywhere in the Euxine system. Attempting to contain it in the Lazaretto was impossible. But that meant nothing to the IHS. It was a matter of pride that they never allow something potentially deadly out of the quarantine. It was a case of laziness; a lack of interest in caring for people.

I know I'm dwelling on details that do not need exposition. I cannot help it. I'm painfully aware that all of this came about because a little child became sick. And if it had happened anywhere else, on any of the planets — including Earth — nothing would have happened beyond this sickness. Yes, Calla would not have been able to travel between the planets, but she would not have been exiled to a world like the Lazaretto. She would have been free to live a normal, happy life with her family and friends.

As I nursed Calla through the worst of the viral attack, I was too tired to fend off the bitterness that grew in my breast. I could not help but hate the men and women who made up the soulless entity known as the IHS. This great and powerful institution was run by little, meaningless creatures who had abandoned their oaths to care for the sick and spent their lives insulating the healthy from the dead and dying. For them, there was no greater good than separating out the weak and the sick. It was a passive attack on the most vulnerable segment of society.

And they would have culled Calla from among us. They would have taken her and thrown her into that void of the Lazaretto from where the sick never returned. Hers would have been a life of darkness without a future. I still feel the heat of the anger that burned within me. Day after day, watching over her, washing her, draining her lungs, and giving her injections to reduce the scarring — all of this built up my determination to keep her free. I would never allow the beasts from IHS to take her away from her father. I would never allow her to be taken from me. There wasn't anything I wouldn't do to protect her.

Calla was strong. I could see right away that she was not in the same kind of danger many victims of that virus encountered. I don't remember when I knew for certain that she would not die, but I remember sitting up all night and crying as I realized that staving off the virus was only half the battle.

She was going to live, yet still I feared for her. Her father, when he learned of my fear, only laughed.

"You've done well." He had come to my room and stood just inside. *His great size dominated the room, despite the fact he had not stepped all the way into it.* *"You should be happy, not sick with worry. I'm told you aren't well. That you don't eat. The others tell me you're living in great fear for*

40

my daughter. Is that true?"

I was shocked that word had reached him on this matter. I knew it was true, that I was overly concerned for the girl, but I had no idea anyone else had noticed. I believed I had convincingly concealed my dread. I would have lied and denied it if I had not been so unbalanced by the news.

"What business is it of theirs?" I allowed myself to become a little indignant. It was all I could think to do.

"It's my business, woman. You're to be taking care of Calla. You can't do this if you are ill. You have allowed paranoia to overwhelm you. Hell, I can see it in your eyes. You even look at me like I'm a threat to the girl."

"If I've been worried, it is only within my duty." I did not like that he was right, and tried to talk my way out of it. "You want me to care for her. This is how I do it."

"You were hired to make her physically better. You were not hired to protect her. That is what I do. And I know what worries you. Stop thinking about it. I won't allow it to happen. I am prepared to go to great lengths to keep this secret. It will not ruin her life. Trust me in this. Do you hear me, Della?"

I only nodded when he asked me if I'd heard him. I was too tired to argue, having been utterly overwhelmed by the responsibility of watching out for the girl. The fact was, I was happy to give up that responsibility. I wanted to. I did not want to keep the responsibility all to myself. I wanted to give it up. I should have. I wished I could have.

14

Gregor Lepov could be a stubborn, prideful man. But when it came to making money, he never allowed pride to get in the way. The Branithwaite case was a prime example. It was a sure bet that he was being hired to check out nothing. The landlord's story had assumption written all over it.

There was little chance that six people had disappeared inside that apartment. There were a dozen explanations why no one had seen them leave. Even the data tag evidence was thin. The recordings of the hallway could not possibly have kept an accurate log of everything that happened in six months. Recorders failed. If Lepov had wanted to, he could have pulled up the Keep's maintenance records and found any number of work orders for recorder repairs.

But Lepov wasn't going to do that. He had agreed to investigate the apartment. The fee was already posted to his account, and he was going to earn as much of it as seemed necessary. There was no reason to overwork the job, but he had to make a good showing. He had every intention of spending two days on the investigation. If, at the end of that time, he had satisfied the customer, he would feel no regret at keeping the third day's fee. It would make up for some of the time lost on that widow's case. And he was certain Branithwaite was dipping into his employer's till to pay it.

That kind of ethics juggling had been standard procedure back on Bukovina. Here in the Lazaretto it was downright saintly. In fact, working on this case for two days would be overkill. It was Lepov's way of salving his conscience. Maybe it was an attempt to keep his friend Ed MacNally happy. Lepov didn't care what most cops thought of him. But he had come to like MacNally, and despite MacNally's natural aversion to Private Detectives, the old Homicide Detective seemed to like him too. There was no reason to give him an excuse to fall back on his old prejudices.

Lepov quickly found the information he needed on the apartment's occupant. Anton Morvees was something of a celebrity. He was a member of a group of men who were well known in the Lazaretto: the Lost Platoon. Lepov had not been in the Lazaretto long enough to remember the story. But from everything he could find, it seemed the story was legendary. It had been so widely spread, Lepov learned, that over the last twenty years or more, whenever the Lost Platoon was mentioned, few details were ever revealed.

Lepov decided he would come back to the Lost Platoon after he'd finished his investigation of the apartment. It seemed to be an interesting bit of history, but he wasn't looking that far back. He was only interested in what had been going on in that apartment over the last year.

Morvees had been the leaseholder of that apartment for two years. The lease records of the ten most recent years were available to the public. Anything dating beyond that time required an official request through Lazaretto Administration Archives. That was something Lepov did not need. He did, however, initiate the request procedure from habit. If he didn't need it, he could always cancel the order.

Morvees was the sole leaseholder on the contract. He had not been married during those two years, and he gave no names for additional occupants. The man lived alone.

He was employed as a Hygiene specialist for one of the largest Hygienics companies in the Lazaretto. That sounded momentarily impressive. Lepov had only to input a few searches on the company to get a clearer picture of what the Hygienics business entailed. Morvees was a janitor. He'd been cleaning offices for years. Lepov didn't know if he should be impressed that the man had endured so many years in such a thankless job or if he should be disgusted that a man had lived so many years with so little ambition.

Lepov decided not to pass judgment on the man. There weren't many people who would think Lepov had lived the most ambitious life. Who was he to judge another man's ambition, or lack thereof? Ambition was a funny thing. Wielded by the right man it could be a glorious and valiant virtue. In the hands of the wrong man, ambition could be an evil and dark weapon. Lepov knew he was somewhere in between those worlds where men and ambition never completely came together.

Lilly had seemed to sense that about him. And she had gently tried to push him in the direction of aiming for something more glorious than mediocrity. It's one of the things about her that intrigued him. Other women would have pushed hard and he'd have fought against them. But Lilly had found a way to push him just enough and not too much. She'd been so good at it that it had alarmed Lepov. It had forced him to back away; just to give him enough space to get a clear picture of what was going on. By the time he'd been ready to close the gap between Lilly and him, she'd gone. Now he wasn't sure if she'd ever come back.

Lepov stared out the window of his office, watching a cloudbank roll over the city. Here he was thinking about Lilly again. He'd have to quit that. He would have to learn how to throw the switch that shut off that part of his brain that wanted to think about her.

Anton Morvees. Janitor. Loner. It was time to get out of the office and see what he could dig up at Chettleham Keep. It was time to find six missing people who may not even be missing. That thought disturbed him. Lepov had not thought of this as a missing person's case. His last one had been such a failure that he'd sworn he would avoid them in the future.

It was hard to know if any of these people were actually missing. The six people would have been logged in as they entered the Lazaretto. But they wouldn't show up again until they attempted to leave through one of the four quadrants. Until then, Lepov had no idea if anyone would notice they were gone.

The landlord had tried to insinuate something sinister was going on. What did he have in mind? Cannibalism? Religious sacrifices? Madness and dismemberment?

That was the stuff of imagination, and Lepov had learned that life never quite lived up to imagination. If something was expected to be exciting, it was never quite as exciting as expected. And if something was feared, it never turned out quite as terrifying as imagined. That was imagination: stuff and nonsense.

People going in and never coming out? Strange containers full of grisly remains? Lepov laughed out loud.

He would close this case as soon as it was practicable. Lepov watched the morning street begin to glisten with rain. He grabbed his coat from a hall tree by the door and mashed his hat down on his head. He was going to throw some water on Branithwaite's imagination and enjoy doing it. And after that, he was going to call MacNally up for a drink and tell him all about it. They were both going to get a great laugh out of this.

The rain was falling hard by the time Lepov hailed a TransitCar and told the driver to take him to Chettleham Keep. Lepov didn't mind the rain. He just wanted to get this case over with.

15

For once, Menya Russell had been a good investigator, and it annoyed the hell out of MacNally. It had taken the youngster no time at all to come up with a probable location for the original resting place of the body: a twelve story apartment building on the western edge of the city known as the Roth Building. To be more precise, it *had* been the Roth Building. Now, it was a deep, square hole in the ground.

"Just follow me and see if this makes sense." Russell excitedly cleared his deskscreen and awaited MacNally's approval to continue.

"Just don't mumble."

"I won't. Look. Let's start here." Russell pulled up documents to support each point. "There are nine work permits issued at this time that involve foundational work. Two of them were issued yesterday. I'm ignoring them, since the body was found yesterday."

"Could have been excavated in the morning and hauled to the dump site by the afternoon." MacNally couldn't help interrupting. He had an irresistible urge to put young know-it-alls in their place.

"True. But I called each site and spoke to the foremen. Neither one actually got around to getting anything done in the way of excavating. One had mechanical trouble; the other one just got a late start. I got the idea he had personnel problems. At any rate, I counted them out. That leaves us with seven construction sites."

"Okay, so then what?"

"Well, one of the sites was all bedrock work. Drilling and blasting. Basically, it was all rock or crushed rock. Two of them were digging down on the southern end, nearest to the edge of the marina. Both of them had contracts with tugs that dumped their debris in the ocean."

MacNally was surprised that only two of the building contractors were using the tugs. It was becoming an acceptable practice to dump waste into the ocean. The majority of Agean, a modest-sized moon, was covered in water. The small bit of land that the Lazaretto occupied was the only habitable land. As the landfills grew, there were fewer arguments about sinking waste in the ocean's depths.

"So that leaves four excavation sites." MacNally raised an

eyebrow. That didn't fully explain why Russell wanted to go to the Roth Building.

"Here's where the soil composition comes into play. I was able to locate the building records of the four sites in question. One of them was new, within twenty years. Its main foundational concrete is saturated in HardTack. Remember, we didn't show any of that. We showed plenty of the metallic fibers. That's called Magtite, by the way."

"I knew what it was called," MacNally weakly defended himself.

"And you were right. The fibers are electrically charged once the concrete has set. It involves the magnetic properties of the fibers. Anyway, one of the last three sites had none of this in its original materials list. That, in fact, is why it's being excavated. Cheapskates built it with only concrete. There's too much moisture here year-round for that. The foundation had crumbled to the point of near catastrophic failure."

"Hell, Russell, are you some kinda engineer now?"

"Actually, I did a little of that in the army."

"You're kidding." MacNally looked down at his partner and tried to do some basic math in his head. "When did you have time to be in the army? When you were twelve?"

"Just two summers. The first one before my last year of school and the next summer once I was out of school. Everyone on Arcobia does it."

"How fascinating for Arcobian teenagers. Two sites left, right?"

"Yeah." Russell cleared his deskscreen of all the supporting documents and replaced them with two single white pages. "The one on the left is the Roth Building. The one on the right is Warren Place. Both of them fit the composition reports. Both of them have had excavation done in the last four weeks."

"So we can check them both out." MacNally liked that idea. It would waste a nice amount of time.

"Not really," Russell said with a rare smile.

"What?" This time, MacNally wasn't sure what the kid had said.

"You might think we need to look at both places," Russell spoke louder, "but we don't. I was able to come up with something else."

"Something else?" Russell had actually peaked MacNally's interest.

"There are several methods for excavation. The tried and true method is the claw and bucket method. This system has been used since man first needed to dig a hole. You just claw at the ground with a sharp object and lift the load out in a bucket. A back-hoe with a front-end loader still does the job. It's a cheap and effective way to get it done. But the bigger contractors now use mulchers. You know how those work, right?"

"Russell," MacNally stared at his partner, "I haven't tried to dig a hole since I was six."

"Mulchers are nothing but a set of grinders that pulverize the ground. A vacuum system sucks up what's left." Russell pointed at the document on the right. "These guys at Warren Place are a high-dollar operation. They rented a mulcher the day they started digging."

"And the mulcher would have turned our body into bonemeal. Is that what you're getting at?"

"That's it, Lieutenant." Despite the fact that Russell usually lacked interest in the job, he managed to look slightly pleased with himself.

"You're a bona fide investigator, Russell. Now, if you can get me an I.D. on the body, I'll let you carry a badge." That had ended up sounding harsher than MacNally had intended. He'd only meant to pick at the kid. Somehow, MacNally left the office feeling like he had seriously insulted Russell. MacNally decided either he was getting soft, or Russell was too easy a target. It didn't help that the young man never fired back at him.

"The VTechs must be having a hard time with their data. They still don't have anything for us."

"Or maybe they're just too busy drooling over girlie magazines." MacNally felt better poking fun at the VTechs. Not only did they deserve it, but he liked to think it made Russell feel better as well.

"Should we talk to them again, see what the holdup is?"

"I don't see what good it'll do." MacNally went back to his desk and grabbed his coat. "I don't think we're in any kind of a hurry. And we can check back with them after we check out the Roth site."

MacNally had done his best not to get angry with the kid. He had hoped they would spend the better part of two days looking at different construction sites. He hoped they wouldn't find anything obvious at the Roth Building. This was no time for Russell to become a proficient investigator. MacNally had seen an opportunity to delay the investigation by a few sleight-of-hand moves but he was quickly losing that window of opportunity. To slow this down he would have to take far more aggressive action than he wanted to. MacNally wasn't sure he was ready to do that.

Slowing down this investigation was harder than he'd expected.

16

The Thief sat hunched over that morning's newspaper. The flimsy paper was covered in grimy cheap ink. There were no flashy color photos in it, no stylish advertisements. *Lazaretto Offline* was a rare example of a vanished breed of information. The few printed newspapers that still existed in the Euxine System owed their existence to the simple paranoia of the lunatic fringe. The majority of people had come to accept the governing controls that facilitated the flow of information through the most commonly viewed NewsVision. Few people subscribed to the old conspiracy theories that speculated on the distortion and fabrication of the news. But those few were loyal subscribers to the low budget 'paper' newspapers that proudly boasted of their freedom from the networked NewsVision. The thief was one of their most ardent subscribers.

With grunts and whimpers he read through the provocative articles, pawing at the paper as if he might rearrange the words into articles more in line with his tastes. The words remained in the order in which they had been printed, and the Thief could only shake his head and sigh, rub his hands together and whine; this unvarnished and unsanctioned news always disturbed him.

His left hand pawed at his head, first scratching at his hair and then attempting to smooth it back down. A pained expression crossed his face. It wasn't there. The body. There was no mention of a body.

That should be good news. The less attention it drew the less interest the police would show. But would the police hide what they knew from the public? Would they censor honest publications like *Offline*? That was impossible, he decided.

He wished the Liar had never told him about the body. It would all come to nothing. They would watch and hold their breath and then—nothing. What, after all, would anyone care about a body from so many years ago? This was the Lazaretto, for God's sake; things weren't neat and tidy like life on the planets. Even the fascist-hearted cops knew that.

The Thief turned the page and spread out the paper. He whispered to himself as he read the smaller headings. *Councilman Found Guilty of Reckless Endangerment.* He shook his head and clucked his tongue at that one. *IHS Investigation Begins.* A great deal of nodding; he liked the sound of that. *Raid Shuts Down Brothel.* "Disgusting," he pronounced, "nasty."

Scanning each story, humming approval where he could—he cleared his throat contemptuously where he couldn't. An article about a politician from the planet Dnepr made him snort in laughter, his long, bent legs kicking first at the floor then at the rungs on his chair. Another story citing a military action against rebels back on Earth made him sit forward in earnestness. He licked at his lips and hugged himself, his elbows sticking out at odd angles as he rocked backwards and forwards. News of combat always had this effect on him. He told himself he wanted to be back in the fray, wanted to feel the heat of battle and the stench of death.

But that would have to wait. He had to stick to the plan. He had a job to do and he'd get no chance to run off into glorious battle. Why, after all, should he risk his safety in war? Hadn't he sacrificed enough? Hadn't he lost his life once already? To be sure; he had already given his all. Let younger men offer up their lives. The young ones had no idea how much they were risking. It was only the older, wiser men who knew how valuable life could be; knew just how much could be lost in death.

The Thief didn't want to think about death. That would have to wait as well. For now there was only the plan. And the plan would bring the payoff he'd dreamt of for so many years. Then he'd have no time for death. Then he'd have the means to truly live; to reach out and take what he'd always known should be his.

The paper failed to hold his interest. It was full of lies, anyway. Propaganda that only fooled the idiots who read it. At least he wasn't ignorant enough to allow that kind of garbage into his home. Papers like *Lazaretto Offline* pandered to the weak-minded. Only the lower classes wasted what paltry monies they had on such nonsense.

The Thief wadded his subscription into a distorted ball and heaved it into the trash. Why waste time when there was work to do?

Uncurling himself from his chair, he scrambled toward the front room where he'd displayed his foil-suit to the Liar. He was pleased with how that had turned out. No doubt she'd been immensely impressed with his demonstration. It was important that she be reminded of his skills. The Thief wanted her to remember her place. Not that it would keep her from causing trouble. But it would be enough. That little bitch was too much to handle if he didn't jerk her chain from time to time.

Check up on him, would she? She would learn. He would be patient. She would see just who was checking up on whom.

Straddling a stool, he bent over an old keyboard as his fingers scuttled over the keys. A twisted smile crossed his lips. It was time to work. There was still much to be done. And if that dead body did force him to ramp up his timetable, he'd have to get cracking.

He'd have to quit worrying about the Liar, the Thief conceded silently. She was a good kid. If her greatest vice was being too careful, he couldn't complain. She was strong-willed. And that was something to be proud of. After all, she'd learned it from him.

17

It had taken Chitti only a few minutes to get Sun settled into the vacant desk beside her own. Sun watched with curiosity as the young woman snatched away the piles of paperwork and tossed them into a new pile in a back corner. In the same way, she cleared the desk of the computer parts and wiped down the deskscreen with a small rag she had fished out of a desk drawer.

"You can use this as long as you need it."

"I appreciate it." Sun slid a finger along the surface of the deskscreen. It was an older model. That was obvious. But Sun made no mention of it. Charities like this did not have extra money to spend on office equipment. "This is more than I'll need."

"Let's not start out lying to each other." Chitti chuckled and returned to the other desk. "That desk model is older than I am. If I remember correctly, I was told it was donated by one of the Lazaretto Administration departments. I can't remember how long ago. But the important thing is it still works. At least, for now it's working."

"I'm sure it'll be fine." Sun sat, placing her palm on the surface. She watched the black screen power up. It was working well enough to pick up her Personal Data Tag signal, though the start routine was a little slow. Okay, it was a lot slow. Sun suppressed an impatient giggle as she waited for the screen to indicate it was fully operational.

"I'm gonna shoot a few things over to you." Chitti was clicking away at her deskscreen with those long fingernails. "First of all, I've got to do a little PR work for the Society's benefit. These files will fill you in on our history and what we've been up to lately. I don't know how much you were able to learn about us back home." She stopped what she was doing and curiously examined Sun. "Where did you say you came from?"

"Fort Mai Ling. That's a military base on Sinop. We have the Euxine System's largest Veterans' Benefits office there. Second only to the home office on Earth." Sun finally spied the pulse of a ready icon on her desk.

"I had an old girlfriend from school that was stationed at Mai Ling. She couldn't stop talking about some little ratty bar just off the base—"

"Fakir's?"

"That was it."

"It's not the nicest bar near the base." Sun gave Chitti a funny look.

"That's what my friend always said." Chitti shook her head. "She and her friends liked to go there for drinks. They liked to see who had the courage to actually drink from their filthy glasses and which of them could stand the creepy come-ons from the ghouls who haunted that place."

"Your friend is tougher than I ever was." Sun smiled politely.

She'd heard of female soldiers doing exactly what Chitti was talking about. There were always stories about men getting injured by the lethally trained females they tried to woo. Sun had always found that kind of behavior ill-befitting the uniform. But the action always happened off base and no one had found a way to efficiently discourage it. At least no one cared enough to put a stop to it.

"Well, she was never a particularly bright or nice individual." Chitti was not at all embarrassed to make such an admission about a friend. "I was glad when she joined up and left home. She was always too eager to get us in trouble. I don't go in for that kind of thing too much."

Sun was impressed to hear Chitti speak like that. It gave her a good feeling about working with her. While Sun could never be accused of being a humorless workaholic by those who knew her, it was true they'd all agree she preferred to get her work done before she relaxed. It just made practical sense to Sun. She had a great sense of duty when it came to work. Fun and relaxation always came later.

"Okay, I see the pages on the Society's work. What's this one?"

"That's most of the data on the Lost Platoon. I have more, but it is far more in-depth, and you may not need that. At least, not yet." Chitti gave Sun an odd smile. "I'm sure you already have the IHS version of this fiasco. But you should know that my documentation is far more accurate. You don't have to believe everything you read in my files, but you'll get more accomplished if you have an open mind."

Sun nodded. There had, indeed, been an official version of how the Lost Platoon had become exiled in the Lazaretto. And the military was not about to stray from that account. Sun had been ordered to assess the proper financial responsibility of the VHB as per the budgetary rider. She had no orders to look for ways to right a wrong that had been committed over a quarter of a century ago. That was for the politicians.

"I look forward to reading the files." It was all Sun could think to say. Chitti would see it for what it was; a vague way of saying she wasn't about to commit to anything. Well, it had been the best she could offer.

The front door burst open, interrupting what had become an awkward moment. Sun felt relief as an elderly woman hurried into the room. She was small, with gray hair pulled back in a tight bun. Despite her shortened stature, it was obvious that she was still strong. *Tough old bird* came to Sun's mind as an apt description.

"Chitti, come quick." Raindrops glistened on the woman as she glanced suspiciously in Sun's direction. Underneath the suspicion, Sun could plainly see fear.

"What is it, Gretchen? Something wrong with Ben?" Chitti was no longer sitting. She'd already stood and grabbed a hooded jacket that had been lying on a stack of boxes.

"He won't let me call a doctor. You know how he is."

"Your husband is going make a widow out of you, yet." Chitti sped for the front door but stopped as she grabbed the old, brass handle. "Sun, I'll be back. I won't be long. Make yourself at home."

"Don't worry about me." Sun barely said the words before Chitti was gone and the door slammed shut.

The late morning glare was strong through the front windows. It was an odd, gray glare. This was, after all, the Lazaretto. The rain had been falling for a few minutes now. Not enough to collect into puddles yet, but the street was more wet than dry. The people on the street were beginning to move with a hint of urgency.

Sun hoped the emergency ended well. She hated to admit it, but she was actually glad of the distraction. It gave her a chance to sit in silence and scan through the files Chitti had given her. Sun was still feeling the effects of her travel and she knew a headache couldn't be too far around the corner. Sitting at a deskscreen—especially an old one with a faded screen—was not going to help. In fact, Sun decided to go ahead and take a few aspirins before the pain kicked in. There was no point in waiting for the inevitable.

Sipping at what was left of her tea, Sun flipped through the opening pages of the file on the *Lazaretto Benevolence Society*. She had been expecting the LBS to be a well-funded charity. She had never dreamt it would be a low-budget operation run out of an insignificant storefront. Sun decided she must have been expecting something on a grander scale due to their rather formal and self-exalted name.

As Sun began to read it became apparent that the LBS was a charity that depended on small donors. There was no major name attached to the charity. In fact, as Sun kept reading, it became apparent that there were no major names tied to the charity in any capacity.

The LBS had only been in existence for five years. They were now the sole charity that dealt in matters connected with the surviving members of the Lost Platoon. Before that, several of the better established charities did become involved with the members of the Lost Platoon, but there had never been a single entity to care for all of them until the LBS.

Sun could find no reason to explain this. Had an anonymous donor decided that the members of the ill-fated platoon would be better served by one charity rather than numerous ones? Had the other charities come together to form this one group? There was nothing in the file to suggest such a thing. She decided she might want to run down the sources of the small donors, but that would have to come later, if it came at all.

Sun stopped reading the file, distracted by the rain. It took her a moment to realize that despite what was now a heavy rain, a man was sitting beside the street. It was difficult to see him through the rain. As far as she could tell, he was sitting on a box. He wasn't shielding himself from the rain. He was simply sitting under the downpour. Had he been sitting there before the rain started? She couldn't remember.

She wondered why he was exposed to the elements. Most people back on Sinop would have feared catching pneumonia. So would anybody else on any other planet. Surely here in the Lazaretto people were even more aware of how deadly pneumonia could be.

As if the man had been able to divine her thoughts, he slowly stood to his feet. It was hard for Sun to see him — his dark shape rose then limped down the street and out of sight.

She would have to ask Chitti about him. She had a good idea that that young lady would know everyone in the neighborhood. People like Chitti Sienté had always filled her with reverent awe; such selflessness was too moving for words. It had been people like Chitti who had motivated Sun to get involved at the Veterans' Health Benefits. It had been her way of giving to those in need.

Sun couldn't be sure, but moments later, it appeared that the same man came wandering back into view as the rain continued to fall. He stumbled across her view, and disappeared out of sight again.

She would most definitely ask Chitti about him. Maybe there was something that could be done for him.

18

Lepov climbed out of a TransitCar. He caught a glimpse of Chettleham Keep rising above him but he couldn't get a good look at it. Hard rain continued to fall. He was forced to lower his head and hurry up the steps. Rain ran along the brim of his hat and poured down at his feet. Cold rain fell on the back of his neck until he pulled open the glass doors of the building and stepped inside.

The front lobby was a good deal larger than most of the apartment buildings Lepov had seen. It had once been an elegant atrium, that wasn't hard to see. Several large settees with heavily worn fabric stood in the center of the entrance. The atrium opened downward into a sunken chat room on the right that had been walled off from the rest of the room with chest high walls covered in low ferns. Inside this chat room were four divans upholstered with something that may have once been velvet, though Lepov doubted it had been real. The furnishings and décor told of a time when this lobby had been more than an entrance; something to come to, not just walk through.

Whenever that had been, Lepov thought, it was too many years ago. He crossed the atrium and stood patiently, waiting for one of the two sets of elevator doors to open. Many elevators he'd run across in the older buildings of the Laz were too untrustworthy to ride. But despite the building's age and tired condition, the doors slid open with enough dignity that Lepov decided the elevator was trustworthy.

Branithwaite had said the apartment in question was on the ground floor. Chettleham Keep's once grand lobby was essentially on the second floor of the building. The ground floor apartments were down one flight. Lepov had no intention of actually visiting the apartment. But he wanted to see the layout of the interior hallway.

No doubt Branithwaite would give him access to the security monitors if he asked. And it might come to that. But Lepov preferred to watch things from a more mobile vantage point. He wanted to be able to see *and* hear what was going on. Lepov knew that all locations had more than just sights and sounds — there was a feel to any place that could only be detected by someone on site.

The elevator doors pulled away from each other and Lepov took two or three steps into the dimly lit hallway. The floor was covered in old carpeting but it didn't fool anyone; it was as hard as rock. A heavily varnished door stood to the left of the elevator with a waist-high crash bar on it. That would be the stairs. An old sign across from the doors had an arrow pointing to the right. *01 – 06* was just discernible in flaked gold appliqués. There were no apartments to the left. The hallway ended a few feet from the stairwell door with a smaller unmarked door.

Lepov walked casually down the hall past apartments 06 and 05, then on past 04 and 03. The odd numbered rooms on his right; these were on the front of the building. The even-numbered rooms were on his left; the back side of the building. He kept walking, right past the apartment that worried Mr. Branithwaite; the corner apartment on the right: 02.

He didn't stop. He kept on until he came to the end of the hallway. If someone had been watching through their hallviewer, Lepov would have looked out of place. He stopped at the end of the hall — no door at this end — and turned and walked back toward the elevator. He slowed down, listening. He heard nothing besides his shoes scratching on the worn carpet. An air vent sighed as a ventilation system kicked on. A low rumble could be heard at the far end of the hall. Undoubtedly, the unmarked door at that end led into a maintenance room where the building's subsystems were housed.

There was little else to hear. No outside sounds made it into the hall. For all intents and purposes, the hall felt like a funeral home.

He used the stairwell to get back to the lobby. The crash bar on the door squealed in shock. The walls of the stairwell had been recently painted, the steps covered with a non-slip composite. For every step he took, Lepov could hear a soft squeak. He consciously lifted his feet as he climbed and the noise ceased.

At the lobby level, he found two doors. One opened into the lobby, a second door opened in the opposite direction. Testing its crash bar—no protesting squeal—Lepov found he was looking down a well-lit hallway that obviously ran to the back of the building. A door at the end was covered with a red sign; *Do Not Leave Door Open*. Service entrance.

Making sure the door to the stairwell did not lock behind him, Lepov followed the service hall and pushed open the abnormally wide metal door. It opened into an alley. A small loading dock hugged the wall just below the door; the alley below accessible by a concrete stair. The surrounding buildings blocked most of the falling rain. Most of what spattered the door were large drops that collected on the fire escapes hanging above.

The alley was wide enough to allow delivery trucks to pass through in one direction. It would have been dark save for a patch of gray light illuminating the brickwork of the surrounding buildings. Lepov held the door open and looked around to his left. Where there had once been a solid row of buildings, there was now a great gap in the row, allowing light into the alley. From the looks of it, a building had recently been torn down directly adjacent to Chettleham Keep.

Movement caught Lepov's attention. Someone poked a head around the corner of the building. A short someone. Lepov ignored the rain that dripped off the brim of his hat and waited until the head appeared again. This time, he could see a face with it. An urchin's little face with big eyes looked at him. When their eyes met, the head bobbed back out of view.

Lepov could hear laughter.

He went back to the lobby.

Lepov stepped down into the sunken chat room, needing a few minutes to think. He would be able to sit along one of the walls without being seen by anyone entering or leaving the building. So far the lobby had been empty, but he didn't want to make a show of himself. It was getting close to lunch time, and he had a feeling traffic would increase before long.

It was going to be nearly impossible to stake out the first floor hallway without being seen. Though not surprised, he had hoped he would be wrong. Sometimes it was irritating to be right. With all the times he'd been wrong in his life, most of them had never been when he'd wanted to be wrong. He would have to use the hall recorders to watch activity in and out of the apartment.

He needed a look inside that apartment. And he could do it. But more than likely he would have to lie his way in. And then Morvees would recognize him; at least he'd know what he looked like. And that would handicap anything he might need to do later.

Lepov smelled the smoke before he saw the cigarette. He'd given up smoking years ago, but he kept a packet of cigarettes in his coat pocket to remind him that he was in control of his desire for nicotine. Some days the smell of smoke nauseated him. Some days it made him lust for a fag more than the curves of a woman. Today was one of the latter days. He sat up and inhaled deeply. Damn, it smelt good.

But if someone in the lobby was smoking, who could it be? The lobby was empty. And he hadn't heard any doors open or close.

The smoke was close. He could actually see it now. It was drifting down into the sunken chat room. Whoever was smoking was sitting on the steps—the smoke hugged the ground. Lepov inched closer to the steps. He couldn't see around the corner, but he heard the smoker cough twice; a small, weak cough.

Reaching around the corner of the steps, Lepov felt rough cloth and grabbed a fistful of it, jerking the smoker into the chat room. The startled smoker cried out and fell into view. For once, Lepov's deductive reasoning had been pretty good. The smoker was the same urchin he'd heard laughing in the alley.

"Leggo!" The urchin wasn't laughing now. He was struggling to free himself from Lepov. None of his gyrations paid off. Lepov might have been getting older, but his strength hadn't yet begun to fade. When it became apparent that the boy couldn't break free he snatched something from a pocket and Lepov saw a glint of steel.

"Stop that." Lepov used his free hand to stick a finger into the boy's armpit, lifting him several inches; an old beat-cop trick that never failed to make a drunk stand at attention.

The boy tried to say something inappropriate for children but he couldn't. All he could do was suck in air. The pain was too great to even allow for whining. The best he could do was stand perfectly still with a face like a tormented demon's. The cigarette in his mouth fell out onto the marble floor. A knife clattered to the floor as well.

"Truce?" Lepov asked.

The boy nodded, a tear rolling down his cheek.

Lepov pulled back, allowing the boy to sink back to his normal posture. He reached out with one hand and began massaging the soft pocket under his arm.

"You crazy old man. That hurt!"

"Yeah." Lepov shoved the boy down onto a bench along the

Jason Phillip Reeser

wall and scooped up the knife. He dug his heel into the burning cigarette then sat beside the kid.

"For one thing, I'm not an old man. I only look like one to you. And for another, I know that hurts. That's why it works. You think your little stick here would have felt good to me?"

"Not if I would've swiped ya good." The boy watched Lepov offer to return the knife. He hesitantly reached out, as if he expected Lepov to turn the knife at the last minute and run it into him.

"Go ahead, take it back. You don't think I want it, do you?"

"How would I know? I don't know nothin' 'bout you, Mister."

"True enough." Lepov let go of the knife and offered to shake the boy's hand. "I'm Gregor Lepov."

"Josh." The boy never hesitated to touch Lepov. He shook hands with a solid grip. Either he wasn't aware of the threat of contagions or he just didn't care. Something in his eyes told Lepov he just didn't care. "And you owe me a cigarette."

"Take it from an old smoker, don't get started on those things."

"Ain't you seen me smokin'? I'm already started on 'em."

"Not likely, Josh. You sounded like you'd never smoke one before in your life. That cough of yours can't fool an old hand like me." Lepov liked the boy's spirit. He wasn't full of anger, but he had just enough vinegar in him to stand up for himself.

"Cigs are easier to get than what I really want."

"And what do you really want?"

"Chewing gum."

"What's chewing gum?"

"Like candy, but you can chew it for hours."

Lepov hadn't been prepared for that. Here was a kid who couldn't be twelve years old who was acting like he was nineteen but wasn't afraid to admit he wanted candy.

"Chewing gum's from Earth. People used to chew it all the time. I read about it once. It's hard to get now. Lots of money. Probably why you never heard of it." Josh said this while examining Lepov.

"Let's make a little deal, Josh. You promise not to stick me with your little dagger and I'll get you some chewing gum. And no cigarettes, too."

"Sure. Like you got the money to buy chewing gum. I might be a kid, but I ain't stupid."

"Kid," Lepov had a hunch Josh was right but he couldn't help himself, "Let me worry about how much it costs."

Josh cocked his head and scrutinized Lepov. His yellow hair was unwashed, though it had been recently cut. He had full cheeks and dark eyes that never stopped moving, watching warily from side to side and any other direction they felt like checking. He was about half of Lepov's height and thin without looking famished. There were faded little freckles sprinkled across the upper edges of his cheeks.

"What do I gotta do?"

"For what?"

"The gum." His wide-eyed glare told Lepov he wasn't an idiot. "You ain't gonna buy me gum for no reason. What do you want?"

Lepov had no intention of bartering something from the boy, but he was so caught off guard by the kid's sharp suspicion that Lepov had to admit it wasn't a bad idea. He made a quick decision.

"I'll get you gum in exchange for a little work. I want to know all I can about apartment Oh-Two, down on the first level."

Josh's eyes drained of interest and he shot Lepov a mocking smile.

"I'll stick with my cigarettes."

"I'm not a cop, Josh." That got the boy's attention. Josh raised an eyebrow, unable to leave the next obvious question unasked.

"You a spy?"

The doors for one bank of the elevators split apart. From where Lepov was sitting, he couldn't see if anyone stepped out of it. But he'd be able to see who it was if they headed for the entrance. He held a finger, cautioning Josh into silent stillness.

Instead of going for the entrance, Lepov could hear steps approaching the sunken chat room. A head came into view as the new arrival looked down into the chat room. The man looked once at Lepov then turned his attention to Josh.

"Just where I expected to find you, boy." The man stared hard at the smashed cigarette on the floor. "Your mother wanted me to find you and send you up. Is everything okay here? Are you bothering this boy?"

Lepov was about to respond when Josh jumped up from the bench.

"He ain't bothered me. We was just talkin'. He was just askin' me what kids like me like to eat. I told what I like. That's all." Josh started up the steps, but stopped and looked back at Lepov. "You do like I said and get some of that for your boy. I bet he'll do like you ask, if you buy him a bunch of it."

Lepov nodded. He heard him make noise all the way to the elevator. All the while, the man at the wall stared icily at Lepov. He didn't stop until the elevator doors closed.

Lepov was alone with the newcomer.

"When I said you shouldn't recognize me, I didn't mean you should be hostile to me. Indifference would have been enough, Mr. Branithwaite."

"I don't want you bothering the Teeg boy. His mother has

enough trouble with him as it is. I'd rather he not get mixed up with you." Branithwaite's icy stare had not warmed up. Lepov had the distinct impression the landlord's hostility had not been playacting.

"I'm not here to get mixed up with anyone. I'm simply here to do the job you hired me to do." He turned and headed for the glass entrance.

"Just a minute, Mr. Lepov. What have you learned?"

Lepov stared out the glass doors; the rain had slowed to a light drizzle. He wasn't paying attention to his client, or the rain. Instead, he was watching a large black car settle down at the edge of the curb. Its air cushion blew puddled water up in a fan that sprayed the sidewalk. He knew that car. And he knew who was going to climb out of it.

The driver's door swung open and a tall, barrel-chested man climbed stiffly out. He was older than Lepov, though not by much, with a mostly bald head sporting a bushy mustache. He was a large man, but he carried most of his weight above his beltline. His name was Lieutenant Ed MacNally. He was the senior detective with Lazaretto Homicide.

The car's passenger door swung open at the same time. The young man with the tight, wavy, red hair was Detective Menya Russell. He was not only young, he was thin with strong shoulders. Next to MacNally, however, he appeared smaller than he actually was. He was a new detective with the department and had borne the unfortunate luck of drawing MacNally as his first partner.

Lepov stepped closer to the door and watched the detectives. They weren't looking in his direction; instead, they were concentrating on something down the street. Lepov chose to stay out of sight. MacNally was a friend but they never liked to share too much from their respective occupations. Not until it became necessary. MacNally didn't like private detectives, despite his friendship with Lepov. He always believed they were interfering with the police. Lepov understood. He'd been a cop.

He was curious to know if they were checking on something related to his own case. But as they moved down the block, Lepov could see they were only interested in the vacant lot next to Chettleham Keep. That was for the best. He had no interest in getting mixed up in one of Mac's investigations.

19

I do not remember the occasion for the party; it's possible I was never told. But there is a great deal I remember about that party. It was the first time I had caught a glimpse of what was going on. At least, I thought I had.

It started with me caring for Calla in her room. She was still draining heavily, but I had found a measure of control that made it easier on the child. Calla was listless at times like that. She would lie on her side, breathing with great effort. I hated to hear her struggle for breath. It made matters worse to see her face; placid, resigned to her little corner of hell. She exhibited the kind of grace of which I could only dream. At such times I would stroke her hair; it did her little good but had a great effect on me.

I had been sitting on her bed, absentmindedly listening to a piano. That meant the party had started. I could barely hear the music even though it was only downstairs and one room over. To me it sounded too far away to be coming from inside the house. I imagined it must have been coming from one of the transport ships still in orbit.

"Is she okay?"

I jerked out of my reverie and stared at Mr. Zoltis. He never seemed to come all the way into Calla's room. Was he afraid of her?

"She was draining some, but it is slowing." I spoke as softly as I could. She was drifting to sleep. I continued to stroke her hair. "She'll sleep now. Maybe two or three hours. She never sleeps more than that."

"You had a funny look on your face when I came in. Are you still worrying yourself for no reason?"

"No," I shook my head. He would think I was lying, but I couldn't help that. "Just listening to the music. It sounded so far away."

"Are you tired?" His question surprised me. "Do you feel well?"

"I'm fine." I could see there was a point to his question. "Why?"

"You should come down and join the party. For just a little while."

"No, I'll stay here with Calla. I'm not one to socialize. Nobody would appreciate my appearance. Besides, I look a mess."

"Yes, you do. But you can clean up. And I thought it would do you good, woman. Not the other way around. The monitors will alert you if Calla needs you, yes?"

The piano was almost too faint to hear. I had to admit I wanted to hear more of it. And by then, Calla had fallen completely asleep.

"Go on," he gruffly ordered me. He couldn't hide the fact that he was pleased to be able to order me around. He never tired of that. "Clean up and put on something nice. And don't take longer than five minutes."

I appeared at the top of the stairs fifteen minutes later.

The piano player was playing with more intensity. I had not been able to hear the rest of the jazz quartet until then; a soft shuffle of drums, the exotic playful call of a clarinet, and a gentle thrum of an upright bass. I stood at the top step and watched men and women dressed for a black tie affair pass through the entrance hall. The women wore grand dresses of black and dark blues. I was going to look out of place; nothing I owned would ever approach that tier of society. Mr. Zoltis knew this.

I tried not to think about the fact that even the servers were dressed better than I was as I descended the staircase. By the time I reached the last step, he was there. I'd been so distracted in Calla's room that I hadn't noticed he was wearing a formal black suit. It did not fit him well. He seemed uncomfortable. Rolls of skin bunched at his collar. He was angry.

"It's all I had to wear," I tried to explain. My dress was made of a creamy green material. I had worn it once to a friend's wedding.

"You look fine," he waved off my dress, impatient as always. "I had to wait for you. Follow me."

He did not stroll through the crowded rooms with charming words for his guests. No one could have guessed he was the host. He bulled through the crowd. He did not nod; he did not make eye contact. I was impressed that he managed not to growl at those in his path.

I followed him to the dining room. A great table full of men and women watched us enter. With growing dread I realized he intended to seat me at one end of the table, opposite from his seat at the head. I yearned to flee. He had never wanted me to come to the party for my general well-being. He had intended that I perform the role of hostess.

I was angry. The entire dinner party had been waiting. Dinner had been held back until the hostess had arrived.

"Well, I found her." Mr. Zoltis stood at the head of the table and waved to gain everyone's attention. "Late, as usual, but what woman ever gets dressed in time?"

He laughed. Every one of the men laughed as did a few of the women. Instinct told me to keep my head. I smiled. I even think I blushed a little; the demure lady of the house. I knew it was important to not anger Calla's father. He was an insensitive ass, but I knew I must never tell him so. I must never do anything that would give him reason to send me away.

No, I had to keep my place. I could not allow Calla to be raised by this man without my influence. I nodded to those seated near me. We ate dinner, and I never once looked up at Calla's father. I could hear him laughing and arguing with his end of the table. Dinner lasted far longer than it should have.

I left the table sick at heart. I'd left Calla only to be used as a centerpiece; a silly bit of décor. I wanted to run upstairs, but before I did, I found myself listening again to the musicians. The clarinet had been switched out for a saxophone. The song was by far the slowest they had played all night. One could almost believe that the quartet was slowly falling asleep, caught in their own magic spell of twilight dreams.

I wanted to let the song lull me to sleep, to forget for a while: Calla, her father, my tacky dress. I nearly nodded off even as I listened. It took great effort to open my eyes as they played a last, long note.

At the end of the hall, I saw Mr. Zoltis exit through ornate French doors. These led to a small terrace overlooking the back lawn. Two men followed.

I recognized one of them, though I didn't know his name. I could not remember where I had seen him. Judging by their careful glances around the hall as they left, the three men wanted to be alone.

Exactly when I had decided to interrupt their meeting I can't recall. But at some point, I had known I would do it. I was still angry at Calla's father for his treatment at dinner. Crossing the hall as the quartet began a little number featuring the upright bass, I drew energy from its strong tempo. Without missing a beat, I put my hand on the French door and pushed.

The men were close to the door. They lifted their heads and stared.

"What do you want, woman?" Mr. Zoltis' voice was cold, unfriendly.

"I'm sorry to interrupt." I could still hear the song behind me until I allowed the door to shut. I took a few steps forward. My employer had never looked so angry. *"I was looking for you."*

"You found me. What do you want?"

"Hello, my name's Della." I nodded to the two men. *"I didn't realize Mr. Zoltis was in a meeting."*

"Yes, I am. I'm sorry about this, gentlemen. This is Della, my daughter's tutor." He didn't stumble over that lie for even a second. *"Della, this is Claude Reno, a man of low rank and low pay in the Lazaretto Administration."*

That was the man I had recognized. He was tall, young and nervous. I knew him from the dinner. I had seen him making a fuss over each course. He had seemed more intent on ensuring he did not drop any food on his lap than on eating.

The third man was tall as well, though much bigger. His muscled shoulders stood out like he was wearing an old-fashioned space-walker suit. His neck muscles held his head rigidly in place. I imagined it must have hurt him to nod.

"This is a competitor of mine, Della. His name is Cam Raley. He's an old trucking hand like me. He's done just about as well as I have, too."

"Maybe a little better." Raley bowed at the waist; an exaggerated gesture that somehow fit his strong physique. Thick blond hair topped off his nearly perfect image. *"May I say that you have no need to apologize for interrupting our meeting? Talking business with Kjarsta is always boring.. I hope you'll stay so we may get acquainted."*

The man's perfect features were no match for his saccharine charm. What he lacked in sincerity he made up for in effort. I disliked him. I could see that Mr. Zoltis didn't like the man's attempts to charm me either.

"No, Mr. Raley. I won't be able to stay." I turned and looked Mr. Zoltis in the eye. *"If you're done with me as a hostess, now that dinner is concluded, I need to get back to Calla. She's not feeling well."*

This last comment was for the benefit of the man from the Lazaretto Administration. Calla's father did not exactly pale when I mentioned that she was ill, but I could see anger in his eyes. There was no way I would endanger our secret. I would do nothing that might compromise the girl. But her father did not know that. I enjoyed watching him squirm.

"Nothing serious," he added, *"just a little cold."*

"I see." Reno, the government man, looked unduly alarmed.

"Was there anything else?" I wanted to make Mr. Zoltis acknowledge my request. I wanted him to see I was upset by what he had done.

"Just go back upstairs, woman. Leave us alone."

I managed to smile and thank him.

"Let's meet again, can we do that?" Cam Raley smiled at me.

"After Calla gets well. I'd like that." I would have liked no such thing, but I knew just saying it would irritate my employer.

Claude Reno said nothing as I left. He just stared as if I were contagious.

They did not resume speaking as I walked back to the French doors. They waited until I shut them completely. By then, I could only hear the plaintive sounds of a muted trumpet and the playful scales of a jazz piano.

Climbing the staircase, I thought about that late-night visitor and what Mr. Zoltis had told him. "You work for me. My partners like to try and call the shots." Since when did Kjarsta Zoltis partner with someone like Reno, the Administration man? And I would never have believed he would work with a competitor like Raley. Both of these men were dangerous to Mr. Zoltis. I wouldn't have cared if I had not worried the danger could spill over into Calla's life.

I wanted to know what was going on with those three men. It would be nothing good. I knew that. I would have stayed well away from them had I not believed that Calla might be endangered.

At that time, I had no way of knowing that I was both wrong and right.

20

The most irritating part about Russell's efficient investigating, MacNally knew, was that the young detective was actually peaking MacNally's interest in the case. In point of fact, MacNally was beginning to feel the tug of curiosity. He wanted to speed things up; to find out what had happened so long ago. If MacNally hadn't decided to work this case on his own agenda, he would have pushed Russell to work even harder; solve this thing as fast as he could.

But not yet. Yes, the details of the murder would be intriguing, but MacNally already suspected how it all ended. Some things, however, should never be exhumed. And that was true for the victim. But if he was unable to keep the past buried, he also knew there would never be enough evidence to secure a conviction. MacNally would have to be careful. He would have to let the case build slowly while he worked to keep the victim's name hidden.

"That was it." Russell stood in the light rain, looking at the excavated site that had once been the Roth Building. They were staring into a hole that was about ten meters deep. The foundation had been scraped clean; rusted iron shoring lined the walls. White chalky patches covered the floor of the dig, rain puddled into the corners, in some places it was over a meter deep.

Barricade bars ran along the lip of the opening. Skeleton steps had been temporarily erected at one corner. The last step was in the shallower puddle.

"You wanna go down there?" Russell had that pained expression on his face again, as if he believed mud could actually hurt him.

"Yeah, I do. We didn't come here to stare at a hole in the ground." MacNally could have suggested they wait until the site dried up, but this was the Lazaretto. His suggestion would make it obvious he didn't want to investigate. When would a hole this size ever dry up in the Lazaretto?

"I was just asking." Russell swung a leg up and over the barricade bar and stepped onto metal grating that connected to the top step of the stairs. The whole structure shook as he placed the rest of his weight on it. The young Arcobian said something that sounded like a curse.

"What was that?" MacNally couldn't help but smile as Russell grabbed hold of the skeleton frame and leaned over to stare hard at the bottom of the hole. "That sounded like pretty strong language for a kid." MacNally climbed over the barricade bar with an exaggerated roughness that shook the stairway all the more.

"You done?" Russell asked, well aware that the older detective was jacking with him. He started down.

Raised serrated treads kept them from slipping on the wet metal. The two men twisted back and forth down the stairs until they came to the last step. It was under water, as was the landing. Russell hesitated, but MacNally pushed past him and stepped into the rainwater. It was cold, and came up over the toe of his heavy shoes.

"So what are we going to see here?" MacNally liked what he saw. A clean site with nothing but mud. There was no chance they'd find a clue.

"Four men are posed to beat us here."

"What?" MacNally wondered what Russell could mean by that.

"I said," Russell spoke up, a little impatient with his partner's hearing problem, "the foreman is supposed to meet us here."

"What foreman?"

"The one over this dig. I called him this morning and he said he'd be willing to answer some questions."

"That's clever," MacNally swore under his breath. This kid was gonna kill him with his bright ideas.

The skeleton frame began to shake as if a giant pile-driver were pounding it into the ground. MacNally looked up and saw two men climbing down. One of them was simply huge. Cold large drops of rain fell from the metal frame and hit him on the face and neck.

"Detective?" A thin reedy voice called down to them.

"Mr. Crawford?" Russell called back in response.

"Yes, I spoke with you this morning." The first man to come down was a miniature man with a hard-caked face; an unmistakable effect from working on an asteroid mine. His bristle-broom hair was completely white. He wore coveralls that might have once been as white as his hair, though that would have been a long time ago.

Behind him, a man-creature in matching coveralls dropped heavily on each step. He must have weighed more than two full-sized men. A small head sat precariously on top of his massive shoulders. He was not simply obese; he was too solid for that. The most appropriate word that came to MacNally's mind was *massive*.

"This is Baen. He's my chief rig operator. I thought I'd bring him along. You said you were interested in details about our dig. He'll know more about it than me."

Beautiful, MacNally thought in frustration, *everyone's got to be clever. Let's all pat ourselves on the back.*

When Russell looked at MacNally for direction, MacNally gestured at him to go ahead and ask his questions. There seemed to be little point in trying to slow him down. MacNally sloshed around on the landing and decided he'd wished he stayed up on the steps. His toes were getting cold.

Russell explained about the body in the landfill. He did not repeat the details of how he concluded the body had come from the Roth site, but he said enough to get them on his side. They were understandably interested and flattered that they could be of help.

"What can you tell us about the site?" Russell asked; a vague question that MacNally was sure would lead nowhere.

"Well, we had to drop the old tower floor by floor. There wasn't any room here to drop it down on one side." Crawford leaned back against the skeleton frame and looked out over the site. "You see, up there, we've got the Chettleham Keep to the south, and north of here is that old two hundred meter tower—I forget its name—ugly, ain't she? Then you got the buildings on the other side of the alley to the east. And of course across the street to the west you got buildings all along the quadrant wall. So we had to dismantle the thing from the top down. There just wasn't a place to set her down."

"So what happened when you got to the basement levels?" Russell asked.

"Oh, from there it got messy." This was Baen talking. He had a raspy voice. "We had two trackjacks that tore up the foundations. Yanked it all out. If you say there was a body in there, I ain't surprised we didn't see it. It gets messy at that point. Just a damn mess of concrete, steel rebar—"

"Magtite?"

"Yeah," Baen nodded and pulled at his coveralls like they were pants that kept falling down, "I s'pose this old building had Magtite. Can't tell from lookin' at it. It's softer than Tack, though, so maybe we'd know."

"But you ran into HardTack." Crawford's questioning tilt of the head was more question than statement.

"No," the rig operator shook his head, but did not seem to be satisfied with his own answer. "No, this was all pretty easy to tear up. Over the whole area." He waved his hand out to indicate the various sections of the dig. "Yeah, none of that gave us any trouble."

MacNally looked at Russell, who was sullenly listening to the contractors. Rain fell on Russell's disappointed young face, his red hair darker now that it was completely soaked.

"Well, how far down past the foundation do you dig?"

"We don't go deeper than the foundation. Just take what was there and stop at the old soil, sand, or bedrock. Whatever was there to begin with." Crawford chewed on his upper lip for a moment. "This is all soil. Bedrock's further down in this area of the city. In fact, there's a good bit of sand in this too. It packs okay for foundation work. You want to know if the body was down below the foundation? That what you're thinkin'?"

"It would help us to know when the death occurred." MacNally made an effort to sound like he wanted answers too. "Below the foundation tells us it was before the building was erected."

"Yeah," Crawford nodded, "or even if it happened during construction—well, it would have had to have been during. If it had been that deep, but below the foundation, it would have happened after the hole had been dug. But I think there's a simple answer to that."

"What's that?" Russell looked hopeful.

"You just check for radiation. There's low levels of radiation in this soil around here. It's nothing gonna hurt ya, I don't guess. The whole Crust shelf has some level or other of radiation." When MacNally and Russell returned blank looks, Crawford tried to explain. "The Crust shelf is just the geological name for this whole region. Lazaretto's built on top of the damn thing. When StarEngine—that's the engineering firm that laid down the original plan for the Lazaretto, Star Engineering—StarEngine decided this area they called the Crust shelf was the best place to build. Other parts of Aegean had higher radiation, and this was fairly low. Good and stable. That and the fact that is was close to deep water wells."

"So the water's in irradiated soil?" Russell's pained expression drew a laugh from the foreman.

"Water's below the bedrock, son. I'm only talking about the soil that's down at this level. But you're missing the point about the radiation. It's not about how bad it is. I'm saying if a body were in the soil for as long as you say, it would have a solid trace of radiation in it. That make sense?"

"Yes, it does." Russell almost looked happy as he turned to MacNally. "Do you remember seeing anything in the soil comps about radiation?"

"No. But it'll show up in the visuals." The boy had looked so frustrated MacNally felt compelled to give him some kind of hope.

"Was there anything else you wanted to know?" Crawford leaned down toward Russell.

"I don't know. You'd know if there was anything out of the ordinary. Was there?"

"Not really, Detective. I wish I could be more helpful. You sure that body was down here?" Crawford's expression said he liked the idea: his dig had produced a dead body.

Russell nodded, his face once more pinched in thought.

"You call us again if you need anything else," Crawford nodded at the two detectives then turned to his rig operator. "Let's go."

Baen turned his head and looked at a section of the wall directly behind MacNally. His face brightened.

"Cholahn's hydraulics. Remember?" He was smiling at the foreman.

"Yeah, we lost two hours that day. Why?"

"Hey, Captain," Baen got Russell's rank wrong, but the look on his face got Russell's attention. "Right over here, along this south side of the dig, one of my rig men had trouble. His hydraulics got beat all to hell. I remember now. I been thinking 'bout it since you were talking 'bout the Magtite and Tack. When Cholahn started in on this side, he was breaking into foundation same as everywhere else, but he was expecting the stuff to break up nice and easy—it's all Magtite, right? But on the side here, he runs into Tack. That stuff is harder to break up. So he should have slowed down. But he didn't since he wasn't expecting it. He overworked his hydraulics. We found a good bit of Tack right over here."

Baen had bulled his colossal figure past all three men and stamped off into the rainwater. He walked about fifteen steps and stopped, facing the walls of the dig to the south. Chettleham Keep rose high above them.

"Right here, I'd say there was a good five or ten meters of Tack. Still a bunch of it there, behind the shoring." Wet, rusted shoring guarded the walls of the dig, ensuring that nothing could collapse into the hole.

Crawford followed his rig operator, ignoring the water that swirled up and over his shoes, soaking the pant legs of his coveralls.

"That's just HardTack from Chettleham Keep, Baen. That don't mean nothin' to these cops."

Baen's eager expression fell. The big man obviously wanted to help. Why was everyone so eager to help on a case that MacNally didn't want to solve? At least the massive rig operator had ultimately failed to give Russell useful information. By the looks of it, Russell knew the trip down into the hole had been a waste of time.

Both detectives began to climb out of the hole ahead of Crawford and his rig man. Neither one of them had to say anything, though they were both thinking the same thing. They wanted to get up the skeleton frame before Baen pounded his way up each step. There was no guarantee it would hold up to that kind of beating.

MacNally had barely been able to keep up with the conversation about soil and radiation and HardTack. What he could actually hear he didn't always understand. What he understood of civil engineering wouldn't have filled one little page of his notebook. That was definitely the kind of stuff Russell enjoyed. Let him figure out all that tedious trivia. Maybe Russell would waste more time than MacNally had hoped for.

MacNally hurried back to the car for his own reasons. Who cared if his shoes were watertight? It did him no good if they felt like they'd been locked in an ice chest.

21

Noon had come and gone. Sun Uijong was still alone. She had not stopped reading to eat lunch. Neither had she taken a moment to wonder what was keeping Chitti so long. Instead, Sun had been sitting hunched over her deskscreen, absorbed in the story of the Lost Platoon. It had taken a strong ache in her back before she realized she was reading from a flat desktop. Searching through desk menus, she was not surprised to see the system had no heads-up-display. She felt along the side of the desk, hoping this older model might have a manual riser. It did. She slid the switch back and the center of the desktop rose to just above a forty-five degree angle.

Relieved to be able to sit back in her chair, Sun stretched her back. Before long, she was engrossed again in her reading.

She had been familiar with the basic tenants of the platoon's history: While returning from combat on Arcobia, the platoon passed through the Lazaretto in route to Earth. The entire unit, twenty-six men, was diagnosed with a blood disease. A debate began over the

Jason Phillip Reeser

fate of these men. General public opinion was on the side of the soldiers; the blood disease was only technically listed as a contagion. There were minimal odds for communicable transmission; almost non-existent. Proponents of Lazaretto protocols demanded strict adherence to the policy, ensuring the health of the populations the Lazaretto had been entrusted to protect.

The debate did not rage for long. The Lazaretto was only twenty years old then. The days of plague were still too fresh in many people's minds. No one wanted to see the Lazaretto's isolation compromised. If that meant the permanent exile of twenty-six combat veterans, then so be it. When the last appeal was denied by a committee that contained members from both IHS and Earth's Military Directorate, as well as members from the Lazaretto Administration, the Lost Platoon slunk silently down the rain-blackened streets of the Lazaretto's Center City into legend.

Sun knew this, she'd read the historical commentaries. Public criticism arose once it was evident that the platoon would never be allowed back to earth. Citizens were now free to complain about the tragic fate of the unit. No one called for them to be sent home; Sun had seen that right away. With the platoon safely exiled, the troublemakers could raise a ruckus without corrective options available to the government. The Lazaretto was often used as a linchpin for unrelated political agendas.

The NewsVision stories moved on to more relevant issues and the general public either lost interest in the unfortunate men of the Lost Platoon or they simply forgot them. Sun found little information on them from about their second year in the Lazaretto to their sixth. In that sixth year, a writer from Bukovina, Kindra Boxovna published a book detailing the years of the Arcobian Rebellion. In her book, she wrote an entire chapter on the Lost Platoon. Overnight, people began talking about the ill-fated soldiers of the Lost Platoon in a way no one previously had.

Boxovna's book reminded everyone of who these men were; hardened men who'd fought an ugly urban suppression war far from home. They weren't just the Lost Platoon. Before that label, they had been the men of the 4th Recon Regiment, Baker Company, 3rd Platoon. Baker Company had earned a gritty reputation for their work in Arcobia's capital city, St. Michel. Nicknamed *Baker's Bastards*, they'd cleared out the heaviest concentrations of rebels in St. Michel's southern hillside *barrios*. A Company decoration had been bestowed upon the *Bastards* a week before they'd been sent back to Earth. The 3rd Platoon had been left behind for a week until relief troops could be put in place. It was believed that during that week, the platoon had been exposed to the pathogen that infected their bloodstreams.

A few men gained fame through the book's publication. Private Emmit Samuels became known for his intrepid attack on the mouth of a cave in a hillside *barrio*. With nothing more than a rifle and an EMP grenade, he rushed the cave opening, dislodging a rebel gun nest that had killed thirteen men during prior attempts to silence it. Samuels had been awarded a StarCross for his selfless duty. Sergeant Lef Montavie was also awarded a StarCross (2V) for his intervention during a convoy ambush. Montavie, blown clear of his Patroller, disabled three of the four rebels despite losing a leg in the attack.

The publication of the book, however, did nothing to raise interest in the plight of the men stuck in the Lazaretto. Most readers enjoyed the book as history, thinking only of the members of the platoon as dead heroes of the Arcobian Rebellion. Nobody wanted to remember that twenty-six men who'd risked their lives for their government had been marooned on a world that was dominated by disease and lonely deaths.

Sun watched the street again, giving her eyes a rest from the electric wash of the raised deskscreen. She was glad to see the rain had nearly stopped. The windows were heavily fogged by then. She felt colder just seeing the whitewashed windows and the rain-soaked streets beyond them. A heavy gray spirit suggested snow might begin to fall. It wouldn't, of course. Aegean's temperatures were never cold enough for snow. But they were cold enough for Sun.

A cold world. Sun wondered what it would be like to be exiled to such a sad, bone-wearying world. She wasn't sure if she could call it a world. It was, after all, a moon. But she'd never been on a moon with an atmosphere. She was aware there were others, but as far as she knew, they were none in the Euxine. Did that mean they were only theoretical? She couldn't remember if any of the other star systems had been reached by an actual live astronaut.

She was getting tired. That was the trouble. Of course she knew that no one had made a trip to any other star systems. That meant it was time to stand up. Time to move around and get some oxygen to her brain. Even better — it was time to get some food.

Her desksystem said 1:30. She wondered about Chitti. Was she still with that woman? Just how much did she help these unfortunate people? What kind of reserves did Chitti have to be able to handle all the little brushfires that crop up every day in a place like the Lazaretto?

What kind of woman could dedicate herself to caring for the men of the Lost Platoon? Sun began to speculate about the woman who had come rushing into the office. Was she a wife of one of *Baker's Bastards*? Was the man who had been mentioned — Ben — was he one of them?

Sun returned to the list of survivors. Was there a Ben? After opening a few wrong files, she finally found a list. Her heart dropped and her eyes watered as she read the pitifully small list. Of the twenty-six men who'd been exiled, only five remained alive.

Sun was appalled. The men's average age should have been around fifty. Instead, twenty-one of the twenty-six men were dead. Sun felt sorrow envelop her. It was too much for her exhausted emotional state. A tear ran down her cheek. All those young men, left to die. Right *here*.

Sun looked up in time to see the same man walking by her window again. It was difficult to see him clearly through the foggy window. But she could see enough to guess he was nearly sixty years old. He was in bad shape. Why did he haunt the front doors of the Benevolence Society? Was he one of the actual members of the legendary platoon? The thought shocked Sun. She knew that despite the fact she had come to help these men, she too thought of them in the past tense. She too thought of them as characters in a schoolroom history book—still twenty years old with more peach fuzz on their cheeks than beard stubble.

The man had stopped to look through the window. As soon as he made eye contact with Sun he backed off and limped out of view.

Sun read the list again. No one with the first name Ben. She did not recognize any of the names; Silva MacDenny, Chaz Grimion, Anton Morvees, Stakka Obenlan, and John Yarmin. The names were as exotic as the story of the platoon—almost alien.

That would have to change. She would get to know these five men. And she would see that they received whatever help she could offer. It was time somebody in the government got off their official ass and showed these men some decent human kindness.

Sun giggled as she realized her comment applied directly to her. *Okay*, she thought, *let me amend that: someone in the government had better get off her pretty, little, official ass.* That was better. The little joke helped to dispel her sense of despair. She would need any help like that she could get.

22

The Thief was angry. He had been betrayed. An ugly word, betrayal; the highest of crimes solely available to lovers and saints. The rotten people of the world could never betray. Betrayal grew out of trust. Rotten people were never allowed a trust they could betray. No. Only good, decent men and women could reach down into the depths of their once pure souls and find the courage to betray a partner, a friend, a lover.

The worst part of betrayal was that the victim was always a pure soul. Trust was something that could only come from a guileless spirit. Trust could never be freely given by a soul bent and distorted by the realities of this world. This purity allowed for the greatest damage once the pure soul was betrayed.

The Thief seethed to think that he had trusted her. The Liar. She had taken advantage of him! It was true he had trusted her. He was not at fault for that. She had deceived him. What else could he have done? He had seen no reason not to trust her. It was his weakness as a pure soul.

And yet her betrayal stung him like the point of a Phasian dagger. She was a woman, after all. He should never have expected anything different.

To think that she had checked up on him! She, who had earned his trust, had distrusted him? She should skulk in dark alleys checking up on the plans he had set? Jeopardize everything he had desired? He would make her pay. He would deal with her. He would hurt her. Make her beg. Her cries would fall on deaf ears. This would come. In time.

But he needed her now. She knew that. His message had been sent over an hour ago. Yet she had been silent. No signal to acknowledge his message. She was baiting him. Asserting her newly imagined importance.

The Thief knew he would have to be alert. Not that she had actually seized any power or position in their partnership. But she was beginning to think so. And that was dangerous. That would make her impulsive. A partner with a crazed sense of power mixed with inexperience might just become unpredictable. She would be hard to hold down.

Where was she? She should have called. Was it possible she was meeting someone else? Had she made a deal with the Strongman? That thought drove him to distraction. Were they even now toasting their new-born alliance, snickering at his downfall? Was she laughing at him in the midst of consummating that unholy coupling?

Or had the Liar gone a step farther? Had she made a pact with the police? Was that her game? Of course, he should have seen it. She'd been so deferential—bootlicking—in her eagerness to please him. Did she think that such dramatics would throw him off the scent? That he wouldn't see through her devices? Rooms in hell were reserved for traitors such as she!

The Thief should have been developing his alternate schedule. He would have to move up the theft far sooner than he had wanted. This ridiculous dead body was the cause. Some dead sonofabitch he'd never heard of. What idiot would get himself buried so close to the secret? The Thief trembled at his appalling luck. How could he have ever prepared for something like this?

The new schedule. Damn, but he'd have worked it out already if the Liar had come as he'd demanded. She would have helped him work out the timing. She would have gladly done that for him. She was good at things like that. She liked to be involved in every step of the process. She—

Every step. The Thief swallowed hard. Could he have been that stupid? She'd been there planning their every move with him. She knew it all. Every step. He must have been out of his mind to have ever allowed that to happen. What had he been thinking? And he'd shown her the suit. The silver suit! He'd been an utter fool.

But fortune favors the lucky, he mumbled deep within his heart. And she's not here. She hasn't come. She doesn't have to know his new plans. And there'd be no reason for her to come. Just to see him alter the schedule? He knew what she wanted—wanted to see every step because she wanted to steal *it* from him—to take it as soon as he had it in hand.

Clever wench. But she'd learn he was more clever than she.

Let her not show up. Defy his summons. It would be her undoing.

The Thief drew in a deep breath and exhaled a smile. Why had he worried? Everything was going according to plan. The Liar would be left with nothing to show for her betrayal. She was lucky he had decided to allow her to live. And she would. At least until he changed his mind.

23

It had taken Lepov most of the night before he realized he hadn't thought about Lilly Stewart since that morning. It was only a small triumph, but he would take what he could get. For the most part, he simply hadn't had time to think about her.

When he'd returned to his office he'd found a message from Mrs. Truiit. She'd demanded that he reopen the investigation into her husband's death, declaring she would never believe he had killed himself. Lepov did not attempt to contact her. If he had, he would have ended up mouthing off about her cowardly husband and her empty bank account. He had actually picked up his phone with that exact intention until he thought better of it. The last thing he needed was some crazy woman showing up with a knife. Even the classiest of women had their breaking point; there was no reason to find out Mrs. Truiit's.

After looking up more information on Anton Morvees, Lepov

had decided to make an early exit. He didn't kid himself. He had no desire to wait around to see if the Truiit woman would decide to make a personal appearance. Just the thought of her was making him edgy. No use leaving himself open to the possibility of becoming embroiled in a fist fight. He could tell he was in the mood to tangle with someone. And while he didn't object to hitting a woman who deserved it, he did like to keep within a certain modicum of civilized behavior.

It was the rain, of course. It always made him grouchy by the end of the day. He was okay as long as he knew he was being unfairly surly. But if he let it go unchecked he could get in trouble. On more than one occasion, Lepov had gotten mixed up with a TransitCar driver when he'd been working too late.

He wasn't that bad yet. But he wished Lilly hadn't come to mind. He was not in the right mood to think about her, though that had never stopped him before.

Sitting in his apartment, a little three-room unit that had somehow become home, Lepov poured a glass of bourbon. That was unquestionably the wrong way to start the night. He stared at the dark liquid, weighing the pros and cons of pouring it back into the bottle. Reaching a compromise of sorts, he tossed half of it down his throat and the other half down the kitchen sink.

Lilly would have scolded him just for drinking half the glass so early in the evening. At least Lepov thought she would have. The truth was, he didn't know. He and Lilly had never spent enough time together. She'd left too soon. And she hadn't come back.

Anger started creeping in. Lepov recognized it. He didn't want to spend the night like that. He stoppered the bottle of bourbon and set it back in the corner of the kitchen counter. He wished he could do the same to his rising anger.

So what if he and Lilly hadn't had much time together? There was nothing to keep him from calling her. Just maybe he'd get to know something new about her.

Sitting back on a couch that was stiff and flat from too much use, he grabbed the phone. Her number was programmed into the database and he spoke her name into the receiver, waiting for a connection. Was she asleep? He'd never been able to keep track of time on the other planets. A solid tone told him the connection was complete. It stopped after just a few seconds.

"Gregor?" She sounded startled.

"Hello, Lilly," he said a bit eagerly. It was good to hear her voice, but at the same time his instincts told him the same could not be said for her. Everything he'd wanted to say felt greatly out of place for an interplanetary call. The damned calls were too expensive to add video. He couldn't even look her in the eye.

"What is it?"

What is it? Lepov felt like he'd mistakenly walked into a crowded women's bathroom. It was too late to hang up.

"It's just me. I was hoping you'd have time to talk."

"About what?"

"Nothing." Hell, he sounded like a sixteen-year-old. What was he supposed to say? *I wanted to talk so we could get to know each other?* He was silently cursing that idiot section of his brain that had decided it was a good idea to call her. "I just wondered how you're doing."

"I'm just fine. Are you meeting with Mac tonight, or are you just sitting around by yourself?" He suspected she knew the answer to that.

"I was just calling you, that's all. Making sure you're okay." That was the safest way to deal with this. Make her think he was just being sweet.

"Well, I'll have to call you back. I'm in the middle of something."

"Don't call back. You said you're fine. That's all I needed to know." He wasn't about to sit around waiting for her call all night.

"Okay." Saying goodbye was even more awkward than their greeting. She killed the connection and Lepov sat with the phone in his hand.

"Sorry to have interrupted whatever the hell you were doing." Lepov tossed the phone aside and closed his eyes. If he knew what time it was wherever she was, he'd be able to tell if she should have been busy. If it was during the morning or afternoon, then yes, she'd be working, meeting with a buyer or a supplier. But if it was night, or even later than that, she shouldn't have been doing anything that would have prevented her from talking with him.

He walked back over to the kitchen counter and put his hand on the bottle.

Someone knocked on his door. Lepov slowly turned around and looked at it. That wasn't MacNally. He always called ahead. That Truiit woman didn't know where he lived. (And in his mood, that was a good thing. If he didn't slap her for her ignorant denials, he'd likely end up offering her a drink. And that would lead to very wrong things.)

Lepov wasn't paranoid enough to grab a shockhammer, but he approached the door slowly. There was no reason to hustle into trouble.

Another knock. Harder this time.

"Hey, old man! You got my gum?"

Lepov swung open the door and looked at the twelve-year-old from Chettleham Keep. "You're a bright kid, Josh. I should have guessed you'd find me. Get in here. And keep that knife in your pants."

"Yeah," Josh nodded as Lepov shut the door. He turned around in a circle, staring hard at Lepov's simple quarters. Disappointment clouded his face. "Dang, I knew you couldn't afford no chewing gum."

"Don't jump to conclusions, boy."

"Lepov, if you ain't got gum, I ain't got anything to tell ya." The boy was bright enough to remember Lepov's name.

"So let's go get some gum."

"You serious?" Josh's eyes grew big.

"You can stay here if you want. But I'm getting out of here." Lepov jammed his arms into the sleeves of his coat and grabbed his hat.

"Wait, I'm comin'." Josh hurried after him.

They walked two blocks east of Lepov's place. Lepov moved at a solid pace, while Josh had to skip to keep up. He was eager to give up his information.

"I didn't want to talk about those guys down there in number two 'cause they give me the creepies."

"What guys?"

"I dunno. Just some guys who go in and out of there. They don't ever smile much. And one of 'em just looks plain crazy. All bent up and ugly like the stump of an old tree. He kind of hisses."

"He what?"

"Hisses. Like a snake. Always talkin' to himself. You sure this place is gonna have chewing gum? We can go back to my neighborhood. They got two stores that sell chewing gum."

"Trust me, boy. Tell me about those guys."

"Well, I don't see 'em too much. Only on the days they bring the boxes out. That's every three days, I guess. I counted 'em for a week. Every three days, out they come."

Lepov looked down at the boy. "You're gonna have to give me more than that. I know about the boxes."

"Yeah, I figured. But you don't know they're gonna send some out tonight." His smile said he knew he was right.

"Tonight?"

"Well, more like tomorrow morning. Early. Before the whole world wakes up."

"You've seen them do this?" The boy nodded. "The boxes—how big? How many?"

"You really gonna buy me gum?"

"You need to learn how to trust a man, son. Bein' cynical at your age ain't the most healthy way to live."

"But it's a smart way to live."

"Okay," Lepov stopped walking and looked up at a brightly lit sign, "I'll agree with that. Now, if you want some gum, we'll have to quit standing out here in the street."

They pushed their way into a small store that had seven aisles packed to the ceiling with strange and oddly shaped items. Lepov had found it when he'd gone in search of a rare brand of cigarettes. He had quit smoking long ago, but he liked to keep a box of the cigarettes as a test of his will; to prove he was in command of his addictions. His old pack of cigarettes had been a casualty of his run-in with a murdering former Administrator of the Lazaretto named Claude Reno. The cigarettes didn't make it through that day, but then again, neither had Reno.

Dneprish Delights was an oddball collection of tobacco products, incense oils, and any number of trivial substances for the most particular travelers. They didn't have the cigarettes that Lepov had wanted, but they'd been able to order them. If his memory was working, Lepov was pretty sure he'd seen something labeled *chewing gum* near the tobacco aisles.

The small room smelled sweet. There was a hint of herbs in the air as well, ones that Lepov could not have identified even if he'd been given multiple-choice answers. The close, sickly-sweet atmosphere was nauseating. Good thing he hadn't had that second shot of bourbon.

"That's it!" The boy rushed forward and stopped in front of a heavily laden shelf. There were small stacks of miniature boxes in white, green, and yellow. "This one!"

Josh pointed excitedly to a green box.

"Get away from that," a short, bald man came from behind a curtain and waved a long finger at Lepov's informant. Lepov figured he must have come from one of the backsides of either Dnepr or Arcobia. The sign on the front of the store notwithstanding, Lepov would have bet he was Arcobian. "You don't touch the gum, huh?"

Josh backed away, both disappointment and anger showing with the same hard twist of his mouth.

"Okay, pop," Lepov stepped between Josh and the old man, "you ought to be ashamed of yourself, talking to a customer like that. Now what would you do if he took his money and business across the street?"

"Who says he's a customer?" The old man wrinkled his face at Lepov. "My system picked you up when you two came in. He don't have a PDT on him. He don't buy nothin' without one. I'm legit in this shop."

"Sure, I wouldn't have thought it'd be any other way." Lepov grabbed one of the little green boxes and turned it over. He did his best not to react to the price. Silly little things cost more than a week's supply of cigarettes. And there weren't but twelve pieces of gum in it. The box bragged that each piece of gum was individually wrapped. Hell, for the price, they'd better be individually waxed and polished.

"Do I get the box?" Josh watched the box in Lepov's hand like a puppy watches a hand holding a scrap of meat.

"I'll take two of these," Lepov said to the storeowner as he made a gesture to calm the impatient boy.

"Okay, you take 'em. I seen your data tag. But you get that little runt out of here. Kids get sticky fingers." The old man pulled a small flat screen from his pants pocket and keyed in a few quick commands. "You can't bring those back once they're paid for. That's my rule."

"I just bought 'em, pop. Give me a few minutes to try 'em out before I attempt to bring 'em back."

The boy led the way out of the store, jumping down the steps of the front stoop, excited that Lepov had purchased two boxes.

"Come on, come on." Josh waved in the light of a streetlamp.

"Okay," Lepov slowly opened one pack with excruciating sluggishness; Josh dancing from foot to foot. Once the pack was open, Lepov drew out a piece of the gum; smaller than a cherry but shaped like one. He held it between his thumb and forefinger and let the boy stare at it. When the boy finally reached to grab it, Lepov pulled it up and out of his reach. "Just a second. Those boxes. Remember the questions? How many? How big? Where do they go?"

"Okay, okay." Josh's eyes narrowed to focus on the gum. "They take like ten, maybe more out each time. They're big enough that I might fit inside 'em. But they look real heavy."

"They carry them?"

"No, wheel 'em out on a little cart. But they gotta lift 'em into the back of the truck, right? And they don't lift easy." Josh bit the inside of his lip, his eye on the gum.

"What truck?"

"That's a different question." He smiled.

Lepov tossed the gum at Josh. The boy snagged it out of the air and it disappeared into a pocket.

"Truck?" Lepov couldn't help but smile to see the boy was wise enough to hold onto his gum for later.

"Nothin' special 'bout the truck. It comes down the alley and they load the boxes onto it. It's just an old truck, not like the big ones that deliver stuff from the shipping port. Smaller like. It don't stick around long. Leaves as soon as they're loaded."

"And they've done this how many times?"

The boy shrugged his shoulders. "Maybe three times. That's all

I've seen. Now come on and give me more than two pieces, Lepov. I'm doing like you asked."

Lepov shook three more pieces out and dropped them in Josh's cupped hand. One of them ended up in the boy's mouth, the others disappeared like the first one.

"You got trouble with cops?" Josh asked as he began to chew.

"What kind of question is that?" Lepov stuck the box of candy into the same pocket of his raincoat as his unopened box of cigarettes.

"I was just wonderin', 'cause that cop's been standin' on the corner watchin' you since we came out of the store. And I never had no trouble with that cop. But I ain't gonna stick around and let him meet me."

Lepov looked back at the street corner. Sure enough, there was a cop leaning on the corner of the building watching him. It was a big cop, too. Lepov didn't know how Josh had recognized the plainclothes detective as an officer, but when he turned back to ask him, Josh was already gone.

This was the second time that day he'd run into Lt. MacNally out on the streets. But this time, he knew it wasn't by chance. Like Josh, Lepov hoped he didn't have trouble with that cop either. For one thing, it was never fun to be on the wrong side of MacNally, and for another he had to grab some sleep before he found an old truck in the middle of the night.

24

The kid noticed they were being watched before Lepov. MacNally caught several sidelong glances from the youngster while Lepov never looked in MacNally's direction. He was too caught up in whatever it was he and the kid were discussing.

MacNally would never have taken a liking to Lepov, a Private Investigator, if it hadn't been for his late partner Arturo Fenelli—more to the point, if Lepov hadn't been with MacNally when he'd learned of Fenelli's death. It had been a real Godsend, having a practical-minded professional along who had been able to keep him from spiraling off the deep end. Lepov was a solid thinker, and he'd been able to help MacNally through those first few days after his partner's murder.

It didn't hurt that Lepov was physically similar to Fenelli. They looked nothing alike in the face, but Lepov had Fenelli's broad shoulders, tall frame, and solid stance. He was thinner than the Italian had been. But they both had passive determination; the types who never gave up.

And most importantly, MacNally missed having a kindred soul

to interact with. He would never have said anything like that while Fenelli had been alive. He never would have admitted they talked in any capacity beyond their daily business. But it was true. Fenelli had been a good friend who'd always found a way to dole out good advice without hammering MacNally with overwhelming judgments and expectations.

Menya Russell would never be able to fill that slot. He was a good kid, just far too young. No matter how well-trained he was, he didn't have the advantage of viewing the world from the back side of four or five decades. Lepov did. And MacNally was looking for advice; although that was something he'd never admit either. Certainly never to Lepov. Lepov would have understood, but he'd have been just as uncomfortable hearing it as MacNally would have been saying it.

Besides, MacNally knew Lepov could figure it out without any help.

"Why is it whenever I don't need a cop, there's one around?" Lepov asked, his hands sunk inside his coat pockets. The boy had run off.

"Take your hands out of your pockets when you approach an officer of the law. I've shot men for doing that with just one hand."

"So shoot me," Lepov pulled one out and the two men shook hands in greeting. Both men were too tired to worry about contagions. MacNally had been there far too long and never expected to leave the quarantine moon; Lepov was beginning to feel the same way. "I get the feeling you've been violating my rights again, Mac. It's not nice to track my PDT with those nasty little machines you've got."

"Well, first of all, this is the Lazaretto, and you don't have any rights. Besides, I went by your place and you weren't there. And you didn't answer my call. This was quicker. You eat yet?"

"Does bourbon count?"

"Oh, wonderful," MacNally led them over to his car, "sounds like I picked a good night to drag you out of your room. You mad at Lilly again?"

"Shut up and take me to a restaurant that's not on the guidebook's cheap list."

MacNally climbed in the driver's side of the car after blowing Lepov a kiss.

"And for the record," Lepov added as he settled into the seat next to MacNally, "you didn't drag me out of my room. I'm two blocks from it."

"And you smell like bad liquor and you're hanging around little kids. What was all that, anyway?"

"Just buying information."

"With what? Looked like you were feeding him fruit."

"It's called *chewing gum*."

"What?" MacNally turned his head to hear a little better.

"Look, you chew it. That's all you do. Stays in your mouth for hours, I guess." Lepov pulled out the little green box and rolled out one of the pieces for MacNally to see.

"What's it taste like?"

"Hell, I don't know. Give it a try."

MacNally reached down, grabbed one of the little green balls, and unwrapped it. He held it up to the light of his instrument panel. It didn't look like much. Sticking it in his mouth, he bit on it a few times and swallowed it.

"I don't see what the big deal is."

"Damn, MacNally. I said don't swallow it. Chew it."

"You did? I didn't hear ya." MacNally held out a hand without taking his eyes off the street. "Let me try again."

"Forget it. These cost too much for you to swallow."

"So what information were you buying from the kid?"

"Nothing important. Just a little case." Lepov gave MacNally a long look. "You didn't see me today, did you?"

"Was I supposed to?" MacNally asked.

"Never mind. I'll tell you about it one day."

"Okay," MacNally didn't push. In the half year that they'd known each other they'd learned to stay out of each other's business. There had been two times that Lepov had needed MacNally's help. But for the most part they'd kept to themselves. It helped smooth out their friendship. Lepov was aware of MacNally's dislike of private investigators. The less said on the subject the better.

They ended up in a little side-street eatery that specialized in seafood. All of it came from Phasis, a planet overflowing with fresh water lakes and hundreds of local fish varieties. Fishing was the major occupation on that world, and seafood their largest export. MacNally and Lepov wouldn't get particularly fresh Phasian seafood in the Lazaretto, but even bad Phasian seafood was better than what MacNally had eaten growing up on Sinop.

"You know," Lepov set his fork down and pushed away from the table after eating only half his dinner, "I'm glad you showed up. To be honest with you, I did actually call Lilly this evening. I wish I hadn't. But I did."

"You did what?" MacNally asked. He hearing was lousy in the busy little dining room. It was getting harder for him to single out voices in a crowd.

"I called Lilly. She didn't sound happy to hear from me."

"She say where she was?"

"No. But she'd last told me she was on Bukovina, I think."

"You don't know?" MacNally did not understand the nature of Lepov and Lilly's friendship. "Don't you two talk?"

"Let's not talk about Lilly."

"Okay." Despite the fact that Lepov had brought up the subject, MacNally let it pass. He changed the subject. "Did you know that I started out as a beat cop in one of the quadrants? I worked Alpha Quadrant for two years. I don't even remember how many years ago that was. Long enough, I guess. I've been thinking about that lately."

"Was that pretty rowdy?"

"No." MacNally realized that Lepov had never been through a quarantine lockdown. He had arrived just over six months ago and had never attempted to leave. "You've been in Delta just before it was locked down, right?"

"Beta." Lepov corrected him.

"Okay, same thing. It is pretty wild while everyone is coming in. But once the doors are shut, you'd be surprised. There's a collective desire to stay in isolation. Kinda like everyone holding their breath. They don't want to get infected by anyone so most of them stay in their rooms. And when they do come out, they don't interact much with each other. It's kinda like back home on Sundays. Streets are pretty empty and there's not too many people making noise."

"That doesn't sound like Sunday on Bukovina."

"Well, I grew up on Sinop. They're a bit more traditional. There were a few predominant religious groups who helped settle it back in the beginning."

"Hence, your near constant state of reverence, Mac," Lepov dead-panned.

"I should expect sarcasm from a secular Bukovinansonofabitch like you. I'll say a prayer for you." MacNally had purposely been profane, though he wished he hadn't. His mother had worked hard to instill in him a fear of all things holy. Most of it hadn't stuck but there was still a deep foundation of something close to reverence. It may have been more along the lines of superstition; whatever it was, it remained. He especially regretted the casual joke about prayer. He hadn't prayed in a long time.

Lepov asked him a question but MacNally hadn't heard him. He was thinking about attending church with his mother as a young boy.

"MacNally, are you deaf?"

"No, I ain't deaf." He didn't like to admit he was losing his hearing; even to those who knew it. "What did you ask?"

"Just wondered if you liked working in the quadrant."

"I was glad to get out of it." And that was the best way to put it.

By the time he'd finally been given a transfer, he'd had all he could take. "Two years of that drove me crazy. It was actually considered a good job because it was so quiet. But that drove me crazy, all that sitting around waiting for one to go off."

"One what?" Lepov waved to the waiter and signaled for a refill of his coffee.

"That's what made the job bad. See, when someone in quarantine begins to exhibit signs of being sick in some way, they can get a little nuts. They begin to realize that they're about to get tagged for a pathogen and they'll never get off the Laz. Some people fight like mad to be allowed to go home, or wherever they were going. And it was our job to restrain them and bring them back into Center City."

"Where they're free to infect everyone else." Lepov shook his head. "I've never understood that one. These IHS people are idiots."

"Yeah, but remember most of what people are diagnosed with ain't that dangerous. And a lot of them end up perfectly healthy. But the policies will never change. No one who is sick in the Lazaretto is ever gonna get out of here. And the ones who are truly sick don't get out among the populace much."

"So what made you start thinking about the old days?" Lepov asked. His expression suggested he already knew the answer. "Feeling mortal? How many years you got till retirement?"

"Something that happened this week got me thinking about my stint in the quadrant." He'd have to decide now how much he wanted to tell Lepov. It was no accident the conversation had worked its way to this. But MacNally still wasn't sure what he was going to say.

What weighed most on his mind was that paper file he'd taken from the cabinet. It was at home now, safely jammed under a stack of backfiles he was supposedly reading.

He wasn't so concerned with *if* he should tell Lepov about the body and what he knew about it. The real trouble was how he would tell it in a sensible manner so that Lepov would be able to understand MacNally's problem. What made it so difficult was that MacNally wasn't even sure he understood all the factors involved.

"You look like you've just swallowed a really nasty pill. Whatever's bothering you, just spit it out."

"It may not be that simple, Lepov."

"Things are mostly simple, no matter what we do to complicate them."

"Like you and Lilly?" MacNally asked.

"Yeah, exactly. That's about as simple as they come. But don't change the subject. What's bothering you? You know, I had a feeling this free dinner wasn't just a casual get together. So tell me what's really going on, or did you want me to beat it out of you? I don't mind beating a cop as long as he's still well enough to pay the check when we're ready to leave this joint."

Lepov could read MacNally as well as Fenelli had.

"I wouldn't want to bore you with a long story." But he had every intention of doing just that.

"Then don't." Lepov yawned, big enough that it forced him to stop speaking for a moment. "I can't be out late. Don't beat around the bush. Say what's on your mind."

"Fair enough," MacNally said after giving Lepov's suggestion some thought. "I may have gotten myself into a mess. Maybe the better way to say it is that someone else has gotten me into a mess. Someone from a long time ago."

"From your days in Alpha Quadrant?"

"Yeah. From those days."

"Did you do something illegal back then? I hardly think you could be held—"

"No. But I may have recently done something illegal." That was only true if he kept the file. So far, he'd simply taken a file that was connected to an open case. Strictly speaking, that could be seen as part of his job. Keeping it hidden was not. Neither was it complying with Department policies.

"Well, damn it Ed, I wish I could sit here and nurse you through whatever this is. But I can't stay. Is this too complicated for you to talk about in small words and short sentences?"

"Did you ever suppress evidence when you were a cop back on Bukovina?" MacNally asked bluntly.

Lepov didn't answer right away. He was too busy staring at MacNally to say anything. He no longer looked in a hurry to leave. He was angry.

"So what, you buy me dinner so you can take shots at me?"

It was MacNally's turn to sit in silence. He had said something he shouldn't have, but he wasn't sure what.

"Who have you been talking to?" Lepov asked with a cynical smile that didn't last. "And why? I had hoped we had become friends—enough that we wouldn't need to dig into each other's past. You've got a lot of nerve, what with the way you cops in this city step on people's toes. I wouldn't think you'd even care about something like this."

"Slow down, Gregor. We just got our wires crossed. We are not talking about the same thing." He still saw anger in Lepov's eyes.

"Have you been checking up on my record as a cop?"

"Why would I do that? I was talking about something I'd done. Not you. I was only asking if you'd suppressed evidence when you were on the force. What's got you so touchy? I guess this means you've suppressed evidence." MacNally decided that it didn't matter if he offended Lepov any more than he already had. Sarcasm seemed to be the best response to his friend's indignation.

"I guess that is my answer." Lepov picked at his food. "I told you once I'd been fired when I was a detective."

"For suppressing evidence? Hell, how could I know?"

"No," Lepov shook his head, "for destroying it."

"I won't ask."

"You don't have to. I'll tell you. I did it to protect someone. And it wasn't me. I did it to protect a good friend."

"I bet he felt guilty as sin when you got fired." MacNally watched the expression on Lepov's face and knew his guess was wrong. "Don't tell me he never knew you did it."

"No, he knew I'd destroyed it. He just didn't know why. But that wasn't the worst part about the deal."

"What was?"

"He was the one who fired me."

"Damn." MacNally cocked his head to one side. He'd always wondered why Lepov was such a pessimist. "Do you wish you hadn't done it?"

"No." Lepov answered quickly. "But that doesn't mean I think I did the right thing. I don't guess I'll ever know either way. But I don't have to, either. What's this all about, Mac? What are you getting into? Don't get yourself fired. You wouldn't be much good to me outside the Department. And there's no way I'd take you on as a partner."

"I won't get fired. The evidence I took isn't something that can be tracked. No one's even aware of it. If I didn't do anything else about it, no one would ever know it existed."

"So what's your dilemma?" Lepov asked.

"This isn't about getting caught. It's about what kind of damage the truth will do. Was that why you destroyed your evidence?"

"No. The evidence I destroyed was fabricated in an attempt to frame my Captain. I was just trying to keep him from going to jail for someone else's crime."

Well, MacNally thought, it was a lot more noble than his own motives. All he'd wanted to do was shuffle evidence around for a little while, something to ensure that the investigation did not come to a premature end. He was just trying to buy time.

MacNally knew what his friend was thinking. But surely he wouldn't think that MacNally was trying to hide the truth because it might damage him. He hoped Lepov knew him better than that.

He had a feeling that he was going to need all the support he'd be able to get in the coming week. The last thing he needed was Lepov thinking he was a corrupt cop. He just didn't know how to make Lepov understand without telling him too much. That body was giving him a headache.

25

It wasn't unusual for me to think of Calla as my own daughter. She wasn't. Kjarsta never told me who her mother was. I never saw any pictures around the house of another woman. He didn't even keep a picture of Calla in his office. There were times I wondered if she were really his.

I would give in to the temptation to speculate on her parentage. More importantly, I would weave complex imaginations wherein I would challenge Kjarsta's custody of the child. I always found a way to keep the girl in my care. That was unsettling. I would begin to believe it was possible. But whenever I focused again on reality, I knew that Kjarsta was far too powerful and determined to ever lose such a battle.

I am ashamed to admit I considered turning Calla in to the IHS. I had reasoned that she would be turned out of Kjarsta's house and I would follow her into the dark recesses of the city, always by her side, caring for her and watching over her. This is no idle confession; no whimsical reminiscing over a silly thought from my past. I had weighed this option with great care. And for a time it had seemed reasonable—even desirable.

Seen from the far end of these three decades, I am surprised by the level of emotion that overwhelms me. I do not wonder at my zealous love for the girl. I do not wonder what drove me to such manic devotion. I have only to access an image from my memory; peer into the stored sights and sounds from that time to understand the great depths of love I had for her.

There was, for example, the night she began to exhibit her first symptoms. She had been sitting cross-legged on her bed, a hairbrush in her hand. Wrapped in a thick, pink robe, she had been counting aloud as she brushed her golden hair. This she did every night—even later, as best she could—two hundred strokes of the brush. She rarely finished, you understand. But not for lack of trying. She would begin with grim determination: one, two, three... It was not uncommon for her to complete the first hundred strokes. But then she would begin to tire. I was never allowed to help. That would have been cheating, she once said. I was only allowed to watch.

That night, she had just finished with her seventy-eighth stroke—I can still remember that number, though I don't know why—when she gave a sudden look of terror. I thought the brush had snagged in her hair and she had yanked some of it out. But I quickly saw I was wrong. The brush fell from her hand as if it had suddenly ceased to be a part of her person. She grimaced in pain. I leaned forward, wanting to reach out and physically remove whatever was hurting her.

She coughed so hard I suspected the spasm had irreparably damaged her lungs. Her sinuses had begun to hemorrhage, fluids pouring down the back of her throat. It caught me off guard. I am sure she could read the terror in my eyes. And I knew I was only making it worse for her.

I wasn't able to pull her forward into my arms. She was coughing again, harder and even more alarmingly than the first time. She tried to ball herself into the fetal position; tried to roll onto her side at the same time. I knew she shouldn't. I was worried about all that fluid in her esophagus. I knew she'd have choked if I allowed her to lie down.

Her coughing had mixed with her crying by the time it was over. She'd been scared by the violence of the fit. So sudden. So exhausting. I was finally able to pull her to me, cradling her face against my breast—careful to ensure I didn't smother her. She was shaking, and I shared her fear. Once, as a teenager, I had nearly drowned in a pond on a relative's farm. Breathing was precious, and never more so than after an incident like hers.

Once I was certain her airways were not blocked with any liquid, I gently laid her down on the quilted bed comforter. She had stopped shaking, though I could still see fear soaking her like raindrops from a cold winter's rain. I lay down beside her and ran my hand along the top of her head, soothing her as best I could.

It was then she broke my heart. Laying on her right side, she began to feel behind her with her left hand. I asked her what she wanted. She wouldn't speak. She just kept feeling behind her. Finally, before I intervened, her little hands grasped hold of the hairbrush she'd dropped. She was still weak and unnerved by the coughing fit, but she managed to lift this antique sterling silver hairbrush and attempted to brush her hair.

"Seventy-Nin—"she struggled to pull the brush through her thick, and disheveled hair. She tried again, her arms slowly regaining enough strength to pull the brush. "Seventy-Nine."

It took her several minutes to make ten full strokes. Forgetting the rules, I reached out and grasped the brush, meaning to help. She was obviously worn out.

"No." It was almost a whisper. More pleading than demanding. She pulled the brush from my hand.

I couldn't help but love her. She was always doing something like that; always reminding me that she was no ordinary flower. She was something stronger, independent; without an ounce of arrogance or rebellion. Perhaps she knew she had a hard life ahead and had determined not to be spoiled or weakened by my care. She allowed me to care for her, but only when she couldn't do it herself.

She'd fallen asleep after the one hundred and tenth stroke. I watched her for a time, amazed at the emotion she was drawing out of me. I knew that night, her first real night fighting that demon, that she was going to come out of it not just alive, but stronger as well. And I determined then, that I would make sure that she not only made it through alive, but that she would get out of the Lazaretto as soon as possible. I did not know how I would make that happen, but I had resolved to make it so.

26

"Major Uijong?" A man's voice called her name from the front desk phone. He actually said *Yoo-jong*. Most people did.

"Yes," Sun resisted the temptation to correct his mispronunciation. *Wee-zhan*. It wasn't his fault. Her name looked much lovelier written in Korean. English might have been convenient as a universal travel language—though she would have debated that—but it could never be accused of being a beautiful language on paper.

"You have a call coming in from Sinop. Would you like me to connect you?"

"Is there an ID with it?" She was tired, and not in the mood for chitchat.

"It's listed as a military call. Colonel Breslau."

"Go ahead and connect me. Thank you." Sun ran a hand through her black hair, making an effort to clear her head. No matter how tired she was, you just didn't say no to the boss.

"Hello Sun, I hope I'm not calling too late. This is the third time I tried to get you." Col. Breslau spoke with a soft, smooth voice that was out of place in the military. She'd always thought he could have been a successful crooner instead of administrating the Veterans' Health Benefits.

"It's fine. It took longer than I expected to get dinner. I had to wait for over an hour before I was even seated. I'm sorry you couldn't reach me, sir."

"Quite alright. I just wanted to hear that you'd gotten in safely and made contact with the *Benevolence Society*."

"I met the director this morning. In fact, I was there all day. I've already done a good deal of work on this. It's going to take a lot less time than I had anticipated."

Sun sat on the hotel bed and pushed off her shoes with her heels. Always careful about spending the military's money, Breslau was unwilling to pay the video charges for the interplanetary call. And without video, she was free to pull off her jacket and unbutton her blouse.

Colonel David Breslau was the kind of man for whom Sun enjoyed working. He was kind, careful never to raise his voice, and saw himself as something of a father for the twelve women working in his office. He was strictly by the book, but that was only because he could not conceive of being any other way. It wasn't a passion for him, merely a set of disciplines that were to be closely followed. He never spent time trying to catch his girls in error; he never imagined they were deliberately circumventing policy. He merely made the effort to guide them back on track if they took a wrong turn.

It had been a unique experience for Sun when she'd begun to work for him. Other superiors had been convinced it was their duty to catch Sun in the act of making a mistake, transforming her into a complete wreck by the time they'd finished with her. She'd become convinced she had made the biggest mistake in her life when she joined the Army.

That had all changed with Col. Breslau. His calm, patient discipline was everything she had hoped she would find when she had enlisted. She liked goals and guidelines, just as long as she was given a chance to meet them without the associated dramatics.

"You anticipate finishing sooner than expected? Why is that?" Sun could tell he did not care if she finished sooner or later. He was simply curious that her schedule might change.

"I can only find five survivors. My assessments will take far less time than we'd estimated."

"Five survivors?" The Colonel cleared his throat, a signal that he wanted to think before he said anything else. Sun had learned early on that it also meant she should remain silent. "I was under the impression that the virus they'd contracted had not been life threatening. I didn't think it had been that many years. I didn't think I had such a poor grasp on history."

"You don't. I'm sure we'd find there were factors other than age involved. But regardless of what happened to them, we only have five soldiers who are still alive."

"I don't like the sound of that." Breslau cleared his throat again. Sun wondered just what that meant. He didn't like the sound of it? She had an uneasy feeling that he was about to make a simple job not so simple. "Sun, we have clear orders to make certain that the members of the Lost Platoon are fairly compensated for being trapped in the Lazaretto after exposure to a virus during combat operations. I hardly think our job is to hand out a few cash settlements to a handful of remaining members of Baker Company's 3rd Platoon."

"I'm not sure I understand, sir."

"It is our duty to investigate these men's deaths. Verify each death and track down any family members that might be eligible to receive this compensation. That would be the right thing to do here. Don't you think?"

Sun would have quickly agreed with him if she hadn't been daunted by the details of Colonel Breslau's suggestion. It would require a great deal of work. But he was right. It was the right thing to do. Funny how the right thing to do never involved less work.

"I know it would mean more work for you, Sun," he said, echoing her thoughts, "but I'm sure you'll do just fine. There is no time issue with this. Don't feel pressured to get this finished by any set date. We don't have much happening back here at Mai Ling. Take all the time you need."

Sun stared out across the hotel room into the black night that hung over the Lazaretto. How much longer would she have to stay within the quarantine city? Even an optimist like Sun had trouble seeing the bright side of this assignment. But there had to be one. For Sun, there always was. And she had to admit she felt a little pride in Colonel Breslau's attitude. He wasn't looking for the easy way out. He wasn't looking for the cheapest way to handle this. He was intent on getting the right amount of benefits to the people who were most deserving.

That went against the grain of most institutions; it was completely unheard of in a military organization. But she was going to be a part of it. She would make sure it happened. Such a noble goal went a long way in easing the discomfort of extending her stay in the Lazaretto.

"Sun, I'm going to work up a directive for you. I'll send it by tomorrow. Do you think you can do this on your own? Or should we consider sending one of the girls to assist you?"

Sun assured him such a move would be unnecessary. She had a feeling Chitti Sienté would be willing and able to help her compile the documentation she would need. Besides, there was no call dragging one of her co-workers out to the Lazaretto. While Sun would find a way to deal with its depressing atmosphere, there was no telling what effect it would have on one of the younger girls.

Sun waited to pull off her blouse and skirt until Colonel Breslau broke the connection. Even knowing there had been no video connection, Sun felt it would have been too awkward to speak with her boss while undressing. It was an even bet that she would have gotten tangled up with her sleeves or stockings, in which case she would have broken out with a severe attack of the giggles. And that would have been difficult to explain to the Colonel.

27

So the Liar was coming after all. The Thief had known she would show up eventually. Her paltry excuse for failing to answer his summons earlier in the day made him want to laugh. At the same time he wanted to shout in anger. Did she think him a fool? Did she think he didn't know where she'd been? There was something reassuring in discovering that the Liar constantly underestimated him. That was an advantage he would exploit one day.

He stood in the center of the cluttered front room, watching his monitors. He would know when she arrived. He would know the truth, then. If she'd joined forces with the Strongman, he would see it in her smug expression. She'd be too confident, too sure of herself. But if she had gone to the police, then she'd be anxious, watchful; unsure if the police would honor their agreement and let her go. She'd try to make him talk, to record a confession from him. God, what arrogance; to think he'd allow her to trap him. Did she think him a child? An idiot who'd never learned how to protect himself? Fool! He'd been through more deals like this than she ever had.

Maybe she hadn't decided yet what she would do. That was possible. She had never been one to think clearly. Making decisions had never been her strong point; a weak-minded female who was good for nothing more than spitting out babies. Maybe she wouldn't even be any good at that. His own woman hadn't been — dead before her little brat began to scream her little head off. That had been an ironic trade; a silly whimpering woman for a helpless sniveling baby.

He would know when the Liar arrived. He would see it in her face; smell her arrogance, her fear. He would know. And he would do whatever necessary to protect the job. He couldn't allow her to ruin his plans. He had waited too long for this. He had put too much planning into it; hung too many hopes on its success. If needed, he would kill her.

His mind had begun to focus on how he might kill her when he heard her key in the lock. He would have to put on a show — never allow her to know he was watching her. Put her at ease.

"I'm sorry you had to make a trip over here, after such a busy day." The Thief put his hands together, took several steps in her direction, and bowed slightly, his voice dripping with apology.

"That's touching," she stared him down until he backed up a step. "What was so important that it had to be said in person?"

What indeed? The Thief had already changed the time line. He wasn't about to tell her about that. So why had he insisted she come over? He knew the answer, of course. He'd wanted to prove he could still make her come. But he could never say such a thing.

"The body." He'd snatched that topic out of thin air. "What have you heard? Are the police investigating?"

"There were no NewsVision reports. But you could have checked that out yourself. Why did you call me over here?" she asked impatiently.

Or was that arrogance? Had she made a deal with the Strongman? No. That didn't make sense. She wasn't one to make liaisons lightly. And she was too shrewd to trust someone like him. So what was her game?

"I've been too busy to spend time with those crooked programmers. What about your source with the police? Haven't they told you anything?" That might hit a tender spot. If she'd gone to the police, she'd avoid discussing her source.

"I haven't spoken with my source since he told me about the body. He's either out of the loop now or he thinks he's being watched. Either way, I haven't heard a thing."

She was too quick to answer. The Thief wasn't sure what that meant. Maybe she hadn't sold him out. Maybe she'd been trustworthy all along. But if that were true, she'd have come when he'd called her. She never would have dared to check up on him. His hands trembled as he puzzled over it all. He needed to think. Needed to know what to do with her.

"Have you been drinking again?" The Liar set her jaw, waiting for an answer.

"That's none of your business, girl. But I'll answer anyway. No, I haven't." The Thief knew she'd expected a different answer. He took pleasure in surprising her.

"Don't start." She stared at an empty bottle of cheap wine on the floor. "With the crazy mood you're in, you'd better stay sober. There is too much at stake for you to screw this up with one of your drunken, psychotic fits."

"I won't take orders from you," the Thief spat. Cat-quick, he clawed across the room and grasped the Liar's throat, shoving her back, bouncing her head against a wall. She exhaled noisily, as if he'd popped a tab that rapidly deflated her. She would have fallen to the floor had his fierce grip not pinned her to the wall.

He stabbed the knuckles of his free hand into her solar plexus. She jerked back, desperate to gain a full foot in height; a vain attempt to suck in air. He kept up the pressure and leaned in, his twitching lips brushing her cheek.

"You have no idea what I can do, drunk or sober. Don't ever demand something like that." He was breathing on her, mocking her inability to draw in sufficient air. "You're in no position to check up on me. Do you hear? And don't ever ignore me again like you did today. I won't put up with that. Do you hear? Do you hear?"

She wasn't able to nod convincingly in answer to his question. Despite the fact that he'd been nearly shouting the question at her, he really didn't expect an answer. He didn't need one. He had her attention. And she had better do as he told her. If she didn't, he'd have no qualms about ending their partnership.

At least he hadn't told her about changing the schedule. That would have been a big mistake. She had no business even asking him about it.

"I changed our time table," he said suddenly. The Thief watched her reaction to that. "We can't take a chance that no one will try to track down the origins of that body. We'll have to hit the Target in three nights."

She didn't bat an eye; she'd been expecting such news. "The Strongman was supposed to be gone when we did this. What are you going to do about him?"

"Whatever has to be done." Was she giving him a clue? Was she worried about the Strongman's safety? "If I have to, I'll kill him. Remember, I'm a soldier. I won't hesitate to kill if I have to. That's how these things get done. No hesitation. I learned that on Arcobia. When the time comes to kill, just kill and be done with it."

"Whatever you say," the Liar said. Was that deference in her attitude?

Of course it was. The Thief smiled in victory. The threat of violence always brought women into line. They had no defense against it. She had been humbled; set in her place. Maybe he wouldn't have to get rid of her after all. As long as she remembered to behave. As long as she understood what he was telling her—he wouldn't hesitate to kill if it became necessary. There'd be no hesitation for anyone. Not anyone.

28

The stained, brown folder sat in the middle of MacNally's kitchen table. It was a small table with only one chair. He had another chair for it, and could have found it if he'd needed to. Or maybe it had broken a long time ago. He didn't remember. He didn't care. He concentrated on the file.

The stains on the folder were from many years ago. Leaky roofs were common in the Lazaretto. There was just too much rain to go around, and water had a way of finding the slightest weak spot to exploit. Once it did, it worked its way down the insides of walls and into the panels of ceilings. Before you knew it, it was raining on the inside.

Rainwater was like that. Hard to contain. It was a lot like the truth. No matter what you did, truth always seemed to find a way in or out. It was an elemental factor of the truth. That was how to recognize it. Lies could be contained. Lies never surfaced unexpectedly. At least not the way truth did. Truth was insidious; dangerous like a wild dog. You might believe you've got it chained in your back yard where it won't get out. You might think you've tamed it for a time. But it was always waiting, watching for its chance. And when it saw the chance, it wouldn't hesitate to break free and run like a maniac. It especially loved to bite.

MacNally had owned a dog like that when he was a teenager. The day it broke free of its chain and bit him was the day MacNally had put a bullet through its head. He never gave it a second chance to bite.

If only you could silence the truth like that.

Drawing in a deep breath, he reached out and pulled the file to the edge of the table and slowly turned over the front cover, exposing the top sheet of the report.

Alpha Security Incident
Security Officer: Edward MacNally
Investigation of Subject: Pan Juarez

It was easy for MacNally to remember those early days on the force. He'd been eager to follow every procedure he ever read. He was gonna be the best cop the Lazaretto ever saw. He'd be a member of the Commission before it was all over.

Well, after all his running around chasing bad guys by the book, he'd never even made Captain.

Over time, he had begun to realize that there were gray areas within the job. But that came later. His two years in Alpha were too early in his career; he was too intent on saving the world to cut it any slack. And as silly as he had looked then from his present day perspective, MacNally still had days now when he wished he had been able to hold on to a small taste of that innocence. But this wasn't one of those days. Sitting at that table, looking at that file, it tasted more like ignorance than innocence.

He flipped the top page over and read the next heading.

Incident Summary

MacNally glanced over the details. He didn't need to read it; still able to recall writing the summary, still able see himself replacing a few of the words to get the thing just right. Back then, he'd been proud to write that report. Like he'd done something invaluable for the Lazaretto. As if he deserved a medal.

All he'd done was follow procedure. All he'd done was recognize a name flagged by Quadrant Security as a possible risk.

The whole thing had been about as silly as it could get. Pan Juarez was an Arcobian dissident who had been shot across the NewsVision spectrum from Arcobia to Bukovina and every planet in between; instantly recognizable by just about every living person in the Euxine system—and just as recognizable back on Earth as well. But when MacNally had investigated the Pan Juarez that showed up in Alpha Quadrant, there had been no question that it had been the wrong guy. Juarez, the dissident, was a dark-skinned Arcobian with patchy chemical stains across his arms and neck that were all too common among that planet's working classes. MacNally's Juarez was a pale-skinned Phasian. The towering Arcobian dissident was known for his self-educated, deep, commanding speech; the Phasian Juarez was a short nervous kid who could barely bring himself to say three words in the presence of an officer of the law.

It had taken no effort to write up a report that confirmed the traveler by the name of Pan Juarez was not a danger to quadrant security. That should have been the end of it.

But MacNally had eagerly followed procedure. And that meant keeping tabs on the traveler during his forty-day quarantine. The security level flagging Juarez had been of the highest priority. He hadn't been labeled a danger because he might hurt someone. The greater concern was that his opponents might come after him. And given his political importance, the danger lay in the bad publicity that would arise if Juarez were assassinated in the Lazaretto. Administration officials had found it convenient to flag him as a security risk. That put the responsibility squarely on the shoulders of Quadrant Security.

Any other officer would have waived procedure. Not only did the traveler not come close to resembling the dissident, but every officer also knew that Juarez was last seen back on Earth. The Phasian traveler had arrived from Phasis. It was simply impossible that the dissident was anywhere near the Lazaretto, let alone Alpha Quadrant.

MacNally remembered that even he had never believed *the* Pan Juarez was in Alpha. He had even conceded the odds of duplicating the famous name were higher than one might expect. Given the total population of the planets in the Euxine system, there was bound to be more than one Pan Juarez buzzing around. MacNally had actually once spoken with an Ed MacNally from Earth. (There had been a banking mix-up that had taken six months to clear up.) There was no telling how often names were repeated throughout the five planets.

But none of that had kept MacNally from doing his duty. He'd done his best to keep an eye on his unremarkable little Pan Juarez. The man was easy to watch. He did nothing beyond staying in his room and coming down to the same little café for lunch and dinner.

That had been one of the most uneventful quarantines that year. MacNally had found plenty of time to examine Pan Juarez. It had become a hobby for him; a challenge. With nothing better to do,

MacNally had watched and waited, writing report after report on this man's activities, or lack thereof. It was all still there in the file.

And then had come the incident with the Motvoi family. In transit from his job on Arcobia back to his home on Phasis, Sam Motvoi, along with his wife and two children, had passed through nearly the entire forty days of quarantine without incident. Just three days short of clearing the quarantine, the Motvoi's youngest child was diagnosed with some virus and the mother went out of her mind. It had taken six officers to get them under control and remove them from Alpha before it was all over. They had the option to leave the child and continue on to Phasis, but of course they had not taken it. But the incident had shaken not only the family, but the officer's as well. Not every official in the Lazaretto was hard-hearted enough to ignore the damage done by Lazaretto policy.

MacNally had allowed himself to become emotionally involved in the Motvoi incident. And that had been his mistake. He had given up watching Pan Juarez.

Weeks later, when the story broke on the NewsVision that Pan Juarez had disappeared in transit from Earth to Arcobia, along with a sizable cache of diamonds, alarms sounded in MacNally's head. Something had been wrong with his Pan Juarez. Something funny had to have been going on. There had been just too much coincidence.

But knowing that he had failed to complete his reports on Juarez, he had decided the safest thing to do was keep his head down. It galled him to do it. He had never before broken procedure. He'd lived in constant agitation for over a year until he realized no one was going to come asking about Pan Juarez. And for thirty years he had concluded that no one ever would.

It was all in the file. None of it had been removed. But MacNally didn't bother to read it. There were details within those reports that would forever remain fresh in his memory. One of them in particular had come to mind the moment he'd seen that body in the landfill. And ever since then, he couldn't stop thinking about the fact that an insignificant traveler from Phasis with the unlikely name of Pan Juarez wore a silver ring with a French Cross on its crest.

MacNally stood up. At his kitchen sink, a row of old canisters were pushed against the wall by a pile of dirty dishes. The big detective grabbed the top of the smallest canister with one of his bear-paw hands and carried it back to the table. Dumping it onto the table, he watched a few scatterings of old rice spill across the pages of the report. In the middle of the rice pattern lay a silver ring with a Cross of Lorraine on its crest.

"Now what am I supposed to do with you?" MacNally asked the

ring.

He knew the answer. He just didn't like it.

It was time he figured out what had happened so long ago.

29

Several options were open to Lepov as he waited in the rain-soaked alley behind Chettleham Keep. He had known there would be a truck that would have to be followed. With that in mind, he had hired a TransitCar to wait for him at the south end of the alley. Josh had told him the truck had entered from the north end and he hoped it would do so again. But if the kid were wrong, and the truck headed out the north end, he would have precious little time to get back to the cab without losing the truck. He was willing to jump onto the back of the truck if it were both necessary and possible. But that was the one option he didn't want to take.

He had been waiting for hours. There was no way of knowing what time the containers would come out of the apartment. And even though Josh had assured him it would be close to sunrise, he couldn't be sure. If Lepov missed them, he would have little to investigate unless they did it again three nights later.

So he waited in the rain. He had found a perch on one of the fire escapes on the opposite side of the alley and about fifteen meters south of the Keep's loading dock. If he stayed back against the brick wall, well within the shadows, he wouldn't be seen. The only mistake he'd made was forgetting to bring something to sit on. The fire escape was an old iron frame, with serrated grating on both the stair treads as well as the landings. Basically, Lepov had been sitting on a gigantic cheese grater for over two hours.

More than once Lepov had been forced to stand to get some relief. He was nearly numb. His long coat had kept his pants dry, but it wasn't doing his backside any favors.

He didn't know why, but staying awake on late night jobs like this never bothered him. If he had been home, he would have fought sleep anytime past ten or eleven. But once out on a job, he never dozed off. His fellow detectives on the force made jokes about it. Mostly they were glad someone kept awake while they grabbed some on-the-job sleep. Lepov never cared.

But as much as the sleep didn't bother him, the rain did. God, he hated the rain. At least on jobs like this. It didn't matter if his coat kept his clothes dry. He felt damp and sticky all over, as if he'd been sprayed with syrup. And it never went away until he returned home and took a shower.

And then he quit thinking about being wet. The Keep's back

door banged open, its shadows cast in a swinging arc. At the same time, light spilled out from the back hall. A shadow figure moved with the door, bent over to secure it in the open position, and then jumped off the small dock. His feet splashed in a puddle, setting off a tiny fireworks display of sparkling water. He looked toward the north end of the alley. That was a good sign.

Lepov looked that way as well. The truck should be coming soon. Both men waited.

A full minute passed—maybe two minutes—before Lepov could hear the truck. The man in the alley spun, watching the south end. That was a bad sign.

Two fat pale lights rocked into the southern entrance to the alley. The route was flipped backwards. Damn.

The truck was everything Josh had said it was. Not a big one that carried supply pallets from the shipping port; those were always rumbling down one of the streets of the Lazaretto, making sure off-world supplies made it into circulation. No, this was an older truck, maybe half the size of the big ones. The bed of the truck was open with no sidewalls. The cab was small as well. There was room for three men if they were no bigger than an average man and didn't mind snuggling during the ride.

A cringe-worthy squeal erupted from the back brakes as the truck lurched to a stop. The man waiting in the alley waved the driver forward a few more meters to line the truck bed up with the dock. Once satisfied, he grabbed hold of the empty bed and tossed himself up, landing on both feet.

"Aren't you a nimble little cat," Lepov mumbled softly.

The cat-man seemed to answer him with a leap from the truck to the dock, disappearing into the building.

The alley grew silent as the driver killed his engine. Rain kept falling, but everything was so wet, most of the rain made little noise as it fell on the sodden alley. A flash of low light from the cab of the truck told Lepov that someone in there was lighting a cigarette. On a night like this, that sounded like a pretty good idea.

Lepov took advantage of the lull to slip down to the landing below, saving time later when he would have to go for the truck. If he had a way to signal the TransitCar, he could have told the driver to swing around to the northern end of the alley. But it was too late for that.

Somebody spoke. They hadn't shouted, they were too careful for that. But someone from inside had come close. It was impossible for Lepov to understand what was said but he pulled back into the shadows in time before a figure came out on the loading dock, followed by a large black container.

The box was made from some composite; it wasn't wood, and it wasn't tin or aluminum. It was maybe a meter wide, not quite two meters long, and about a half a meter high; a small coffin.

Now he was beginning to think like Branithwaite.

Two more men came out with it, and all three men wrestled it onto the truck. It was heavy. Josh had been right about that. But what was in it? Five more of them were loaded next. Straps were thrown over them, but no tarpaulin. That would have been too convenient for Lepov. They seemed determined to leave him no safe place to stow aboard.

If the men who'd loaded the boxes jumped onto the truck, Lepov was in trouble. He'd have no way to stick with the truck. And there he caught a break. One of the men climbed into the passenger side of the cab, the other two ducked back inside the Keep and let the door swing shut.

Covered by the noise of the old truck's combustion engine, Lepov hurried down the last two flights of the fire escape and jammed his ankle as he dropped two meters onto the alley floor.

The truck began to move.

With his ankle on fire, Lepov ran along the shadowed edge of the alley; he had to catch the truck before it turned into the street. That was going to be easy enough. The driver was in no hurry. But Lepov knew that once he caught the truck, he was going to have trouble pulling himself up onto the bed while it was moving. Ten years ago he'd have been able to do it with little effort.

Just as the truck slowed before turning out of the alley, Lepov reached the truck and was able to catch his foot on a piece of the bed's framework. At the same time a small dark figure flipped onto the front of the bed near the cab. The movement startled Lepov, who did not yank himself up soon enough before the truck swung into its turn. Nearly dragged by the foot that was jammed into the frame, Lepov cursed out loud and grabbed wildly at empty air.

"Here!" hissed a whispered voice. Someone seized Lepov's hand and guided him to a solid handhold.

It took several concerted efforts for Lepov to drag his body up and over the edge of the truck bed. He lay still, trying to catch his breath as he felt the truck pick up speed. Once he'd regained some control of his shaking arms, he pushed up enough to look around. A figure was seated against one of the containers.

"You almost didn't make it, Lepov." Two starry eyes sparkled at him out of the darkness.

"Kid, what are you doing?" Lepov recognized Josh as lights from the passing buildings flicked over them.

"You got any gum?" That infuriating little smile was easy to see despite the shadows.

"You earned two pieces of gum for saving me back there." Lepov made no attempt to reach into his pocket. "But you lose three pieces for being dumb enough to jump onto this truck. What are you doing out here?"

The smile was quickly replaced by a scowl. Lepov had hurt the kid's feelings, but he didn't care. The last thing he needed was the boy getting hurt and his mother climbing all over his back about it.

"The next time this truck slows down or stops, jump off. Got it?"

Josh didn't say anything. He simply turned away from Lepov and pulled himself tight against one of the containers. His wet hair shone like polished boots in the darkness. Lepov said no more, and slid further onto the truck bed, setting his back to the same container.

"So maybe it's a little too dangerous to be jumping off trucks." Lepov's voice trailed off as the truck slowed down. At the risk of being overheard by the men in the cab, he mussed the boy's wet hair and laughed.

Lepov knew enough about Lazaretto geography to realize they were heading toward the eastern edge of the city. That confirmed a suspicion of his. He had speculated that the containers weren't going to the shipping port or one of the quadrants. That left either the roads that led out of the city into the barren hills to the west or the docks to the east — down toward the marine harbor.

And if the containers were going to the harbor, that meant they were going to be dumped. And that meant he needed to get a look inside them before they were loaded onto one of the sea barges. But the truck's cab had a back window, and anything he did would eventually be seen.

And so he waited. The truck made many turns through the heart of Center City, making an obvious choice to stay off the main streets. Every time they turned east, the streets dropped lower; they were getting closer to the harbor.

At the marine gate, unmanned sentry gates allowed the truck through. Lepov was pressing his luck staying on the truck, but he had known the gates were unmanned, and he only wanted to get inside the gates. Once inside, he knew the dock lights were too bright for him to stay hidden on the back of the truck. The first time the truck slowed to make a turn, Lepov grabbed Josh and slid off the back. Josh landed easily on his feet and wisely ducked into a shadow off to the side of the well-lit street. Lepov was much slower, but only a few steps behind the boy.

They kept the truck in sight, and moved down the street, trailing it while staying out of the lights as much as possible. They had been forced to hurry around three different corners before they saw the truck slowly backing up to a concrete jetty.

Lepov was surprised to see a salvage vessel alongside the jetty. He had been expecting one of the big waste barges to take the containers. Instead, the truck was preparing to unload onto the salvage boat. A great A-frame winch stood uncertainly in the stern well. The deck amidships was cleared, ready to take on the containers. The A-frame could double as a loading crane.

"This is where we go our separate ways, kid." Lepov shook his head, anticipating Josh's refusal to be left behind. "Don't give me that look. You wanted to come along, wanted to get in on the job, right? Sure, you did. So now's when you gotta take orders from me. If you can't, you got no business workin' for me. Agreed?"

Josh, lit by the first wisps of a cloudy morning, nodded sullenly.

"Okay, then. You stay put. Most importantly, you stay out of sight. But you better stay alert. When this old scow gets back, you need to make sure I get off. If I don't, go find that cop you saw the other night. His name's MacNally. Tell him to come looking for me. Course, by my calculations, that would be too late."

Josh's face had brightened. He had clearly been expecting to be sent home.

Before the shrouded sun began to wear away the darkness, Lepov patted Josh on his head and pulled off his coat. He balled it up and handed it, along with his hat, to the boy.

The night's rain had turned to mist. All eyes were on the loading process on the starboard side of the scow. Lepov slipped across the dock, heading to the jetty that stuck out from the dock on the scow's portside. A good ten meters of water separated the jetty from the salvage scow.

That water was gonna be freezing. Lepov was beginning to think he'd lost his mind. Was he seriously about to swim through foul, cold, harbor water for that busy-body Branithwaite? No, he wasn't. But he couldn't help but admit that he'd become curious about those containers. Too curious. Because cat-killing curiosity was about to make him do something he knew he would regret.

Bending down to slip off his shoes, he saw a smaller pair of shoes next to his.

"You do see the boat, don't you Lepov?" Josh pointed toward the end of the jetty. "Don't tell me you were gonna swim across."

There were times he had to admit the kid was pretty sharp. But he wasn't about to say it out loud.

"Josh, I told you to stay put. Now I mean it. Don't make me cuff you to this jetty." He didn't tell the kid that he hadn't seen the little dinghy. He also didn't tell him that he wasn't carrying handcuffs.

"Okay, okay. I know. Stay out of sight."

The mist was thicker near the end of the jetty—enough that Lepov wondered how Josh had seen that dinghy. It was also enough to ensure that he would have no trouble getting aboard the scow. Under this cloak of water vapor, he found a small corner that offered him concealment as the boat's crew turned the bow of the old salvage boat east, heading for open water.

Once clear of the harbor, the crew disappeared below deck. The navigational system must have been modern enough that no one was forced to stay on deck or in the small wheelhouse. And it didn't take long for Lepov to discover why they'd all disappeared.

The wind. This was no ordinary ocean breeze one found on Phasis or Bukovina. This was more like something he would have expected to find on Arcobia. Wind buffeted the scow from nearly every corner of the compass. It didn't matter what hiding place he burrowed into, the wind sought him out like a hungry predator. To make matters worse, he was going to have to climb out of his hole and make an attempt to see what was in those stupid boxes.

Why had he left his coat with Josh?

At least his bum knee had been repaired. He would never have crossed that deck on a bad knee. Not the way the deck was playing peek-a-boo with his shoes. Now you see me, now you don't. One step on the deck, one step on nothing but sea spray.

He managed to reach one of the boxes and found that they weren't sealed or locked. A simple clamp latch held the hinged lid down in three places. It took a great deal of coordination to lift the lid. It worked best to do it as the scow dropped down into a trough between swells. With the lid open, Lepov held his balance long enough to examine its contents.

At first, he wasn't sure his eyes were working right. It was true he had allowed Branithwaite to excite his imagination to the point that he had been expecting something strange, even macabre. It had been disappointing to stick his hand into a box full of dirt.

As the mist and sea spray began to soak the contents of the container, Lepov did his best to examine it. Most of it seemed to be sand, crushed rock. He tried to feel around in it with his wet, freezing hands. There were no bones, no bizarre matter. He was going to get pneumonia, maybe even swept off the deck and out to sea, all over boxes of dirt.

He was tempted to go knock on the hatch and ask to be let inside. These guys weren't killers. They were simply what they appeared to be: sailors hired to dispose of rock and dirt.

But they were disposing of rock and dirt from Chettleham Keep. That was something he would have to think about. And that wasn't good news. That meant his only option was to crawl back into his hole until they dumped their load in the sea.

If MacNally could only see him—no, Lepov wasn't going to think about that. Tucked in between one wall of the wheelhouse and a stack of lashed down crates, Lepov drew his knees up to his chest and put his head between them. Thinking of Lily was about the only thing that might possible keep him warm.

30

It became too difficult to keep Calla's sickness hidden from the rest of the household staff, despite my best efforts. I was forced to clean her clothes, her bed sheets, her washcloths, and towels. Mr. Zoltis would not allow me to bring in one of the younger girls on the staff to help me. He would trust no one.

But it was more than just the work that had become a problem. Calla's cries were getting louder. Her fits more often. I may not have been allowed to inform anyone on the staff about her illness, but that was quickly becoming a moot point. The others knew already. If they didn't, they would figure it out sooner than later.

I said the same words to my employer.

"You think so, do you?" He stood impatiently in front of his desk. I had come to his office just as he was preparing to leave. "And do you know what I will do with any of them who do figure it out?"

I did not reply.

"They'll wish they had minded their own business. They'll never get a chance to speak of it. I'll see to that."

I may have been too tired to respond properly. His boast should have chilled my heart. I knew what he was suggesting. But I couldn't help but see the humor in what he was saying.

"What the hell are you smiling at, woman?" He clinched his hands as if he wanted to strangle something.

"Your suggestion."

"I wasn't suggesting anything. I told you what I would do."

"Yes, I understand. Only, does that mean you're willing to kill any members of the staff if they hear Calla crying all night and speculate that she might be ill?" He narrowed his eyes when I used that word kill. I lowered my eyes from his and tried to keep from smiling. "Forgive me, I mean silence. Do you mean to silence them, then, if they make a logical assumption? You've not hired idiots, Mr. Zoltis. And you can't silence them for the natural act of logical deduction. You'd have to kill all of them eventually."

This time he did not make a gesture to correct my wording. He only scowled deeply and reached over his desk and mashed a button.

"Cancel the meeting. My little girl's foolish tutor has just made me

aware of a problem I'll have to attend to. She can't seem to handle things herself."

He was either speaking like that to play a part in our charade, or he meant that I should have dealt with this problem of the staff myself. I knew that even if I had, he would have disapproved of my doing anything without consulting him, so I took no offense at his words.

Mr. Zoltis stood still for a moment. He was working out a solution then and there. Never one to dither with decisions, he attacked problems with a prescient ability to see and choose the best options available without hesitation. His arrogance and crude manners aside, he was impressive, at times.

"Pack up Calla's things. I'll get you within the hour. Have what you need to nurse her. Don't worry about your clothes. I'll deal with that later. Just have her ready to move when I get back. Is that simple enough for you, woman? Or do I need to lead you by the hand and do it myself?"

"I can manage." I did my best to suppress my curiosity. I knew any questions I asked would only irritate him, knew that he had found a solution for the problem, and I was glad to see it. I wanted to keep Calla's secret safe. I also did not want any of the staff to get into trouble with Mr. Zoltis. That would have been dangerous for Calla. The police might have started asking questions if members of the staff began to disappear.

He returned in two hours. Calla still lay in bed, though I had dressed her. I was not sure if he had meant to move her on a gurney or if he would want her to move on her own. There were days when that last option wouldn't have been possible, but she could have managed that day with my assistance.

He shouldered his way into the room. Calla's face brightened when she saw him. I hated to see that. She was such a sweet, innocent child; he a crude, dangerous man. I realized I was thinking of her more as my child than his. I did not like to see him near her.

"Can she move?" He addressed the question to me, never looking in her direction.

"She can. With our assistance."

"And this." He kicked at the three bags I had packed. Awkwardly, he gestured for me to pick them up, then just as awkwardly blocked me as I reached for them. He grabbed them, muttered "Wait here," and left. His inclination would have been to make me carry the bags, but I had the feeling he did not want to be left to deal with the child.

I often thought he was an awful man for that; a father who cared nothing for his daughter. I wanted that to be. I wanted to believe he had forfeited his right to her. That would have been best for her. I suppose I mean it would have been best for me. But over the years, I could never feel comfortable believing this. No, time always allows for greater objectivity. And I now know that he did care for her. Loved her. However, this powerful, corrupt, and resolute man did not know how to deal with the prospect of his daughter's illness. He could not command the illness to leave; could not intimidate it, bribe it, or manipulate it. He was unused to such impotence. The rest of us learn to deal with our limitations. Not Kjarsta Zoltis. He could not. And it ate at his heart.

We did not leave through the front entrance. Patiently, I helped Calla to the back of the house, where Mr. Zoltis had a TransitCar waiting. This surprised me. I had never known him to travel in anything but his private vehicles. He did not climb into the back seat with us. I shut the door, eager to keep Calla from the cold.

"You have the address," he said to the driver. "No stops."

He smacked his hand on the roof of the TransitCar, and it rose slightly, heading for the back gate. The interior smelled of industrial cleaners. It should have given us a sense of cleanliness, but it only made me wonder why it had needed such a heavy cleaning. I hugged Calla close in my arms.

"Where is he?" she asked. The walk had tired her, she was shaking.

"You'll see your father again, soon." Where had he gone, indeed? I had expected him to reveal his plans. I had delayed asking questions because it was logical that he should eventually tell us what was happening. I grew angry. I had no idea where the driver was taking us.

"Can't say," the driver answered when I asked the address he'd been given. It was evident Mr. Zoltis had been persuasive, if not downright threatening.

It wouldn't have mattered if the driver had given me the address. I was not familiar with the Lazaretto. As we moved through the streets, I did not recognize streets or landmarks.

I grew angrier. Not with the driver. With myself. I should have demanded an explanation from Mr. Zoltis. I never should have moved Calla from her room until he had given one. It wasn't that I believed her father would put her in danger, but I could not take care of her if I did not know what to expect. Before he had decided what to do, I should have been consulted.

The TransitCar turned into a concrete alley. Passing under the imposing shapes of large brick and glass buildings, we eventually shushed to a stop. The driver made no move to open the doors.

I grasped the handle for the back door and twisted it. It remained locked.

"Hey!" I tried not to panic as I demanded that the driver open the doors.

"We wait here." It was all he would say.

I was in no mood to be compliant. I could feel the eyes of all those back-alley windows staring down at us. I knew that no matter how many windows there were, no one would see what happened in the alley. No one would try. Had the driver followed Kjarsta's instructions? Or did he work for one of his rivals? I had no idea who such rivals might be, or what they would be capable of, but it scared me nonetheless.

And then, as if by magic, Kjarsta appeared at our door. It made no sense to me, but I had never been so happy to see him. I wanted to cry. Calla too reacted strongly to seeing her father. She didn't hesitate to cry.

"Come. Don't sit there staring at me." He jerked open the TransitCar door. "Come on, woman. Move it!"

We rushed into a hallway that was covered in a fresh coat of green paint; the heavy paint odor a relief after the overwhelming smell of the TransitCar. A young man I did not recognize guided us down the hall through a door into a stairwell. Calla's father followed with her bags. We dropped down one flight of stairs and hurried into another hallway.

Our guide, a serious-faced man with a peach-fuzz beard, inserted a key into one last door. It only occurred to me after he closed it behind us that we had been driven by an unseen urgency. I actually felt relieved when we left the hallway. Calla's safety lay in our speed and secrecy.

In the silence that followed, I examined the room in which we stood.

It was an ordinary suite of rooms: a large front room, an adjoining kitchen, a doorway into a bathroom, and a hallway leading off to the left. The floors were covered in thick carpet, a decorating fashion that had been out of date for thirty years, though the carpet itself appeared to be fairly new. The walls were bare. No pictures hung on them, no religious icons, nothing that would give a clue about the occupant. The ceilings, though of average height, gave off the impression of being low. It was the dark spirit of the place; no windows, no brightly colored decorations or upholstery. It felt more like a bunker than a home. It didn't help that we had urgently stolen our way through the tunnel-like halls as fugitives.

And that's what I couldn't stop imagining. We stood catching our breaths in a semi-circle, with Calla standing against me. I expected her to collapse at any moment.

"Calla needs to lie down," I told Mr. Zoltis. He cocked his head and looked at me as if he'd forgotten we were there.

"Show her the room," he ordered the young man.

I followed him into the little hallway and we entered a room on the left. I noticed a door leading to the right, but it was closed and I gave it no further thought as I busied myself with Calla, pulling her out of her jacket which had managed to get wet during the brief trip from the TransitCar to the building. I hadn't even noticed the rain. It alarmed me to see her in wet clothes, though in reality it had only been the jacket. Her blouse and long pants were still dry.

Pulling these off, I slipped an oversized heavy cotton sweater over her head and fit her arms into it. The clothes I tossed aside to be dried later. The room had two small beds, a bureau, and one chair. I folded Calla into the bed farthest from the door, reassuring her that everything was going to be all right.

The young man watched us during this procedure, never offering to help and never taking his eyes off me. His predatory stare unnerved me.

105

"Tell Kjarsta to bring me a cup of hot water for tea. She'll need it to take her medicines."

He turned and left. I had purposely used Mr. Zoltis' first name. I had a feeling it would be to my advantage if the thinly bearded man knew I was not just another servant. I had framed my request as an order for the same reason. I didn't imagine many people dared to give Kjarsta Zoltis an order.

The young man delivered the water. I had tea powder ready along with Calla's medicine. Once she was asleep, I found Kjarsta waiting in the front room. He pointed to the young man.

"That's Bernham. If you need something, you tell him. He tells me."

Bernham watched me as before. He made no attempt to speak.

"And while you're here, you stay out of the second bedroom. Under no circumstances are you to go in there. Is that understood?"

I nodded. A strange smile appeared on Bernham's lips.

"I want a private word with you." I did my best to sound authoritative. Bernham must have picked up on it because he didn't wait for a sign from Kjarsta. He slunk off in the direction of the forbidden bedroom. I waited until I heard the door close before speaking. "Mr. Zoltis, am I right that you plan to leave us with this man? You're going to have to tell me everything. Who is he? Where are we? And how long do you plan to keep us here?"

"You'll be here until Calla is free of this thing. Where is not important. As for Bernham, he will not trouble you. He knows the penalty if he does."

"Do you mean he would trouble me if you weren't restraining him?"

"God, woman. You worry too much. Bernham works for me. That's all you need to know." He narrowed his eyes, examining me. "Did you think I'd put you in danger?"

I was caught off guard by the sincerity of his tone; I had never heard him speak in such a manner before. There was a hint of kindness.

"If we are to be here awhile, there are things we will need."

"Bernham," he interrupted me. "Tell Bernham."

"And does he know? About Calla?"

"He knows the girl is sick. That can't be hidden. But he thinks you are her mother. He does not think I am her father. Keep it that way."

That might account for the predatory stare. Bernham assumed I had a child, and that it wasn't Kjarsta's. I didn't like that at all.

"Mr. Zoltis, is this necessary?" He was so much taller than I, but I blocked his exit. "Are you certain he won't be any trouble?"

"Always guarding that virtue, aren't you, dearie?" His kind tone was gone, replaced with something easier to recognize: disdain. "You'll be fine here. More to the point, Calla will be safe. That's all that matters."

I wasn't sure about that. But I had no choice if I was to stay with Calla.

31

He should have slept for most of the day. He didn't want to get sick. And his body had taken quite a beating out on that scow. But no matter how much he lay in bed, Lepov could not sleep.

Scraping off his wet clothes, he'd dropped into bed as soon as he'd returned to his apartment. Sleep had come soon enough—he'd been too tired to eat, too tired to keep his eyes open—but the sleep had only lasted for an hour and a half. Just enough to warm him up, but not enough to reenergize him. He felt funny—head all full of water and wind. Closing his eyes didn't help. The gray rolling sea invaded his inner vision. There was no place he could turn that wasn't covered with water the color of iron—nearly the same color as dirt.

He sat up, tired of fighting it. That was the thought he couldn't avoid: dirt. Why were they dumping dirt? He had always assumed Branithwaite was wrong. He had assumed there would be nothing of interest about that apartment. But the fact was Branithwaite had been right.

And the hell of it was, he couldn't sleep because he wanted to get inside that apartment.

He'd warmed up enough to want to eat. And as he did, he considered his next move. It had only taken one and a half bowls of store-bought soup to make up his mind. Grabbing his coat and hat—Josh had faithfully returned them at the pier—Lepov took a SubTransit to Alpha Quadrant SubTransit station.

A heavy cough rattled his frame as he climbed out of the station. If Lilly had heard that, she'd have argued that he needed to stay in bed. He wouldn't have listened, but she'd have said it.

The station was only two blocks away from Chettleham Keep. And for once, it wasn't raining in this miserable Lazaretto. A brisk walk might have been just what he needed to clear the sea salt out of his head. The sidewalk rolled beneath him. He'd been off the salvage boat for hours, but the motion hadn't gone away. The best he could do was focus on the buildings ahead of him. That minimized the rise and fall of his imaginary horizon.

Before entering the Keep, Lepov circled the north end of the building, where apartment 02 was buried in the corner. He'd forgotten about the construction site. The great void left by the crews who'd torn down the Keep's neighbor intrigued Lepov. It was a simple explanation for the dirt.

At least it should have been. But judging by the solid shoring that stood alongside the Keep's exposed foundation Lepov had to admit it didn't make any sense at all. The digging had been done on the other side of the shoring, not on the apartment's side. Why would there be debris from digging inside the apartment?

He let that question roll around in his head while he went in search of Branithwaite. It was time to get a look at the hall recordings.

Branithwaite was harder to find than he should have been. Lepov finally found him on the seventh floor, trying to appease a woman who was upset about the plumbing in her apartment. Something about clogged pipes and many attempts by maintenance to free them. Lepov had to wait until Branithwaite calmed her down with promises that were too large to keep.

"I've been looking for you," the landlord said with some irritation.

"You've been looking for me?" Lepov couldn't help but parrot the man.

"The boy was out late last night. This upset his mother."

"What does that have to do with me?" Lepov frowned, not willing to admit that Josh had been with him. "Boys are hard to control at that age."

"Now—"the landlord began to whine, but Lepov cut him off.

"I want access to your security room. The recorders, to be exact. Let's go take a look at them, okay?"

Branithwaite would have protested further but Lepov just walked away in search of the elevator. The landlord was forced to follow.

Just as the lobby's former elegance spoke of a once grander past, the Keep's security room spoke of a time when greater attention was lavished on the safekeeping of the Keep's occupants. Located on the main floor, but separate from the lobby, the security room was nearly the size of one of the smaller apartments, consisting of two rooms of equal size.

The first was a waiting room with a few chairs and couches off to the left and an imposing desk on the right. Beyond this Branithwaite led Lepov into the second room where the bank of recording screens filled the back wall. There were sixteen screens all told, though most of them were no longer working. A center console and desksystem sat in the middle of the room, facing the screens. A communication station was on the console's right. The left side of the room had a sink, countertop, small table, and cabinets. At one time, security personnel obviously weren't allowed to leave their workplace, and ate on the job.

Lepov knew better than to get his hopes up as he studied the extensive system. He touched the console's deskscreen. The security system's logo appeared in the center of the desk.

"How much of this works?" he asked skeptically.

"Most of the recorders throughout the building. Only five of the screens on the wall. The archives will hold a year's worth of recordings, but I'm afraid the security processor won't analyze anomalies and threats."

"But you noticed people had disappeared in that apartment."

"That was simple. It sends me an alert when there is an inconsistency in the total number of residents and visitors over a seven-day period. The original landlord charged extra for visitors who stayed longer than a week. The system simply looks at the number of people who enter as opposed to those who leave."

"So what's the bad news?" The system sounded too good to be true. Nothing this old ever worked this well in the Lazaretto.

"Most of the recorder's signals are sent by the original generation of transmitters. Highly susceptible to interference by transmissions coming out of Alpha Quadrant. Much of the visual recording is jumpy and gets too much static.

"Is there anything else you need?" Branithwaite asked.

Lepov dragged a chair to the console, shaking his head. The landlord left him alone.

Lepov found the recordings of the previous night. The cat-man was there, as were the two other men. Both of them looked too stupid to know what was really going on. They looked like their only interest was to move the containers. But the cat-man was careful in his movements. He kept a watch on the corridors as he moved in and out of the apartment. He might be someone who knew something.

The recording package had no image indexing. Lepov was forced to hunt and peck his way through the data. His best guess was that the three men were the only ones who regularly entered the apartment. If any of them were Anton Morvees, he couldn't tell. The file photo of Morvees was an old one from his days with the Army. The cat-man could have been Morvees, but Lepov suspected his nimble movements meant he was too young.

As Lepov accessed data from the older storage cache, he noticed movement on the live feed monitor from the hallway. Lepov watched three men leave the apartment. Judging from what he had seen of the recording footage, no one was left in the apartment.

Lepov thought about the implications of that. Was the apartment empty? Would they be gone long? That would depend on what they did once they left the building. If they left on foot, it might mean they were only going for a short time. Of course, Lepov was considering going in to the apartment. He had to consider it. But the question was: how much time would he have?

He awkwardly tried to follow the three men with the recorders. He changed his field of view from the first floor to the back entrance. They weren't there. Had they left by way of the lobby?

He wanted to toggle his view from the loading dock to the lobby. Most of the labels on the recording console were unreadable. He had to wipe away dust and grime in order to find the switch he needed.

The old system was in worse shape than his desksystem back at the office. For a moment the switch seemed inoperable. Finally, the monitor's field of view shifted, and he could see the men standing out on the street in front of the main entrance.

A TransitCar slid into view, and the two big men climbed into the little car. The third man waited until they were gone before walking away to his left. He might have been heading for the SubTransit station. That meant Lepov had time to get inside.

Maybe if he'd gotten more sleep he'd have been thinking more clearly. But if he'd gotten more sleep, he'd still be in bed instead of preparing to force his way into that apartment.

Lepov left the security room and headed for the stairs. The security room was near the stairwell. It took him only a few minutes to get to the door of the apartment. Branithwaite had been unable to give him a key; the locks had been changed by Morvees years ago. But that didn't bother the former policeman in the least.

Most locks that still required a key were fairly simple mechanisms. If the lock had been a digital lock, that would have been a problem. Lepov could still have worked his way in, but he would have needed a wristcomp with an illegal logarithm protocol. Such things were not only illegal, but they were in constant need of costly upgrades. His equipment hadn't been upgraded since he'd arrived in the Lazaretto. That made it nearly obsolete.

But Morvees had taken cheap security measures, and his keylock did not prevent Lepov from quickly entering the apartment.

The front room was empty, save for the five containers stacked on a far wall. As Lepov expected, they were empty. A cluttered table stood alone near a doorway into a kitchen. No chairs. The kitchen was moderately clean; no piles of dirty dishes, though the cabinet tops and cooking surfaces hadn't been scrubbed in a long time.

Noticeably, the apartment lacked any sense of personal use; no pictures on the walls, no shoes lying around, no books or newspapers. Another item obviously missing was a desksystem. Lepov hadn't seen too many homes that didn't have one. There might have been one in the back rooms, but Lepov couldn't think of the last time he'd seen a house that didn't have one in the main living area.

Maybe Morvees was just eccentric. Lepov sampled a piece of hard candy from a jar in the kitchen, then walked into the back hall. The floor plan he'd seen earlier showed two bedrooms on either side of it. The door on the left opened into a nearly empty room. A single bare mattress sat in one corner. A small ugly chest of drawers crouched in another corner. In the center of one wall, a crooked, faded picture of an angel hung by itself. The image seemed terribly inappropriate.

The room across the hall was locked. And Morvees hadn't been cheap about this one. A high-grade digital lock protected whatever was on the other side of the door. Lepov had seen a few just like it on Bukovina. These locks were a nightmare for cops and private investigators. They weren't fun for their owners either. A number of people had been locked out of their homes when they'd forgotten their complex keycode. And there were no shortcuts or backdoors to get the code reset. Once, Lepov had actually had to use an axe to open the door for an elderly lady who'd locked herself out of her house and needed her medicine.

Why would Morvees need such a lock? He might have to take Branithwaite more seriously. Maybe he'd pursued this case ass-backwards. He might have been better off checking out the missing people. If he could have verified that they were indeed missing, he might have approached this thing with more caution. As it was, he'd charged headlong into Morvees apartment without knowing how much time before anyone returned. That had made sense when it seemed Morvees had nothing to hide. But just the presence of that digital lock was setting off alarms in Lepov's fatigue-soaked brain.

He shouldn't be standing in that hall; he shouldn't even be in the apartment any more. The time to get out of there had been five minutes ago.

But as Lepov strode quickly to the front room, he stopped dead next to the containers. Now that he had an idea something was actually wrong, he was processing information with greater ease. And he didn't like the end results.

Those black containers looked too much like coffins. But if that's what they were, Lepov couldn't see the point. They'd been full of rock and gravel. If Morvees had killed those people—for arguments sake, Lepov was willing to go along with that theory—why wouldn't he have sent them out in the containers?

No. He shook his head at that question. Too hard to dispose of them somewhere else. So that must have meant that he'd buried them in the building's foundation. Lepov had a strong logical balance, and did not scare easily. But he couldn't stop the chill that ran through him. In a moment of clarity, he could see a possible reason for the contents of those containers.

If someone buried a body in the foundation of the building, some of that foundation would have to be removed: rock and gravel. More than likely, it was busted concrete he'd been looking at. Busted gravel filling five small coffin-shaped boxes.

He had to get back to his office and start tracking down the names of those people who had gone into the apartment. With the gaps in the recordings, he had figured they had simply left without being seen. But he had failed to recognize the other side of that coin. It was just as possible that during those gaps in the recordings, *more* people could have entered the apartment. There had been multiple deliveries of the containers to the harbor.

Suddenly, Branithwaite's fears were all too understandable. Lepov wasn't going to jump the gun and run off shouting 'serial killer'! But he sure wasn't going to hang around that apartment any longer. He was going to get out and start taking this investigation seriously. And he was going to keep Josh out of it.

He would be busy the rest of the day. And he was going to earn every bit of his fee from the landlord. He already wished he'd passed up the job. But that wasn't his biggest wish. What he really wished for was a back door to that apartment. Because after wasting all that time, the front door lock turned and the door swung open.

Lepov was just an arm's reach from it. He had only a second to recognize the cat-man standing in the doorway. Before he could say a word, Lepov threw his body into the younger man's and they tumbled into the corridor, Lepov landing on top. Both hands held down the squirming cat-man. Lepov knew the cat-man would break free as soon as he let go. But Lepov had to let go to get off the floor. His best advantage lay in his weight. The cat-man must have been fifty to sixty pounds lighter than Lepov. Drilling his knee into the man's upper leg, Lepov let go and clawed his way to his feet.

The knee had been effective. His opponent did more than move like a cat. He squealed like one too. By the time Lepov broke away from him, it sounded like he'd broken the man's leg. Maybe he had. He caught a glimpse of the cat-man rolling around on the floor, clutching his leg. That gave Lepov time to run.

He couldn't go far. Cat-man's two brainless partners were were blocking the hall. And this time, they held the weight advantage. Lepov's only hope was the momentum he'd built up as he ran down the hall to where they stood blocking the exit.

He hit directly between them at the best possible speed for his age and physical shape. To get by them he had to hit them just right, so they would split apart from the impact. As Lepov's shoulder crashed into them, he knew he hadn't hit them just right. He hit them just wrong. Stars shot through his eyes and one of his opponents hit him with a hammer. Lepov couldn't see what they actually hit him with, probably just a hand. But it felt like the sonofabitch was swinging a hammer. And that was all that mattered.

Lepov could remember hitting the wall, sliding down it. His cheek smashed against old green paint. Then, mercifully, his brain shut down, not allowing him to remember any more.

Since that first evening, when the body had been discovered in the debris of the landfill, MacNally and Russell had been waiting for the crime scene visuals. This data, collected by the VTechs, was the bread and butter of a criminal investigator's day. There were not many detectives left who relied on the traditional methods of investigation. Ed MacNally was one of the last of his kind. He'd been doing his best to teach Menya Russell the rudimentary skills necessary to seek out the truth. All he hoped to do was get the kid to stop relying so heavily on the results of the visuals.

Crime scene visuals were taken with a multistage camera that recorded six aspects, or levels, of the crime scene. Aspects one and two were a range of physical surface images that allowed investigators to view all images at their original aspect or magnified up to 48 times their original size. The clarity of the magnification was dependent on the High Data rate used in the recording. The greater the HD rate, the deeper the visuals that were taken. But for each increased level of HD there was a corresponding increase in the cost to process the larger storage cells. The remaining four aspects recorded thermal images, chemical scans, CT scans, and radiation scans.

Chemical scans could tell an investigator the exact chemical makeup of any substance found at the scene. CT scans allowed them to see beneath the layers that could not be seen by the naked eye. Radiation scans were most often used to determine the rate of decomposition, the age of anything at the scene, as well as chronological sequences of injuries or damage.

With that much information at their disposal, investigators tended to become lazy. MacNally always recognized the value of visual data, but he only ever saw it as a useful secondary tool, not a primary one.

Whether he was getting through to Russell on the subject or not, at least Russell had learned to temper his comments with restraint when they received the visual report.

"Chem scan verifies what the soil samples told us." Russell's head was buried in the report.

"What?" MacNally looked up from his copy.

Russell just shook his head.

"Detective?" A fresh-faced VTech stood off to one side waiting for MacNally to acknowledge him. From MacNally's point of view, this kid made Russell look downright middle-aged.

"Well?" he prompted the technician.

"Would you like me to stick around? In case, you know, you

have any questions about the data."

"Were there any problems with this? Any gremlins?"

"Any what?" The VTech gave MacNally a funny look.

"Any irregularities." MacNally pronounced each syllable with exaggerated care, as if he were speaking to a puppy that would never understand his master's language.

"Oh, no sir. None whatsoever."

"Then what took so long? Were you college kids too busy drilling holes in the walls of the women's locker room?"

"Sir?" This time he knew perfectly well what MacNally was saying as evidenced by the red glow about his face.

"It took you guys forty-eight hours—" MacNally watched the kid's eyes glaze over. It looked like he was about to cry. "Oh, forget it."

The VTech made a hasty retreat out of the Homicide office.

"What was his problem?"

"Why do you do that?" Russell was in an unusually brave mood. "Can't you treat anyone with kindness?"

"How was that unkind? I'll be damned if I know why people get upset talking to me. All I asked was why it took so long for the visuals. How is that wrong?"

Russell's response was too low for MacNally to hear. The big detective growled a bit as he returned to the report. He knew they were wasting their time. Whatever information the visuals could give them, it wouldn't help them. MacNally already knew all that he was going to be able to know. What he needed to do was get away from Russell for a while so he could make an attempt at identifying the ring with the French Cross.

"MacNally, did you realize you always get grouchy when you start looking over visuals?" Russell wasn't just feeling brave; he was apparently feeling cocky. "I'd be willing to bet you feel threatened by this technology. Maybe you even see it as evidence of your own obsolescence."

"That's pretty good, boy. You learn stuff like that at some Arcobian psychotherapist?" MacNally pulled a cigarette from a nearly empty pack and stuck it in the corner of his mouth. "Why don't I just let you go through this report alone? It'll be a chance for you to show me just how competent you're getting at this job."

"And what will you do?"

MacNally lit the cigarette and blew a cloud of smoke in Russell's direction. "That won't be any of your business."

MacNally didn't think he'd been acting particularly grouchy, but it had been a good enough excuse to get away from his partner. Russell would spend forever going through that report with a fine-toothed comb. That should give him the time he'd need to get a few minutes alone with Puzzle Pete.

Pete Landon was an underachieving beat cop who'd been pulled from the streets when it had been brought to his superiors' attention that he was a puzzle whiz. Not that old jigsaw puzzles captured his attention. He was a word sleuth and numbers wizard.

With the math skills of a professor, and the word skills of a linguistic genius, Pete had no desire to make a living from either one of his gifts. He enjoyed being a cop, and spent his off days solving meaningless puzzles. He had been forced to leave his patrolman's position by the Precinct's Captain. From Pete's point of view, the increased stress from a job with greater responsibility was never worth the increase in pay. It was a simple equation that Pete could see clearly in his head. But the Captain had been terribly persuasive— four weeks of the late night shift, combined with forced overtime for each day off, was enough to force Pete into accepting the offer of working special assignments.

Pete had an office down on the first floor of the precinct, close to the duty sergeant's front desk. It was noisier there than upstairs. The stewpot of patrolmen, suspects, and just about anybody else coming and going through the main doors of the precinct at all hours of the day and night was just the kind of atmosphere that Pete preferred. The cold rainy weather blowing in through the constantly opening doors helped his concentration even more. It was his way of staying close to his old job.

"Hello, Pete." MacNally pushed open Pete's door. Pete had been a friend of MacNally's former partner, Arturo Fenelli. The puzzle jockey was younger than Fenelli by maybe ten years, but they had been close. Pete had been the last person to speak with Fenelli the night he'd been murdered. He'd lost a bit of his boyish outlook on life that night. And though he and MacNally had not been particularly friendly prior to that, they had found common ground that was slowly evolving into friendship.

"Lieutenant MacNally, what a surprise." Pete sat with his feet propped on the edge of his desk. He had a head full of dark, curly hair that fell to his shoulders like a lion's mane. "Just imagine, I hear talk that the VTechs send you their report, and you show up down here within the hour. I expected you ten minutes ago."

"I ain't here about the visuals." MacNally reached behind him and pushed the glass door shut. He took two steps forward to the edge of Pete's desk. "I'm here about this."

"Very pretty," Pete swung his chair around and set his feet on the floor, taking the ring from MacNally's outstretched hand. "You getting married?"

"That's funny," MacNally said without a smile. "I need to see what you can find on this. I'm looking for anything that might tell me about the ring's owner. Think you might dig something up?"

"Sure." It was Pete's primary occupation at the precinct. He had a knack for tracking down information, as long as it was in circulation on any of the planets. He was like a ferret. There wasn't a hole he couldn't get into. "Just have your Captain tell my Captain that he needs this right away and I'll get right on it." He wasn't trying to be difficult; he was always getting requests for work. His Captain was in charge of setting his priorities. If he didn't, Pete would never have a free moment away from his job.

"That's a problem." MacNally's cigarette was almost too short to keep in his mouth, but he kept it tucked deep in the corner of his lips, unconcerned that the burning tip was close to setting his mustache on fire.

"And that explains the closed door." Pete sat even straighter as he peered more closely at the ring. "What am I looking at here?"

"That's what I want you to tell me."

"No, don't be obtuse, Mac. I mean, is this a personal matter? Or are you in trouble with your boss?" When MacNally said nothing, Pete gave him a hard look. "Okay, first of all, I won't ask any more questions. And I'll do this for you, but only because it requires absolutely no skill or time to do it. That's a French Cross."

"I know that," MacNally whined to the puzzle expert as he took the ring back. "I want to know more than the obvious."

"It's actually called a cross of Lorraine. Anywhere else I'd say it's as insignificant as a Fleur-de-lis. Could have been made by anyone, anywhere. A tourist's bauble. A cheap commemorative trinket. It's nothing. And you wouldn't be able to find anything about that specific ring."

"You said *anywhere else*. What does that mean?"

"Yes, well, I did say that." Pete scratched at his chin. The long mane of hair slid from the back of his neck around to the front as he leaned forward. "Here in the Lazaretto, you simply have to know a little history to recognize it. I'm surprised you haven't already. Look inside at the inscription."

MacNally turned the ring so he could see the engraving. Two letters were nearly impossible to read, but they looked like two capital *B*'s.

"And what is *BB*?" MacNally hadn't noticed them before.

"That narrows the owner down to being one of twenty-six people. Do you know who *Baker's Bastards* are?"

"Sounds familiar."

"That ring belonged to one of the members of the Lost Platoon."

Pete gave MacNally a weak smile. "Is that all you need?"

"Hold on. The Lost Platoon was one of many platoons in Baker Company. How can you be sure it's from the Lost Platoon?"

"Aren't you a detective, Detective? Don't you recognize deduction?"

"I recognize a shot in the dark when I hear it."

"I'll give you *educated guess*, if that's what you call it. But either way, I simply know how to put two and two together. Was the ring found here in the Laz?"

"Yeah," MacNally said.

"So the best logical deduction—*guess*—is that it belonged to one of the Lost Platoon, given the fact that none of the other platoons were marooned here thirty years ago. We could speculate that a member of, say, the 2nd platoon came back this way years ago, lost the ring or pawned it, then left without it. But why take a ride like that when the obvious answer is the Lost Platoon?"

"That's it?" MacNally pinched what was left of his cigarette with his thumb and index finger and dropped it in a waste can at the corner of Pete's desk. "That's the best you can do?"

"You look disappointed. I feel just terrible." A smile crept over Pete's lips. "I did spot the engravings on the back, you know. Don't I get points for that?"

"No." MacNally shoved the ring deep into his pants pocket.

"I don't know how Fenelli ever worked with you." Pete spun in his chair until he was facing a bank of cabinets. "Let me finish what I was working on. I'll be done in thirty minutes or so. I'll check into your ring."

"I'd say thank you," MacNally said, "but you practically made me beg, so you don't get any gratitude."

The playful grousing came to a noticeable halt as Pete turned back to look at MacNally. "Have you been by to see Lynn lately?"

"No," MacNally hesitated, ashamed to admit it. Fenelli's wife was good as gold, but MacNally had a hard time talking with her. They had not known each other well, despite the number of years he had worked with her husband. In time, they had both become jealous of the other; she for all the time her husband spent at work, he for all the love his partner devoted to her. MacNally knew that his attitude had been childish. Lynn had been given the raw end of the deal. She'd spent a lifetime waiting for her husband. And in the end, he never came home, fulfilling her worst fears.

"She asked about you." Pete did not shy away from making eye contact with the big detective. "She's worried about you."

"I'll give her a call."

Both men knew he was lying.

33

Chitti Sienté looked dubiously at Sun, highlighted by her wrinkled brow. She was sitting down and looking up at Sun, who nervously stood in front of her desk.

"That's a great boss you got there."

"He is," Sun protested. "I can see why you might not think so."

"And why does he want all of this?"

"So we can absolutely confirm that the money we are distributing gets to everyone who deserves it. Not just the original members of 3rd Platoon."

"Okay," Chitti said. "You do know this will take some time."

"Time is something that I have plenty of." Sun smiled, relaxing a bit. It looked as though Chitti would help after all.

"But the surviving members don't have all that much time left, you know." This was said with more than a hint of annoyance. "I'd hate to see them wait around while you and I chase down old death certificates and obituaries."

Sun had considered that same point as she tried to get to sleep the night before. While it made sense to get started on the bigger job of tracking down and verifying the deaths, those five men ought to be given their dispensation as soon as possible.

"You ought to go ahead with your assessments on the survivors," Chitti said, "while I start compiling the documentation you're going to need for the families of those members who have already died."

"Would you? Really?" That had been exactly what Sun had hoped the Society's Director would offer. She had been too afraid to suggest it earlier. She didn't want to appear to be too demanding. "I don't know how to thank you."

"There's no need. I want to see this done as much as you do." Chitti stopped for a moment to think about what she'd just said. "Actually, I'm sure I want to see this done more than you do."

Sun knew Chitti was only speaking the truth; she did not mean to brag. It was one of the growing number of characteristics that Sun admired about this young, single woman. Businesslike, Chitti was a no-nonsense administrator/nursemaid who cared deeply about her wards without allowing her emotions to control her. The more time Sun spent in the Society's office, the more she realized Chitti was something special to watch.

She badly wanted to know why Chitti Sienté put so much effort, gave so much of herself, toward the welfare of the men of the Lost Platoon. It might have made more sense if she were more like Sun; emotional, driven by nearly impossible to control empathy. But that wasn't Chitti. Chitti gave off the impression that was deliberately setting out to help, as if it were a cost and yield equation. Sun burned to know more of Chitti's story but had to concede that she could only be patient, and allow Chitti to reveal more of herself at her own pace.

"Well, if you're sure you don't mind doing all the hard labor, then I could go ahead with my interviews."

"This kind of research is not something I'd call hard labor," Chitti said. "But what do you mean by interviews?"

"I'll need to interview each of the survivors." Sun read alarm in Chitti's expression. "Is that a problem?"

"To a degree. When you said you needed to assess each of the survivors, I assumed you meant a financial assessment, maybe with a medical one. I had hoped you wouldn't need to speak with them."

"Why?" asked Sun.

"There are several reasons. I'll start with the more obvious one. Several of these men are not what you would call genteel. They were soldiers, and since that time, they've been stuck in an ignominious exile. To be plain—they're raw, grouchy men. But that won't be your biggest obstacle. The real problem will be their pride. Though it's true they need assistance from departments like the Vets' Health Benefits, they're gonna have a chip on their shoulder whenever they deal with the military. They won't be cooperative with you. The last thing they'll want to do is admit that they need you. You'll have to take that into account."

"I think I'll be able to." Sun knew what Chitti was trying to tell her. None of the men were going to show gratitude for the help that was en route. When she said this to Chitti, she was surprised to see Chitti shake her head.

"That's not what I mean. We're talking about animosity, not ingratitude. Your department is bringing aid that should have been given thirty years ago. These men were left to die on their own. Worse than that. They were left to *live* on their own. I hope you can see their point of view here. It will help alleviate the offensive behavior that you are bound to see in an interview."

"I guess I can do that," Sun answered hopefully. She already didn't like the sound of what Chitti was saying. She could already feel a weight settle over her; something unpleasant had just contaminated the enthusiasm that she had held for this project. Within those few moments she had begun to see this job as an ugly duty, an assignment to be avoided and put off. She hated to think it could change so quickly.

"Don't take it to heart." Chitti could evidently read all of this in Sun's face. "This doesn't mean you aren't going to do them some good. I was only saying you should be prepared for a certain degree of attitude from them. It will make your time spent with them that much less frustrating. You understand?"

"Yes, I do." She didn't feel any better about it, but Sun did know what Chitti meant.

"So let's get you started." Chitti motioned for Sun to draw up a chair. "First thing you need to do is look at these five guys and decide who you want to speak with first. Come on."

And now Chitti was taking care of Sun, just as she did for the countless others who came to the Lazaretto Benevolence Society. Only now, she was acting as nursemaid for a Major in the Army; a woman trained to overcome her emotions with discipline and focus. For Sun, it was a bit embarrassing. She could see it all happening, but with a detachment that did not allow her to correct the situation. She knew that Chitti must recognize it as well, but this only illustrated her earlier observation that Chitti knew how to manage people and situations with great skill.

"Four of them should be available any time. None of them have busy schedules." Chitti displayed the list of five men on her deskscreen. "Anton works during the day. He'll be harder to catch."

"Anton Morvees?" Sun was reading from the side of the desk, craning her neck to see the names.

"Yes. You know what? I'd suggest you start with Lieutenant Yarmin. He's always home. Lives on the north end of town. Near the shipping port."

"What's he like?"

"Well, to be honest, he's gonna be one of the most cantankerous ones to deal with. But you might as well get him over with, right?" Chitti smiled sympathetically. "The thing to remember about John is that he's all bluster. He's the officer of the group. He's tried hard to keep control over the men. Only, he never could. Not once it was announced that they were going to be spending the rest of their lives in the Lazaretto. Most of the men held onto some respect for John, but the rest just turned their backs on him. He's bitter about that."

"Was he a good officer?" That was always the question that came to mind for Sun. Officers had a job to do, they all did. But there were good ways to do those jobs, and bad ways. It was that simple; you could be a good officer, or you could be a bad one.

"From what the others have told me, I would say no. He was easily angered. Quick to take his anger out on the platoon. He was mostly interested in what he could gain. He lost a great deal when he got stuck here. He lost a lot of opportunities. He's told me many times of his plans once he'd been discharged. None of them involved getting marooned in the Lazaretto with a virus."

"Should I try to see him today?"

"I better call him. He won't like you arriving unannounced."

"I would appreciate it if you called." That unpleasant feeling was still heavily upon her, but Sun could tell that Chitti's efforts were helping.

"Okay," Chitti said. She did not seem surprised, however, when she could not contact the Lieutenant. He was, she guessed, either at a local bar, or in a sour enough mood to refuse to take calls. "That's not uncommon with him. What I'll have to do is visit him this evening, talk with him, and then you can meet with him tomorrow."

"Someone else on the list?" Sun suggested.

"I tell you what; maybe I better talk to all of them first. The more I think about it, the better that sounds. You said you weren't in a hurry."

Sun began working on the list of platoon members who had already died. She still had that check on her spirit. All she had wanted to do was come and be a part of helping out a group of people who deserved assistance. Instead, it seemed she was going to be the representative of a system that had not only failed to help these men, but was now riding in to save the day much too late.

Her mood grew worse when she began to look over the details of the deaths in the platoon over the last thirty years. It was going to be a long and gloomy afternoon, Chitti's level-headed assistance notwithstanding.

34

He didn't like getting called in like that. There was nothing to do but go, of course. But that didn't mean the Thief had to like it. When his men told him they had caught a fish, they'd thought it was funny. But that also didn't mean the Thief had to think it was funny. And he didn't. Not one bit.

Caught a fish, did they? And what was a filthy fish doing poking its fish-nose into the Thief's business? Didn't fish know what poking around got you? Didn't every good fish know what happened to the stupid cat that poked around? The spotted little thing got skinned alive and eaten by a Chinese family of ten, that's what poking around got it.

And now this Fish had disrupted everything. Just his presence was unbelievable. What did it mean? Who was this Fish? Who sent him? The Thief wanted to scream when he dwelt on it—when he put real thought into it. How could someone's luck get this awful?

It all came back to the Liar, he muttered in his soul. It *has* to be her. She'd never counted on her Fish getting hung up on a hook. No, she never would have risked it if she had. But what would she do now? What would she be willing to do to save her Fish? Or would she sacrifice him to save herself? That was the most likely result of this. She'd rather let him gut the Fish than make any kind of move to save him.

The Thief shook his head when he realized just how cold-blooded she could be. If she hadn't taken this turn against him, he would have actually been proud of her.

While mulling over this, he had been forced to take the SubTransit to get across town. There was less chance that someone would take notice of his movements if he arrived at a SubTransit station. Taking a TransitCar was too easy to track. But that also meant he would have to walk several blocks to see the Fish.

Standing hunched over the end of a bench on the SubTransit, the Thief focused his attention on a woman near him. She was delicious-looking despite the fact she was buried under a full-length skirt and long-sleeved blouse, all of which was covered with a leather coat buttoned up to the throat. But he knew about the skirt and blouse since bits of them stuck out at the ends of her arms and her ankles.

The woman swung her eyes up just enough to get a look at the Thief. He smiled at her and she swung her eyes away. It didn't matter that she made an effort to be discreet. No matter how plain she wore her hair, no matter how many layers of clothes she hid behind, the Thief knew she was drawn to him. He knew she wanted to reach out and touch him.

All that kept her in check was the poor rags he wore. She could feel his magnetism, but women naturally held a distaste for poverty that was just as strong as their taste for wealth. So for now, as the SubTransit swayed along its route, the Thief was content to sway over the woman, knowing how fully aware she was of his leg rubbing against her own. Soon a woman like this would no longer be forced to repress her desire for him on account of his financial status. That was all about to change.

Or was it? Some little Fish was trying to nose his way into the deal. And why? Was he out to get a cut of the deal? Or was he trying to break up the deal altogether? Either way, that Fish had no idea how bad a crack he'd gotten into. Nobody was gonna ruin everything he'd worked for. Not a Fish. And not a Liar. No one.

His anger fueled his walk from the SubTransit station. He was so engrossed in his mental agitations that he never noticed the rain that began to fall. The only thing he did notice was that the afternoon was still too bright for his liking. He shouldn't have been moving around at this time. Too many people could see him.

Aware of this, he was forced to enter the building from the back entrance. Once inside, he made his way to a stairwell, then shuffled down one flight and emerged into a dark hallway. It was time to deal with the Fish.

"Where is he?" The Thief asked as he came into the room.

"In there," one of his men said, jerking a thumb in the direction of a back room.

"Well, I didn't come here for the fresh air. I want to see him."

The Thief followed his three men down a hall and into the room. One of them nodded in the direction of a black container. There was a nervous pause from all three men. The Thief looked at each one of them and then looked at the container.

"You put him in there? Why did you stuff the Fish in there?"

"I dunno," one of them answered honestly.

"How long's he been in there?" the Thief asked.

"An hour," another one of them said.

"Well," the Thief did a few calculations in his head, then said, "that's airtight, you know? He's probably dead."

One of the men turned and looked at one of the other men, who was busy looking at the last man. None of them looked at the Thief.

"There's no point in worrying about what's been done. I still want to see him."

One of the men, one who had argued against putting the Fish in the box, hurried to unlatch the lid and swing it open.

The Thief stepped up to the container and peered inside. A man lay stuffed in the fetal position. He was a big man, and there wasn't room for a big man in that box, so he didn't look like a man at all. He mostly looked like a bundle of clothes jammed into a suitcase, except for the side of a face visible in one corner.

There was just the flutter of movement from the Fish's eyelids to indicate he wasn't quite dead, though the Fish's face wasn't the right color. It was gray and yellow, like congealed grease at the bottom of a used cook pot.

"Well, let the air get to him for now. I want to talk to him. Did he say anything?"

The man who'd opened the box shook his head and said "no."

"He wasn't really awake," one of the other men said. "I hit him on the head pretty hard. He ain't really moved since then."

"So maybe air won't do him any good, anyway." This was said by the one of the men, though the Thief wasn't paying attention to which one of them said what. He was too busy trying to plan what he should do next.

The best way to play it would be to get the Liar to come down and take a look at the Fish. The Thief could watch her reaction, see if she recognized him. See if this Fish was working for her. Then, if he could prove that, he'd dispose of them both. Maybe see if was possible to jam a Fish and a Liar into one box at the same time. Now that was a funny thought. Mashing them together like that would serve her right. If she wanted to take on a partner, it was only fitting that they should get together. Get extra together.

But the Thief had to remind himself he had no proof yet that the Liar and the Fish were related in any way. The first thing to do was to summon her. And this time, she'd better come when he called.

"By the way," the Thief said to one of the men after making the call, "have you spoken with the Engineer?"

"Not since this morning. He's still inside." This time he jerked his thumb toward the other room in the hall. "He's been down there since early this morning. And last night, after we made the delivery, he was still down there. I'm not even sure he came out of there at all last night."

"You two wait with the Fish," he said, nodding at them. Pointing at the other man, he said "wait out in the front room for her. When she gets here, don't let her in to see the Fish unless I'm there. Understand?"

All three of the men nodded. They understood.

The Thief stood over the box one more time, carefully examining the Fish. Who was it? He shrugged and turned away. He would find out soon enough. There was little point in worrying over it. Whatever the Fish had been planning was over now.

And if the Engineer had finished his job, then it would be time to hit the Target.

35

There was a period where Lepov could remember noise. Somebody had been trying to scream. But the sound was muffled — too far away to understand what all that yelling was about. Like the sound kids make when they smash a cup over their mouth and chin and yell crazy words into it.

Lepov started to get the insane idea that the noise was coming from him but decided that couldn't be right. He hadn't been a kid since he was young. In the end, he just wished that whoever was yelling would shut up.

There was shame realizing that he was actually the one yelling. It didn't matter that he'd only been a kid. It didn't matter that he had finally quit screaming. He'd only done so because he'd grown up. That had been years ago, all that yelling, crying and fighting for breath. A long, long, time ago. Surely he'd aged during that time. And with age came wisdom and discipline. The kind of discipline that maturity taught you; how to accept what fate deals out.

And so all the yelling and crying had come to an end, despite the fact that age had dragged in a whole new set of woes. His body could feel the effects of time; his back felt like it had been twisted and then bent in half. His hip was no longer in the natural position he had come to enjoy as a commonplace biped. It was shoved up and into his lower back, while at the same time he knew he was doing his best to kick one foot up and behind his shoulder.

But that was age, for you. He'd tried to tell Lilly that—age had a way of painting aches and pains all over you when you weren't looking. He could tell by the look on Lilly's face that she hadn't believed him. She simply hadn't gotten to that age yet.

But what Lepov couldn't understand was why his neck had been set on fire. That wasn't something he had done as a young man. And it certainly wasn't something age would do. Setting fire to specific areas of your body was illegal; at least Lepov thought it was. And even if it wasn't, it was certainly stupid. So why had he set his neck on fire?

Maybe he'd done it to distract him from the thunderous pounding in the back of his head. Yeah. That might have been why he'd set his neck on fire. If he had, the fire was doing its job. Most of what Lepov could concentrate on was the fire. That pounding in his head wasn't nearly as remarkable as the fire.

But the fire couldn't suppress the fireworks that blinded him. They were everywhere. Best fireworks he'd ever seen and he couldn't enjoy them. Some idiot had set them off too close, burning his eyes, leaving him sightless, as the afterimages bled white, yellow and red, melting into troughs on the far edges of his peripheral vision.

As the last of the fireworks display fell off and out of sight, Lepov was overwhelmed with a sense of melancholy. He didn't know why—maybe it had to do with his growing up, his aging process—but whatever it was, he became convinced he'd never see fireworks again. There was something inspiring in their starry, explosive little shows. And never again would he sit under a cloudless summer sky and shriek at the colorful presentations. He regretted that. He would have liked to see fireworks again. Maybe someday when his body quit hurting so much.

The blackness that followed on the heels of the last exploding shell was absolute. Lepov wanted to bow his head in deference to the hand of fate, but he couldn't move his head. His chin was resting on his knee; at least he thought that's what it was. It was hard to be sure. It was also getting hard to care much about it. All he wanted to do was let the blackness wrap itself around him and carry him away. Away to a place where he could stretch his back and get some relaxing sleep. Was that too much to ask?

He had expected an answer to that question, but no one said anything. But who would have been there to answer him? He puzzled over that for several years and the only person who came to mind was Lilly.

And then he slept. How much he slept was up for debate. Lepov only knew for sure that when he woke, he could no longer feel the fire that had been burning on his neck. To be honest, he could no longer feel his neck either. That wasn't right. No matter how good it felt to be free of that searing pain, he should still have been able to feel *something*. Who had decided that he couldn't feel his neck anymore? Or his whole body, for that matter? Was Lilly doing this? Was she mad at him for hiding in the Lazaretto?

If Lepov had been able to, he would have broken into a panic sweat right then. At that moment he realized he couldn't feel any part of his body, and that was the time to panic if ever there was a time. Maybe he did break out in a sweat. He would never know. Not if he couldn't feel the sweat bead up on his forehead. Not if he couldn't feel sweat trickle down the small of his back.

Sweat wasn't the issue. He had to concentrate to understand what it was that made him feel sick; what it was that opened the door just a crack to allow terror to slip in. And terror couldn't be allowed to enter for only a few seconds. Terror had a way of pushing further into the room until it overwhelmed everything else that had been there before. And terror was certainly doing that. Lepov could feel it gripping him; an iron grip around his throat. Maybe terror hadn't invaded the room as much as it had sucked all the oxygen out of it, leaving Lepov unable to breathe in the cold vacuum left behind.

And it wasn't even a room, damn it. And for just that instant, that split second of realization, Lepov could feel the hair stand up on his neck. Because the truth was too much for even the terror to hold back. And the truth was, Lepov was not in a room. Lepov was in a coffin.

"Open it!" Another muffled voice. Not the voice that had been screaming.

Yes, yes. Open it! Lepov couldn't agree more.

Bright light flooded him. Lepov wanted to burrow away from it, but there was nowhere to go, and he had no control over his arms or legs.

"I didn't say close the lid again." This voice was clear and angry.

"You didn't say not to."

Not to! Lepov tried to shout, just so everyone was clear about that.

"Whatever," said the angry voice. "I don't guess it hurt anything."

Are you kidding me? Lilly? Are you hearing this?

"She's here, in the other room."

"Okay, okay. Go get her. I want her to see this."

What she? What her were they talking about?

"Let's see if she'll admit that she knows who this Fish is." The angry man was not so much angry anymore. He had a funny kind of chuckle that scared the wits out of Lepov. Lepov hadn't yet worked out why the man couldn't see that Lepov was smashed inside a little box. But at least the air had come back into the room. Whatever had grabbed hold of his throat had let go. Lepov couldn't suck in air like he wanted to, but he knew he was getting some of it. And that seemed to be important. He was beginning to get feeling back, at least in his head. And despite the fact that the pounding had resumed on his skull, he had never been so happy in his life.

"What is this?" The mysterious *she* had come into the room. Or maybe she had come into the coffin. Lepov had no way of knowing the difference.

"I was wondering if you might know what this is."

This is me, dammit! Why didn't anyone see that?

"I have no idea what it is."

It? Had she just called him *it*? That was low. Even Lilly had never called him *it*.

"Why is it here?" She just kept calling him *it*, and that was beginning to piss off Lepov.

"That's what I want to know. All we do know is that he was snooping around in here. I think we'd better find out who he works for. See what they know about the Target."

"Well, if he won't talk, and you can't find out who he works for, you need to get rid of him."

Damn you, Lilly, what did you say that for? Lepov would have sat up and slapped the double-crossing slut if he could have, but he had no idea how to do that since he had no idea which way his arms were pointing at the time.

"Are you sure you didn't hire this Fish? You know, checking up on me?"

"Don't be an idiot. And don't wait around to try and figure out what he knows. Just kill him."

Lepov was shocked that Lilly would say such a thing. She'd never been like that. The pain that was beginning to register all over his body was nothing compared to the pain he felt in a deeper hole. A hole so deep that Lilly's words echoed inside it for weeks on end.

"You are a cold woman," the man said, chuckling again. "Okay, close the lid."

The coffin, the room, the whole of the Lazaretto became deathly quiet as Lepov tried to speak. Somebody had to say it. Somebody had to remind that man that they'd all agreed not to close the lid.

"Don't stand there like idiots. Close the lid!"

And then all those years slid off Lepov like an avalanche off a mountain, and he was six years old again, with that silly cup jammed over his mouth and he was screaming and yelling and crying and nobody could hear him because the pounding in his head was louder than the words bottled up in his throat.

But this time was different from before. With all the effort he could manage, Lepov drew his knee back and actually found a way to throw his head back against the side of his tomb. Pain shot through him, his head was tender there already. And the pain gave him clarity and for the first time in many years, he understood where he was, and what it meant.

He was in one of the shipping containers.

And then Lepov knew that clarity wasn't always a good thing because he had an idea that he would have a long time to understand with greater and greater clarity. Even worse, those faraway voices were closer now, and no matter how he tried to ignore them, he understood everything they were saying.

"I've already called for the truck. It should be here in just a few minutes."

Lepov felt the container tip, and heard the squeal of metal on metal. Wheels. A thrumming below him told Lepov what he had already guessed. They were wheeling him out of the apartment.

His voice hadn't come back yet. No matter how he tried, he couldn't get any words out loud enough to be heard outside that box. It didn't matter. No one was going to listen. Not even Lilly.

That was absurd, and he knew he'd better quit thinking like that. Lilly was thousands of miles away on another planet. His mind had been playing tricks. Oxygen deprivation had filled his head with confusion and nonsense. That woman was not Lilly.

A queasy feeling hit him in the stomach. That was the elevator. They were taking him up to ground level. And they weren't being gentle about it either. Twice Lepov felt his body weight shift with the movement of the container. Once he felt his neck jam. And the fire came back. It had never occurred to him before that his head was cocked at an angle that should have been impossible. He could picture that container from the outside, and he knew that a body as big as his own should never have been able to fit inside it.

With all too accurate vision, Lepov paced through the procedure even as he heard the rumbling engine of the truck. They would load him onto the truck bed. Drive him through the streets, each turn bringing him lower and closer to the marina. The automated gates, the arrival at the pier. The A-framed winch swinging out to latch onto the container and swinging back to drop him on the salvage boat.

Irritatingly, Lepov felt each step of the journey mockingly matching his prediction with copy-cat precision. Even the pitch and yaw of the boat was exactly as he had expected. The sea might have even been rougher. It was hard to tell in the darkness of his coffin. And that was what this container had truly become.

Incredibly, the walls of his coffin did not keep out the biting wind that swirled over the water. Lepov could feel cold digging into bones, even as he began to lose feeling again all along his twisted body.

The stars must have found a way to shine down through the constant clouds of the Lazaretto because Lepov was able to see them through the lid of that coffin. White stars shooting across the heavens. It should have been beautiful. He knew it would be the last time he ever saw the stars. But there was nothing beautiful about them. They were as cold, and distant and deadly as a woman. Hadn't she told him that there were flowers on Earth with her name? What a poor choice, to name her after a flower. Lilly was the wrong name. Name her for a star. A cold, distant, murderous star that winked in mockery at a dying man.

How many men had died under the cold, impassive gaze of millions of stars? How many men could boast that a star—a star they had loved—had ordered their death?

Lepov had never seen so many stars in the Lazaretto. Funny that he should see so many now, as they exploded in his head, showering his mind with brilliant cold light.

Far away, light-years from his star-field, Lepov imagined he could see the winch swing around and pick up the little man in his black coffin. It was sad to think that no one had come to the funeral. No one had bothered to break away from his busy schedule to see a man off to his grave.

The tiny little coffin tilted as the gravedigger picked it up with one hand. Lepov cried to see it. The big man, who was obviously too big for the little coffin, was now turned upside down, held over the water and about to be dropped headfirst into it.

Somebody should say something. Somebody should say anything. Anything was better than those last words that Lilly had said. Anything was better than hearing Lilly say "just kill him."

At least his head had stopped hurting and the fire had gone out on his neck. That had to be worth something.

He couldn't even feel the queasiness as the elevator dropped him straight into the ocean. About the only thing that he could feel was exasperation. And that was only because that little kid was screaming again. And Lepov just wished he would stop. But he never did.

Book Two

Execution

36

The first time I ever heard the name Fortunado was our second day in Calla's new home. Hearing Fortunado's name was no big event. To look back on it now, I am tempted to suggest that I knew then and there how important that name would become to Calla and me. But the facts do not support such flights of fancy.

In what would become a common routine, I cleaned Calla after breakfast, and dressed her in soft, loose cotton clothes. Her father spared no expense on her wardrobe, despite the fact that I had warned him how unnecessary it was to put her in expensive outfits. She was, after all, extremely ill by then, and I was forced to change her clothes often; they were usually soaked in her sweat, often soiled with phlegm or mucus. But he insisted she wear only the best cottons—no synthetics. The pants and shirts were nothing more than pajamas, but he spent the money and made certain that I dressed her with them.

Once this morning schedule was complete, I would sit with her as she tried to take a late morning nap. Most nights were hard on her and she needed to sleep whenever possible. I usually kept an eye on her for half an hour before I left her alone and went in search of something to eat. I never allowed myself too much time for this, being uncomfortable with the idea of leaving her for too long.

I was usually alone in the kitchen, fixing my meal. Bernham, Kjarsta's man, was rarely seen. But on that first morning, he came into the kitchen as I was brewing tea. I could tell he had only come out of the back bedroom to gawk at me, as if I were some department store display. He walked in and watched me, making no pretense of having anything else to do.

This would become his habit if I did not immediately put a stop to it. As my father had often advised, the best defense is a strong offense.

"I'm glad you're here, Mr. Bernham," I wanted to sound as if I were speaking to a servant, though I had to be careful. There was no sense in angering him. I only intended to annoy him. "Kjarsta said I was to let you know whenever I needed anything. Since I am not allowed to enter your room, it would be best if you came out at this time every morning. I'll be sure to have a list of things that Calla or I require. I'll try to have them written down on paper so you won't have trouble remembering them."

His sly look quickly turned to alarm. He did his best not to show it, though his face was easy to read. He began to speak, but I interrupted him.

"Don't worry," I added, "there's no list for today. I will need a day to think through exactly what I will need. Then, tomorrow, you'll be able to begin working on the list I make tonight. I wouldn't be surprised if it were a long list at first. The lists should get shorter over time, after I've made sure we have what we require."

"It's like working with Fortunado all over again," he said, his lip curled.

131

I did not know much about Bernham then, and so I could not know what effect my words had on him. Judging by the disappearance of his predatory stare, I decided my words had done some good. After fumbling about for a drink—a quick shot of some sort of liquor—he retreated to his back room.

I had no way of knowing, but I hoped that Bernham would leave us alone after that. Unfortunately, my plan went all too well. I did not see or hear from him for days. In the end, this was to have a great impact on us. But at the time, I felt I had done something right. This was merely ignorance on my part, not arrogance. But throughout history the best of intentions have been felled by both ignorance and arrogance without any great difference between them.

For those few days, however, we were left alone. Our food supply was restocked as we needed it. I never saw anyone do this; it was brought into the apartment during the night while we slept. I had no doubt it was done at this time to avoid questions from anyone outside the apartment. I was still forced to clean Calla's clothes, and did so in the bathroom. I had to do my own as well. I did not mind. I understood that a regular supply of a child's dirty laundry might raise questions.

All of this work kept me busy for the majority of each day we lived in that apartment. It was difficult not to allow the work and Calla's sickness to wear me down. We never saw sunlight. We never felt fresh air. I did my best to keep my spirits high, especially whenever Calla was awake and conscious of my presence. I knew this isolated existence was hard on her. Not only was she battling that virus, but she had to feel the oppression of our life in those confined quarters.

And so I sought out Bernham after those first few days of solitude. I decided we needed something more than just food and cleaning supplies.

"What do you want?" he asked, cracking open his door enough to peer at me with one eye. "I won't take any kind of list from you, lady."

"Please come into the kitchen, Mr. Bernham. I would like to speak to you, and I don't want to do so with a door between us."

He narrowed his eyes and waited for a moment in silence, hoping I would change my mind. When I turned toward the kitchen, I could hear him mutter as he pulled open the door and followed.

"Well?" He exaggerated his question with a shake of his head.

"Please tell Kjarsta the girl needs a leisure-system." I was unaware how rare and expensive such gaming/entertainment computers were in the Lazaretto. But I had an idea when I saw Bernham's crooked grin.

"Ask him yourself, Lady. Don't waste my time with this. Kjarsta don't like silly ideas. I was right about you—you've got as much sense as Fortunado. Did you have any serious reason for asking me out here?"

"I want some art work for my girl. She sits in that room all day staring at bare walls. If she's to get healthy, she'll need something cheerful in the room. Do you understand what I mean?"

The young man dropped his mocker's grin and bit down on his bottom lip. I had obviously said something that caught his attention.

"Does the girl need medicine? Do you need more food?" His sober expression surprised me. "If not, then stop bothering me, okay?"

"Kjarsta—Mr. Zoltis specifically told me that if there was anything I needed, I was to ask you and you would pass my request on to him. He did not tell me to limit my requests to medicine and food. Are you refusing to pass on my request?"

"I can pass on every silly request you can think up, Lady. But that won't mean that Mr. Zoltis will listen to me. All I'm trying to do is keep you from wasting everyone's time. Now why don't you go take care of the girl and forget about this, okay?"

Bernham meant to maintain control over me. It was more than a game to him. I could feel his hatred. I was unhappy to see that we were going to get locked into a battle of wills. It was all so unnecessary. I was no threat to this man. And if he only knew Calla was Kjarsta's daughter, he would understand it was in his interest to take care of her in the best possible way. Instead, he was working against me in an effort to retain some little bit of territory he felt was in jeopardy.

"Are you telling me you refuse to speak to Kjarsta for me? Is that your final word on the subject?"

"I never refused, Lady." He was no idiot—at least smart enough not to allow himself to be backed into a corner. "I'll pass your request along."

"Thank you, Mr. Bernham. I will leave you be, now." I hurried into Calla's room, shutting the door behind me. For two people living in the same apartment, we were not getting along well. I didn't like that. Calla's safety hinged on this man's cooperation. I was having trouble remembering that. I hoped I hadn't made an enemy of Mr. Bernham.

I couldn't sleep that night. Or the night after.

With a big, beefy hand, MacNally reached over and tapped the face of the man lying in the hospital bed. The face was gray. Too gray. MacNally had seen dead men before, and this face had come as close to dead as one could get.

"You there?" MacNally saw movement that suggested the patient was beginning to awake. "Wake up, old man."

"You've got nerve calling me old."

"You remember anything?" MacNally cocked his head to one side to get a better look at that gray face. Despite the fact that the patient was talking, the color just wasn't coming back to his cheeks— or his eyes, for that matter.

"What am I supposed to remember?" A hand to the face,

scratching at his stubble as if the answer to his question were written in Braille.

"Start with the simple stuff. Do you know who I am? Do you know who *you* are?"

"MacNally, I may feel like the inside of a dead dog, but I ain't stupid." A look around the room. "Is this a hospital?"

"And Gregor Lepov proves just how sharp a detective he can be." MacNally leaned in close to Lepov's ashen face. "I guess it's too early to ask questions."

"Have you got dirt under your fingernails?" Lepov asked.

"What?" MacNally twisted his wrists and inspected his nails.

"You should have dirt under your nails. If you're the one who dug up my grave. Did you dig up my grave?" No humor in his tone. A serious question.

"I'll explain it all to you later. Just try to sleep again, okay?"

"Tell me, Mac. Was I really buried in a coffin? You asked me if I remember anything. That's all I can remember. Don't wait to tell me. I'm all right."

MacNally stared at his friend. It wasn't hard for him to see that Lepov wasn't all right. But he knew that if the roles were reversed, he'd want to know just what was going on. And MacNally's own curiosity was bugging him as well.

"Well," MacNally cleared his throat, "just what do you remember?"

"I remember a lot. But I have no idea what order to put it in. Let's not wait around to see if I can make sense of this mess. You tell me what you know, and then I'll work from there."

"Okay." The big detective sat back in his chair and pulled out a pack of cigarettes. "Russell and I were reading through paperwork when that little kid of yours showed up at our office."

"Kid?"

"The gum-chewer. Josh. That's who you've got to thank for being alive. He remembered my face, and tracked me down. Gave us a story about you poking your nose around some apartment, and how you went inside and some other guys went inside and you never came out."

"How'd he know all that?"

"From what we could understand, he'd been watching you. The last he'd seen, one of those boxes was being loaded onto a truck. He took a guess that you were in the box and he had an idea where it was headed."

"And you believed all this?" Lepov watched MacNally's lit cigarette with mild interest.

"You want one of these?" MacNally held the pack out. "You've been through enough to earn one."

Lepov shook his head, but kept watching the lazy wisps of smoke escape the glowing end of the cigarette.

"Suit yourself. And yes, I did believe him. That kid's pretty sharp. And I knew you'd been involved with him. His story was urgent enough that I figured it wasn't worth the risk to sit around and question him too carefully. We took a patrol shuttle from the roof and tried to get to the marina in time but we were too late. It took some time to identify the vessels on the water, but we finally located the boat just as they were dumping you into the deep."

"And the guys in the boat?"

"We didn't get them. I had to let them go. We were too occupied with getting to you. The box was air-tight, so it stayed on the surface. But it wasn't going to for long. As it was, most of it was underwater. And the shuttle didn't have a way to grab it."

"Let me guess," Lepov interrupted, "you jumped into freezing water and pulled me out of my little coffin. Is that it? Am I gonna have to thank you for the rest of my life?"

"No. You're gonna have to thank Russell. For once I was glad to have a kid who's less than half my age as a partner. Even Fenelli couldn't have done what Menya did. I was actually proud of him."

Both of them sat in silence, watching the smoke ascend to the white-washed ceiling before it dissipated. It was hard to read Lepov's thoughts. MacNally figured his friend was just now realizing how close he'd come to dying. MacNally wondered why he couldn't have saved Fenelli the way they'd saved Lepov. Lepov always worked alone. And there was always that chance something would happen to him with no one there to watch his back. But Fenelli had not worked alone. Fenelli had always relied on MacNally to watch his back. And MacNally had not been there to save him.

Even the little kid Josh had been a more faithful friend to Lepov than MacNally had been to Fenelli.

"So now you're gonna tell me what this is all about, right?" MacNally tried to focus on something other than the death of his partner.

"I'll try." Lepov reached out for a cup of water that was sitting on a small table beside him. "I'd like to say everything is clear and I know just what happened, but it ain't and I don't."

"You'd better start at the beginning, and tell me what you were working on."

"Yeah, I better do that." Lepov turned his head to one side and stretched his neck. "I feel like I was packed in some lady's purse and sent through the mail."

MacNally was about to tell Lepov that he *had* been packed into something no bigger than a purse, but he was stopped by Lepov's sudden look of anger. "You just remembered something important."

"Maybe. I don't know. I need to think about it." Lepov looked around the room, his eyes never stopping to look at any one thing. "Start at the beginning, right? Yeah, I gotta do just that. But answer a question for me first, MacNally. Did you and that kid partner of yours find a dead body at the site of that demo'd building next to Chettleham Keep?"

"How would you know that?" MacNally must have looked as surprised as he sounded.

"Well, it doesn't take a genius to figure out I just stepped into something pretty big. People don't try to dump you in the ocean because you've stumbled upon a petty crime. Mac, I don't think that's the only body you're gonna find down there. I have a feeling there's at least four or five more."

"What are you talking about?"

"The landlord of Chettleham Keep has recordings that show six people going into a basement apartment, and none of them coming back out. All within the last six months or so. At first I thought they were being taken out of the apartment in the boxes. Like they did with me. But when I followed the boxes, they were emptied into the ocean. Just rock and dirt and sand. And it finally occurred to me that the bodies were buried in the foundation somewhere, and the excess debris was being dumped at sea."

"You act like your memory's coming back. Is it?" MacNally gave Lepov a skeptical look. "Are you sure that's what this is? Memory? Or could it be something else? The recollection of a dream, maybe?"

"What does that mean?" Lepov tried to massage the back of his neck. It was obviously bothering him.

"That body we found—the one we think was buried under the Roth building, next to this Chettleham Keep—can't possibly be one of those people you mentioned."

"And why not?"

"Because," MacNally said with confidence, "the body we found has been buried for thirty years or more."

"Thirty years?" Lepov took another drink of water and began to tell MacNally everything he'd been doing since being hired by the landlord. His story held together until he came to that hammer hitting his head. He wasn't sure what happened after that.

"Well," MacNally offered, "we know what Josh told us, that several people went in after you. And we know you came out in that box. You remember that? Being in the box?"

"There was this guy who kept talking about a fish. I remember that. I remember fish, and fireworks. And—"

MacNally saw that same look on Lepov's face again. There was a lot of pain, but mostly anger. He waited for Lepov to speak.

"Maybe that's it. I don't know." Lepov tried to move. Tried to roll onto his side, but something seemed wrong with his back and he grit his teeth and settled back to his original position.

"You're remembering something else, Gregor. What is it?" MacNally didn't want to push too hard, but judging by the look on Lepov's face, something important kept crossing his mind. Lepov shook his head. MacNally didn't buy it. "You ain't in a position to hold out on me, Gregor. You need help, and we need to deal with these guys who tried to kill you. Now what is it that's bugging you?"

"It's stupid, Mac. Forget it."

"Damn it. Talk to me."

"She was there." Lepov's voice cracked. MacNally had never heard the private detective sound like that before. "I know it's impossible, but I can't shake the image of her standing over me in that damned box."

"What?" MacNally wasn't sure if his hearing was giving him trouble or if Lepov was too tired to speak up. "Who is *she*?"

"It doesn't matter who she is, because it wasn't her."

"Come on, Lepov. Cut it out."

"It was Lilly! Okay? I can't shake the idea that Lilly was the one who watched them seal me into that coffin and then told them to dump me in the ocean. I'm out of my mind, okay? I know it wasn't her. You know it. But my stupid little brain keeps placing her there at the scene."

Lepov's hands were shaking as he did his best to slow down his breathing. He wasn't making this up. MacNally could see that plainly enough. Whatever had actually happened didn't make much of a difference. This image of Lilly haunted him.

"Okay, Gregor. Like you said, there is no way that was Lilly. We both agree on that, right? So what you gotta do is start visualizing something else. Picture another woman in that scene."

Maybe Lepov was doing just as he'd suggested. Maybe he was visualizing someone else where Lilly had been. Whatever he was doing, he certainly didn't look like he was in the mood to talk any more. MacNally cleared his throat.

"I better leave you alone for now. With what you've told me, I can go in and arrest these guys."

"Don't," Lepov shot MacNally a quick look. "I need more time. I need to wait and see what's going on."

"They want to kill you, Gregor. You can't go back there."

"Who knows I'm still alive?" Lepov asked.

"Half a dozen people, I guess. There's been no announcement, if that's what you mean. I doubt this guy knows anything. What was his name?"

"Morvees. Some relic from the Arcobian Rebellion." Lepov sat up, but let out a gasp of pain as he slipped his legs off the bed and tried to sit upright. "My head's gonna explode."

"What are you doing? Lay down, you idiot." MacNally jumped from his chair and grabbed Lepov by the shoulders. "And don't get back up, you hear? What kind of a relic?"

"I'm fine. I'll be just fine. I want to sit up." Lepov brushed away MacNally's hands. "I can sit up, for God's sake. What do you mean what kind of relic? Morvees? He's more like a celebrity, I guess. Part of some group of soldiers who got stranded here after leaving Arcobia forever ago. He was part of that Lost—"

"Platoon?" MacNally's eyes narrowed as he thought about what Pete Landon had told him. "This guy who owns that apartment was a member of the Lost Platoon?"

"Yeah, why? He still is I guess, wouldn't he be?"

MacNally nodded, but didn't say anything. He was trying to decide just how to proceed. After working out a few details in his head, he nodded at Lepov.

"Okay, you get some time. I won't arrest these guys yet. But that's because I'm gonna look into this Morvees. But you don't go near him again, understand?"

"You're worse than Lilly. At least she let me do my job."

"What?" MacNally had heard him just fine. But he wasn't about to acknowledge the insult. "You stay in this bed. You didn't see how bad you looked when we popped the lid on that coffin. I'm told you got lucky. You didn't have any air in that thing, you know? It's lucky your brain's so small it didn't need much air."

"I'm just supposed to lie here?" Lepov didn't try to get up, but he was ready to, the moment MacNally left the room.

"Just let me do my job and poke around, okay?" MacNally put a hand on Lepov's shoulder. He should have said something reassuring. Something that let his friend know that he was worried about him and wanted him to sit out of whatever was going on. But that was easier said than done. He was all too aware that Lepov wasn't going to take suggestions like that favorably.

MacNally also knew that if the roles were reversed, he wouldn't feel comfort in any kind of platitudes designed to keep him sidelined. He knew he'd be chomping at the bit to get out of that bed. What he should do is tell Lepov to get his pants on and get back out there.

"Don't you leave this room as soon as I leave, you understand?" So much for the daring side of his personality.

It didn't matter what MacNally told Lepov. There was no chance

Lepov would lay there for more than five minutes after MacNally left. And MacNally understood completely.

38

As Lazaretto mornings went, the Aegean sunlight was practically blinding. Sun had never seen the cloud cover so thin. She could actually make out the shape of the star as it began to rise above the eastern horizon. Even stranger was the shrouded image of the planet Sinop as it hung at a quarter crescent in the western sky. Sinop was farther from Aegean than the Earth was from its moon, but its coloring was lighter than Earth's, making it hang brighter in the sky. Most of the time, the inhabitants of the Lazaretto were unaware of the planet spinning above them, but on days like this, Lazars were given a gentle reminder that they were living on a waterlogged rock held captive by Sinop's gravitational field. For some, it was reassuring to know that they were indeed connected to the colonial worlds; they did belong to that greater social order known as the human race. But for many, it was only an unwelcome reminder that they were trapped on a barren world, unable to return to the worlds of civilization.

Sun embraced the more positive response to seeing that sliver of Sinop. But she understood that there were countless men and women who must hate to see any portion of that free and spacious world hanging in the sky. She shuddered to think there were children who felt the same way and pushed the unsettling image from her mind.

Sitting in the back of a TransitCar, she closed her eyes and tried to clear her mind. Worrying about the luckless life of a Lazaretto exile was not going to do her much good. She needed to focus on her job. Needed to be sure she had a plan for how she would approach Lieutenant John Yarmin, the most senior officer of the Lost Platoon.

Despite the fact that Chitti had spoken to Lt. Yarmin the night before, Sun still wondered if the old officer would actually speak with her. She hoped not to be sent away before getting a chance to talk with him. Sun thought she could win the man's trust if she only had a few minutes in which she could convince him that the military was truly sorry for the Lost Platoon's fate and sincerely wanted to make significant reparations.

Chitti had been unsure of Sun's chances. The Lieutenant had been drinking when they'd finally spoken and his attitude was difficult to judge. He'd been irritated when told about the Veterans' Health Benefits representative. But Chitti pointed out that he'd have been irritated if he'd just won the lottery. Most of the time, she told Sun, he was a mean drunk. There was nothing charming about him if he'd had too much to drink. And that night, he'd had too much, if not more than that.

After all of Chitti's efforts to smooth things over, the fact of the matter was, Sun would have to do this without any aid from the solid and pragmatic Chitti Sienté.

Sun thanked the TransitCar driver and stepped onto a street that was nowhere near as clean as the street in front of the Lazaretto Benevolence Society. It hadn't been cleaned in ages. Well, she decided, if she was on her own, it wouldn't matter if the neighborhood was spotless. She was going to have to charm the inveterate drinker John Yarmin. There was no way around it.

Yarmin lived in an eight-story walk-up that looked like the oldest building in the Lazaretto. It stood in the northwest corner of Center City, just across the street from the Shipping Port. Most residents were afraid to live so close to that portion of the Lazaretto. Lazaretto Administrators insisted that the Shipper's Formula — a powerful anti-viral application that was sprayed on all cargo in the shipping port — could never cross into Center City; few people relied on their confident assessments.

From what Chitti had told Sun, John Yarmin didn't believe the big shots either, but he had been forced to take his lodgings near the Shipping Port due to a run of bad luck at one of the gambling rooms in the West End. Additionally, he had refused Chitti's help on more than one occasion. She had scolded him for his stubborn pride but continued to keep an eye on him.

The West End had once been the only residential district in the Lazaretto. Its twelve square blocks of apartment buildings had been the main housing for IHS employees at the opening of the Lazaretto. Many of its first occupants had been the builders of the Shipping Port. Once this automated phase had been finished, the workers had cleared out of the Lazaretto for construction work on the fast growing planets of Dnepr and Phasis. As the size of Center City grew, many West End residents moved out to the residential zones south of Terran Park, especially after rumors spread about the dangers of the Shippers Formula.

By now, most of the West End was empty, save for a few hundred holdouts. At street level the businesses that had once been grocers, clothing stores, newsstands, small restaurants, and coffee shops had been replaced by liquor stores, strip clubs, gambling houses, pleasure brokers, and fortunetellers. Most of them thrived on the business of traveling Lazars who had not yet been locked down in quarantine.

On a previous trip, one of Sun's failed romances had tried to take her to the West End before they entered lockdown. Unfamiliar with the West End, she had only objected after they had entered a filthy little bar that catered to the military crowd. Sun couldn't remember the name of it, but that was on purpose. She had tried to purge the memory of that night from her mind.

The open stairwell in Yarmin's building smelled of mold—a lot of mold. It wasn't uncommon in the Lazaretto, but Sun wondered how anyone could live with such an overpowering odor. She knew that the sense of smell could adjust to any odor, but she wondered just how long it took before someone in this building quit noticing the stench.

Yarmin's door was on the fourth floor. Sun pulled at her dress uniform before she knocked. She wished she had fixed her hair but realized it was too late as a voice from within mumbled something she couldn't understand in a flat tone.

"Lt. Yarmin?" She knocked again. Two doors down, she heard a small but loud dog begin to bark incessantly.

That same voice from the other side of the door rose and shouted something. It might have been aimed at the machine gun barking of the dog in the other apartment, but it was impossible to tell. The dog must have decided the harsh words were for him; he stopped barking and Sun never heard him again.

"Lt. Yarmin? I'm Major Uijong. I believe Chitti Sienté told you to expect me."

Nothing. Sun wasn't sure if that meant she should speak louder, or if it wouldn't matter either way. She waited a few moments. The stillness was broken by a clattering from the door handle; a frantic action that made Sun think someone was fighting to get out. The abruptness startled her. She imagined Yarmin was in trouble and was tempted to grab the handle and shove open the door.

"What about Chitti?" A low voice spoke after the door was opened enough to allow a sliver of light to escape from within.

"She spoke with you last night. Do you remember?"

"No." The door shut.

"I'm authorized to make a deposit into your account." Sun spoke loud enough to be heard through the door, but she didn't yell. She also wasn't going to stand there much longer. She knew when she was being toyed with. She didn't believe Yarmin. He knew exactly who she was. And Chitti was right. He was being thickheaded just for the fun of it. "Let Chitti know when you're ready to talk to me."

She would have turned to leave, to give the threat some credence, but she decided it might be worth it to wait. She had guessed right. The door opened wide.

"Impatient officers don't live long in combat." John Yarmin stood in the doorway staring down at Sun.

"Good morning, Lieutenant Yarmin. My name is Major Sun

Uijong. May I come in?" Sun put on her best smile and waited for the old soldier to let her pass.

The Lost Platoon's ranking officer stood a full head and shoulders taller than Sun. He was in his mid-fifties but looked more like a man in his seventies. Thin white hair lay scattered across his spotted scalp. A hawk-beaked nose and a pair of small eyes drew the front of his face away from his cheeks, giving the impression he was perpetually thrusting his head forward in search of prey. There was little meat left on his frame. He hunched forward despite the lack of weight on his frame, walking and moving about like a spider; all legs and arms without the support of a backbone.

"I guess you can." He watched her enter.

There was a level of poverty that Sun could comprehend, but it was difficult to comprehend the state of Yarmin's apartment. There were no old and tattered clothes lying in heaps. There were no filthy dishes piled in the sink. That would have suggested Yarmin had more clothes than just the ones on his back. It would have suggested he had food enough to use a plate to hold each meal. Yarmin's place was empty.

Aside from a stained and torn chair beside the window, Sun could see nothing more than a bare room with doorways leading off into a bathroom and a kitchen. The bathroom was dark, but she could see the outline of a commode. The kitchen was lit by a window she could not see and had a sink in it. No refrigerator, no stove. A small cabinet hung precariously on the wall above the sink. It had no door; its shelves bare. Beside the sink, Sun could see an empty can against the wall.

The rooms were clean. With the door to the hallway closed, she could only smell the mustiness of the stairwell if she put her mind to it. The apartment itself did not smell bad, though it did not smell good either. The windows were reasonably clean. Even Yarmin appeared to have kept himself washed. His clothes were old and stained, but it was obvious he did the best he could with them.

It dawned on Sun that she was staring at both the room and Yarmin only after she noticed him watching her. She felt guilty and tried to hide behind a weak smile.

"I didn't mean to barge in on you like this," she began. He just stared at her as she tried to find a way to explain why she'd come. "I thought you would be expecting me. You don't recall speaking with Miss Sienté last night, Lieutenant?"

"Let's try this." He never stopped staring at her with those close-set eyes. The look was both one of mockery and distrust. "You don't call me Lieutenant, and I won't salute you. That make sense, *Major*?"

"Oh, yes. I didn't mean to—" she never finished the sentence.

The truth was, she had no idea if she had insulted him or if he was just being difficult. She couldn't help from looking back over the room; its barrenness was mesmerizing.

"Pretty little place I got here, huh?"

"Mr. Yarmin, I'm here on behalf of the Veterans' — "

"You said that already. Outside. Something about a deposit."

"Yes," Sun nodded. Trying to avoid gawking at the room she turned directly toward Yarmin. His face was white with stubble. When he opened his mouth, she could see blackened teeth and gaps where teeth had ceased to exist. "I've been asked to interview you and your men and see what steps need to be taken to help you."

She knew how weak that sounded. To suggest to men who'd been abandoned for thirty years that the military had decided to help them was ludicrous. Looking at Yarmin and recognizing the heavy toll those thirty years had taken on him underscored the point. Sun felt worse than ludicrous: she felt party to a criminal act. Yarmin might have agreed with her.

"I know how inadequate this must sound, Lt. Yarmin. But we deeply regret our failure to take care of you and your men. From my own personal point of view I can only imagine how worthless this gesture must seem to you."

"Don't start to cry over it, Major. We're grown men. We learned to live with it long ago. And don't be so sure your help is inadequate." Yarmin examined his shirt and smoothed out a wrinkle. "Do you know why someone has suddenly taken an interest in us?"

Sun did not have an answer for him; best to keep quiet instead of stumbling around for an answer that could only be a guess.

"I'm the reason, Major. Me! I've been fighting for a long time to get someone to come out here." His tone grew harsh. "Are you the only one they sent? Is that all they sent out here, one woman?"

"At least your persistence has paid off, Lt. Yarmin. And as disappointed as you might be in me, I'll do everything I can to make sure you get compensation that will improve your life here."

"That's just great, Major." Yarmin turned to look at her. "But I don't care about your money. If I'd wanted money, I could have had that a long time ago. Don't look so upset. Complete your interview, and make sure you talk to every one of my men. Make sure you are as thorough as you can be. Just like the Army taught you. But keep your eyes open. You just might see something you hadn't expected."

She wasn't sure what the old officer meant. Was he mocking her? It certainly sounded like it. The more she spoke with him, the more uncomfortable she became. His penchant for staring flustered her. Conducting an interview in this manner was near to impossible.

She had planned to stop by Anton Morvees' place after Yarmin's.

Now she wasn't sure she should. If he were anything like his commanding officer, it would be too much for her in one day.

"I won't bite, Major. Ask your questions." Yarmin spoke in a tone that said he seriously believed Sun was afraid of being bitten.

"I only have a few of them. It won't take long." Sun fought to regain her composure. She scolded herself for allowing Yarmin to unbalance her. His aggressive presence was only an act. He was playing with her, and laughing at her.

She took a breath and counted to five. She would not cut this interview short due to a case of nerves. And she would not skip Morvees' place for the same reason. She was, after all, a Major in the Army, and well trained to handle difficult situations.

That was the theory anyway. And she was going to stick with that theory no matter how little faith she had in it.

39

The Thief hated waiting. Waiting for something drove him nuts. Waiting for *someone* made him insane. And he'd been waiting for the Engineer for three weeks.

He had to admit that the Engineer had come through in the clutch. It was a lucky thing he'd been able to do the work. All that slide-rule-weight-bearing-maximum-minimum-safety-parameter-yap was too much for the Thief to worry about. But *that* wasn't something he would ever admit.

Why would he admit it? The Thief knew the Engineer was all too aware of how much he was needed. And that made the Engineer too smart for his own good. Too clever, he was. That was always the problem with educated twits like that. They never knew when to keep their clever little brains in their pockets. Always taking them out and showing them off. Didn't they have any idea how annoying that was to the rest of the world?

Of course not. Because no one ever did anything about it. No one ever snatched that brain out of their hands and squeezed the life out of it. It's what everyone should do, but they never would. They were always too impressed with the cleverness. Too much in awe of how polished the little brain was. Shiny little brain.

But the Thief knew that smart ones like the Engineer never understood the single most important truth about their miserable little brains. Although there were times when those brains were required for important tasks that made them indispensable, there would always come a time when the task would be completed, and the shiny little brain wouldn't be needed anymore.

The Thief's Engineer clearly didn't understand that. If he had, he wouldn't have been wearing that smug look on his face. He wouldn't still be showing off his brain, tossing it from one hand to the other, making sure the Thief saw just how big and shiny it was. No, the Engineer would have kept it tucked deep in his pocket, far from sight.

"You were beginning to think I wouldn't finish, weren't you?" The Engineer nudged the Thief with his elbow, a wry smile on his lips. "I know, I know. But I told you I would get this done."

"That's great," the Thief said. There was no wry smile on his lips.

"I'll admit it was tricky. That stuff down there is crazy. Digging's not the problem, as you know. But there is so little to work with. The sand is packed, sure. Been packed forever. But once you dig into it, man, it's like water. And what with all the disturbance from that construction crew on the other side; well, that was nasty."

"Yes, I know." The Thief let the Engineer show off his brain a little while longer.

"Come down and I'll show you what it looks like now." The Engineer left the kitchen and walked down the hallway, never turning to see if the Thief followed.

At the door of the back bedroom—the bedroom with the digital lock—the Engineer tapped in a code and waited until the lock scrolled through its mechanical sequence. The Engineer nodded as each of the four bolts tumbled into their unlocked positions. He liked things like that, systematic precision. The Thief couldn't have cared less. It was only a lock, for God's sake.

Behind the locked door, the two men crossed to a far corner where a second door lay flush with the floor. A rope had been tied to this door, run up to a pulley, then down to a counter weight. When the Engineer pulled up on the door, the counterweight propelled it open with a powerful force.

A stairway descended into darkness. The Engineer dropped down this stair, motioning for the Thief to follow. The Thief did, unable to believe how stupid the smart little Engineer really was.

A tunnel led away from the stair. The Engineer paused on the edge of the light that spilled down from the room above.

"This is all part of the old tunnel, which held up pretty well if you think about it. I'm proud of that, you know. We weren't sure it would. I wasn't, anyway. But as you know, time took its toll. Of course you know. You're the one that told me it had to be repaired. I'm telling you things you already know. I'll stop."

That's the kind of thing the Thief was talking about. Right there. Why would anyone say idiotic things like that? Showing off. Plain and simple. And the Engineer probably thought he was being humble. What an ass.

"So anyway, here we go." The Engineer reached over to a panel on the wall and touched a sensor. Bare lights popped on in sequence, starting about a meter away from them and moving down the corridor at intervals of ten meters. Blue-white light illuminated a tunnel that was not quite two meters wide. "All of this was still in good shape. That's because of the building's foundation. Good solid stuff."

As the Engineer made a fist and hammered the wall of the tunnel, the Thief shook his head. The man was tedious.

"The trouble started after this first ninety-degree turn."

"I know. I showed you where the trouble started." The Thief did not mean to get into a pissing contest with the Engineer, but it was hard to keep his mouth shut.

"Exactly, right in here. Now this is what I was talking about. See this here? Put your hand on it. Gritty, right? *Sand.* We had to start the sealant here. Of course, you can't just slap it on willy-nilly like. There's a right way and a wrong way to do it."

"Which is why we called you."

"I know. You did the right thing."

The Thief, at some point, just quit listening. The Engineer was too far into his shtick now, and nothing would stop him. He had that little shiny brain out like it was a yo-yo and he was a yo-yo wizard. With hands quick as magic he tossed, twirled and shuffled that brain around, first one way and then another. The show would have been dizzying to most people. But the Thief was not most people. And this wasn't the first time he'd seen the show.

"Here's where the trouble really started. This branch." The Engineer stood looking down a second tunnel that met the first tunnel at another ninety-degree turn. The lights for that tunnel were not on until he touched a second sensor. "This section had always been a problem for us years ago, from the moment we began to dig it out. We'd never seen anything like this before. I suppose it might be common here, but certainly never on any planet I've ever worked on. Most of this looks like clay. But there are all these little veins of sand running through it. You think you've got solid clay above you, but there's just a thin layer of clay, covering another layer of sand."

The Thief did his best not to start shouting at the Engineer to *shut up*. As long as the Engineer kept walking it was okay. The Thief allowed him to continue his show.

"Sealant wouldn't do the trick, because the sand was holding the weight of the clay. The sealant only made it heavier. So we had to remove the layers of clay to reach the sand. What's this?"

They had come to a portion of the tunnel where a cavity had been dug into the wall. The sand and clay from the cavity had been piled beside it. The cavity was about one meter high, one meter deep, and two meters long.

"You did say you were done with everything, didn't you?" the Thief asked.

"I thought we were, yes. But what is this all about?" He squatted down and peered into the cavity. "This didn't just happen. Somebody dug this out."

"I dug it out." The Thief stood over the Engineer.

"I hope you aren't going to tell me you're planning on starting a new branch. This is the worst possible place to do that. Straight back behind here, if I have my bearings right, is a natural aquifer, or at least this is where the drainage lanes lead to the aquifer. We're a good twenty meters from it, and that's enough to protect us, but we can't get any closer to it."

The brain was out of the pocket again. And the Engineer was back to his sleight of hand tricks. That shiny little brain was the star of the show.

"I don't give a damn about any of that." The Thief was relieved he wouldn't have to sit by and watch any more of that droll show. He finally got to do what he had wanted to do all along. He simply snatched that shiny little brain out of the Engineer's hand. And once he got a hold of it, he wouldn't let it go. Surprisingly, the little thing tried to jump free. It wriggled around in his hands, and the Thief had to be careful not to let it slip free. The Engineer grabbed at it too, wrestling with the Thief for it, but the Thief had it and wasn't about to let it go.

And he didn't just want to hold on to it. He started to squeeze it. He had to crush it so that once he did let it go, the Engineer would never get to use it again.

The Engineer, who'd fallen to the floor of the tunnel, kicked his heels against the walls, fighting for leverage. The Thief had not expected the Engineer to put up such a fight. It didn't matter. The Engineer was too small to overcome the Thief. He wasn't nearly as strong either. And that was the deciding factor. No matter how hard the frantic Engineer tried to pry the Thief's hands off the brain, he couldn't do it.

And just as the Thief had expected, the Engineer couldn't say one intelligent thing without his brain. He whimpered a great deal and cried out in simple, one-syllable words. But he had nothing clever to say. He couldn't even calculate how much longer the brain could survive the crushing pressure of the Thief's hands. The truth of the matter was, without his brain, the Engineer was nothing more than a little animal, scrambling for its survival.

And as he shoved the Engineer's lifeless brain into the cavity, the Thief knew that was all the Engineer had become. A dead little animal in a muddy hole in the ground.

40

Lepov ignored MacNally's advice and crawled out of bed as soon as he'd left. The old cop was right, of course; Lepov knew he should stay in bed. But who cared how bad he had looked when they'd fished his coffin out of the sea? The fact of the matter was, he *felt* like death had come early in his life. But while he was in no condition to start wandering around the Lazaretto, there was no way he could have lain there in bed. True, he wanted to get on with his job, but that wasn't the driving reason to get back on his feet. Something else drove him. *Someone* else.

Lilly.

Whether it was from some damage incurred from his oxygen deprivation, or from the blow to his head, Lepov didn't care; he could not get the image of that man talking with Lilly out of his head. It wasn't Lilly. Lepov knew this. But this woman — this non-Lilly — looked more and more like Lilly the more he thought about her. He'd told MacNally that he had never been able to see her, but Lepov could swear he was beginning to remember seeing her. And what he remembered was too much like Lilly.

And that was why he couldn't lay in bed all day. Because he knew that was ludicrous. He had not seen a woman who looked like Lilly. He hadn't seen a woman at all. But the longer he lay there, the more he convinced himself he'd seen Lilly and she wanted him dead.

The man he'd seen must have been Morvees. And for once, MacNally had good advice. Lepov wanted to stay well away from Anton Morvees. But that was going to be a problem if he wanted to find out what was going on — if he wanted to find out why they'd wanted him dead.

Lepov's best course of action lay in coming after Morvees through one of the other people in the apartment. There had been the three younger men who'd stuffed him in the shipping box. They would know *something*, though Lepov had little faith they would know anything important. These guys were hired help, nothing more. What Lepov needed was to find Morvees' partner, if one existed.

And that brought him right back to the woman. She had spoken with far too much authority to be hired help. How often did she come to the apartment? It was, unfortunately for Lepov, the only way to find her. He did not know her name; he would never recognize her. Aside from his persistent faulty memory that told him she looked like Lilly, Lepov knew absolutely nothing about her.

Lepov climbed out of the Alpha Quadrant SubTransit Station and into the brighter than usual afternoon. The cloud cover was high, allowing Lepov a rare feeling of elbowroom. Most of the time, the Lazaretto was crowded by low clouds; at times Lepov would notice he was walking with his shoulders hunched, seemingly afraid to hit his head on the overshadowing cloudbank. Days like this — high clouds — were a relief; a Lazaretto sunny day.

Maybe it was the weather. Lepov was feeling better though his head still hurt. And his back still felt like someone had tried to bend his spine into a circle. But the more he moved around, the more he loosened up. He knew that most of the pain was held in check by the painkillers the nurse had given him. That was good enough for now. He'd deal with the pain when the drugs wore off.

But until then, he wanted to get back to the Keep's security room. He wanted to see the recordings from the day of his deep-sea excursion. He had a feeling that the woman wouldn't be identifiable on the screen for one reason or another, but it was worth a try.

Digging through the archive, he accessed the recordings on the first floor hallway. He was shocked to see clear images. But his luck ran out when the woman entered the frame. She'd been wearing a raincoat, complete with hood. She was more than hired help; Lepov was now certain of that. She was involved enough that she knew not to allow herself to appear on the security recording.

Lepov settled into the console chair and waited. He was going to have to watch for the woman. And that might take forever.

That also meant he was alone with his own thoughts as his only interaction. Once again he could see that image of Lilly standing over his coffin.

It was going to be a long day. The temptation to pull out a cigarette was stronger than he'd felt in a long time. Something would have to take his mind off Lilly, or he was going to drive himself crazy.

He tried to concentrate on the lobby. Every time someone came in through the front doors, he watched them, trying to guess if they were visitors or if they were residents. A dozen people came and went as Lepov paid attention to their dress, how much they were in a hurry, and if they were familiar with the layout of the Keep. Four of them were women, but all of them rode the elevator to the upper floors. It occurred to Lepov that he could sit there for weeks without ever seeing the woman. And if she didn't show up soon, it would be better to abandon his plan right away rather than wait two weeks and then abandon it.

He was understandably surprised, then, when he watched a woman enter the lobby and proceed to ride the elevator *down* to the first floor. It had to be the wrong woman. She must be heading toward one of the other apartments. She was lost, or had pushed the wrong button in the elevator. Lepov kept thinking of rationalizations like that the whole time she walked the length of the hallway. He was trying to come up with more of them even as she stopped in front of 02. He gave up looking for alternate explanations as she ran her hands down her overcoat and then ran one of them through her short black hair.

When she reached for the bellpad beside the door, Lepov sat straight up and prayed the recorder's archive was functioning properly. Once she got inside the apartment, Lepov would have to decide what to do next. He was already reviewing the images of her as she came into the lobby from the front entrance. The archive had worked. But whether deliberately or not, the woman had never lifted her head enough to allow a clear view of her face.

If only Lepov had MacNally's PDT reader. That would have made his job simple. He'd know exactly who she was.

He was so intent on trying to catch a solid shot of her face on the archive that he almost didn't notice that she never went into the apartment. A glance at the recorder screen was enough to catch her as she headed back toward the elevator.

What had happened? Lepov didn't have time to run the archive ahead to the point where she had touched the bellpad. She was already back in the elevator and would be heading back through the lobby before he could scan the archive. Had she dropped off a package? He hadn't seen her holding anything. Had she picked something up? No, he was fairly confident that the door had not even opened. He would have caught that movement out of the corner of his eye.

But what then? And what should he do now? The elevator was opening, and she stepped out of it, heading toward the front doors.

There was no time for Lepov to process everything that was going through his mind. He considered following her. He knew that if she slipped out of sight, he'd lose a chance to clear up his confusion about Lilly. He also knew that if given the chance, he might be able to intimidate this woman into giving him the information he wanted. She was a small woman—small enough for him to dominate without much of an effort. Small enough to make her hard to follow in the growing crowds of the late afternoon.

In a later moment of clarity, Lepov would be able to recognize what he did. But as she walked across the lobby, he yanked open the door of the security room, never once aware of his panic. All he could do was move. Act. Do something.

"Excuse me," he called, barely suppressing his rash state of mind.

"I'm sorry?" The woman turned her head to look back at him. She slowed down, but did not stop.

The lobby was empty. Somewhere in the back of his mind, Lepov noted that under the open lapel of her coat she was wearing a uniform of sorts. Behind her, a TransitCar slid across his field of view. People were moving on the sidewalk. She was closing on the steps leading down to the glass doors.

She sped up. Lepov wanted to shout at her. He wanted to demand that she hold still. He never said a word. He didn't have time for that. Instead, he reached out, grabbing her wrist. She jerked her arm away from him but his grip held. She stared wildly at him, her free hand scratching at his face.

Lepov knew he could not fight her on the open stairs. Someone would see them. Wondering if he had lost his mind, he jammed his fist into her stomach; not a full swinging punch, but enough to knock the wind and fight out of her. She doubled over, moaning as air escaped from her lungs.

Still gripping her wrist, Lepov swung her arm up and over his shoulder as he snatched her around the waist. As a variation on the fireman's carry, it was easy to do. She didn't weigh much. Lepov hurried across the lobby, disappearing into the security room unseen.

Once back in the outer room, Lepov allowed her to slide off his shoulder and down onto the larger sofa. She was still conscious, though she shook her head in confusion. Once she caught her breath, she glared at Lepov; the fear in her eyes replaced with anger.

"What are you doing?" Her eyes took in the room from one side to the other.

"Now take a minute to catch your breath. I'll do the same and then we can come to some kind of understanding." Lepov held his hands out, expecting her to make a run for it.

"Who are you?" she demanded.

Lepov's mind had begun to work more clearly. The more his thoughts came into focus, the more he realized how much of a mess he'd made. His best bet, no matter how much he knew he'd screwed up, was to keep up the play he'd started. If he stopped now he wasn't going to get anything out of her. Unless you counted the lawsuit that was sure to come.

"You're gonna tell me who *you* are. And then you're gonna tell me what is going on here." Lepov took a step in her direction and she obediently backed up against the corner of the sofa. "Now let's get the ground rules straight before you say anything.

"First of all, I ain't a cop. So I don't have a lot of rules that protect you. Second, you and your pals tried to kill me. So that eliminates most of my rules that would have protected you. So your best move is to start talking while you still can. Otherwise, I'll hurt you."

To back up his words, Lepov grabbed a ceramic lamp from a

table and smashed it down on the table's corner, shattering the ceramic into a dozen jagged shards. He dropped what remained of the lamp and snatched up the largest shard.

The woman wasn't angry any more. Fear had returned. Lepov was disappointed. He had not given the attempt on his life much thought; he'd been too preoccupied trying to decide if Lilly had been involved. But the more he did think of it, as he stood in front of one of the killers, the more furious he became. He realized he wanted to use the ceramic shard on her.

"I don't understand—what is it you want?" She addressed her question to the sharp edge of the shard.

"Let's start with your name. Who are you?"

"My name is Sun. Major Sun Uijong."

41

The big man in the wrinkled suit loomed over her silently as Sun tried to explain why she had knocked on Anton Morvees' door. Part of her knew that she need not defend her actions; the rest of her knew it mattered little. She had obviously been mistaken for someone else and this man looked ready to carve her up. She saw no reason to provoke such an obviously violent man.

He did not back away. He was too close; she felt him as much as saw him. Brutish anger flowed from him so that he barely contained it. He might have even have been sick—his face too gray. He seemed out of breath more than he ought to have been, even for a man his size. All of this prevented her from thinking and speaking clearly.

"I've never met Mr. Morvees," she patiently repeated herself. Although he had scared her, Sun had recovered her composure and worked at calming the man. "If you were watching me, then you know that I knocked on the door and there was no answer. I don't believe anyone was home. I'm simply attempting to meet with him to arrange some financial assistance from the government.

"Now, if you'll take a step or two back, maybe you can tell me who you are and what this is all about."

The man ran his thumb up and down the glazed side of the ceramic shard as he tried to decide what to do. Sun's answers had clearly not been what he had expected from her.

"Okay," he took two steps back and set the shard on the table beside him, "Sit right there. If you try to get up, I'll put you right back in the same spot, only not as gently as before. You don't know me, but you need to believe me."

"I do." Sun nodded slowly, she had no intention of trying to run anywhere. Not yet, anyway.

"I'm a Private Investigator, but I'm not going to tell you my name. You're gonna have to prove some of what you've told me before I tell you my name. And we're gonna do that with the help of a friend of mine."

Sun watched him reach for a phone from the desk behind him. She didn't like the sound of that: a friend.

"Who's your friend?" she asked.

"He's a cop. Does that bother you?" The man smiled.

"No." Sun wondered if this were a good cop or a bad cop.

"Mac," he said into the receiver, after waiting a few seconds, "I need some help. No, I'm not at the hospital. Forget about that. I need you to look up a Major Sun—" he shrugged his shoulders at her.

"U-i-j-o-n-g."

"Yeah, I'll tell you after you get me her information." The man's eyes never strayed from Sun. He didn't trust her to stay put. The cop on the other end of the line did not take long to give him what he needed. "Yeah, I'll check it.

"Okay, Major," he was still holding the phone while he was speaking to Sun, "put your data tag on the desk here. Slow. Real slow."

Sun had to undo the buttons on her coat to reach into her uniform and pull out her PDT. It was in a dragonfly pendant on a chain around her neck. She unclipped the pendant and climbed off the sofa. Carefully, she crossed the room and set it down on a corner of the desk. The deskscreen blinked in recognition and her personal information came up under the tag. Sun backed away and allowed the man to examine it.

He expanded the document and took his time reading it. When he was done he started speaking to the cop again.

"It looks okay. Do you have it yet? Jeeze, I don't even know if this old desk will transmit. Okay, good. Look okay to you?"

Sun saw that the man's attentiveness had wavered. He was only glancing at her every now and then. Either he had forgotten he didn't trust her or he was beginning to believe that she was not the woman he had believed her to be.

"Thanks Mac. No, I'm not gonna tell you where I am right now. I'll get back to you." He paused then added, "So I lied. Come and arrest me."

He set down the phone and turned his full attention back to Sun.

"I guess I'd better start explaining who I am and what I'm doing and why I got a little rough with you. And I will. But first, are you okay? Did I hurt you?" He picked up her PDT and offered it back.

"Yes, you did." Sun took the dragonfly and clipped it back to the chain. "And yes, I do want to know what this is all about. And I may

153

also want to call the police."

"That's only fair. But I hope you'll listen to me first. I'm not as crazy as I must appear to be. Only a little impulsive and maybe a poor decision maker."

"Okay," Sun sat back down on the sofa. "Go ahead."

The man's name was Gregor Lepov. And the story he told was difficult for her to believe at first. He was thin on details, but she understood enough to know that Lepov believed Morvees had tried to kill him and that he had help from a woman whom he did not know. He told her she could verify all of this with Detective MacNally of Lazaretto Homicide, the man with whom he'd just spoken.

Her first instinct was to call the police. It did not matter if his story was true. He'd assaulted her and that was too much to overlook. She was an officer in the military, after all.

But the more she watched this Lepov, the more she was intrigued. She could see that when his color returned to his face he would not be an unattractive man. He was worn down, but he had a boyish aspect that made up for the weary lines on his face. Despite his rough manner he was not arrogant. There was something more in the line of fatalism directing his actions. She could believe he could see no other way to act, despite the fact he didn't like it.

And if his story were true, she had to know more of it. If Anton Morvees were involved, then she needed to know about it. Criminal activity would definitely disqualify him from the compensation list.

Was it possible that good could come out of being roughed up by Gregor Lepov? She would have trouble forgetting his willingness to manhandle her, as well as his threats with the sharp edge of a lamp. But she was willing to believe that he was not in the healthiest frame of mind after the attack on his life; both physically and mentally. It was enough, at least, for her to work with.

"So do you want to call the police now?" he asked after he finished explaining why he had assaulted and kidnapped her.

"Not yet. I may later. But I think you and I can help each other."

"How's that?" he asked, suspicion on his face.

"I told you I'm here looking into the current status of the Lost Platoon; living and dead. You're a private investigator. I have a feeling you could help me get the information I need to complete my mission here."

"So I do legwork for you, in exchange for your silence? Blackmail's a big step for an Army officer. You sure you wouldn't want to start with something a little easier, like a drunk and disorderly charge, maybe? Or possibly petty theft would do the trick."

"Says the man who kidnapped me."

"Well, now that's not exactly the first time I've crossed the border into the criminal world. But I'm assuming you're new to this." Lepov was clearly making fun of her now.

"If you'd rather I call the police I'll gladly do it. Only I have a feeling you'll have trouble investigating Morvees from a prison cell."

Lepov cocked his head and smiled. "I think I've got a tiger by the tail. Have you eaten dinner yet?"

Sun didn't want to admit it, but she knew Gregor Lepov was doing his best to charm her, and she was falling for it. It didn't hurt that he was getting some color back in his cheeks. Was she having a warming effect on him? It was a complimentary thought, but she tried to ignore it. All he was doing was trying to win her over to keep her from pressing charges.

That might just work, she thought.

"Dinner? After tossing me on the sofa, I thought you'd never ask."

"Well, trust me, Sun Uijong," his pronunciation was close enough, "I can't remember the last time I asked a woman to dinner *after* I'd thrown her on the sofa."

As they left through the glass doors of the lobby, Sun could not stop shaking her head; she couldn't believe she'd actually used a line like that.

42

It hadn't surprised MacNally when Lepov's call came in about Major Uijong. He had known Lepov would be busy despite the attempt on his life. He was glad to hear it, though he had to sound upset with Lepov if only to show that he cared for the man's health. He sincerely hoped the private investigator made some progress because MacNally was getting drawn into his own investigation. He was beginning to think he might have been wrong about that long-dead body in the rubble.

He hadn't been too interested in Pete Landon's history lesson on the Lost Platoon until Lepov mentioned that Morvees was a member of that crew. And every indication pointed to the excavation directly adjacent to Morvees' apartment as the body's original location.

It had taken MacNally an hour to verify that the Arcobian dissident Pan Juarez had no connection whatsoever with the Lost Platoon. Baker's Bastards had fought against the Arcobian rebels while Pan Juarez had been drumming up support for the rebellion on Earth. Juarez had, in fact, never been on Arcobia during the actual rebellion. He had been there just before the fighting erupted, stirring up dissent, but had left before the first shot was fired.

So what was the connection? The Pan Juarez that MacNally had investigated in Alpha Quadrant was not the Arcobian dissident. But the dissident Pan Juarez who disappeared after leaving Earth had been bound for the Lazaretto. He had to pass through there to get to Arcobia. Yet he disappeared at the same time that there was a second Pan Juarez in the Lazaretto. Thirty years did not change MacNally's impression that such a coincidence was preposterous.

And that led him to the same conclusion he'd come to thirty years before. *The* Pan Juarez had employed a double to get through Lazaretto Quarantine as quickly as possible.   Doubles weren't anything new. Administration officials knew that doubles were used from time to time. It was extremely costly, and difficult to stop. And the prevailing attitude among the administrators was that if a man had money to hire a double, it was improbable that he had any kind of a virus. These were men who moved in the highest circles and had the best possible medical care available to them. For the most part, the practice of quarantine doubles was overlooked.

For thirty years Ed MacNally had secretly held the belief that Pan Juarez had disappeared after being murdered in the Lazaretto by his double for the diamonds he'd brought to buy votes for Arcobian independence. It was the sole reason for hiding that foolish file. It wouldn't have done the Lazaretto any good for the public to know that Juarez had been allowed to be assassinated in the Lazaretto. Add the fact that MacNally would have taken the fall for it, and he had every reason in the world to hide or even destroy that file.

But for the first time in his life, MacNally had an idea who Juarez's killer might actually have been. And he had to decide if he should go after him. If Anton Morvees had actually been the double, and killed Juarez for the diamonds, there was a chance for MacNally to redeem his thirty-year-old mistake. Even if it wasn't Morvees, it might have been one of his fellow *Bastards*.

It was too early to bring his Captain in on it. MacNally wanted to be sure he could prove who had killed the famous dissident before he publicly *discovered* the file. But he was going to have to tell Pete Landon. As much as he didn't want to, he would also have to tell Russell. But considering that Russell was Arcobian, he didn't want to involve him just yet. Instead, MacNally decided he would ask Lepov for help.

So he was content to know that Lepov was chasing Morvees. MacNally would spend his time looking for the proof they'd need to hold him once they caught him.

"Did you get a chance to look at the visuals?" Russell walked up to MacNally's desk and looked over his partner's shoulder.

"Enough of it," MacNally had the document up on his

deskscreen. He'd known Russell would come asking about it. "Radiation played hell with the DNA."

"But that engineer we talked to was right. I talked with a labtech, and he used the radiation readings to estimate how long the corpse had been buried. He thinks maybe thirty years. Give or take. That eliminates the possibility of the body being below the Roth building. It was built forty-eight years ago."

"Don't tell me you think the body was buried somewhere else." MacNally was too sold on the body's proximity to Morvees to want to hear any other theories.

"No, I don't think it was. That just means someone took the time to bury it in the basement. I'm already looking into the history of the building, and who had access to it."

"You could try to drag up someone who was familiar with it. Someone who might have noticed fresh concrete down there way back when." MacNally hated to send Russell after a bad hunch, but it would keep him out of the way for a little while longer.

"I'll work on it." Russell stared at MacNally, wanting to say more, but didn't.

"That's good, Menya." MacNally knew the kid was waiting to hear what MacNally planned to do next. "If you can take care of that, I need to follow up on a few leads Gregor Lepov gave me."

"I thought you said he didn't know much about who tried to kill him." Russell's stare had only grown more accusatory. He wasn't stupid, and MacNally would have to stop lying to him soon.

"He just called a few minutes ago and was able to give me a few more details. It seems his memory is slowly coming back." So today wasn't the day to stop lying. But it was a great day for a headache. He lit a cigarette to block out the pounding in his head.

"Okay." Russell turned to leave but stopped and swung his head back around. "I forgot to mention Officer Landon came looking for you earlier. He said you should call."

MacNally called Pete immediately.

"Ed," Pete's tone clearly meant he was enjoying himself, "did you know that nearly all of the members of the Lost Platoon are dead?"

"Sure they are. They were exiled here for some deadly disease. It makes sense, Pete." For a puzzle wizard, he wasn't too bright.

"If they had all contracted a terminal disease that would have simply been bad luck. But what makes the story of the Lost Platoon so tragic is they had a mild one. They were sick, but it wasn't fatal. They were left here to die for something like a nasty cold. Incredibly, if the quarantine had run another two or three weeks, the virus would have cleared up and they'd have gone on their merry way."

"You're kidding." MacNally had never paid attention to the

story all those years ago. He'd been too busy trying to be the perfect security officer in Alpha Quadrant.

"No. That's why it's so odd so many of these guys are dead."

"And the ring?" MacNally didn't like talking about it over the phone, but he was too tired to drag himself down to Landon's office.

"It was something like a citation for combat performance."

"A Unit Citation?" MacNally asked.

"This is where you're in luck." Pete sounded like he was rubbing his hands in glee. "The ring was only awarded to three members of the 3rd platoon."

"Son of a gun."

"You got something to write with?"

"I don't need it. Tell me the names, I'll remember them."

"The rings belong to Lt. John Yarmin, Anton Morvees, and Silva MacDenny."

MacNally nearly dropped his cigarette into his lap. *Morvees?* He was alive. Did that mean he was the double? Had he killed Juarez after he put on the ring to assume the identity Morvees had established? It was too tidy. It made too much sense.

"There's just one more thing, Ed." Pete had to be smiling. He was good, MacNally thought, but he was a pain in the ass as well.

"And what's that?"

"All three of these guys are still alive."

MacNally's curse was sufficient to spit his cigarette out onto his desk.

"That good enough for now?" Pete's smile was *audible.*

"Well since you're so pleased with yourself," MacNally had one more question for the puzzle man, "and I probably owe you a dinner, I might as well get into debt just a little bit more. This one is a favor for Gregor Lepov."

"What does Lepov need?"

"Some peace of mind." If MacNally were going to enlist Lepov's help, he wanted to be able to bring him proof that Lilly Stewart was far away on Bukovina and nowhere near Morvees. The last thing MacNally needed was Lepov fixated on Lilly.

43

I had no idea what was about to happen that day, or just how monstrously it would influence the rest of our lives. I did not particularly have any idea what day it was either. Living in that windowless apartment made it impossible to distinguish between night and day. We had a clock, as well as our internal clocks, but that kind of existence made it impossible to keep track of the passing of time.

Most of the days passed with nothing more remarkable than a bad bout with Calla's sickness. She might have had to fight through an especially harsh coughing fit, or her sinuses might have drained so heavily that she passed out from an inability to take in enough oxygen. But such attacks, while violent and unpredictable, were getting rarer as the weeks passed by.

This fact turned the smallest occasions into exciting moments.

And the exciting moments could dazzle you enough to make you miss the more important ones that were as mundane as they were life-altering.

"Swallow all of it." I was forever trying to force Calla to eat. It was hard for her—sometimes even painful—but I knew that she needed every spoonful I could coax her to take. I wasn't always pleasant about it. Calla could be stubborn, and I had to be more so for her sake. "Now one more."

Calla choked on the soup and spit most of it onto my blouse. I gave her a hard look, not fooled by her I-couldn't-help-it eyes. We were getting on each other's nerves.

That time I gave up. I wasn't always as hard or strong as I needed to be. I just took the bowl and left the room, in search of a towel to wipe the soup off my blouse.

Without consciously thinking about it, I had assumed Bernham was in his room. He was always in that room. It drove me mad when I thought about how much he was in that room. But at the same time I had come to expect it and there was a security in that kind of consistency.

As I wet a hand towel and dabbed at the soup, the front door opened. I knocked over a small glass of milk. I hadn't seen the front door opened in many weeks. Bernham stepped inside, and shut the door.

I knew milk was running along the countertop and I should wipe it up but I couldn't help staring at Bernham. He watched the milk, then me, and finally he spoke.

"Mr. Zoltis said I should give this to you."

He was holding a large package. I hadn't even noticed until he held it out to me. It was wrapped in paper, and was obviously a framed picture.

"Thank you," I said as I set it down against the counter. I wanted to tear the paper off right then and there but I forced myself to clean up the milk first. I could tell Bernham was still watching me closely even though my back was turned. Perhaps he was as curious as I was about the picture.

I resisted the urge to take it into our room unopened so that Calla could see me open it. I wanted to see it first, to make sure it was appropriate for her—not something that would upset her. But I also did not want Bernham to enter our room to see it. And he seemed curious enough to do just that if I did not let him see it there in the front room.

The paper was tightly wrapped and secured with strong tape. I had trouble tearing it. Bernham reached into a back pocket and withdrew a pocketknife that looked terribly long and cruel after he unfolded it. I hoped he did not notice my negative reaction as he took the framed picture and sliced the paper diagonally across the back. I always did my best to hide my fear from him. I had the distinct impression he enjoyed making me uncomfortable whenever possible.

"Thank you," I said, unable to take my eyes off the curved steel blade until he had folded it back into itself and slipped it back into his pocket.

The picture, once revealed, was stunning. I'm sure I let out an audible gasp. Maybe it was a combination of our stark existence and my physically and emotionally weary state; tears blurred my vision. For that moment, I was unable to hide this vulnerable reaction from Bernham. I had no idea if he was aware of it or not. All I could do was stare in wonder at the picture in the ornate gold frame.

It was the image of an angel; a tall, glorious angel. She was standing at the foot of a bed. Its occupant lay in shadow, and it was anyone's guess who that person might be. I immediately assumed it was someone like Calla; sick and in need of God's touch. But the body in the bed was not the focal point of the scene. The angel was not in the center of the frame, but it didn't matter. The viewer's eye was so strongly drawn to her that it appeared she was the center. And there was no doubt the artist had intended just such an effect.

Golden hair cascaded down the back of the angel's head; it was in fact the source of light for the scene. Her skin was neither white nor gold, but a magnificent blend of the two colors that created a skin so vibrant I always had trouble not staring at it. And if I did stare long enough, it seemed to come alive. There were times I wanted to reach out and stroke it; to feel the glory of that angel burn through my fingertips.

She was wrapped in a bronze robe that ran from her shoulders down past her feet, its folds forming a soft pedestal around her. The artist had managed to give this rich fabric both a silky texture and a strong, solid texture. I often wondered if he could not decide whether it was made of bronze colored fabric or it was in fact an impenetrable armor plated bronze. I came to understand his dilemma; there were times I wanted it to be as soft and tender as God's grace, and other times hard and dense like a shield.

Artists never tire of bestowing wings on angels. But this artist—I had never been able to discover his name—had found a way to portray the power of her wings that I had never seen before. These wings were folded. But they did not fold into her robe as mere decoration. They looked more like folded, muscular arms that were ready to spread out at the slightest provocation. There was intensity stored in them impossible to ignore.

But all of these aspects of the angel—her skin, robe, and wings—could not compete with the angel's face. No matter how many times my gaze strayed to her hair or the complexity of the robe, I was always drawn back to that face. And each time I gazed at her, I always saw a different expression. The first time I looked upon her, I could see her compassion for the bedridden patient. I knew the angel would do all she could to intercede on the patient's behalf with the Great Healer. But there were times I disagreed with that first impression. She could be compassionate, but I had also read despair in her eye, anger, even laughter.

I knew, as time passed, that I was projecting my own emotions into the portrait, but I had never seen a face like hers before, and I came to both love and hate the raw emotions that were mirrored back at me.

I didn't notice all of this right away. As I unwrapped the frame, I was simply overjoyed to have such a beautiful angel to keep watch over Calla. Kjarsta had not only responded to my request, but he had outdone himself. I was glad he had not brought it himself. I would have been embarrassed as I tried to find the right words to thank him. I'm sure it would have embarrassed him as well.

I hung the picture on the wall directly across from Calla's bed. She could lie on her back and see the angel any time she opened her eyes. I could see just how happy it made her and it brought tears in my eyes. That was unusual for me. But that was an unusually happy time for us.

And that was why I paid little attention to what happened afterward.

The door to Bernham's room opened, and a man emerged whom I had never seen before. I hardly paid him any attention; I was still caught up in watching Calla look at the angel. Only later did I consider it enough to realize that I had never seen anyone go into the room. Just a man coming out of it.

But whether or not I was paying any attention to him, he was paying particular attention to me. It would not have happened if I had closed our door. But I had been too focused on Calla and the painting. Had I closed the door, a great deal of sorrow would have been erased from all of our lives.

But I had left it open. And the man stood watching us.

When I did pay him some mind, I knew he was a man that should not be around Calla. He was small; not short, but a small man. His face was small, as were his hands and feet.

I remember little beyond this odd visual measurement. As soon as I saw him there, I saw Bernham come into view, and he saw what I was seeing. Bernham, the quiet petulant tenant in the room across the hall, bellowed at the small man.

"Fortunado! Get back in the room. Have you lost your mind?"

I had time to remember that I had heard the name before. And I also was able to match the man's features with those of the man I had seen at Kjarsta's house in the middle of the night.

A stab of fear hit me as I finally understood the man was not looking at me. He stood staring at Calla. An alarm coursed through me and I immediately put myself in his line of sight, cutting off his view of the girl.

"She's an angel, that one." Fortunado turned and spoke to Bernham. "I'll keep that one in reserve. Might come in handy."

"Shut up!" Bernham boldly stood toe to toe with the small interloper. He seemed greatly wound-up over what had just happened.

"Okay," he smiled; his words too easily recognizable as mockery.

And just like that he was gone. He could not have been there for more than two minutes. Maybe just one minute. But it had been enough.

I made an effort to put that awful man out of my mind. I did not want to spend any time worrying over him. I see now how idiotic that sounds, but at the time, it was a valid choice to make given the facts I had. Unfortunately, I had few, if not none of the facts that I would need.

44

Sometime after they had taken their seats, Sun wondered if she had lost her mind. It was ridiculous. That was the only word that came to mind. Ridiculous. She was eating dinner with a man who had assaulted her and threatened to slice her up—possibly even kill her. But after discovering he was a private detective looking for the people who had tried to kill him—none of this verified, no less—she had consented to eat with him at the same table.

This was the kind of thing that had driven her mother crazy as she was growing up. Sun liked people, and never shied away from interacting with them. She'd even once been found serving make-believe tea to an escaped patient from a nearby mental health facility. Maybe, Sun thought from her removed vantage point, she too was in need of mental health treatment.

But her instinct whispered assurances to her. Gregor Lepov, the detective, was no one to fear. His *assault* was all show and no substance. The more time she spent with him, the less she believed he would have ever used that ceramic shard on her.

"Do you like Bukovinan game?" Lepov sat hunched over his menu. "You might want to try the seafood if you aren't used to the game. It can be a little wild for most people with domestic tastes."

"I'll try it," Sun shrugged her shoulders. "What sort of game is it, exactly?"

"Well, that's the real question, I suppose. You see, back on Bukovina, we colonists found all sorts of little furry things running around in the bushes. Scared the devil out of us."

"You're from Bukovina?"

"Well, that's what my mother insists on telling me anyway." He allowed a little smile at which Sun couldn't help but giggle. "Yeah, I guess you know what I mean. Anyway, all these little creatures running around came in all shapes and sizes. They were mostly the same sort of animal—something like large rabbits, I suppose. But the darn things never looked the same. Colonists finally gave up trying to name all the subspecies after they'd seen about forty of them. Scientists had some fancy name for all of them, but the farmers never were comfortable with it. They just got to calling them game, and hunted them every chance they got. Like I said, they're a bit strong, but we grew up on the taste and enjoy it."

"You've got me worried. Maybe I'll try the seafood." Sun wasn't about to lie to herself. He was charming. And she let him keep at it.

"The fantail will be the closest thing to fresh," Lepov said.

"Oh, I can't eat fantail." When it came to seafood, Sun was picky. "But I enjoy grilled tuna."

"If you like seafood we could duck out of here. There's a Phasian Seafood place close to my apartment."

"No, this'll be fine." Sun answered a little too quickly. She knew she hadn't liked the idea of going so close to his apartment. She was being silly, of course. But she had to draw the line and make sure it was pretty easy to see. He was charming, but she would have to make that call to the police before she would put any kind of real trust in this man.

He ordered the game. She ordered the tuna. They both picked at bread as they settled in to wait on the chef.

"So," Lepov stopped chewing to ask a question, "tell me about your connection to the Lost Platoon. Where do you fit in with them?"

"How well do you know their story, Gregor?"

"Just what most people know. The basic story."

"That's all I'd known until a short time ago. Old history, right? But the truth is, this history is still going on today. These men are still alive, and they've been terribly mistreated for thirty years. I hate to think that we as a people had anything to do with this. But you know, it's good to know that we're taking steps to correct it. That's why I'm here. To see that we make an effort to give them some kind of dignity."

Sun explained the government's decision to make restitution and her role in making that happen. Lepov let her speak, not interrupting. He was content to sit back in his chair and give his full attention. At least, she hoped that was what he was doing. He was beginning to look a little discolored again. She hoped he wasn't fading out of the conversation.

"So you're having trouble finding these men, is that what you need me for?"

"Well, we've only just begun."

"We?"

"I'm working with a local woman who runs a charity here in the Lazaretto. The Lazaretto Benevolence Society. Have you heard of them?" Lepov shook his head. "Well, it's a small organization. And they are almost completely set apart as a charity for the benefit of the members of the Lost Platoon. The Director and I are just beginning to go over the list of members. I'm not just tracking down the living members, but I'm also trying to verify what happened to the members who have passed away already. I'm looking for any relatives who could be eligible for this money."

"I don't guess your job is going to be much fun. Trying to apologize for years of neglect and abandonment with a monetary deposit could look a little insensitive. Maybe I ought to offer you my protection and come along with you."

"I won't say your idea is without merit, but I think I'll be okay. The first man I spoke with today was difficult, but he was no threat. Just an unhappy man who's life has been stolen from him."

"And he's had thirty years to sit around and think about it. That makes for an uncomfortable friendship between you two."

"I don't have to earn his friendship, Gregor. I only want him to believe that we're sorry. And he doesn't even have to believe me."

"That sounds a little more pessimistic than I'd have thought you'd be. I had you figured as the sunshine-on-my-window kind of girl." Lepov caught himself and tried to make amends. "I meant to say *woman*. I didn't mean to call you a girl."

Sun wanted to laugh. But she didn't want to have to explain why she was laughing. It was hard to keep a straight face when Lepov said something like that. His boyish face was accentuated as he tripped over the apology. He was no boy. That was certain. She guessed Lepov had to be around fifty years old. His hair was already showing signs of gray around the temples. But the face just didn't match that estimate even with the deep lines that time had folded into his loose skin.

"I'll admit you're right about the sunshine and pessimism." Sun paused while a waiter set their orders down on the table. He mixed them up, and Sun and Gregor had to exchange plates after the waiter left. They looked over their meals and tried small bites.

"So go on," Lepov prompted. "Sunshine and pessimism?"

"I was always getting labeled an optimist. I got to where I hated it. I wanted to be a pessimist. Like wanting red hair, I suppose."

"Well, you're getting your wish. You seem pessimistic about the job ahead of you. Or are you being cynical?"

"No, not that." Sun hadn't given it much thought, but she knew herself enough to know that cynicism wasn't the problem. "I'm just trying to be practical, I guess. Or I just don't want to get my hopes up. Especially after meeting the platoon's Lieutenant. My conversation with him wasn't anything like I had expected. I'm going to have to have an open mind about this. I just don't want to expect too much."

"You're going to have trouble finding information on the members who died." Lepov stopped speaking to chew on his

Bukovinan game. "In the short time I've been here, I've learned that record keeping isn't a virtue. It's a bit of a lost art around here."

"On a quarantine planet?" Sun had trouble believing that. "Wouldn't health records be a priority around here?"

"Major Uijong," Lepov used her title playfully, "nothing has priority in this way-station beyond the primary goal of the Interplanetary Health Service. No man or woman or any *thing* living or non-living will leave this moon with a contagious pathogen. End of story. They don't care too much about the dead around here, as long as they're disposed of in a manner that doesn't endanger the general population."

"Then I may need your help after all." Sun liked that idea. She wanted to see Gregor Lepov again. If only for the fact that they were halfway through dinner and he hadn't made a pass at her all evening. Not since he'd hit her in the gut, anyway. But she could overlook that. Most men she'd dated were far more obnoxious than that.

"You might do better with someone else's help," Lepov said.

"You're being modest." Was he trying to avoid her? Maybe he was only making a play. Maybe he was only playing her for a sucker — wine and dine her until he can get away without obligation.

"Not modest. Just honest. There's a friend of mine who might be the right person to help you track down these old records."

"Another *friend*?" Maybe there'd never been anyone on the other end of that call to the police. "Let me guess, another policeman?"

"Yes, as a matter of fact. Only he's not your average cop. For one thing, he's got a fully developed brain. And for another thing, he knows how to use it."

"So give me his name. I probably won't need it. But just in case."

Lepov wrote the name down on a napkin and slid it across the table. She folded it and slipped it into a pocket.

"You aren't eating. Bad Tuna?"

"No," Sun looked down at her plate and saw that she'd only taken two small bites of the grilled tuna. "You just ask too many questions."

"All part of the job." Lepov pushed his plate away. "You made the right choice. The game is just a tad too *gamey*. It's doing a solid job of trying to kill me. I don't know what bush they found this creature under, but they need to take it back and bury it beneath it."

45

A quick search through the PDT tracking system told MacNally what he'd wanted: Lepov was eating dinner at a restaurant. That was no surprise. But it was surprising that he had a companion. A *female* companion. On any other night, MacNally would have been glad to see it. But not this night. Not with the kind of news he had for Lepov.

He supposed Fenelli would have told him to wait, not to interrupt the man's dinner. But MacNally knew he'd have ignored his old partner; Fenelli had always been too interested in other people's feelings. In this case, MacNally needed to speak with Lepov. That he should wait until the man was finished eating dinner made no sense whatsoever.

By the time MacNally had driven to the restaurant, he'd read over the basic information on Lepov's companion. It was the woman Lepov had called about earlier. She was a Major with the Army; some kind of office clerk. Approaching the table, he could see that she was more attractive than the image file supplied by the military. She looked like a child next to the solid frame of Gregor Lepov.

"Hello, Lepov." MacNally walked right to their table, grabbing a chair from a second table. He sat down without an invitation.

"Have a seat," Lepov said sarcastically, "Sun, this is that friend I called earlier; Lieutenant Ed MacNally. Mac, this is Major Sun Uijong."

"Lieutenant," the woman nodded in welcome.

"Major," MacNally gave her a moment's inspection then turned back toward Lepov. "You still look like something I dragged out of the ocean."

"I was hoping food would improve my looks. That's what we're doing here. We're eating. That's what we'd like to keep doing." Lepov wiped his mouth with his hand. "Don't be embarrassed that you interrupted something. I'm sure you hadn't thought we'd be in the middle of something. But I can find you later, after we're finished."

"Gregor," Sun had taken the napkin from her lap and set it on the table, "it's quite okay. I need to get going. I have a few things to finish up tonight before I call it quits."

"Now just hold on, Sun." Lepov glared at MacNally.

"No, I've taken too much time as it is." Sun smiled graciously at MacNally. "You've provided me with an excuse to return to work."

"Just how late a day do you put in?" Lepov looked at his watch.

"I had an interruption this afternoon, if you'll recall." She stood. "I may take you up on your offer, Mr. Lepov."

"I'm easy to find."

MacNally and Lepov watched her leave. MacNally hadn't said anything to keep the Major from leaving. He was glad she'd gone.

"What was she all about?" he asked.

"What do you care? And what are you doing walking in on us like that?"

"I figure it's time I told you what I was working on. Your work and my work seem to be crossing paths."

"And the cop is gonna fill me in on the details?" Lepov's face said he knew better than that. "What is it you want?"

"To be honest, I need your help."

"So we're back to that?"

"What?" MacNally was tired of people mumbling.

"I said *we're back to that?* From the other night? You and your dilemma about that evidence?"

Lepov was quick. Quicker than MacNally had expected.

"Let's get out of here and find someplace we can talk."

"You worried we'll be overheard here?" Lepov asked.

"No," MacNally answered. "I just can't hear half of what you're saying."

They left the restaurant. Rain was beginning to fall, and the sun had dropped low enough that most of the streetlights had powered on. MacNally drove through the light rain, content to keep driving the vehicle instead of looking for a place to park.

"So is this about that body?" Lepov asked. "'Cause if it is, I got to tell you I don't remember too much about our conversation this morning. At least not the details. There was something about this Lost Patrol everyone is talking about. And then this body."

"Whaddaya mean *everyone* is talking about? Who else is talking about the Lost Platoon?"

"My dinner date you scared off. She was talking about them. So were you. And I was reading about them. Is that what this is about?"

MacNally was nearly as confused as Lepov, and he was the one who was trying to explain things. He put out a hand, cutting off Lepov. He needed to start from the beginning.

"This goes back a long time."

"You and Alpha Quadrant, right?"

"Yeah. I want to know if I can trust you to just listen to me. Don't ask questions until I'm done. And then I'm gonna need you to help me on a few things, okay?" MacNally knew he was handling Lepov with kid gloves, but it was necessary.

"So tell me."

He did. MacNally started with the story of Pan Juarez, his suspicions about the old corpse, and the fact that only three people could have owned that ring. He took his time, and Lepov was patient enough not to ask questions until Morvees' name came up.

"My guy? This guy who tried to kill me? You don't think the corpse is Morvees, do you? That someone else has taken Morvees' place?"

"No," MacNally shook his head, "that's not what I mean. I think that one of these three guys won't have their ring, and that they somehow gave it to the corpse."

"And one of them is this double? One of them was set up to pose as Juarez to do the quarantine time, then step aside as the real Juarez took their place?"

"Maybe, and when the deal goes down, the double sees the opportunity to take the diamonds and kill Juarez."

"That's stupid, Mac. I hate to say it, but it makes no sense."

"And why not?" MacNally didn't like being contradicted, even when he was wrong.

"Because if that had happened, the double would have split. He never would have stayed here. Not with diamonds. And considering most of the quarantine time had been served, it's a no-brainer. He simply gets out as Pan Juarez. Your theory doesn't scan."

MacNally cursed. "You're right. But I ain't happy that you are. That's why I wanted you in on this. I need someone else who can think through this. Another pair of eyes and another brain."

"Well, I can offer two out of three of those," Lepov chuckled. "But I'm not sure what your next step is. Do you try to track down what happened to Juarez? Does that even do any good? Or do you grab Morvees and make him talk?"

"If I do that, then everyone knows what I know. That's what I'm trying to avoid. That's what I've been trying to avoid all along. That's why I need your help. I can't do this like I normally would."

"Does Russell know all of this?" Lepov asked. MacNally shook his head. "Anyone else?"

"Pete knows a little. Knows about the ring, he's the one who told me which guys had these rings. He doesn't know much else."

"Mac, if you're trying to keep this under wraps because you slipped up a little as a kid cop, you're wasting everyone's time. Hell, as rookie mistakes go, it doesn't even register in the minor category. Your pride can't be that sensitive."

"It's not about that," MacNally assured him. "This thing will hit the NewsVision in ways I don't want to think about. If that is Juarez in our morgue, Arcobia goes nuts. Their favorite son was murdered here? Something fishy with the cops? My boss, his boss, everyone's gonna lose two or three fingers in this. I ain't worried about my reputation, but no one's gonna believe this was a solo mistake. They're gonna see conspiracies in every corner of the Lazaretto.

"If it's not Juarez—if it's someone from the Lost Platoon—then we can let it go public. And I have a feeling that's all it's gonna be. But I gotta know for sure."

"So we need to see inside that apartment again. But in that back room." So Lepov was going to help. And why not? MacNally knew that his information had not changed Lepov's case. Lepov's goals would stay the same. "That tells us what is currently going on with these guys. But at the same time, we need to track down these rings. See who's missing their ring."

"And I go back over Juarez's movements." MacNally lit a cigarette at the same time he made a left turn in heavy traffic. "I don't think that'll do much good—historians have been going through that data with a fine tooth comb. But I already know more than they do. Maybe I'll see something they missed."

"Have you taken this to the next level yet, Mac?" Lepov gave MacNally a funny look. "Where this might just lead?"

"I know. If someone had hired a double for Juarez, and there was a system in place to get Juarez into the Laz, somebody important was behind this. Somebody who's not gonna want us to get involved."

Lepov nodded. He didn't suggest that they should stay out of it. And neither did MacNally. They weren't the kind of men who shied away from trouble. But they weren't reckless either. They had seen what could happen to a man who had allowed clues to lead him to his death. They didn't need to mention Fenelli. They were both thinking of him, and of the lessons they'd learned.

"What was your dinner date saying about the Lost Platoon?" MacNally asked, a sudden change in topic.

"She's here to get them some kind of government funding. But she has to track down what happened to every one of them, dead and alive. The ones who are alive will have to be screened. I explained that record keeping here is spotty at best. I offered to give her a hand."

"It'll be nearly impossible."

"So drop me off at my office and I'll get started."

"I'm not done." MacNally had already steered them to Lepov's office, and he pulled to the curb and set down the car. Rain started coming down with a vengeance. "I'll come in with you."

Lepov silently climbed the stairs to his office. MacNally followed in the same manner. The only sounds were those of their wet shoes on the painted wooden steps. MacNally wasn't looking forward to what he had to say next.

"Okay," Lepov said, once he'd closed the outer door to the office and pulled off his wet coat. He tossed the coat onto the back of a chair and dropped his hat on top of it. "I thought all of that was the bad news. But now it looks like that was the good news. So what is it?"

"I didn't want to do this. But you were gonna find out at some point. And I need you to be stable right now. I don't need you running off with an axe to grind."

"Come on, MacNally. What is it? Just tell me," Lepov

demanded.

"It's Lilly."

The room grew as silent as the vacuum of space. He had the irrational idea that Lepov was about to pull a knife on him.

"What's Lilly?"

"I asked Pete Landon to just run a check, you know, to verify — "

"What's Lilly?" Lepov repeated his question. His hands curled into fists and his voice had dropped an octave.

" — to verify that you were right. That the woman in your fuzzy memory wasn't Lilly. That she was on Bukovina. I was only trying to put your mind at rest."

"Did something happen to her?" It was a cold question, as if Lepov were only asking out of duty.

"No." MacNally stared at Lepov and didn't want to say what had to come next.

"Where is she?" An even colder tone.

"Lilly arrived in the Lazaretto seven days ago."

"The hell she did. We talked two or three days ago. She was on Bukovina." The response was automatic. Lepov didn't sound as if he believed a word he was saying.

"Now first of all, don't assume this means anything. You know as well as I know that this doesn't connect her to what you thought you saw or heard."

"So I'll get to work on Morvees," Lepov circled his desk and sat down. "Let me know what you find on Juarez."

MacNally was tempted to mimic Lepov; to act like nothing was wrong. But he knew he couldn't leave Lepov like that. He had to make sure Lepov didn't go off the deep end.

"Gregor, listen to me. Women do funny things, you know? She'll have a dozen reasons why she didn't tell you she was coming through here. Most of them won't make sense to you, but they will to her."

"You're gonna tell me about women? Mac, you've got a more intimate relationship with Menya Russell than you do with any woman."

MacNally was tempted to take the bait and hit Lepov with his fist but he managed to let it go. "All I'm saying is don't make the mistake of convincing yourself Lilly was in that room. You know as well as I do, she wouldn't be mixed up in something like that."

"For a cop," Lepov looked up at him, "you're pretty stupid. You know as well as I do that neither one of us knows Lilly Stewart enough to make that presumption."

As much as MacNally didn't want to admit it, Lepov was right. What did they know about Lilly Stewart?

"You want me to stick around awhile?" It was a stupid question and MacNally knew what Lepov would say, but he'd had to ask the question all the same.

"You want to hold my hand? Is that it? Maybe you could take my mind off Lilly by running over to the West End and arresting a hooker for me. Bring two and we'll have a party."

As MacNally left Lepov's apartment he had to admit he'd been wrong. He hadn't expected Lepov to say anything like that.

46

The Thief sat under a tin awning, listening to the rain hit it like the scurrying feet of dozens of rats. Rain bounced off the concrete sidewalk, occasionally hitting the tips of his shoes. He was sitting at a small table outside a trashy sandwich shop run by a couple of filthy Arcobians. No one ever ate there. The Thief suspected they made money the old-fashioned way — they sold drugs out the back door. They also did a pretty solid business selling cheap beer. Young people started showing up late in the evening; the closer to midnight the greater the number of barely-legal drinkers and their younger friends.

But it was too early for the kids to start drinking, and the Thief had agreed to meet the Liar there as long as they left before the crowds arrived.

The Thief watched the Liar. He had spotted her walking up the street. Covered by a hooded coat, she walked briskly, her hands sunk low in the hip pockets of the coat. He would have recognized her anywhere. She had always made an effort to walk as if she were unaware it was raining. If she had adequate protection from the rain, then there was no point in hurrying.

She sat beside him and slid back the hood, letting it fall around her shoulders.

"What did he say?" she asked without preamble. "Is the tunnel finished?"

"It's finished," the Thief nodded in pleasure. "It's finished, and he's finished."

"He's...?" She raised an eyebrow. "Don't tell me you — "

"Shut him up? What's so wrong about that? I never trusted him, and you didn't either. I simply took measures so that we could trust him. Believe me," the Thief's smile was most evident in his eyes, "he's completely trustworthy. I'd trust him now. I must confess, he'll likely not keep his mouth shut. I don't even think he *can* shut his mouth. But that's not important."

His manic smile turned to one of amusement as an image of the Engineer popped into his head. Stuffing a man's mouth with sand

and clay was the definitive way to shut him up. The Thief couldn't suppress a giggle.

"That was foolish." The Liar spit the words out with a surprising amount of bitterness.

Did this mean she had been in league with the Engineer? Could she have been plotting with that little idiot? Lovers, maybe? The Thief made sure to control his facial expression. He could see she was watching him. It wouldn't do to expose his suspicions.

"What did you want me to do with him? Drop him at the police station so he could turn us in as soon as possible? I'm beginning to wonder whose side you're on." He allowed her to see a little of his suspicions; it would look even more suspect if he showed complete trust in her.

"I'm beginning to wonder whose side I'm on too." She stared him down, daring him to hurl more accusations her way. "You didn't need to kill him. And now you've created a complication."

"No complication, dear. He's gone and buried. Won't be found."

"They'll have to find him."

"What are you talking about?" the Thief hissed at her, leaning across most of the little iron table. "They won't find him. *Can't* find him."

"Someone's looking for him."

"*Who's* looking for *him*?"

"From what I've heard, the government is looking for him. And they'll have to find him."

Was she joking? It was the only explanation.

"And how do you expect them to find him? Unless they bring shovels into that tunnel, no one will ever find him."

"Then you'd better get a shovel." She wasn't joking.

The Thief wanted to grab her by the throat and choke that arrogant spirit out of her. She was too smug; too certain that he would have to listen to her. Just like that Engineer. Too smart for her own good. Too crafty to be trusted.

He didn't choke her. He was smarter than that. And he was too crafty to ignore her strictly on the grounds that she annoyed him. There had to be truth in what she was saying. And if someone was looking for the Engineer, then the Thief knew that the Liar was right; he would have to make sure someone found him.

"I have to get back," the Liar jumped up. "You fix this."

Fix it. That was something he would do. Fix it. *Fix you.* He was sure he would do that. When he had finished the job, when he was ready to leave; he'd fix her then. If he was going to have to drag that little brain out of the hole he'd shoved it in, then he might just use the Liar to fill it back up. But he'd have to squeeze hard to make her fit into the hole where he had stashed that brain. Squeeze and smash her down to the size of an overinflated brain.

He giggled out loud. He just might look forward to that. But he'd have to wait. He'd have to get the job done first. And before that, he was going to have to go dig that brain out of the tunnel. Then he would have to decide where to dump a smashed little brain so it could be found.

47

The trick was to get inside the apartment again. Lepov had to figure that out before he did anything else. But what chance did he have? And how was he to get past the lock on that back bedroom door? Pete Landon might be able to give him a hand with that. It wasn't that Lepov couldn't get past the lock, but he wanted to do it without letting Morvees know he had been there.

But it only mattered if he could actually get back into the apartment. That was the trick. At least, that should have been the trick. Lepov shook his head and tried not to think about the even bigger problem.

The real trick was figuring out how he was going to stop thinking about Lilly. And that was going to be almost impossible; the truth was, he didn't want to stop thinking about her. He wanted to figure out what she was up to.

He tried to tell himself it didn't matter. That wherever Lilly was, he had work that did not involve her. But he was amazed how easily he had forgotten that Lilly was possibly involved in everything. The facts were too damning.

She had lied to him. That was undeniable. She had said she was on Bukovina. They'd even spoken on the phone. Nothing. Not a word about her arrival in the Lazaretto. A detail impossible to disregard. MacNally had suggested she might have dozens of reasons for lying, but Lepov didn't buy it. There could not be a reason for her to lie unless she had something to hide.

And that was another of those facts he had to consider. Lilly was hiding something from him. Something important enough to maintain her pretense for over a week. Maybe longer. She had to know she was coming to the Laz, which meant she'd known about this for more than seven days. How long? Two weeks? Three? God knew how long she had known she was going to lie.

He wondered, how long had she been working with Morvees? It was an absurd question. It was a stretch to say she was working with Morvees. He had no facts to support the idea. Only his addled memory of Lilly and Morvees standing over his impromptu coffin.

Lepov needed to think like an investigator, not a scorned lover. He would have to prove that Morvees and Lilly even knew each other before he could suggest they were working together. And that seemed unlikely. All speculation aside, what he needed was hard evidence. And that meant he'd have to discover what Lilly was doing.

MacNally hadn't said where she was, but that wasn't a problem. Lepov's job was to find people. He could have just asked MacNally where she was, but he knew the old cop would have told him to stop thinking about her. What MacNally didn't realize was how impossible that was. He hadn't been able to stop thinking about her when there had been no reason to suspect mischief. How could he stop now, knowing something was wrong?

Ask an investigator not to investigate?

Not that he intended to spy on Lilly. He would simply find out where she was staying and go see her. That was the adult thing to do. He wouldn't cause any trouble. He wouldn't make a scene. Just talk with her, find out why she had misled him.

But, if there were the slightest chance she was involved with Morvees, talking with her would tip his hand. And she would have a chance to cover her trail. She'd be able to warn Morvees. She might even be shocked to see him alive if she had been the one who suggested he be dumped in the ocean.

This kind of back and forth logic-trap held Lepov's attention for much of the night. He tried to ignore it; tried to concentrate on Morvees' apartment. But on that front he had few alternatives.

He could ask MacNally to arrest everyone in the apartment on false charges and, while they were busy with lawyers, he could get inside. But that would be too aggressive. Too obvious.

Sun Uijong was an option. But he didn't like that. Yes, she needed to see Morvees. But using her to distract Morvees, or get him out of the way, was too dangerous. He had an immediate interest in Sun that surprised him. He didn't like military types, but she was different. She seemed out of place. At any rate, he didn't want to put her in any danger.

Josh was off limits too. The boy had to be kept out of this from now on. If these men had been willing to kill Lepov, might they also be willing to kill a nosy kid? He was out of the question.

Lepov imagined finding Lilly and forcing information from her. But the image was a mirage. Lilly wasn't mixed up with them. He repeatedly had to remind himself of that. She was most likely moving a piece of art through the Lazaretto for a client who demanded discretion. That was the logical assumption. To think anything else would be paranoia.

Still, Lilly would not have passed up the chance to see him while she came through quarantine.

He fought to return his thoughts to the apartment. He was missing basic information. The body had been in the ground for thirty years. The people who had disappeared into the apartment had come through in the last six months. If Lepov wanted to tie these two facts together, he would have to link thirty years in the past with the present via the apartment.

The question he needed to first address was one to which he hadn't yet paid attention; who had lived at that apartment during that time frame? Had Morvees been there for thirty years? If so, then that would tie the body more securely to Morvees.

Lepov lowered his hand to his deskscreen and waited for the old machine to power up. He didn't think he'd have any trouble accessing lease or real estate records. But as he had warned Sun, recordkeeping in the Lazaretto required great patience and diligence for anyone who was determined to find anything.

If he were diligent enough to find records on the apartment, Lepov could then take a few minutes to look for Lilly. He wouldn't interfere with her, but it wouldn't hurt to find out where she was.

48

It was too early for Sun to call it a night. Besides, she would have felt guilty if, after telling Lepov she had work to do, she then went on to the hotel and curled up with a book. But that was exactly what she wanted to do. She was tired. The tension from speaking with Yarmin had worn her down. Gregor Lepov's scare had not helped. On top of it all, the seafood was making her sick.

She resisted the temptation to go to the hotel and headed back to Chitti's office after realizing that for all her effort, she really hadn't accomplished anything. And even though her commanding officer was willing to allow plenty of time for completing her assignment, she didn't want to push her luck. She needed to accomplish something.

There was a significance in the way Lt. Yarmin had told her to investigate every member of the platoon. He expected her to find something wrong. Then there was Gregor Lepov's story of Morvees and his attempt to kill Lepov. Was that the simple key to Yarmin's insinuation? Was Yarmin aware Morvees was dangerous?

Those two went back a long way. There was obviously bad blood. But from which direction? Yarmin could have been lying. How could she know?

"Chitti," she said as she came into the front room of the *Society*, "I was afraid you would have gone home by now. I'm glad you didn't."

"At least someone's glad. I'm not. I should be at home with a good book."

"That's funny," Sun said with a chuckle, "I was just thinking the same thing."

"Then there's something wrong with both of us. We know what we want, but we aren't doing anything about it." Chitti was working on her desksystem but used Sun's arrival as an excuse for a break. She rolled her head and neck in one slow circle. "Did you see John?"

"I met him," Sun nodded. "Lt. Yarmin is interesting."

"I always think of him as a jackass." It was an unusually unkind comment from Chitti. Sun had expected her to be more charitable.

"I guess he has an excuse. Life has dealt him a mean hand."

"Sun, John Yarmin was a jackass before he ever came to the Lazaretto. His buddies were dealt the same hand. None of them ever behaved the way he does."

"I didn't realize…" Sun silenced herself with a hand to her lips.

"Have you eaten?" Chitti looked at an old clock on the back wall.

"Yes, I have." Sun pulled up the list of living platoon members on her deskscreen. "I'd like to try to contact one of these tonight."

"It's getting late," Chitti warned her, "wait until tomorrow."

"I guess, but Sgt. Morvees wasn't home, and I just feel like I haven't done anything. I'll try to see this one —" she touched a name on the list — "MacDenny. Silva MacDenny. It says here he lives between here and my hotel. I can just go see if he's home."

"I doubt you'll find him there. He spends a lot of time in the bars. And I wouldn't suggest you go look for him in a bar."

"Maybe I'll get lucky." Sun smiled in an attempt to convince herself she was right. "By the way, how familiar are you with Lt. Yarmin and Sgt. Morvees? I mean, how well do they get along?"

"Nobody gets along with John Yarmin. You can guess why."

Sun nodded. She didn't tell Chitti about Lepov, or his accusation about Morvees. But surely Chitti would know if Morvees were capable of any criminal activity.

"Have any of the men had trouble with the police?" Sun asked. It was a lame way to ask if Morvees were capable of attempted murder but Sun couldn't bring herself to be so blunt.

"John gets picked up every now and then for causing trouble after he's been drinking. But no, none of them have ever been in any trouble. Why?"

"Just checking," Sun tried to think of a simple explanation, "it is part of the assessment. Anyone convicted of illegal activity above a misdemeanor will be ineligible to receive compensation. I'm glad to hear none of them will have that problem."

"Well," Chitti shut off her deskscreen, "you might have eaten, but

I haven't. I was going to take you to a great little Terran place close to your hotel. Maybe tomorrow. You'll like it. They make great pizza. But since I'm on my own, I'll get something spicy tonight."

"I like spicy," Sun said.

"Not this spicy. This spicy hurts if you aren't careful."

"Then I'll look forward to the pizza tomorrow."

Chitti pulled on her coat and stopped to look out the front window. It was completely dark; the sun had been down for almost an hour.

"You'd better wait to see MacDenny until morning. This is no time for you to be out in his neighborhood."

"I'll only just go to his place and see if he's there. I won't take long. Like you said, he may not even be there." Sun was determined to stop at his place.

"I was afraid you'd say that. Come on. I'll go with you." Chitti cut off the lights and pulled open the front door. The sound of rain filled their ears.

"You don't have to do that, Chitti. Besides, you're hungry."

"I won't be able to eat if I'm worried about you."

Both women stepped under the awning and waited until they saw a TransitCar approach. Chitti walked out into the rain and waved down the car. Climbing in after her, Sun gave the driver the address. He spun the car around, heading toward Center City.

"So before we see him, what can you tell me about Mr. MacDenny?" Sun felt cheered that Chitti had decided to join her. It made her feel lucky. MacDenny was sure to be home.

"He's quiet," Chitti said after giving her question some thought. "Very smart. Sad, as well."

"Not angry like John Yarmin?"

"Oh, no. Nothing like John. The drinking Silva does is not to embolden him. He drinks so he won't have to face his exile. He's a sweet man, but weak."

Here again was a challenge. Yarmin's anger wasn't the only emotional obstacle Sun would have to overcome. If MacDenny were the sad case Chitti declared him to be, then Sun would have to find a way to see beyond his tragedy. She would have to make sure she did not become emotionally hung up on his misfortune.

The rain kept beating hard as the TransitCar dropped them in front of MacDenny's building. A massive brick affair with hundreds of small square windows, it bore absolutely no distinguishing marks to set it apart from the neighboring buildings, save the white steel numbers over its door.

Sun dashed up the steps and pushed her way through one glass door. She turned around expecting Chitti would be right behind, but saw Chitti was still climbing the outside steps. Sun went in search of an elevator.

The elevator she found rumbled in response to a punch of its round yellow call button. Sun could hear it descending its shaft. It arrived on the ground floor just as Chitti caught up with her.

"I'm surprised you found an elevator to work in this old building. I wouldn't have even tried the call button."

"Maybe it's an omen," Sun joked. "Maybe this means Mr. MacDenny will be here."

"Sure, I guess so." Chitti looked suspiciously around the small carriage as they stepped inside. The old doors slid shut; heavy wooden doors covered in thick layers of glossy lime paint, thick flakes curling where the paint had begun to peel.

Sun pushed the button for the fourteenth floor. The elevator rumbled for a moment, but never began its ascent. The two women looked at each other and waited. After a pause, the doors slid back open. They were still on the first floor.

"You see what I mean?" Chitti stepped out of the carriage. "We'd better just take the stairs. Even if this thing did start to move I don't think it would be wise for us to be in it. We might as easily get stuck between the thirteen and fourteenth floors."

"I can't remember the last time I climbed fourteen flights of stairs," Sun laughed nervously.

"Here in the Lazaretto we get used to things like this." Chitti led the way to a door with an emergency sign hanging in the middle of it. She hit the crash bar and they entered the stairwell.

The old, steel staircase was narrow and open in the center. As they began to climb, Sun leaned out and looked up. A dizzying array of steel spun above her. The building must have had thirty floors or more. She could see most of them before the vertical shaft narrowed to a point. Pale lights clung to the wall above the door for each floor.

"Now, if I lived someplace like this, I wouldn't have to watch what I ate every day," Sun said, pointing out the silver lining.

"People living in a place like this can't afford to eat like we do. For them, gaining weight would be good." Chitti, as always, pointed out the starker realities.

Sun didn't know how to respond. While she had not been raised in a wealthy family, she had never known hunger. And the military had always provided a decent living for her. The job was not lucrative, but it was comfortable. She was unfamiliar with poverty, and for that reason, unsure of how to react to it. She had been caught off guard, walking into John Yarmin's apartment. Perhaps she would be prepared this time.

They were near the fourth level when a large black bundle fell past them through the open center of the stairwell. A hint of breeze followed it when they heard it hit the bottom—mostly a soft, smacking sound—though Sun also faintly heard a metallic crack followed by a vibration like a tuning fork.

"What—" Sun grabbed the inner handrail and leaned out to try and see what had flown past them. She could see a bundle of rags. "What is that?"

"You mean who." Chitti had one hand on the rail and stared at the bundle.

"My God, do you mean—?" Sun started back down the stairs. "Do you think that was a *person*?"

"I think that's what it was. I saw a hand as it went by."

Sun felt sick. Chitti showed no reaction.

They descended the steps quickly then slowed near the bottom. She wasn't eager to reach the bundle. It was still just a bundle in her mind. Until they confirmed Chitti's guess, that it was indeed a body, Sun preferred to think of it as only a bundle.

Chitti must have sensed her hesitation, and she pushed past Sun. Sun should not have allowed it. She was a Major in the Army, after all. Death was not supposed to be something feared. But that was all just theory. Sun had never been in combat. She might not have feared death, but it was unfamiliar and disturbing.

"I don't believe this." Chitti had reached the concrete floor of the stairwell and the body. She knelt.

And that was what it was. Sun could no longer deny it. It was a body. It lay crooked in a ragdoll pile. From where Sun stood, she could see a large bald spot on the back of a man's head. The smell was overpowering.

"What happened?" Sun asked, as if Chitti would know.

"I don't know. But I do know who this is." She frowned at Sun.

"You mean—?" Sun's voice faltered.

"This is Silva MacDenny." Chitti stood, retreating several steps.

Sun tried to back up as well but tripped on the stairs behind her. Falling, she caught herself on the rail in time to prevent injury. Easing herself to a sitting position, she stared at the bundle. At the body. At Silva MacDenny.

Calla was getting better. She was sleeping more. A blessing for the both of us. I was beginning to relax, though only a little. I knew by then Calla was going to live. The chances of dying from the infection were low, but I knew she was not getting the best medical care, and I worried that my inadequacies might be the death of her. It was a selfish concern. But it

bothered me nonetheless.

My focus shifted then. No longer working just to keep her alive, I was able to put extra effort into diminishing – eliminating, if possible – the telltale signs of her fight with the plague: scar tissue. There was nothing I could do about the scar tissue in her lungs. That was beyond my skills. It was unlikely a surgeon could have done much for her. Fortunately for Calla, the Lazaretto screeners did not have the equipment or the inclination to conduct such a thorough examination. The lungs would not be a problem.

The real problem would be with her sinus cavities. A basic visual exam was usually sufficient to expose the presence of scar tissue in the nasal cavities behind the nostrils. These paranasal sinuses of a *Euxinus Spirare* survivor were often covered in a crisscross pattern of scar tissue. Application of a nasal irrigation could greatly reduce this scarring. The irrigation could be frightening for a child as young as Calla. The nasal cavities would be flushed with a mixture of salt water, liquid vitamin E, and several other additives to promote reduction. The human body being programmed to reject the presence of fluids in those cavities, the body would send out alerts to the brain, assuring the patient they were drowning.

Once again, Calla displayed grace under pressure. She did not understand why we had to perform such intimidating treatments, but she trusted me when I told her they were necessary. My heart broke to see her face the treatments with such silence and firm resolve.

After a session of irrigation, I would always retreat from her room, once she was asleep. It was emotionally exhausting to put a child through something like that. I would invariably sit alone in the kitchen with a glass of wine, trying to calm my own nerves. We were only a few weeks away from finishing the treatments. There had been a time I wasn't sure I would make it. But I was beginning to see light at the end of the tunnel.

One such night, I was sipping wine, Sinopese wine, an expensive vintage on which Mr. Zoltis spared no expense. I had been crying. Not for Calla, and not for myself, but simply crying at the thought this would all be over soon. For reasons I could not understand, it made me cry. I blamed the wine.

There are times when we can be certain fate delights in bad timing. This was one of those times. Not only had I been crying, but I was also in need of a bath. The night's treatment had been rough on Calla and the salt water had caused her to vomit. I had intended to clean up after the wine, too wound up to do otherwise. And it was this moment when fate chose to play its trick.

As I drained the last drops from my glass, the front door opened. A large man stood in the doorway. I knew him. He was handsome, muscular, with wavy hair that had to be manufactured. He was simply too perfect to be of the same species as the weary, disheveled woman sitting in the kitchen.

He shut the door, then looked around until he saw me. His eyes brightened as he came across the room and into the kitchen. It did not take me long to put a name to the face. This was Cam Raley, rival of Kjarsta

Zoltis and now his partner. I remembered, in the brief moment before he spoke, that I had not liked him at our first meeting. I also remembered coming away with the distinct impression that he might be dangerous.

"I'm so happy to run into you again, Miss Della. I was beginning to think I would never again have the pleasure. Already, this appointment has been worth my while. No one mentioned you would be here. I'm so glad you are." His smile covered the entire lower half of his face.

He took my hand and kissed it. Just barely, of course. But for a greeting in the Lazaretto, it was unusual. I had an idea he would have welcomed far more physical contact than just our hands. I was suddenly reminded why I had not liked him.

"I'm Cam Raley. We met at Kjarsta's. You interrupted us."

"Yes, I remembered you, Mr. Raley." I was wondering how quick an exit I should make. I felt worse than I looked, and I knew I looked awful.

"Is there more wine?" he asked. His mischievous smile said he knew he was being forward. My only answer was to pull out a glass and pour some Pinot Noir. He thanked me, tasting it first before quickly downing the rest.

I tried to leave. He casually blocked my exit. He was such a big, solid man. I had not noticed it in the poor lighting of our first encounter, but there in the kitchen, I could see that Cam Raley's physique was perfect; too perfect, as if he'd been carved from plastic. I knew that look. He had obviously used chemical sculpting to achieve his muscular appearance. I hated that. It was a growing fad that I hoped would come to a quick end. There was a sickening arrogance which accompanied it. Though Kjarsta Zoltis was an arrogant man, his arrogance was bred from accomplishment and accrued power. Raley's arrogance came from something he'd bought and paid for; something that came with instructions.

"I seem to be early. Kjarsta asked me to come down and meet him." He moved closer. I backed away until I was against the counter. "I really had no idea you were here, or I might have arrived earlier. Are you still tutoring Kjarsta's daughter?"

I panicked at that. If Bernham were to come out of his room and hear the question, he would likely guess that Calla was not my daughter. The thought upset me, though I couldn't say why. It was Kjarsta who had devised the subterfuge. But I had a feeling there was a good reason for it, one which I did not want to jeopardize.

"Yes," I answered. I couldn't decide which answer was the safest course, so I settled for the least complicated.

"Is that your only obligation here?" He brushed my cheek with the back of his hand. The combination of his oily smile, his manufactured comic-book-hero shape, and his sleazy come-on was more absurd than disgusting. I drew a slow breath and suppressed the desire to scratch him. "You must be special if Kjarsta trusts you with his only child."

This time, he put both hands on me; one grabbed my wrist before I could push him away, the other on the back of my neck to pull me closer. I turned my face from his and cried out. Bernham was standing in the hall watching.

181

I had never before been so happy to see that queer, truculent man.

"Bernham!"

Raley did not release his hold, but turned his head toward Bernham. Only after he had given Bernham a long stare did his grip relax. I pulled away and retreated into a corner.

I don't know what would have happened afterward had Mr. Zoltis not entered the apartment. Would Bernham have interfered? Or would he have backed away and left me to Raley? But my employer had come into the apartment, and Cam Raley immediately ignored me.

Kjarsta was no fool. He was too sharp to miss the subtext in the room. I'm sure he could see the panic on my face and could not help but feel the tension. He stood in the center of the front room staring contemptuously at the three of us. He knew what was going on, of that I had no doubt. But I could not read his reaction. He could have been angry with Raley, or he might have blamed me. I did not want to stay and find out.

Even after I had left them, and was back in the room with Calla, I never understood the importance of what had transpired. Raley was obviously dangerous, an unknown factor in our attempts to keep Calla's secret. But what I had not realized that day was that Bernham had just discovered something about the woman and child with whom he had been coexisting. I only knew I was grateful that Bernham had come when he did.

Of course, for thirty years I've wished the man never had.

50

Officially, a new day had started. But that was only a technicality. It was two minutes past midnight when the call came in. MacNally had only climbed into bed a half hour before that. He never should have slept; a few minute's sleep poisoned the soul.

"Where we going?" MacNally asked Russell as he climbed in the car. Russell had eagerly offered to pick him up. Apparently the kid had been out on the town instead of home in bed like a good little boy.

"Not far, now. Apartment house outside Center City." Russell looked fresh. "You look awful, MacNally. You get too much sleep?"

The kid's smile was nauseating. If MacNally had the energy he would have punched him in the eye. As it was, he simply leaned his head back and closed his eyes.

Russell pulled in behind two police cruisers and shut down his engine. The street was empty of vehicular traffic, but there was a steady stream of pedestrians wandering both sides of it. Rain had fallen earlier; it was now just a heavy mist. The hit and miss lighting there cast slick shadows and reflections off the puddles and windows.

An IHS van sat on the opposite side of the street. Two uniformed officers stood outside the doors to the brick apartment house.

"Hello, MacNally," the oldest officer nodded and pulled open the door. "Nice of you to finally drag yourself out of bed."

"Your daughter just wouldn't let me go, Sergeant." MacNally shook the Sergeant's hand. "Russell, say hello to an old pain in the ass, Sergeant Cawper. Phil, this is my new partner Menya Russell."

"How ya doin', young salt?" Cawper nodded but did not offer to shake hands.

"I think I'm doing better than you, sir," Russell said without hesitation.

"And why's that, boy?" Cawper asked.

"Cause MacNally's not impregnating *my* daughter."

Cawper threw his head back and laughed. It sounded more like a dog's bark than anything else. "You're right about that, old salt. I like this kid, Mac. He's just what you need."

"Yeah, he's a real riot."

After they entered the building, Russell asked, "Does that guy even have a daughter?"

"What?"

"Does that guy even have a daughter?" Russell raised his voice.

"Not that I can remember." MacNally was irritated that Russell had trumped his joke and didn't want to discuss it.

They followed the directions of another uniformed officer and found the body lying in the bottom of a stairwell. A man in an Interplanetary Health Services uniform stood just inside the stairwell.

"You waiting for us, Davis?"

"Yeah, I am, as a matter of fact." Davis was a short, bearded man with white, matted hair that looked like something growing on the back of a stray dog. He had a long, perpetually smiling face. "Your guys finished with the visuals about an hour ago. Where you been?"

"An hour ago?" MacNally turned to Russell for an explanation.

"I don't know. They called me at the same time they called you."

"Dispatchers," MacNally shrugged his shoulders. "Sorry you had to wait."

"That's okay, MacNally. I've just been standing here getting acquainted with your dead man. He's got quite a story to tell."

"One that starts with the line *I leapt to my death for love*?" MacNally pulled on a set of protective gloves.

"I don't think so. That jump was no jump. Unless his ghost came back from the grave to make it happen." Davis was smiling, but he wasn't joking.

MacNally looked at the IHS tech. "You a detective now?"

"I'm not blind."

"So come show me." MacNally gave Davis room to explain.

The body was lying face down. Most of it was. The legs were twisted backwards at the knees, toes of the shoes pointing up. One arm was caught under the torso, but the other—the right arm—looked like it had been yanked from behind, rammed back and up into the shoulder blade. The head was down, with only a slight shift to the side. MacNally could see one eye and part of the mouth.

The mouth was open.

"Well, let's start with the obvious," Davis squatted near the head. "There's no blood, even though we can see the skull hit the concrete. See the tear in the skin? I'd estimate this guy dropped from at least ten stories. So there would have been a lot of blood. But there's not."

"What's that?" MacNally knelt down on one knee and pointed at the dead man's mouth.

"The second obvious fact. Tests will confirm it, but my guess is that is dirt. Mud, really. His whole mouth is jammed with it."

MacNally knew the man was right. The open mouth was packed with mud, a solid cake of dried mud. Some of it had broken loose and was scattered across the discolored lips.

"I'll spare you the details, MacNally, but the simple fact is, this body's been dead awhile. And from the looks of things, it was actually buried before it dove through ten floors of the stairwell."

"There's mud under his fingernails, too." MacNally held up a finger of the right hand to better study its tip. "See that? Fingernail's torn. Poor bastard was fighting for his life. This wasn't no suicide."

"Let me lick 'em, and you can have him." Davis turned and looked at Russell near the door. "Hand me that bag, will you?"

Lick 'em and bag 'em was not a technical term. It was, however, a fairly accurate description. Davis first laid an adhesive strip on the neck of the body. He counted to fifteen before peeling it back off. After carefully sealing the strip in a plastic envelope, he stuck a hypodermic needle into the same area of the flesh and extracted two vials of blood.

Lazaretto protocol was unique at a crime scene. If a body could not categorically be identified as a murder victim it first had to be sampled and removed for testing. The threat of disease—whether from virus, pathogen, or biological origin—had to be assessed and identified immediately. Even if a detective declared a death to be homicide, the on-site IHS representative had to sign a waiver releasing the body to the police. Tests would be conducted on the blood and the skin swatch at IHS, but the body would be taken to the police lab for the investigation.

Knowing full visuals had been taken of the crime scene, MacNally and Russell gave the labtechs the go-ahead to take the body. An officer informed them that the two ladies who had discovered the bodies were in the front lobby.

MacNally sent Russell up the stairwell to find out the exact location where the body had been dumped over the handrail. The elevator was not working and MacNally wasn't about to climb ten or more flights of stairs. MacNally dug out a cigarette and went in search of the women.

They were not in the lobby, but in a small adjacent room. It was an office, probably for a maintenance man or landlord. The women were seated on a couch. One of them was asleep, a small woman with short red hair. The other woman saw him coming and sat up. Tired as he was, MacNally knew her instantly.

"Lieutenant MacNally?" The woman smiled, visibly exhausted.

"You're Major Uijong." MacNally looked at her with a puzzled expression. "You found the body?"

"Yes, we were on the stairs when he fell."

"But what were you doing here?"

"We were coming to see him. To interview him."

"Interview who?" MacNally asked.

"*Him.* The man in the stairwell. His name is Silva MacDenny."

MacNally cursed, and the cigarette between his lips fell out. He caught it with a big beefy hand, was burned by it, dropped it to the floor, and rubbed at the burn. He had noticed none of this.

"That's Silva MacDenny?" MacNally scratched at his balding scalp and realized absent-mindedly he had forgotten his hat at home. "Major, are you sure that's Silva MacDenny?"

"I'm positive that's him." The redhead stirred from her sleep and sat up. "I've known Silva MacDenny for years. That's him."

MacNally introduced himself. "What can you tell me about him?"

"There isn't much to tell, Lieutenant. He's a—was—an engineer; a veteran from the Arcobian Rebellion. A quiet man. Kept to himself. I can't imagine why he'd do this."

"Do what?"

"Kill himself."

MacNally said nothing about murder. That would come later. "Did you ladies hear anything, before or after MacDenny fell?"

They looked at each other. The Asian girl's eyes were wide; apparently, she was still shaken by the event. The darker skinned one—a cute little thing—seemed more at peace with what had occurred. Both of them shook their heads.

"I don't think we heard anything. We didn't even hear MacDenny as he fell." The Major shuddered at the memory.

"Okay, we'd like to speak with you again in the morning. Could you come by the station? Say, around nine."

Fenelli would have apologized to them for making them wait so long. That wasn't MacNally's department. Russell should have been there to say it. But with Russell busy climbing the steps of a man-made mountain, MacNally was forced to try and apologize. He tried to think of what Fenelli would have said, then gave it his best shot.

"Thanks for waiting so long. We would have been here sooner but one of those dumb girls at dispatch dropped the ball. We didn't get the call until just after midnight."

That was enough apology for one night. MacNally nodded at them, again conscious he was not wearing his hat, and headed back toward the stairs. The labtechs were wheeling out MacDenny's body on a gurney. They'd wrapped him in heavy plastic; Lazaretto crews never took chances.

MacNally might have been tired, but he was awake enough to know something screwy was going on. He had just found three suspects tied to that ring, and one of them had just been murdered. Somebody was playing games. MacNally hated games.

Russell wouldn't answer MacNally's call. The kid was somewhere up in the stratosphere, and MacNally couldn't get him to answer. After waiting another thirty minutes, he angrily decided he was gonna have to climb those stairs anyway. And all because Russell wasn't answering his calls.

He was probably just ignoring him so MacNally would have to climb the mountain. Russell would be lucky if MacNally didn't throw the kid off the tenth-floor landing.

51

It was disorienting to wake up in the wrong place. A hangover only exacerbates disorientation.

It took Lepov three times to open his eyes and figure out where he was. On that third try, he recognized the cracked window wet with condensation. A turn to his left confirmed his guess. He'd slept in his office. He was on the smashed cushions of his musty couch, still in his suit. He hadn't even removed his jacket.

He was glad to see a bottle of bourbon sitting on his desk still half-full because he felt like he'd downed the whole thing. No, he hadn't drunk much at all. The bottle had only been three-quarters full to begin with if he remembered right. But considering the way his head felt, he might not have been remembering right.

He sat up, running his tongue around the inside of his mouth. He had never been fussy about oral hygiene, but he wished he kept a toothbrush in the office. Water wasn't going to help him much. Someone should have looked after him, made him go home.

That was the wrong thought to allow in his head; the next logical thought left a worse taste in his mouth.

Lilly.

No, it hadn't been necessary to drink that much to feel this way. He'd felt like hell before he started drinking. And even as the pale morning light worked its way down between the towering buildings of his street, Lepov knew he wasn't going to feel any better — even if he found a toothbrush.

Get up. It was the only thing he could do. If he sat there much longer, he'd do something he regretted. He had to move, get his blood moving.

A small box caught his eye. The green box sat on the corner of his desk; Josh's chewing gum. With nothing to eat and no coffee in the canister — he'd run out a day or two before — the chewing gum was his only choice. Peeling back the cardboard top and unwrapping two round pieces, he hesitantly dropped them in his mouth. The fruit flavor edged out the awful taste in his mouth for a short while.

"Not bad," he said. "Better than a morning cigarette."

Lepov staggered to the windows and pulled one open. It was freezing outside. A cold front had come in late during the night but it felt good for a minute or two. Lepov closed his eyes and let the chilly air bite his neck and ears. He could feel it run through his thin hair, exposing the bare spot at the top.

Why had he spent the night in his office? He tried to remember what he'd been doing. The easiest way to work it out was to check his deskscreen. He shoved the window closed and walked back to the desk. His coordination was already improved. The gum and the cold air were doing some good.

He stared at the desk and saw it was still activated. He hadn't been asleep all that long. It would have automatically shut itself down after four hours. Or was it three? It didn't matter. It just meant he hadn't slept enough. That was nothing new.

From the look of things, he'd been searching through the Lazaretto's residential archive. That made sense. He'd been trying to backtrack the owner of Chettleham Keep's apartment 02. Morvees had leased the property in only the last few years. Before that, the lease had been under a woman's name, Sandella Sahdjec. She had held the lease for twenty-eight years. Before that it had been leased under the name of Francois Bernham.

Another page lay open on his desk, one which had nothing to do with residential archives. This one was an open script still executing its last command. A blue symbol in the shape of an eye glowed in the center. The eye's pupil moved from right to left in constant rhythm.

Clarity came back to Lepov with the suddenness of a fist to his gut. *The MoleRunner*. It had taken two solid drinks of bourbon before he had been able to do it. And even afterward he had felt like a real ass. But he'd known he would do it before the night was out. The bourbon had only emboldened him to get to it without further delay.

The MoleRunner was an illegal script that dug through Lazaretto PDT archives, running down any matches for a particular PDT signal. He had Lilly's PDT signature on his desksystem. He had simply released the mole to run down any and all entries in the current archive. He set the mole to start its run eight days back, to catch her at the moment she entered Lazaretto Registration. There was no way for her to get around that. After she was in, the mole would see every one of her movements that had been caught by a reader; hotel registration, any dining purchases, everything.

The archives were massive, and the mole was running as fast as could be expected. Its accuracy was over ninety-five per cent; it would miss a few of Lilly's movements, but not many.

Already it had tracked her through the first day and a half. She was staying at a modest hotel near Alpha Quadrant. Lepov was a little shocked to see that; it meant she wasn't planning on staying long. Alpha was close to its quarantine lock down. If he didn't have his days mixed up, there were only about four days left.

He shuffled the Molerunner to the bottom of the deskscreen; not wanting to be distracted. He had only decided to run it as a precaution, in case he wanted to find her later. Let it run, he thought. He wanted to concentrate on the apartment.

His best bet was to locate the Sahdjec woman. She'd had that place a long time. Lepov wanted to talk with her without delay.

It had taken him about an hour to get cleaned up. He took the time to shave. A day's growth was beginning to make him look like an old ape he'd once seen in a shoddy little zoo back on Bukovina. The old ape had never moved; just sat in his cage staring at the passing visitors with eyes that looked ready to cry. That had been when he was a kid. He hoped that old monkey hadn't lived long.

Maybe he was beginning to look like that to people; maybe they hoped he wouldn't live much longer either. It took two cups of coffee from Comic Joe's to burn off his self-pity. Unfortunately, Comic Joe's only reminded him of Lilly. It had been where they'd first met. More cold air out on the street and two more pieces of the chewing gum got his mind off Lilly and back on Ms. Sahdjec.

She lived on the south side of the Lazaretto, not in one of the newer homes there, but in a small house sitting in the middle of a small yard that was well-kept and high enough to slope rainwater away from the house. Most of the houses on the south side of town were expensive. This one was on the lower end, but it wasn't cheap. This Sahdjec woman had money.

Lepov stepped out of the TransitCar and walked up the stone

steps that crossed the slope of the front yard. It was impossible to tell if anyone was home. There were no lights on inside, but the morning was far enough along that someone could have been inside without needing them. Lepov knocked loudly on the front door. He hated doorbells. Most of them were muted; people rarely welcomed interruptions to their day.

He pulled his overcoat tight as a stiff breeze snapped coldly at him. He wouldn't wait long. If she weren't home, he'd go in search of Francois Bernham. From what he could see, there had been no Lazaretto exit records or death certificates issued for either Sahdjec or Bernham. One of them was bound to be home.

The sound of an inner lock told him luck was on his side. He backed away from the door—so Ms. Sahdjec could get a good look at him—and stood straight, despite the fact that it gave the wind a free shot at his neck.

"Can I help you?" The voice from inside was stronger than he had expected. Sandella Sahdjec was close to seventy years old.

"My name is Gregor Lepov, and I'm looking for Sandella Sahdjec." Maybe he had the wrong house.

"What do you want with Sandella Sahdjec, Mr. Gregor Lepov?" It wasn't a promising reply.

"I'm a private investigator who has a few questions for her. Is this her home, or did I knock on the wrong door?" He hunched his shoulders again. Whoever was inside had been given enough of a chance to see him. That morning breeze was too much on bare skin.

"You've got the right door." And with that, the outer door swung inward. A large black woman smiled at him and stepped off to the side, indicating he should come in. "Cold out there, isn't it? The weather people still can't predict this weather here. You'd think after fifty years they'd get it right. I really don't think anyone cares enough to put the effort into it."

Lepov walked into a warm living room covered in soft fabrics. The furniture was covered in soft cotton prints, the plush carpet was the color of a lion's mane, and the walls were seemingly lined with burgundy silk. It was all synthetic, of course, but all quality work.

"Ms. Sahdjec?" Lepov had seen the woman's picture in the archives. She was older than the most recent image available. She had a face full of kindness; her eyes warned she was no pushover.

"That's me. But if you would allow me to call you Gregor, I'll allow you to call me Della. Come into the kitchen where we can talk while I make us coffee. You drink coffee, don't you?"

"As many pots in a day as my heart can take."

"I know that's right. My heart can't take as much as it used to. A young man like you don't have to deal with that yet. But one day..."

"I might be older than you're giving me credit for." Lepov sat down at a worn table and felt right at home. It was like coming home to one of his grandmothers.

"I hope I'm not interrupting anything. I won't take too much of your time." He didn't say things like that often. But he didn't get a chance to interview decent people like Della Sahdjec often.

"Do I look like I was doing anything? Six months ago I would have been sleeping off a night shift. But that's all in the past, now. I'm retired."

"From what?" He watched her set a cup of coffee down in front of him and nodded his thanks.

"Nursing. You're looking at a lifelong nurse."

"Here in the Lazaretto?"

"Mostly," she said, sitting down in front of her coffee. She drank it black. After a sip, she looked Lepov in the eye. "I'm sure you already know all of this about me, Gregor. Why don't you tell me why you're here?" Again, the eyes told him to be careful; she was no fool, and would not suffer foolishness from him.

He hadn't met a woman with that kind of iron since Lilly.

"Della, I'm here to talk with you about an apartment that you leased in Chettleham Keep." Lepov saw an unpleasant look in her eyes, a total lack of recognition.

"I don't think I understand," she answered carefully. "Just where is Chettleham Keep?"

"A block from the entrance to Alpha Quadrant. There are records indicating that you had been leasing the apartment for twenty-eight years." Lepov watched her, looking for signs she was putting on this charade of ignorance: an inability to look him in the eye, hands fidgeting with the hem of her blouse, biting her lip. There were any number of ways body language could warn him someone was lying.

But not Della. Either she was telling the truth, or her performance skills were flawless.

"I hate to refute the record, but I have been living in an apartment on the south side of Center City for a most of that time. I only moved here six months ago, after I retired. But I have never lived near Alpha Quadrant." Della took a long sip from her coffee, then added "perhaps you have the wrong name."

"That's not impossible with the poor record keeping in the Lazaretto." Lepov smiled at her, and decided he didn't believe he had been given the wrong name. There was no reason for him to think that yet, but he had a feeling he would find a reason if he spent a little more time with her. "If you don't mind, Della, I'd like to ask you a few questions anyway. I won't take long. I had planned on trying to look up the previous owner — the one listed before your name."

"And what was his name?" she asked.

"Francois. Francois Bernham."

This time she was unable to mask her emotion. Bernham's name electrified her. She had been holding her coffee and set the cup down so suddenly, Lepov was surprised it didn't shatter.

"You know the name?" Lepov gave her an encouraging smile. "Maybe you know the apartment I'm talking about. It's on the ground floor, more like a basement level, I guess. Two bedrooms, a kitchen, and no windows."

"Mr. Lepov," Della's tone and manners became rigidly formal, "I do not mean to be rude. However, I will tell you that I know little about such an apartment. However, since you have mentioned Mr. Bernham's name, I believe I can tell you who had the lease on that apartment. It is possible that this person used my name as a leaseholder without my knowledge. The man you need to speak with is Kjarsta Zoltis."

The name was familiar to Lepov, though he could not remember why.

"I do not think you will find Mr. Bernham. That will be a dead-end for you. But if my guess is correct, then both Mr. Bernham and I were listed as leaseholders by Kjarsta Zoltis. Unfortunately, Mr. Zoltis is a dead end for you as well. He died six months ago."

"Do you know why you were listed as the leaseholder?"

Della stood and walked to the sink. She ran water over her coffee cup and set it upside down on a towel. Turning, she faced Lepov, her hands on her hips.

"Mr. Lepov, I won't be able to answer any of your questions. Are you finished with your coffee?"

"I'd take a little more if you don't mind. You knew this Bernham?"

"I'm afraid we finished the last of the coffee." Without a hint of shame, she took hold of the half-full coffee pot and poured all of it into the sink. She took Lepov's cup and cleaned it in the same manner as her own.

"If you should remember anything," Lepov said, pulling a small paper card from the inside pocket of his jacket, "I would appreciate it if you gave me a call. I'm worried that people's lives are at stake. A few may have already been killed. It's important."

He did not get the chance to stand before she asked a question.

"Mr. Lepov, are there truly lives at stake?" For a moment the fire had gone from her eyes. The question did not come from curiosity; he heard despair in her words.

"I won't lie to you, Della. We think several people have already been murdered. We only want to keep this from happening again."

Della came back to the table and sat; her hands on its surface, palms down. Closing her eyes a moment, Lepov thought she was about to pray. Instead, she raised her head and took a deep breath.

"This apartment you're asking about—I do know the apartment. I didn't live there. But I did stay there for a time. But only temporarily. I'm sorry, but I cannot say more than that."

Some witnesses are tough to crack, but Lepov could always tell they would eventually give the interrogator what he was looking for. It was the tough guys who nearly always had a breaking point; the inflexible iron rod that breaks under pressure. But Lepov could see that Della was not like that. She did not deny having the information. She only said that she could say no more. The conviction in her voice told Lepov she meant her words.

"I'm sorry, Mr. Lepov."

"I thought you were going to call me Gregor," he reminded her.

"I'm sorry." Della led him to the front door, a tired smile on her lips. "Please don't come back. I won't change my mind."

"Thank you for the coffee, Della." Lepov put his hand on the door and looked back at her. "Why did you call Francois Bernham a dead-end?"

"Goodbye, Mr. Lepov."

"I look forward to seeing you again, Della."

The TransitCar was still waiting for him. Della Sahdjec had already closed her door and turned the lock.

If he would not be able to find Bernham, Lepov thought, then he might as well see if the Molerunner had come up with anything more on Lilly. It didn't matter if it had. He would hold on to the information. It wasn't like he would go after Lilly. He had a better head on his shoulders than that.

52

Sun stepped through the doors of the Center City Precinct a few minutes after eight o'clock. She was alone. Chitti had not come with her; there was an emergency with a man who had been stranded in the Lazaretto after being diagnosed with Phasian Hepatitis. He had been there only three months, but his condition had been aggravated by an infection. Chitti had accompanied him to a hospital.

It was a busy morning for the police. She elbowed her way to the front desk and gave her name to a fat man with curly hair.

"I'm here to see Detective MacNally." Sun smiled at the officer.

"Just a second, ma'am." He leaned to one side and stuck his finger in the air. "Bobby, you see that? You see that clock? That thing's moved from the twelve to the one. That means five minutes have ticked by. Now why are you still in my station?"

"I'm goin', I'm goin'." Bobby, a shaky young man with hair going in all directions, didn't go. "If you'll just give me a minute, I can explain—"

"Did you hear me say I wanted an explanation?" The officer glanced at Sun and rolled his eyes before continuing with Bobby. "Out! Now!"

Sun heard the offender-in-question say something in a garbled, outer planet language. She decided it was best that she couldn't understand. She smiled again at the officer, this time to sympathize with his frustration.

"Now what can I do for you?" He gave her his full attention.

"Detective—no, that's not right. Lieutenant MacNally." Sun liked this man. He had a pleasant face.

"He's upstairs. I mean, his office is. But he won't be in for a while. He doesn't work much in the morning. Is there some way I could help?"

"I'm here to talk about finding Mr. MacDenny's body last night."

"I don't know anything about that. Sit down if you can find a seat. I'll have the desk send me a flag when he gets in. Okay?"

"Thank you, Officer O'Brian. You're very helpful."

"I'm Irish. We're always helpful."

Sun giggled when she heard the Irishman resume his argument with Bobby.

Sun fought the temptation to leave; to go back to Chitti's office and let MacNally find her when he was truly interested in hearing her statement. After all, she thought, she had already told them all she knew. It made no sense that the detective wanted her.

One reason she hadn't gone back to the office was that *she* wanted to talk with MacNally. She wanted to find out what he thought of Gregor Lepov. The two men were friends, it seemed, and she was going to take the opportunity to learn what she could.

A woman came into the station crying loudly. An officer led her off to the right and they disappeared through a door. A short angry man rushed in after them, asking where "that cop took my wife." A crass reply from someone in the crowded center of the room nearly touched off a brawl. The curly-haired fat man at the desk barked an order and two uniformed officers intervened, walking the short angry man through the same door.

The sight of all those policemen reminded Sun that Gregor had given her the name of one of these men who might be able to help her get the information she needed on the Lost Platoon. She still had the name he'd written down for her: Pete Landon. She stopped a young officer passing by.

"Excuse me, could you tell me where I can find Pete Landon?"

"Sure, he's right over there." The officer pointed toward the far end of the room. "Office in the corner, the one with the door open."

Sun thanked him, and he fumbled his attempt to say it was no problem. It was nice to see a young man who could become a little shy when speaking to a woman. Sun followed his directions and stopped at the open door.

A man lounged behind a small desk that clearly held every item that had ever been set on its surface. It was hard to judge how old he was; his face was lined enough that he couldn't have been as young as Sun, yet his head was covered in long, thick, curly hair. His eyes were closed and his feet propped on a stack of books. She could see the trace of a smile on his lips.

"Hello," he said, not opening his eyes. His smile grew. "Come on in."

"Are you Peter Landon?" It would have felt odd to call him Pete, too presumptuous.

"Not Peter." His eyes popped open; the smile in full bloom. He dropped his feet and sat up. "Pete. Anyway, I heard you walk up. But I didn't hear you pass by or go back, so it only stood to reason you were waiting outside the door."

With all the noise coming from the main room, Sun wondered if he were joking. She started to introduce herself, but he interrupted.

"Just sit down. You're Major Sun Uijong. And no, I'm not that clever. My deskscreen's proximity reader has lit up your name right in front of me."

Where he might be reading her name on that crowded desk was anybody's guess. Again, Sun wondered if he were joking. She decided she liked him. He reminded her of her youngest brother, a genius full of foolishness.

"I'm curious why a lovely lady like you would know my name and be looking for me. I hope this is an interesting story."

"I was told that you were the man to see if I ran into a problem with the information I am researching. You come highly recommended."

"Well, that's flattering. However, I don't generally hire out to someone outside the office. I'm kind of a homebody."

"I'm sorry, I didn't mean to presume. Gregor Lepov gave me your name, and I just wanted to meet you. Gregor thought I'd have some trouble with the recordkeeping here, though I haven't so far."

"Lepov is a friend of yours?" Pete chuckled. "I was unaware Gregor Lepov had friends beyond MacNally and me. Old friend from the home planet?"

"No, not an old friend. I'm not old enough to have those."

"Well, no. I didn't mean old." He blushed.

"We only met yesterday, in fact. Have you known Mr. Lepov long?" Sun was glad she'd gone looking for Pete Landon.

"A little while, sure. We have a drink together now and then."

Sun couldn't think of a simple question to ask. Here was her chance to find out who Gregor Lepov really was, what type of man he was, and yet she couldn't formulate a question that sounded natural. She knew she couldn't come right out and ask if he were an honest man or ask if he were an upstanding citizen. But she should have been able to think of some question that would provide her with the information she needed.

Instead, she smiled nervously and said nothing.

"So what research?" Pete asked, breaking the awkward silence.

"I'm here with Veterans' Health Benefits and I am arranging compensation packages for members of the Lost Platoon. Do you know their story?"

"Wait a minute," Pete looked down at his deskscreen, "I knew I'd seen your name before. You were in that report on MacDenny."

"Yes, we were there when he fell." Sun winced at the memory. "Silva MacDenny was a member—"

"—of the Lost Platoon," Pete said it before she could. "I know. I was looking at some of this Platoon stuff just the other day. This makes only four survivors now. What sort of research were you doing?"

"Could I ask you a question first?" Sun was thinking of John Yarmin and his suggestion that she take a close look at the other living members. "Why were you investigating the Lost Platoon? Are the police aware of any illegal activity?"

"Well, no. I was just looking up some things for a friend."

"For Gregor Lepov?"

"No," Pete shook his great mane of hair. "I can't say. But we don't suspect anything illegal is going on."

"I see. Well, I'm not just tracking down the members who are still alive. I also need to find out how each of the others died and look for any surviving relatives. That was Gregor's worry. He didn't think there were good records on deaths in the Lazaretto."

"Unfortunately, he's right. Have you had any trouble yet?"

"I'm not sure. I'm getting some help from Chitti Sienté, the director of a charity here that focuses on the Lost Platoon. She was doing the initial research on the members who had already died."

"She was with you last night. I saw her name on the report."

"Yes, and I came down this morning because Lt. MacNally wanted to ask us some more questions."

"At eight in the morning?" Pete gave her a funny look.

"I'm afraid I was a little early. Military habit."

"Why the question about illegal activity?" Pete leaned forward. He had intense blue eyes that did not allow Sun to avoid the question.

"If there is evidence of anything illegal, then the compensation will be forfeit. So I was curious when you had said you were looking into the Lost Platoon." Sun paused, trying to decide if she should say more. She couldn't think of a reason not to. "There's another reason I asked, though. It has to do with a Lt. John Yarmin."

"The Platoon's commanding officer. He's still alive."

"Yes, and I've spoken with him. He suggested that I speak to all of his men, and keep my eyes wide open. He seemed to be suggesting I would discover something illegal. He didn't say that in so many words, but it was the impression he gave."

"John Yarmin has a habit of that," a voice said from just outside the door. Chitti stepped into the little office and nodded at Pete. "Hello, I'm Chitti Sienté. Sun has been using my organization's office to research the Lost Platoon. I have worked closely with the few survivors."

"Hello, I'm Pete Landon. Major Uijong and I were just discussing your boys in the Lost Platoon."

"Well, like I said, John Yarmin is not psychologically balanced. He has always tended to imagine conspiracies and betrayals. He once told me he believed that the platoon's exile had been staged, a ruse."

Sun wondered why Chitti hadn't told her that before.

"I wish you had told me before what John said to you, Sun. I could have saved you the trouble of worrying about it."

"I guess so, though it certainly hasn't caused me any undue worry. I had intended to look into this diligently anyway."

"Weren't you going to talk to that big detective from last night?" Chitti asked. "Or is Mr. Landon here filling in for him?"

"No, I'm just waiting for him. How is the man doing, the one you took to the hospital?"

"He's not doing well. I don't think he'll live very long."

"You didn't have to come down here, Chitti. You could have stayed with him." Sun didn't even know the sick man but she felt tears beginning to form as she thought about his condition.

"There was nothing to do. He's not conscious anymore. And the nurses are taking care of him as best they can. I decided I'd better come see what I could learn about Silva's death."

Sun had forgotten that Chitti knew Silva MacDenny.

Pete offered to take them up to MacNally's office where they could wait in a relatively quieter location. The two ladies thanked him for his offer and were soon following him to the Homicide office.

Sun hoped the interview wouldn't last long. She needed to get back to work. There were still two platoon members to interview. And with MacDenny's death, her job had taken on a new urgency. If only the government had tried to help just a few years ago, Silva MacDenny might have found some peace in his last days. As it was, he had not even heard that help was on the way.

Sun wanted to cry. It was unfair; Silva MacDenny and so many others had suffered needlessly under a draconian policy that had stolen their lives and dignity. She had to finish her job, quickly. The delays had to cease. Those four men deserved to get the help they needed as soon as possible. Sun vowed that she would personally make it happen.

53

He woke with a sense of urgency. *Today is the day.* This was it.

His hands shook as he tried to climb out of bed. It wasn't nervousness. That was impossible. He'd faced combat with steel resolve. He'd do the same today.

The Thief took a soiled shirt from the floor and stumbled into the small washroom outside the bedroom. Jamming the light switch, he squeezed his eyes shut to avoid the painful light. Through this narrow, blinded view he spied his reflection. Most of the hair on his chest was gray and looked like cobwebs. His beard had started to spread again; a gritty, sandpaper shadow which made him resemble an ancient desert Bedouin.

His first duty was to shave. He'd better not let himself go. That wouldn't do. The women wouldn't like that. They liked a man with a solid, smooth jaw. Shave first.

Instead of pulling on the old shirt, the Thief crumpled it in his hand and rubbed a clear spot on the mirror over the sink. The reflection became clearer — still spotty — but clean enough. He scraped the stubble off his jaw and neck. The blade was dull and he didn't bother using hot water. It hurt but he didn't care. The pain helped to clear his head.

He was tempted to bemoan the condition of his body — his knees hurt, his shoulders were sore, he even felt pain deep in his belly — but he knew he was in much better shape than the Engineer.

He laughed at that. Who wasn't better off than the Engineer? After all, the man's brain had been demolished. Smashed to bits. It had annoyed the Thief that the Liar wanted him to dig up the brain so it could be found. But once he'd begun the process of uncovering the brain and taking it up to the Engineer's home, it had really become a good bit of fun.

The brain had been much heavier than he'd expected. There was no denying that. And it had taken him forever to drag the brain up those stairs. It was the elevator's fault. It just wouldn't move. Dragging the dead weight of an overinflated brain up ten flights of stairs was a noble but nearly impossible task.

But such noble deeds weren't without their funny moments. And the Thief could think of none funnier than the moment he had rested the brain on the banister and seen it slip into the stairwell's void.

After watching it fall all the way to the ground, he had thrown himself against the stairwell wall and just laughed, had discovered he couldn't stop laughing. Even now, the next morning, the laugher came with regularity. Seeing that brain fall for such a long time, he had thought it would bounce; had the funny idea it would bounce all the way back up to the tenth floor so he could grab it again.

He would have to stop laughing at some point. There were things to do. He had to distract the Liar so she wouldn't know that he was planning to do the job that night. That was going to take a cool head. He had to keep her guessing, make sure she was not ready for what was coming.

Yes, something was coming, all right. He had decided he had no choice but to deal directly with her prying. He was no longer able to overlook her spying. She knew what she was doing. She knew how serious her betrayal had been. Check up on him? Keep an eye on him? That would stop.

Didn't she know how dangerous it was, peering too closely at something that doesn't want to be seen? That was an easy way to lose an eye. Just as easy to lose two eyes. And the Thief could guarantee such.

Just a little planning and execution. Allow the eyes to see what he wanted them to see; then blind them just when they caught a glimpse. Those double-crossing little eyes would never know what hit them.

54

Leaving Della Sahdjec's, Lepov knew he should have gone looking for Francois Bernham. He had every intention of doing so. But he knew that before he did, he would wind up at his office. And he knew what he would do as soon as he stepped through the door.

He would check the MoleRunner.

The mole had tagged Lilly's movements from her arrival through the first two days. He could have suspended its run and redirected it to find her current whereabouts, but not yet. He wanted to see all of her movements; see if she'd ever been anywhere near Chettleham Keep—there was no point in denying it. She'd lied to him. As impossible as it had seemed, there was no denying that the woman in Morvee's apartment could have been Lilly.

But he was getting the itch to find her, to know where she was now. It was still early enough in the morning for Lepov to have a decent chance of finding her at her hotel. He was tempted to tell himself that Lilly was not an early riser, but again, that was one of those things he knew little about.

The less he thought about it the better. But that was easier said than done. He simply wanted to be able to trust Lilly; he'd never met a woman who had impressed him this much. All he really wanted was to be with her.

It felt good to get out of the cold wind as he descended the steps of the SubTransit station a block from his office. Would Lilly give him a reception as cold? She'd done that before; after he had falsely accused her of setting him up when they had first met. The guilt he'd felt from that mess was a factor in his decision to stay behind in the Lazaretto when she had left. But now he was beginning to wonder if he'd been completely wrong about all of that. If Lilly were now lying in regards to her whereabouts, maybe she had lied six months ago.

He was startled by that train of thought. A great deal had happened in a short time during his first case in the Lazaretto. There were still many unanswered questions. But did that mean he should suspect Lilly of conspiring with Morvees to kill him?

Lepov sat back against the bench of the SubTransit car and closed his eyes. He thought about Lilly, allowed an image of her to fill his mind. Lilly Stewart. Lilly was an incredible woman. Was she capable of murder? Until yesterday he would have flatly denied it. *Impossible.* So what had changed? The fact that she had lied? Did that automatically make her a murderer?

Nonsense. Lepov knew it was nonsense. That's what made Lilly special. In the short time he had come to know her, he had seen that despite being a tough woman in a tougher environment, she had never become a hard woman. She still retained a measure of grace and honor that Lepov had not seen anywhere else in the Lazaretto. Hell, he knew that his own measures of grace and honor were sorely lacking. What right did he have to suggest Lilly was capable of such deception and ill intent?

So what did that mean he was doing? Running off to confront her just so she knew he was aware she was lying? To embarrass her? To force some sort of concession? To win her favor by putting her in a position where she not only owed him an explanation but owed him reverence as well?

He couldn't do that. Not to Lilly. Even if she had lied, there had to have been a reason. All it took was a little faith; faith in a good woman. Was that so hard?

He didn't think it was impossible. Hard, yes. But not impossible. He simply had to make a decision and stick with it. Believe that Lilly was worthy of trust, or believe she was unworthy of such a thing. And if it came down to that, he knew the answer was the former. She was trustworthy.

As he climbed the steps out of the SubTransit station just a block away from her hotel, he decided he had to trust her. He would have gone in search of Bernham if he hadn't been so close to her hotel. As it was, it made sense to go ahead and see if he could find her. There'd be no reason to embarrass her. He'd simply say he was on a case and was surprised to run into her.

He might even be able to ask her to join him for a late breakfast or an early lunch.

He was definitely going to shut down the MoleRunner script when he got back to his office. That had been unnecessary. Childish, even.

Caution hadn't been tossed entirely to the wind. Coming into her hotel, Lepov found an empty chair in one of the corners of the reception room and sat down with a view of both the entrance and the elevator doors leading up to the rooms.

He couldn't just ring up her room and invite her down. He was going to have to be patient. He'd wait until she came out of the elevator and crossed to the entrance before he would stand up and *run* into her. He was beginning to feel good about his decision to come and find her.

Famous last words.

When he did see her, she wasn't coming out of an elevator. She was coming into the hotel through the glass entrance. She wasn't alone. A tall, powerful man with a full head of wavy hair walked with her. He was laughing, telling her not to worry about something. She laughed in return.

The sonofabitch was twice her age and his chiseled physique was obviously fake. The hair had to be as well. A real clown, Lepov thought.

"I have to admit," Lilly said, now within earshot, "I wasn't expecting breakfast. That was unnecessary. I could have fended for myself."

"I was happy to do it." The man's voice was deep and Lepov decided this had to be a lounge lizard who had started following her, from whom she could not break away.

Lepov left his chair, moving at an angle which would intercept them before they made it to the elevator. He put his head down and walked at a pace guaranteeing a collision. He was only a few steps away when he belatedly recognized the man, though from where he couldn't recall. Alarms rang through his brain but it was too late to avoid her. He had to stop abruptly; he had timed it so well that he actually almost ran *into* Lilly.

"I'm sorry," he mumbled just before making eye contact with her. He wasn't sure which of them was quickest to show recognition. Maybe both of them said each other's name simultaneously. He only hoped he sounded as surprised as she did.

"Gregor, what are you doing?" She stopped walking but stood with her hands at her sides, making no move to greet him.

It was like his last call to her; *what did you want?* All of his prepared greetings burned up on reentry. He wore the best, confused look he could conjure and asked "what are you doing in the Laz?"

An odd expression came over her features and she covered it poorly with a smile. "I just got in. I was going to surprise you."

As lies went, it was terribly weak; but for a mood killer, devastatingly effective. Lepov felt heat rise from his neck. Even the man beside her looked uncomfortable.

"I'm surprised." He tried to think of the man's name. Riley. Or Rally. The man had held a party that first day Lepov had met Lilly. "Did she surprise you too?"

"He was expecting me, Gregor. This is Cam Raley—"

"Yeah, I remember."

"—who hired me to bring a piece that he wants kept out of the news."

"Well, Mr. Raley, it's nice to see you again. I'm sure your secret is safe with Miss Stewart. She's so good at keeping secrets, even her friends think she's still on Bukovina. Lilly was clever enough to make fools of them all. Or at least a few of them."

"It's nice to meet you as well, Mr. Lepov. I remember our meeting. And Lilly has spoken of you several times." That chiseled face and equally chiseled hair was irritating as hell.

"Well, sometimes it's easier to talk *about* me than it is to talk *to* me."

"Cam, I'm afraid I'm going to say goodbye to you here, do you mind?" Lilly turned toward Raley casually, ignoring Lepov for the moment.

"Of course not. I've overextended your hospitality as it is. You'll still be around for a few days, right? I may need you again. Just minor details."

Cam nodded at Lepov, his chemically sculpted body stiff at the neck, and smiled as he walked away. Lepov had the funny notion that Raley was as pleased as the cat who has just swallowed a prized mouse.

"You," Lilly pointed at Lepov, "follow me."

And just like that, Lepov felt that he was the transgressor. Lilly was angry with him, despite the fact that she had been the one telling lies.

He followed her.

The ride to the fifth floor was silent, uncomfortable. Lepov tried not to start thinking like a guilty defender. He had the axe that needed grinding here. Not her. He would have to remember that.

They were inside her room with the doors closed before she turned to face him. There was no doubt at all; she was mad as hell.

"What is this all about? Why did you come here?"

"I'm on a case. Did you think I came here to see you?" She wasn't buying it. "How would I know where you were? And what are you doing here? I just talked to you a few days ago and you said nothing about this."

Her eyes flared. "What kind of obligation do you think I'm under? Don't treat me like a wife that didn't ask permission to go out for the night."

"I don't think you're obligated to me." He changed his mind on that immediately. "Unless you consider the good manners from one friend to another an obligation."

"Gregor, don't be silly. I was more concerned with the good manners — no, not manners — the good faith practices of my profession toward my client."

"Raley?"

"Yes, Cam Raley. He specifically stipulated that I not inform anyone of my travel arrangements. People know what I do for a living. He didn't want anyone speculating about what I was doing for him. He is determined to keep this transaction as discreet as possible. And yes, if he didn't want me to tell anyone I was coming into the Lazaretto, then that included you."

"And did this secret delivery include an early morning breakfast?" He regretted the question, just not quickly enough to stop it from coming out of his mouth.

"Yes, it did." Her answer was cold; a temperature low enough to freeze the outer layer of his soul. He knew there was more. "He paid for all of it except the sex. That was on the house."

Lepov's thoughts irrationally turned to the MoleRunner and the need to kill the script before Lilly found out about it. He was already in deep and he wouldn't need her finding out about anything like that to make it worse.

"You took that the wrong way," he weakly protested.

"Really? I hope so. The man's nothing more than an old friend. More like a father or an uncle, okay? Now, was there something you wanted? I mean besides an explanation and complete confession. Was there a reason you came looking for me?"

"Is there anything wrong with wanting to see you? Do I have to have a reason? I haven't seen you in six months. Don't you think I'd want to see you after I found out you were here?"

"Ed MacNally told you, didn't he?" She shook her head and sat at a small glass table. "I was worried this would happen. I've been sick at my stomach worried you'd find out and do this."

"What did I do?" Lepov asked in exasperation.

"Make a scene," she sighed. Lepov tried to argue but she stopped him. "If you want sympathy because you haven't seen me in six months, remember why that was. You stayed here, Gregor. And you never left. You've been hiding here — why, I don't know. But I figure you'll have to work it out on your own. In the meantime, I wasn't going to sit around crying about you. I have a business to run. And this is part of that business. People hire me as an art broker. Not because they want to get me into bed."

"I said you misunderstood me."

"Fine, whatever. Let's just stop right there, okay? I'm not feeling all that well." Lilly reached up and let her ponytail down. Her white hair fell down around her shoulders and she ran her hand through it.

"And then what, you're going to leave? That's it?"

"I don't know, Gregor." Her acerbic reply backed him up several steps. "I wasn't proposing a definitive schedule for the next four days. I just said we need to stop for now."

Had the call from the front desk not come at that moment, Lepov might have kept talking and made the whole mess worse. Instead, he was caught off guard when Lilly took the call and then handed him the phone.

"You've got a call." There was no spark in her eyes; her voice like a stranger's.

"This is Lepov," he said.

"Mr. Lepov? I'll connect you."

"Hold on. Who's looking for me and how did they know where to find me?"

"A young lady called the front desk and asked if we had seen you. As a licensed Hotel, we have a legal proximity reader that tracks the movements of hotel guests and their guests. It was no trouble to determine that you were in Miss Stewart's room. Don't worry, Mr. Lepov. We haven't told the lady where you are. She will only know that you are in the hotel."

"So connect me," Lepov frowned and tried to guess who the caller was. Was it Della Sahdjec? Had she changed her mind?

"Gregor?" Sun Uijong's voice was a welcomed change.

"Hello, Sun," Lepov couldn't help but smile. "How did you know where I'd be?"

"I was just with your friend, Peter Landon. I mentioned that I needed to find you and he said he would have no trouble tracking you down."

"A clever boy, that Pete. Why did you need to find me?" He turned his back on Lilly, who was pulling off her shoes and paying little attention to his call.

"I need your help, if your offer stands."

"Of course my offer stands. Promises made over dinner, especially Bukovinan game, are never made lightly. I'm all yours." Lepov couldn't remember the last time he'd said anything over the top like that. Maybe once or twice with his wife before the marriage had soured, but if so, he couldn't remember it.

"You don't have to," Sun objected.

"I'm just glad you called and asked for my help."

It wasn't until he put down the phone that he became aware of how the call must have sounded to Lilly. He didn't mind in the least. In fact, he liked the idea. It might serve a purpose.

"I'm gonna go now." Lepov watched her, baiting her for a reply.

Lilly busied herself arranging her shoes against the wall. She did not ask what the call was about or who was on the other end. She kept busy until she could find nothing more to do. She finally made eye contact.

"I'll call you," she said.

"Okay." Lepov didn't ask when. It was probably best if they stayed away from each other until their tempers cooled.

55

If at times I have been too focused on the seemingly irrelevant it is because there are parts of this story painful to recount. If I could, I would skip them. But as painful as they are, they are necessary. They are indispensable to the tale. I have no choice but to bring them out. I wish it were not so. I wish I could let these things go.

I had been so fixated on keeping Calla's secret, so fixated on keeping Calla safe, that I never saw it coming. This is why I blame myself for so much of what happened. But that does no good now except to salve my conscience just a bit. But not enough.

Bernham said nothing to me after the incident with Cam Raley. But I felt something was different. I only hoped that it was my imagination. After all, what else could I do?

I don't blame myself, really. I know how all of that goes. How the victim cannot accept the fact that life is cruel, at times, without explanation.

How the victim turns inward and tries to find blame—anything to cover the shame of being victimized. How this gives the victim a small measure of control in a situation in which they never had control. If I could blame myself, then I could believe I had some control in the outcome.

I had no control whatsoever. Bernham had all the control. How could it have been otherwise? I had no idea where we were. I had no control over our provisions; no way to contact anyone beyond Bernham. I wasn't even sure of night or day; whether it was cold or raining. Everything in our world sifted through Bernham.

Moreover, he enjoyed it. The only thing keeping him in his place was Kjarsta Zoltis. He did not know who we were, and that was another layer of security that came from Kjarsta's protection. Bernham stayed away from us because he was unsure of our importance.

All along he had suspected that the only important thing was that we stay out of sight. Kjarsta never understood the damage he had done not telling Bernham who Calla really was. That would have been enough to protect us. Bernham was not crazy enough to risk angering a man like Kjarsta. But for all of Kjarsta's shrewd ways, he had miscalculated his young, bearded employee.

So had I. If I hadn't, if I had understood then what I do now, I would have told Bernham everything. Before it was too late. But what does that matter now?

Bernham had kept his distance until the incident with Cam Raley. Raley's reckless actions changed everything. They changed Bernham.

He knocked on our door two nights after Raley had come and put his hands on me. I opened it as quietly as possible. Calla was already asleep.

"Come on," he gestured toward the front room.

I grabbed a shawl and wrapped it around my shoulders. The front rooms were always too cold. After checking to make sure he hadn't wakened Calla, I followed.

The shock from his attack was brutal enough to render me unable to fight back. I was unable to take a breath, unable to say a word or cry out. He grabbed me by my hair and threw me on the floor of the front room. I lay on my back, stunned. I remember my fingers digging into the heavy carpet. It felt like coarse, gritty hair.

Bernham stood over me, cruelty on display from ear to ear. He knelt beside me and grabbed me by the collar of my blouse, pulling me head and shoulders off the floor.

"That's good," he was looking into my eyes, reading them. "None of that arrogance you like to show-off. You're afraid. But not enough, I don't think. Still thinking that Kjarsta Zoltis is protecting you."

That was more chilling than the violence. I was slowly regaining control over my mind and body, though my spirit was still locked in fright. But I held still. I didn't know what he was doing or what he meant. And I had to find out what he was thinking.

"Now you're going to listen to me," he said. That was hard to do while his right hand grabbed my ankle and slowly pawed its way up my leg. A Phasian spider would have felt better than that dreadful hand. I tried to block it with my own but he smacked it away. The sound of his hand cracking against mine rang in my ears.

That hand was up on my blouse then. I felt ants crawling all over me. But the look on his face kept me from fighting him off. I could see it was what he wanted. He was waiting for me to struggle.

"It's time we quit playing games, woman. It's time you quit thinking I work for you. Yeah, I know that's how you saw me. A goddamned peasant. But I wasn't going to put up with that forever. Is that what you thought? That I'd just keep duckin' my eyes and doing whatever you told me?"

I couldn't believe, as terrified as I was, that I was still able to concentrate enough on what he was saying to realize he was out of his mind, that he was delusional and crazy. I also knew there was no way to fight his accusations. They were firmly rooted in his mind and there was nothing I could say or do to eradicate them.

"I know what you're thinking. You think Zoltis will come down here and stop me. But he won't. Not now. I've had a little talk with Cam Raley. And it didn't take long for us to find out we had mutual interests. That's business. Two men combining their resources in pursuit of mutual interests."

I had managed to crawl back from him just a little as he spoke. He watched with predatory anticipation; waiting for the moment when I would try to spring for the door.

I backed up until I hit a wall. I wanted to crawl into it and through it until he couldn't reach any part of me. My back pressed against it but it refused to allow me in.

Closing the gap I had managed to create, he caressed my cheek and his hand slid over my mouth. Bile rose in my throat. I remember fighting back tears. He was looking for things like that. I didn't want to give them up for his gratification.

"Raley knows who the girl is. Knows it's his. And Raley wants her. With her, he can control Zoltis. I don't give a damn either way. But you're what I want. And Zoltis won't let me have you. I guess it's obvious why. He just doesn't want to share." His hand—that same vile hand—pressed down along the front of my blouse. His eyes dilated and his breathing grew ragged. He had to be responding to my fear, no matter how hard I tried to hide it.

"You're wrong," I said. I knew it didn't matter even if he believed me, but I said it anyway.

"But Raley doesn't want you," he continued, ignoring what I said, "and so he doesn't care what I do with you. So he gets the girl. Funny little thing, isn't she?"

And that's when I ceased to fear anything he might do to me. Calla.

My heart burst to think of her; of what Raley had in mind. I didn't know. I was too unbalanced to be able to think it through. But I knew that whatever it was, it would be too much. It would be more than the both of us could bear.

"So I think it's time to sample the wine, you know?" Bernham shoved me sideways and I slid down the wall.

Calla. I concentrated on Calla. How in the world was I ever going to protect Calla?

Bernham's hands tore at my blouse and I started to scream. But at the same time, he started to scream too—a scream that was cut off and ended in a long, grating gurgle, as if a demon had taken possession of his tongue. He let go of me and his hands clawed at the air around him. He kicked me once, but then his legs kicked feverishly at the floor and wall.

I balled my body against the wall as tightly as I could, hands covering my face. I was crying by then, no more bravely hiding tears. When Bernham ceased thrashing, I lowered one arm and dared to look at him. He was sitting with his legs stretched out like a marionette set in the corner of his traveling box. I'd never seen a man's face distorted so.

Behind him, a man held Bernham in a choke-hold. One arm was bent, locking the other arm in place. After what seemed like a full day of terrifying silence, the arms slowly relaxed and Bernham slid to the floor. His phantasmagoric face far too close to my own.

Stooping over Bernham was the man who had choked the life out him. He was the little man named Fortunado. I shook when I finally saw him. Instead of feeling safe with my rescuer, I knew that I had only traded one madman for another. The madness wasn't in his eyes and smile like Bernham's. It was in the way he blinked at Bernham's body; a playful, elfin expression on his face, a child winning a fun and nonsensical game.

"No tasting the wine, Bernham." Fortunado was on the verge of laughing. He must have sensed my fear. "Don't you worry about me. I don't like wine. I bet Bernham don't like wine much anymore either." This time he did laugh. And before I could say anything or do anything, he retreated down the hallway.

By the time fear for Calla fueled my efforts to stand and return to her room, Fortunado was gone. He had vanished into that locked room.

I locked Calla's door as soon as I was in the room and blocked it with the dresser. Bernham's throttled body lay just on the other side of the wall. I couldn't stand to think of it. I pulled her bed away from the wall, then lay down at the foot of it and cried. I have no idea how long. When I awoke, Calla had crawled from her end of the bed and curled against me.

I dreamt of ants and spiders.

56

Once he had finished with Major Uijong and Chitti Sienté,

MacNally poured a large cup of coffee and sat at his desk. This MacDenny affair was a problem. Russell was busy with the thirty-year-old cadaver; MacNally had to work on MacDenny. That meant he had limited time to search for Pan Juarez and the missing diamonds.

It should have been the other way around. He should have given Russell the MacDenny case. Then he could have worked on the John Doe and looked for Juarez at the same time. But it would be tough to make the switch now without attracting attention.

MacDenny's apartment had yielded no clues. As expected, the recorders in the stairwell had been inoperative. In fact, without Major Uijong, they wouldn't have any clues at all. But she had told them that MacDenny's former commanding officer, an old grouch by the name of Yarmin, had hinted at something illegal going on. It was a place to start.

MacNally had Yarmin's address and planned to go there. But before he did he wanted to look at MacDenny's background. He had a hard time believing it was coincidental that another member of the Lost Platoon had just popped up on the radar. Especially when this one had a ring identical to Yarmin and Morvees.

Yet they'd found no ring on the body. Did that mean the ring in MacNally's rice can was MacDenny's? Maybe. But he had not established if Morvees or Yarmin still had theirs.

The best way to profile anyone in the Lazaretto was to pull up their employment records. These would give MacNally a list of associates, tell him where that individual had spent his time geographically, as well as an idea of his financial status.

The most recent employment status for MacDenny was *retired*. A quick run through the previous five years showed him working for a construction contractor as a civil engineer. Knowing Russell would point out the obvious, MacNally checked and found it was not the same contractor that had demolished the Roth Building. MacDenny had worked for the contractor for ten years. Before that, there was no listing for Silva MacDenny as an employee anywhere in the Lazaretto.

That wasn't impossible to swallow. Some exiles, sick or just in despair, chose to live off the government dole. They had that option, though it was not comfortable. They were provided with a place to sleep and sufficient food. But that was all. The living quarters were usually barracks-like, the food hardly sufficient, let alone nutritious. It was hard to believe someone of MacDenny's education and skill would take this option.

MacDenny had degrees in both civil engineering and mechanical engineering. The fact that he had joined the military led MacNally to assume MacDenny had a checkered past. A man with such an education did not just join out of patriotism. He was either running from a woman or the cops. Half of the original planetary colonists fit into that category. But as the planets became more settled and began to mirror Earth's penchant for law and order, the military had been the last refuge for men fleeing their past. With so much more land and employment opportunities available on the colony planets, it became harder to find willing volunteers to fill the ranks. Military regulations had been relaxed to open a new segment of the population from which recruits could be drawn; petty criminals, dead-beat fathers and husbands, and even the mentally unbalanced. Over time, the face of the Combined Euxine Military machine had transformed from Earth's elite fighting men into something more closely resembling a resurrected French Foreign Legion.

Cops like MacNally tended to overlook a man's past, as long as he left it behind before coming into the Lazaretto. Rapists and killers were the exception. Those kinds of stains never came out; the grimy atmosphere of the Lazaretto brought out the worst in a man.

But MacDenny's record was clean. If he had been running from something, it had been personal. Probably a woman, MacNally concluded. Weren't most men running from a woman? A mother, a lover, a fiancée who'd been left at the altar and never stopped calling for years on end to remind you of how much of a stupid ass you'd been to leave her waiting like that without even telling her you'd left her to become a cop on some god-forsaken moon she'd never heard of? MacNally shook off that last thought and decided he wasn't satisfied with MacDenny's records.

There was no chance MacDenny had sat around unemployed for twenty years. Had he been too sick to work? How sick had the boys of the Lost Platoon really been? According to Pete Landon, they hadn't been sick at all. Was that true for all of them?

He checked on the employment records of the other living platoon members. As the system compiled data, MacNally called Russell to his desk.

"Menya, you got anything new on that corpse?"

"I might." Russell grabbed a chair from an empty desk and sat down. MacNally envied the way the young man could do that with such ease. It had been a long time since MacNally had been able to move around in such a way. Just dropping into a chair was beginning to be a delicate operation. Russell, unappreciative of his pain-free status, explained. "I've been running a few tests with one of the labtechs. I didn't want to tell you something in case it didn't work out. It's all pretty much guesswork for now. But basically, we think we might be able to reconstruct the DNA. From what I understand of it—and there isn't much that I understand—we can reverse the effects of the radiation, but only slowly. Like picking sand out of a sugar bowl one grain at a time."

"And what are you doing while the labtech's picking sand out of this sugar bowl?" MacNally had never heard of a process like that.

"I've been mapping out that hole where the body was. We have a good idea where, and I'm trying to get us closer to the actual spot."

"What good does that do us?"

"The basement of the Roth Building had been segmented into storage rooms for all of the residents. If I can find out exactly where this guy was buried, I might be able to find out who put him there."

Again, MacNally was tempted to switch places with Russell, who apparently had time to chase down absurd ideas. But Captain Jenkins was bound to ask questions if he changed assignments midstream.

"Can I get a favor from you?" MacNally asked.

"I suppose."

"When MacDenny's visuals get back, would you look at them? You read that crap quicker than I do. You see a lot more."

"Sure, MacNally."

"Keep up the good work, Menya." MacNally knew that sounded stupid. But if Russell thought so, he wasn't saying anything. He just thanked MacNally and went back to his desk.

The Lost Platoon's employment data search was complete. MacNally spread the files onto his deskscreen to examine them.

Stakka Obenlan had been employed for nearly the entire thirty years. The job was nothing to brag about; he'd been a repairman for an elevator company. Come to think of it, MacNally smiled, that was definitely not a cause for boasting in the Lazaretto. Shame might have been more appropriate.

Chaz Grimion had been employed in a Morse code sort of way; a year on, two years off, four on, one off, three on, one off, and so on. Not the most stable individual, but not surprising for a soldier who'd gotten a raw deal. Probably made just enough money to keep himself in drinks and cigarettes and went back to work when he'd run out.

Nothing about him grabbed MacNally's attention.

Yarmin and Morvees, on the other hand, caught his attention right away. Both of them were listed as unemployed the first twenty years, like MacDenny. That was tough to swallow. An officer, a noncom, and an educated engineer without the ambition or inclination to provide for themselves? That wasn't just improbable. That was simply impossible.

It took him an hour to figure it out. He was mad when he finally did. He should have thought of it even before the employment records. There was one entity in the Lazaretto that harassed any man, woman, or child who was exiled to life in the Lazaretto for their first two years: IHS.

The Interplanetary Health Service demanded regular health check-ups from all individuals labeled *nullus exitus* their first two years there. The check-ups were nothing but a frustrating exercise in futility. Once officially diagnosed with a pathogen, no one ever had a chance of being released from the Lazaretto. To add salt to the wound, IHS never offered assistance to the sick. The check-up was nothing more than a data-collecting protocol.

But the advantage to this nonsense was the last and most frustrating part. Each man, woman, and child was required to fill out a redundant set of forms every check-up. And check-ups were scheduled every three months.

Once the data search had combed the IHS records on Morvees, Yarmin, and MacDenny, MacNally quickly found what he needed.

All three men had listed their employers at each of the three-month check-ups. MacDenny had listed four companies, Yarmin had listed six names, and Morvees had listed as many as ten. All in a two year period. But all of them, at one time or another, had worked for the same companies.

The most important name he could find in the ownership records of those companies was Kjarsta Zoltis. Zoltis had been the head of a large shipping conglomerate working evenly between legal and illegal trafficking, which no one had ever been able to prove. And Zoltis died after a long and painful murder just six months ago. That these men had worked for Zoltis was no surprise. It looked as if Major Uijong's hunch was correct. Something wasn't right.

Cross-checking the ownership records gave MacNally one other prominent name, that of Cam Raley, another big name in shipping, though he had never been linked to anything illegal, either officially or speculatively. Raley was one of those pillars of the community who just seemed to rub MacNally the wrong way, always too good to be real. But MacNally attributed this to the man's personal character, not his business practices.

If these soldiers had gotten involved with Kjarsta Zoltis, MacNally suspected there might have been more from the platoon involved as well. He set his desksystem to run a search combining the platoon members and Kjarsta Zoltis' businesses. He included IHS records in the search. It would have to run a while.

Maybe the best thing would be to talk with Cam Raley. Despite MacNally's personal reservations about the man, Raley had always been cooperative. Two separate incidents had involved employees of Raley's charged with murder, the first a drunken bar fight that had ended in a manslaughter conviction. The second had been a lover's quarrel involving two of Raley's people. Both times Raley had extended the police every courtesy possible to ensure the investigations were quickly resolved.

But before he approached Raley, MacNally wanted to grab something to eat. Then he'd see what Raley knew. And maybe after that, Lepov would have some news. He hoped so. They needed to find out what was going on before another MacDenny dropped dead from the sky.

57

"I feel funny asking you to do this." Sun had trouble looking Lepov in the eye when he came into his office.

"I don't see why," he said, "I'm happy to help." He actually looked it.

Despite having asked Lepov to accompany her on her next interviews out of worry for her safety, she was excited he had agreed to come along. She no longer worried. Lepov was big enough and shrewd enough to make her feel safe. All she felt now was an embarrassing giddiness which she tried to hide.

"From what you told me, that Lieutenant you went to see was pretty hostile toward you, and of course I warned you that Morvees tried to kill me, and the last man you went to speak with tried to fly from the tenth floor of a stairwell. I'm glad you called me. If I'd have known you were going to interview more of the Lost Platoon, I might have insisted I come along before you had the chance to ask me."

He walked around his desk, sat, and reaching down, pulled out the bottom right drawer. A dull gray box lay at the bottom. He set it on top of the desk. Entering a three-digit number into its keypad, he unlocked the lid and flipped it open.

"Is that a gun?" Sun was unable to see the contents of the box clearly from where she stood.

"Something like that." He pulled a slender device from the box and dropped it into the right outside pocket of his coat. Sun did not get a good look, but it was silver, long as a man's hand but not as wide.

"If I'm not mistaken, Mr. Lepov, shockhammers are illegal in the Lazaretto." A shockhammer was nothing more than a palm-sized cattle prod. It didn't disable a man, but it knocked him on his back long enough to give someone an advantage in a fight.

"Major, any kind of weapon is illegal in this miserable place." Lepov smiled. "And no, Ed MacNally wouldn't cut me any slack if he knew I had one. He's a fanatic about things like that."

"I thought you just liked to jab people in the gut," Sun gave him an evil glare.

"Only women," he shot back. "Guys need more than a tap above the belt."

They went in search of Stakka Obenlan first. Chitti had given them an address located in a quiet neighborhood near the marina. The houses were old and small, with practically no space to separate each one from its neighbor. The district might have once been quaint, but now it was merely sad. These weren't abandoned homes, but she knew the people in them had been abandoned long ago.

Stakka Obenlan turned out to be the man Chitti had called *Ben*. He and his wife Gretchen had lived down by the marina for over twenty years. They were more than happy to see Sun. Ben examined Lepov warily—the soldier in him must have recognized that Lepov was no benefits administrator—but warmed to Sun right away.

"Take a seat, take a seat," Gretchen shooed them into the tiny living room. The little house was dark. A few small lamps made pools of golden shade on the shadowy floor. In contrast to the cold wind blowing outside the house, the room stifling.

"This all looks quite cozy," Sun politely observed. She made no mention of having seen Gretchen back at the office. If the woman had remembered it, she had chosen not to say anything. Perhaps she was embarrassed. At any rate, it was not Sun's place to mention it.

"It's home, you see?" Ben smiled at her and sat on the arm of Gretchen's chair. He put an arm around her. The gesture was a habitual intimacy but Sun could see it was also a habitual move to protect his wife. "We don't have much, just the two of us. It's enough, though, huh?"

Gretchen looked up and smiled with her great red cheeks. Even in the poor light Sun could see them glow.

"I've been sent by the Veterans'—"

"We know all about it," Ben waved away her explanation with his free hand. "Chitti explained all of that to us already. We're happy to hear it, of course."

"A great thing you are doing, Miss Weshaw." Gretchen's poor attempt at Sun's name was sincere and Sun felt no desire to correct her. The older woman's gratitude couldn't have been more obvious.

"I just hope it isn't too late. We are so sorry for the neglect your husband has suffered." It was going to get difficult for Sun to hold back her tears. The dark room might just be a blessing.

"Who's suffering?" Ben asked, playfully patting the top of Gretchen's head. "A man who finds a woman like this is never suffering."

"Oh, now he's showing off." Gretchen lowered her eyes and brushed his hand away. "It has been tough on him. Don't think it hasn't been. After all, I was never able to give him children."

"That's not your fault," he objected. He explained: "We were told we shouldn't have children. They would be forced to live here, you see? No one wanted to bring a child into this place. It would have been cruel. They would never have been allowed to leave."

Sun glanced at Lepov and his stoic presence gave her the strength to resist more tears. The kind of grace Ben and Gretchen Obenlan shared in the face of an unfair life was rare. The difference between this man, who had found a partner to share his unfortunate life, and John Yarmin, who had lived alone all these years, was immeasurable. The difference between life and death. Sun could think of no other comparison.

They talked for thirty minutes or more, Ben being the biggest talker, though Gretchen managed her fair share of comments. Sun asked a question now and then, but mostly allowed them to talk on their own. They seldom received visitors, so this was a rare opportunity to interact with someone outside of themselves. Lepov, Sun noted, never spoke.

By the time they finished, Sun was tempted to invent more questions just to stay and visit. Such a friendly couple was hard to find on Sinop, even more so in the Lazaretto.

"If there is anything else you need, please let us know." Ben held the door as they walked out. He nodded at Lepov — still reserved toward the large, silent man — but asked permission to hug Sun briefly. She knew she could have refused without offending him — this was the Lazaretto after all — but she didn't want to. He placed his hands on her shoulders and pulled her close, his hands never really touching her, but only briefly brushing her coat. When he turned his cheek to hers she felt only a blush of contact.

"Weren't they wonderful?" she asked Lepov as a TransitCar took them back toward Center City.

"They were cute. I have trouble believing that man was in the same unit as Morvees and Yarmin." They were the first words he'd spoken in over an hour.

"I noticed how quiet you were in there." Sun enjoyed his obvious discomfort at her words. He was far more vulnerable than he liked to portray himself.

"I wasn't there to talk. That's your job. I didn't want to get in the way."

"And I thought that maybe you were intimidated by them. You don't see happiness in your line of work too much, do you?" The question came out harsher than she had intended.

"I don't see it at all." There had been no self-pity in his comment. Sun was startled to realize that he was merely stating a fact.

"Let's hope for two in a row, okay?" She was rapidly becoming aware of his large, solid presence in the back of the TransitCar. He was not a man to fidget; always looking for a more comfortable position, unsure of what to do with his hands. He sat still, comfort the furthest thing from his mind. An air of resignation hung over him, the one thing that kept him approachable. Without it he would have been a statue. The absence would have been too much for her.

"Two in a row? Oh, you mean the last member of this dwindling platoon? What was the name?"

"Grimion. Chaz Grimion." She put a hand on his arm. "You feeling okay? You look a little better than yesterday, but not much."

"I'm fine."

"Then is something wrong?" She couldn't say why, but it felt like his mind was elsewhere.

"I don't see happiness too much, remember?" He stared sternly at her before allowing a smile that was both soft and a little forced.

"Maybe that's what I'm for." She belatedly realized her hand was still on his arm and she withdrew it. He seemed to take no notice of her touch. She settled into her seat and tried to relax. Maybe Chaz Grimion's interview would be just as delightful as the Obenlan's.

"Come in!" Chaz Grimion bellowed from inside his apartment. Sun had an idea they weren't going to be so lucky.

"What do you people want?" The old man answering to the name of Grimion was round, with white hair. He wore an old leather eye patch over his right eye. He was sitting in a fat, stuffed chair in a bathrobe that came down to just above his knees. Below the robe, a striated pattern of blue and green blood vessels showed through his white pasty skin. He wore a pair of sandals. White hair puffed out where the robe opened at his neck.

The room was freezing.

Sun had to stand close and nearly shout to make him understand her. A radio playing in the room didn't help but he made no move to turn down the volume.

After Sun had to repeat her words a third time, Lepov stepped over to the radio and shut it off. Grimion scowled at Lepov, who scowled back, and Grimion returned his attention to Sun.

"Do you need medical attention for your hearing, Mr. Grimion?" Sun had to speak loud and slow to avoid repeating herself.

"What for?" the old man shouted back. "I got no one to hear 'cept you people. When you go away I won't have no one to hear."

Sun hoped that Chitti had enough rapport with this man that she could get him in to see a doctor. That was the point of her mission here, to make sure these men were taken care of. It wasn't always about money.

"Do you have any family, Mr. Grimion?"

"Of course I got family," he sneered at her. "What do you think I am? Something they hatched in a lab? My mom and dad are back home. I ain't seen or heard from 'em in a long time. Probably been a month or more. But yeah, I got family. Don't you?"

He gave Sun and Lepov a frantic going-over with his one eye.

Sun tried several ways to explain the purpose of her visit, but each time he started talking about something else entirely. He eventually gave up and concentrated on the view through the window beside his chair. Pointing at each window in the building opposite his, he patiently tried to count each one, but lost count when switching his view from one window to the next. He sighed in frustration.

They left him like that; he did not seem to care or even notice their exit. Sun felt a disturbance in her gut. This was the kind of thing that should have been addressed early in the man's life. Such mental imbalances had to be caught early enough to prevent permanent damage to the man's mind. Once again it seemed her job had been too little, too late.

As they stepped into the elevator, Lepov seemed to sense this despair in her, putting a hand on her shoulder, to which she couldn't help but respond. The human touch was so alien in the Lazaretto she was shocked how easily she leaned into him, allowing his arm to encircle her. She laid her head on his chest and left it there as the elevator dropped to the first floor. Lepov was warm.

"You need a new job." The doors opened and he gently righted her again. "This kind of stuff might be too hard on a light spirit like yours."

"Is that your professional opinion, Gregor Lepov?" She stumbled, and tried to regain her balance. Reaching out, Lepov caught her by the hand. "I'd say the same for you. A man with as much melancholy as you shouldn't spend his days rubbing elbows with the darker edges of society. Especially ones like the Lazaretto's. You need something to pull you out of the gloom, not something that pulls you deeper into it."

"Yeah? I don't suppose you know how I'd go about doing that, hmm?"

They were face to face, his hand still around hers. She wanted to pull him closer, bring him down enough so she could lift her head and kiss him. Even with the weight of the Lazaretto's paranoia, she wanted that. But he was resisting her. Not fiercely, but noticeably.

"If you don't know how, then I doubt I'd be able to tell you." She hadn't meant to sound trite. "I hope you don't think I wasted your time. It appears I didn't need you after all."

"I'm not so sure about that." He let go of her hand and she saw a twinkle in his eye. "Old man Grimion might have beat you with his radio if I hadn't been there to turn it off and stare him down. He looked crazy enough. Who knows what he was capable of?"

"Don't," she shook her head, "don't be unkind. I can't imagine what these men have been through. It's awful to say, but I'm glad there are so few of them left. I'm not sure I could handle seeing more of them in this state. And I haven't even seen Anton Morvees yet."

"I don't think you ought to. You need to stay away from him."

They left Chaz Grimion's building and walked down the stone steps to street level. Lepov stopped at the last step and lifted his head so that his eyes were not hidden by the shadow of his hat brim.

"I'm serious about that Sun. And I can't go with you if you try to see him. He can't see me."

"I'll be okay, I guess." She shuddered at the lie. But after seeing that poor old man in his bathrobe, she did not want to miss an interview with Morvees. Perhaps Lepov was wrong. Maybe Lepov had the wrong man. What if he were just a harmless old man who needed to know that someone out there cared about him? That's all any of these men had needed for thirty years. Ben Obenlan had found that someone. But how many others had? Was Ben the only one?

"Call Ed MacNally and get him to go with you, or even Pete Landon. Don't go alone, Sun."

"I'll think about it. Maybe I'll take Chitti. I think I'll go back to her office and see what she suggests."

That had satisfied Lepov. But his resistance had broken the idyll of their time together, and they both seemed to realize the need to retreat to their respective offices. Lepov made sure to put her in a TransitCar before hailing one himself.

Sun was glad he had not asked her to lunch. There was too much for her to consider. The Obenlans had left her off-guard and Chaz Grimion had thrown her off-balance. The awkward moment with Lepov had left her needing time alone. She did not wish to go back and see Chitti. A quiet lunch was all she needed. After that, she'd try Anton Morvees' door again.

58

Lepov knew the best thing to do was get back to work. He needed to forget Lilly Stewart and Sun Uijong. Both of them were distracting him from getting what MacNally needed. So far, he wasn't any closer to peering inside Morvees' back room.

And how could he peek inside, constantly thinking about Lilly and the way she was running around with Cam Raley? That was a slimy one. Too slick. Nobody became that successful without dirtying his hands. Lepov knew he was being petulant, but couldn't help it. It wasn't impossible Raley was a bad egg. One thing Lepov had learned in the Lazaretto in his first six months was that anyone making money there was either breaking the law or about to break it.

The Lazaretto had a way of doing that to a man. The threat of disease and death lowered the safeguards society had built against the corruption of man. Here, where men should have worried what lay beyond death, they had found a tortured craving to make a last grab for the prize. Lepov had been there long enough to feel that tug; he just hadn't been there long enough to give into it.

MacNally seemed to have found a way to defeat it. But Lepov suspected MacNally's success had more to do with the solid morality of Arturo Fenelli than Ed MacNally, though it had become habit enough that he would probably stay clean even though the man's former partner was dead. Maybe, Lepov thought, MacNally could do the same for him: keep him on the straight and narrow.

Kjarsta Zoltis had given into it as soon as he had arrived in the Lazaretto. Lepov pulled up information on the Shipping Magnate and scanned the highlights. Zoltis had won the maintenance contract for the Shipping Port—the completely automated zone of the Lazaretto—during the Lazaretto's early days. If rumors of Zoltis' illegal business ventures were true, then this tie to the Shipping Port was bad news. A man like Zoltis with such access would have too much freedom. Without oversight, he would be like a kid in an ice cream parlor.

And that was where Zoltis' partner came in. Lepov had learned the hard way that the former Administrator of the Lazaretto was as corrupt as Zoltis. Claude Reno had been able to keep his partnership with Zoltis closely guarded. For how many years? Hard to say, but Lepov had a feeling they had been collaborating for decades. Reno had been too eager to kill Lepov, Lilly and anyone else who threatened to expose his secret. If he had turned corrupt only recently, he might not have been willing to go so far. No, he had been corrupt for a long time. Possibly even as far back as the day Zoltis won his maintenance contract.

The contract had to be their common interest. A little digging in the archives gave Lepov verification of this; Reno, as a Councilman, had been part of a Shipping Port Commission. If Zoltis was going to play games in the Port, someone on the Commission would have to get a piece of the action and run interference for him. Who approached whom? Had Reno discovered Zoltis' game? Or had Zoltis offered Reno a chance to get involved? No one would know; both men were dead. Either way, it didn't matter anymore.

But all this data on the Shipping Port raised another flag for Lepov. If Zoltis was in a position to manipulate shipping in the Lazaretto, with protection from Reno, what did that mean for Raley? Raley's business was based on shipping as well; mostly wine from Sinop, other luxury commodities, and coffee. Lepov was shocked to see the amount of coffee moving through the Lazaretto. If he understood the shipping data, it was one of the most shipped commodities among the Euxine planets. Math was never Lepov's strong point, but he wasn't entirely stupid on the subject. He understood enough to see that money flowed like a swollen river through that Shipping Port.

None of this meant Raley was crooked. But it reminded Lepov that Raley's ethics were not above suspicion. At the least it suggested to Lepov that it would not be a waste of time to dig around in the man's affairs. But that would have to come later. And only if he thought Raley was a danger to Lilly.

It was a shame that both Zoltis and Reno were dead. Zoltis certainly knew what had been going on in that apartment. And there was a chance that Reno knew as well. But without either of them alive to reveal old secrets, Lepov and MacNally would have to dig them up the old-fashioned way. That was how the old corpse had come to light. Maybe the digging that had to be done was more literal than metaphorical.

Lepov wondered if he ought to go poke around the site of the dig. Would there be anything to see? He doubted it. But the key had to be down there somewhere.

He cleared his deskscreen and wrote the number *one* at the top of it. He had to start with what he knew. And the first item was Branithwaite's missing persons. Lepov had never taken the landlord seriously about the missing persons. It made more sense to believe that the recorders simply failed to catch the missing people in question as they left the apartment. But his opinion changed when he came to point number two. Morvees had tried to murder Lepov and dump him in the sea. For point three, Lepov noted the loads of clay and dirt being dumped in the sea. The fourth point was the body discovered by MacNally. The obvious conclusion was that there were more bodies buried under that apartment.

With Branithwaite's data tag, Lepov took a careful look at the recordings showing the people entering the apartment. As Branithwaite had said, there were six people. Each of them could clearly be seen as they left the elevator. Unfortunately, the recorder did not have PDT recognition. All Lepov had was their facial signatures.

He called Pete Landon.

"Can you do it?" he asked the puzzle man, after explaining the problem.

"I can't run a full facial recon on these guys. That's gonna take authorization from someone with bigger feet than me. But don't let it get you down. Send me the recordings, and I'll see what I can do."

Lepov packaged the six shots and punched them through the system. "This is all I got, Pete." He waited for Pete to tell him they had come through.

"I hear you went and got yourself a friend," Pete said.

"Did I?"

"Why can't I meet a nice girl like that? She asked questions about you."

"Who are you talking about?" If Lepov had been forced to guess he would have said Pete was pulling his leg.

"I had the good fortune of meeting Major Sun Uijong this morning."

"Well, that explains your problem, Pete. You can't meet girls like that because the smart ones don't attend puzzle conventions. Neither do the pretty ones. In fact, I'd lay odds that women — any of them — don't go looking for puzzle gurus."

"I knew I was doing something wrong," Pete sighed dramatically.

"Pete, let me give you some advice. A woman is the one puzzle you should stay away from. There's no basic equation that can make sense of them."

"Spoken like a true misogynist." Pete's laugh was cut short. "Okay, here are your head shots. Let me see if they're good enough to work with."

Lepov waited. He was surprised that Sun had already gone to Pete, but more surprised that she had been asking questions about him. He was tempted to ask Pete what those questions were, but decided he didn't really want to know. He was having enough trouble with Lilly; there was no reason to start worrying about Sun.

"Wait," Pete broke his silence, "I've seen this guy."

"Which one?" Lepov hoped they had just caught a break.

"This last one. I've seen the face before, but I can't remember where."

Lepov said nothing; he wanted Pete to have a chance to think without interference. A ten-count passed before Pete spoke again.

"I'll have to think about it." Pete apologized.

"Call me back if you think of it," Lepov suspected the puzzle man was shaking his long mane of hair in frustration. "And don't apologize. I'm thankful for any help you can give me."

Lepov broke off the connection with Pete and looked at the image from the last man, the one Pete had said he recognized. The face was unremarkable. As old as Morvees, or even older. It was hard to tell. Did that mean he was one of the Lost Platoon? No, that didn't make sense. Those still alive were all accounted for. And most of the other five were younger than Lepov.

None of them were women. That led to another thought: had Lilly ever shown up on this recorder? He would have to pull up the archive from Chettleham Keep if he wanted to check on that. It would require a lot of time to scan the images.

No. There was no point. The MoleRunner would tell him if she'd been there. There were several PDT proximity readers on either side of the Keep's entrance. If she had stopped in there during the last seven days, he'd know about it soon enough.

He needed to eat. He needed to get something in his stomach to settle the funny feeling he got every time he considered another move to spy on Lilly. It wasn't enough that she had lied. He still couldn't get that image of her out of his head; Lilly standing over his coffin, ordering his death. If he didn't exorcise that memory soon, he knew the memory would grow out of control. Before long, he'd see her standing over his grave, ordering spider-like demons to drag him down to hell.

At least he hadn't begun to suspect Sun. And if he ever did, he knew that hell wouldn't be far away. He wouldn't even have to dig a six-foot grave to reach it.

59

The Thief left his dingy little apartment for the last time. He no longer needed computers and electronic equipment. And he no longer needed more sleep. He slipped out of his grungy neighborhood and headed across the Lazaretto to his basement apartment. The time had come to stop hiding. No one would be able to stop him now. It did not matter if the police eventually connected him to that miserable dead brain in the bottom of that stairwell. By then, he would be gone.

He carried a travel bag with him. The foil suit was inside it as well as his one decent set of clothes. When this was over, he would slip away forever. Thirty years of patience. And now it was time.

He was outside the basement apartment's door when he thought about the old, dull razor. He'd left it at the other apartment. He would need it. It wouldn't do to leave without it. No, he couldn't go without shaving. The women wouldn't like that.

The Liar could go back for it. Yes, he'd tell her to go get it. But would that be wise? Would she guess he was leaving? No, not if he were careful. He would have to tell her he was moving from the one apartment to the other as a precaution. Maybe he would tell her he was afraid of the police. Or maybe tell her that he wanted to test the tunnel by sleeping in it? It didn't matter. No matter what he told her, she would believe him. She was a fool and she would believe him.

He stepped through the door of the basement apartment and dropped his bag in the kitchen.

And besides, he quickly thought, what did he care about a razor? He would be able to afford new razors. Even Lazar-razors. It was silly to worry about an old, nicked up razor. That was from the old life. He was about to gain a new life. And with a new life would come more than just new razors. There would be new clothes, new women, and new apartments.

For the Thief, anything new would be close to paradise. He had been stuck in the Lazaretto so long that he had trouble remembering life outside of that black-hearted chamber. But in just one night, all of that would change.

He jumped when he heard the knock on the door. No one was supposed to be coming. The men he had hired to move the containers were no longer there. He had sent them on their way, wages paid in full. They knew nothing about his plans and had no reason to return.

Was it the Liar? Had she come early? Was she nosing around again? Spying on him? Did she hope to find out what his time schedule really was? He wouldn't stand for that. He'd already decided to stub out those shiny little eyes. One at a time, of course. Put each one of them out with a sharp stick. That was the way to deal with eyes that peeked into corners they had no business being in.

The knock again. It had to be her. She was trying to catch him unawares. She wouldn't be knocking unless she had some sneaky little plan. The Thief wasn't about to be caught off guard.

He pulled the door open a crack and peered through. It took him a moment to realize it wasn't the Liar. It was a woman, to be sure, but it wasn't *her*.

To the Thief's utter surprise, this strange woman called him by name.

"That's me," he admitted. "What do you want?"

She was from the Army. It hardly seemed probable. No one from the Army had contacted him since he'd come to the Lazaretto. What did the Army want after all these years?

"May I come in?" Her face was all smiles and sweet intention. The Thief did not like her.

"You can tell me what you want."

She began to talk about the Thief's misfortune, his exile, and his present condition. Her mouth had a ridiculous way of both smiling and frowning, sympathizing with him while she also continued to feel good about it all. But what did she know of his condition? What did she know of misfortune and neglect? The Thief decided she was a horrible woman. It was a horrible mouth.

It didn't help that she looked like an inhabitant of Sinop's Mao Province. Those squinty-eyed rats were worse than Arcobians.

She was still standing in the hallway; the mouth still talking about money and regret. Pathetic.

"That's enough," the Thief stopped her, still watching through the crack in the door. "I don't want your money. You can't seriously think I need your money, do you? I won't take it. Not tonight. I won't need it after tonight. I wouldn't have taken it two weeks ago, but I especially won't after tonight. You're not needed anymore."

The woman looked like she would cry. The mouth trembled. Such a weak mouth. The Thief wondered if he ought to drag that mouth inside and treat it like he had treated that smarmy little brain.

He grew bored listening to her ask again and again if she could come in and talk. He really should let her in. How easy it would be to let her in the room, let her into the back room, and then let her down *there*. That would serve her right, after she'd interrupted his day. She was a dainty thing; it would take little work to smash her still-talking mouth into the hole he'd dug for the Engineer's brain.

Let her in. A fine idea. That mouth just kept moving. *Please, please let me come in and explain.* He really should let it in.

The mouth was small. Much smaller than the brain that had jumped and fought to free itself from his crushing grip. Would the mouth put up much of a fight? Pity he had left his razor behind.

"If you should change your mind…" the mouth said, calling him by his name one more time. "Please let me know. Call me."

And just like that, she handed him a small card and walked away. The Thief stood with the door cracked, trying both to see her as she walked away and read the card in his hand. He was overcome with a great longing and disappointment as he realized he'd missed his chance to shut her up. That much noise coming from one mouth was too much. But he had been too indecisive. In the future he was going to have to act quickly. The next time he had to act, it would be with speed, no hesitation.

60

MacNally had called ahead, and Cam Raley was waiting as he stepped off the elevator. The well-kept, fully functioning elevator opened directly into Raley's two thousand square foot apartment. The man's wealth could have been measured by the size of his personal living quarters. Living space was prohibitively costly in the Lazaretto. But the real testimony to his wealth lay in the large penthouse's décor.

"Lieutenant MacNally, what a pleasure to see you again." Raley stood in the middle of an open room, nodding his welcome.

"Thanks, I'm glad you remember me." MacNally looked around and saw Raley's place was not jammed with fancy furniture and useless flotsam. It was almost bare.

"You've noticed my Spartan tastes?" Raley smiled. "I don't put my money into many *things*." That last word lingered too long. "You can be sure I'm not a monk, Lieutenant. I just spend my money differently than most."

"Okay." MacNally didn't care.

"I'll give you an example. You see the floor you're walking on?"

MacNally glanced at the white and grey swirls under his feet.

"This floor was made of true Earth-mined marble. Not marble recycled from older buildings from the Industrial Age of the Twentieth Century. That kind of marble is actually easy to acquire. This is Virgin Marble from the dwindling quarries of Monte Altissima. Have you heard of them? They once supplied the ancient sculptor Michelangelo for many of his famous works. And even though my interior walls are paneled with wood from a giant sequoia that once stood on the Californian north coast for nearly two thousand years, I would rather point out the trim that surrounds them."

MacNally wanted to tell Raley he didn't give a damn about trees and marble but he held his tongue.

"The molding and baseboards are made from a tree twice as old as the sequoia. More than half the wood of a bristlecone pine of the Sierra Nevadas was wasted to cut and shape the trim. I always find that a valuable lesson. To create a masterpiece, one must be willing to destroy something beautiful and priceless. Greatness comes from the ashes of former greatness."

"I'll keep that in mind." MacNally followed Raley through a door at the end of the open room.

"This is my private office," Raley pointed MacNally to a chair and then sat in an identical one just a few feet away.

The office was not as barren as the first room, though it was much smaller. The walls of the office were covered in framed works of art.

"My real treasures, as you can see." Raley nodded at the canvases. MacNally was supposed to know what he was looking at.

"They're real nice." The images meant nothing to him.

"None of these paintings is a copy. You see the Van Gogh there? *Starry Night*. My agent had to pay double the price to acquire it."

MacNally looked at the heavy blue and yellow colors and

decided a five-year-old must have painted it.

"I have a dozen of them here: Monet, Degas, Wyeth, Hopper." Raley stopped in front of a canvas that depicted a lonely house sitting in the middle of a field. A girl lay in the grassy foreground. Fallen, perhaps? An invalid? Raley nodded at the girl.

"That's *Christina's World*, 1948. Andrew Wyeth. She used to be my pride and joy. But not anymore. I'm ashamed to say that I've been unfaithful to her. Another woman has stolen my heart. If you'll turn around..."

MacNally turned in his seat to see a painting that clearly held center stage on the back wall. It was the simple image of a heavy woman with long black hair. MacNally decided immediately that it was unremarkable.

"She is *La Gioconda*, from 1519, the simple portrait of a nobleman's wife. But as you can see by the expression on her face, she knows she is much more than that. She knows her true worth, though she is also aware that this value is a deeply held secret. This simple portrait has been called the zenith of Man's artistic expression on Earth."

"It looks familiar." This was the closest MacNally could come to a compliment.

"I have only had her in my possession since yesterday. She has cost me dearly. But, she is worth every penny."

"Raley, I'd like to get right to the point, if you don't mind," MacNally changed the subject, ignoring *La Gioconda*.

"Not at all." Raley sat stiffly in his chair. MacNally had forgotten that Raley had a chemically sculpted body. He had a moderately muscled frame that was just a step below that of a body-builder's. The Sculpting might have been a good choice for a man to make at one time, if it didn't make the whole man look like a plastic mannequin. Even his blond hair had been sculpted into a wavy, rock-hard style. Nobody had paid for a chemically sculpted body in decades. Anyone who paid for the procedure discovered only too late that it could not be reversed.

"I have records showing that you employed a number of soldiers from the Lost Platoon soon after their infamous exile here in the Lazaretto. I have their names here, and would like you to look over them and tell me what you can remember about them."

"Of course," Raley took the data tag and placed it on his desk, sitting forward so he could see his deskscreen. Having chosen to sit before the desk with his guest, he had found it necessary to grab the electronic display and spin it around in order to read it. "This is going back a few years, Lieutenant. Many, many years."

MacNally made no comment as he watched Raley read the names

and dates. He wasn't going to see much reaction in that manufactured face, but he tried to watch the eyes. They would be the only place he might find an unprotected reaction.

"I might have to pull up some old files for you, Lieutenant. I'm not recognizing the names, though I am not surprised. I do recall that we made a decision to offer our assistance to many of the soldiers. We just felt they had been given a raw deal. Can you imagine fighting a war for your government, then being sentenced to exile here?"

"You don't mind it here too much, do you Raley?" MacNally knew that Raley chose to live in the Lazaretto. It was a singular eccentricity of the import/export wine merchant; instead of keeping an office on Sinop, the Euxine System's preeminent supplier of fine wines, then shipping the wines through the cargo quarantine — which consisted of chemical treatment with only a ten-day incubation — Cam Raley actually warehoused his stock of wines in the Lazaretto.

"That's just good business." Raley's smile was mischievous, even a little dark. "I set up my wine business within the quarantine to make it *more* difficult for buyers to purchase my stock. You might think this obstacle would turn buyers away but you would be wrong. The obstacle is irresistible. It's human nature. My customers are convinced that the more readily available wines in the planetary shops *must be* inferior. I have simply harnessed the power of the Lazaretto and strong-armed the forty day waiting period to work to my advantage."

"So what would these men have done for you?" MacNally was unimpressed with Raley's arrogance.

"I'm not sure, to be honest. I know we made an effort to give them employment. That's all I can say without calling up a detailed report."

"I'll keep that in mind in case I need more information." MacNally could see the idea annoyed Raley. "I also found that many of these men were employed by Kjarsta Zoltis. Can you tell me about that?"

"I'd be surprised to hear it." Raley's eyes narrowed; not by much, but MacNally caught the gesture. "I never liked Kjarsta Zoltis. The man was a crook. I stayed as far away from him as I could. I'm not surprised to hear some of the Lost Platoon worked for him — the military tends to hire men from the rougher edges of society. But I would be bothered to learn we hired some of the same men. Oh, I don't mean to say you're wrong, Lieutenant. Our oversight in those days wasn't what it is today."

"Were you aware Zoltis died a short time ago?"

"I heard about that. It was good news." Raley's smile was gone. "Was there anything else, Lieutenant?"

"No." MacNally stood and grabbed the data tag from the desk.

"I'm sorry I wasn't of much help."

"Me too," MacNally said truthfully. He stopped in front of *La Gioconda* and gave her another look. He didn't like her. Like most women, she seemed to be laughing at MacNally.

"If this little tart is worth as much as you say she is, you've got a funny way of protecting her. She's a bit out in the open, don't you think? Women have a way of straying, you know." He chuckled at his own joke.

"She's well protected. I own the building, Lieutenant. And there are only two ways in and out. As you may have noticed coming in, there are multiple layers of security. My girl won't stray. I have more faith in her than you have in your wife."

"I'm not married, Raley." MacNally stopped at the elevator, smiling at his host.

"My mistake. And thank you for your concern. You think like a cop. I like that."

MacNally hit the button on the elevator, "I *am* a cop, Raley."

Russell called as soon as the doors had closed, but with too much interference on the call. MacNally had to wait until he was outside the building before he could make a solid connection.

"You're gonna want to hear this, MacNally." Russell sounded excited.

"Well, what is it?"

"I looked at the labtech report on your stairway jumper."

"MacDenny? What about him?" MacNally stood under the front awning and watched rain flood the street. The afternoon was prematurely dark. The weather was only getting worse.

"His mouth was stuffed with the same composition."

"Same what?" MacNally could not hear his partner.

"Same as the body from the landfill. Sand, clay, even a bit of Magtite. The stuff in the corpse's ribcage was the same thing in this guy's mouth."

MacNally heard him well enough this time. To Russell's credit, it was worth getting excited about. It was time he told Russell the truth. And then it might be time for them to make some real progress. Lepov would need to know about this as well.

MacNally endured the rain as he left the shelter of the awning. Maybe things were going to start working in his favor. That would be a welcome change.

61

I don't know how long I lay in Calla's bed. If you asked me to give a definite answer, I would say it was three days. That's impossible, of course. It could not have been longer than twelve or fifteen hours. But that made little difference to me. I feverishly tried to sleep, and when I could not do that I tried to think of what I should do next.

I wanted to take Calla and run. But there was nowhere to run. It was the Lazaretto, after all, a prison like none other; a city where one lived and died surrounded by the mirage of normal life whose inhabitants knew full well they were trapped in a deadly world they could never leave. As trapped as we were in that windowless room, we would have been just as trapped had we fled outside its walls.

Bernham's body preyed upon my heart. It was still there in the front room. I could not do anything with it. All I could do was thank God Calla could not see it and try to ignore it as I crossed through that room from the hall into the kitchen. I still had to make meals for us. I still had to care for Calla like nothing had happened. It wasn't by choice. I had no way to contact Mr. Zoltis. And Fortunado had not come back.

The angel in the frame, I suspected, would share my horror at what had transpired. But I was shocked to see her face; the face was not just disturbed by it all, it was also pleased. Had she had wanted this to happen? Every time I saw this expression I turned away, terrified at the implications. Was I pleased? Had I wanted Bernham dead? Could I have killed him to save Calla, or even my own honor? The angel knew the answer. I detested her for the silent accusation and dared her to prove it. But she could not prove it and I could not disprove it. Fortunado had interfered and the truth had been put on hold. But the question burned within me: could I have fought back enough to kill the man?

Removing Calla's dinner dishes from her room, I carried them to the kitchen. I had become so accustomed to the idea of a dead man lying in that room that I was startled to see a figure standing in the center of it as I passed. I dropped the dishes and I'm sure I cried out.

Kjarsta Zoltis stood over Bernham's body, a puzzled expression on his face. He gave me a hard stare, his eyes moving from me to Bernham, then back to me again.

"Mr. Zoltis," I barely managed to whisper. I'd been controlling my emotions just enough to take care of Calla. But seeing her father there meant I did not have to bear this alone anymore. I could feel the shakes begin to overtake me. I tried to explain what he was seeing. "He...Bernham...he tried..."

"Are you hurt?" he asked dispassionately.

"Bernham tried to—"

"Shut up, woman. I can see what's happened. I asked—are you hurt?"

"No," I shook my head.

"Dumb sonofabitch tangled with the wrong cat, huh?" I could see he wanted to smile but his lips ended in a grimace.

"But I—" he wasn't in the mood to let me finish a sentence.

"I don't want to hear any of it. Do you understand? How's the girl?"

I was mortified to realize he thought I had killed Bernham. He did not simply accuse me of being capable of such a thing, but had flatly assumed I had. I did not correct him because I was also disturbed to hear him call Calla the girl, as if she meant nothing to him. I assured him she was safe.

"Then get back to her. Stay in your room and I'll handle this." *He looked down at the heap that had once been our queer and surly roommate, no longer hiding his amusement.*

I did as he commanded. I stayed in the room the rest of that day. Later on, I could hear men moving about in the front room. Afterwards, it became quiet. I wasn't sure if Zoltis and whatever men he had called in were finished and gone. But I did not come out to see if the body was gone. I was too content to stay hidden.

Mr. Zoltis finally came back. And he had brought a new man with him.

"This is Morvees. He'll watch over you now."

"Hello, Miss." *The young man nodded to me. He rocked forward in a half-bowing motion that I was sure he meant to be taken as subservient. Maybe it was because of my recent ordeal with Bernham, but I took his bowing and scraping to be something more like the motions of a predatory bird watching its prey.*

"And where's the little chitti, eh?" *Morvees ducked his head and looked around the room. "I'm sure she's a fine little chitti."*

"She's no concern of yours," *Calla's father warned him. "Stay away from her."*

"Oh, absolutely, Mr. Zoltis." *He pulled back and wiped at his mouth. "The little chitti won't even know I'm here. I know all about how delicate chittis can be. Hope to get one of my own one day."*

I did not speak with them long. I went back to the room and locked it. Our situation had not improved in the least. I was finally beginning to see that I was going to have to take charge of Calla's future. If she were ever to get free of the Lazaretto and live a normal life, I would have to make it happen on my own.

I knew I had to get her out of there, with or without her father's help.

62

Sun hurried back to Chitti's office, in need of the younger woman's solid, no-nonsense presence. Meeting Morvees had scared her. She should have taken Lepov's advice and gone there only with Lt. MacNally or Pete Landon. It wasn't uncommon for Sun to call herself *stupid* from time to time, but this might have been one of her more prominently stupid moments in life. That old man's eyes, which had been all she could see through the crack in the door, were frightening. She could believe he had tried to kill Lepov. What might he have done to her? It chilled her all the more to remember her insistence that he let her into the apartment.

She decided not to tell Lepov about the incident. He would be angry. And that was the last thing she wanted. She didn't want him to start thinking she was a bubble-headed woman. Despite the disturbing run-in with Anton Morvees, Sun still had the presence of mind to guess that Gregor Lepov did not take well to women who couldn't use their heads. And she certainly wanted Gregor Lepov to take well to her.

Chitti was unfazed when Sun told her about Morvees.

"You're just getting a little tired, Sun, too caught up in all of this."

"You don't think Anton Morvees is dangerous?" Sun considered telling Chitti Lepov's story about the attempt on his life but decided against it.

"He's about as dangerous as John Yarmin. They're both old soldiers who have been abused by a cruel system. There is no question these are disturbed men. But I would not label grouchy, bitter men as dangerous. They're annoying, I'll grant you. But that's all."

"You don't seem to mind them." Sun sat at her borrowed desk and tried to keep Chitti talking. Chitti's self-assurance was doing wonders for Sun's anxiety. "Why are you here? What is your interest in these men?"

"I have a personal stake in the Lost Platoon." Chitti hesitated. "My father was a member of that unit. He's dead now. But I still have all his memories. He filled my head with stories of the combat glory of *Baker's Bastards*. He didn't know that I soaked up all the sad stories too. Of the exile, and how he and his friends were so badly mistreated. The lost dreams and hopes of so many men. They used to get together from time to time, and talk about what might have been. But that didn't last long. It was too hard on them. They all ended up drifting off to be alone in their despair."

Sun was shocked to hear Chitti speak like that. Emotion was the last thing she had expected to hear from this hard-edged woman. Even as she told her tale, there was no hint of self-pity, no blush of acrimony. Sun would never have guessed that Chitti had personal ties to any of this.

"And now you're doing what you can to help them all."

"No one else was doing it."

"So I'm here for you," Sun thought out loud, "you're one of the survivors we are trying to help."

"I don't really need help, Sun. I'm happy to stay right here. Even after the last of the platoon dies, I'll be here. There's always someone to help."

Sun thought about what the Obenlans had told her. The platoon had been told not to have children. Children would not have been allowed to leave the Lazaretto. Chitti would never be allowed to leave the Lazaretto. This tough young woman would be forced to live out her life in this filthy, deadly city. The thought was overwhelming to Sun. She turned away from Chitti and looked out the window to keep from tearing up.

It was still raining. Did it ever not rain? Maybe the Lazaretto could not help but cry as well. Maybe the rain had only come after the years of despair and sorrow had saturated this moon. It had once been thought that the actions of men could melt the Terran icecaps. Was it possible that here, the wretched lives of men could coerce the heavens to weep?

A worn and shaggy face caught her attention on the street. It was the same man she had seen her first day there. He was sitting on his box again, staring at the Society's front windows. Sun could not tell if he could see her or not, but she saw a weak smile cross his lips. Was he smiling at his own reflection? Or was he just flinching against the rain that fell on his cheeks?

"Chitti," Sun asked, still watching the man in the street, "do you know that man?"

Chitti had to lean over to see the man. She nodded as she answered. "His name is Cecil."

"What's wrong with him?"

"Nothing." Chitti turned back to her desk. "Cecil's perfectly healthy. He could leave any time he wanted to. He likes coming down here because he wants sympathy. He wants to be attended to like a child. I've told him to go away. To go back home. He won't. And I won't coddle him anymore. There are not enough resources here to waste on him."

Seemingly able to hear them, Cecil stood and stretched. Scooping up his box, he limped out of sight. Sun couldn't decide which part of Chitti's story was worse; Cecil's obvious craving for attention, or Chitti's pragmatic dismissal of him.

Sun had neglected her paperwork and it was time to correct that. She activated her deskscreen and began to fill out assessments on each of the living platoon members. It would be a long afternoon.

As she began her personal assessment of Anton Morvees, she repeated her question to Chitti about his potential for violence.

"Chitti, do you really believe Anton is not capable of violence?"

"Sun, let me show you something." Chitti reached down and picked up a black satchel. "I carry this bag everywhere. And here's one reason why."

Chitti withdrew a small black object and set it on her desktop. Sun recognized it immediately.

"That's a Para-Lazer." She'd only ever seen them in the Army. They delivered a surgical shock to the nervous system that rendered the victim immobile for as long as twenty hours. Lepov's shockhammer was a child's toy in comparison. "I thought weapons were illegal in the Lazaretto."

"They are. I keep this with me for protection. But you see, someone once told me this gun was more dangerous to me than to anyone else. Statistics suggest that I'll end up being shot by my own weapon rather than someone else's. But I don't believe that. There is nothing inherently dangerous about it. But if I mishandle it, or allow someone else to get their hands on it, then it becomes dangerous to me. But as long as I'm careful, it can't hurt me. Anton is not dangerous as long as you're careful with him. But that's the way most people are."

"Okay, but I can't help but think about what John Yarmin said. He clearly wanted me to investigate each of these men. I am sure he was warning me that one or more of them was up to no good. And when you consider what happened to Mr. MacDenny—"

"What do you mean?"

"Well, it is hard to believe Mr. MacDenny died either accidentally or through his own will. And consider that we were going to talk to him after John Yarmin told us to investigate everyone thoroughly. Now, if Anton Morvees knew I was going to speak to Silva MacDenny, isn't it possible he got there first? That he did not want us talking to Mr. MacDenny?"

"How imaginative, Sun. But I think it's a little *over*-imaginative." Chitti turned completely in her chair to give Sun her full attention. "I told you John has a tendency to indulge in conspiracy theories. And even if you're right, that would make Ben and Chaz suspects too."

"Well," Sun smiled, "I didn't suggest they could have done it after seeing both of them. Ben is such a sweet man. And Mr. Grimion does not seem to be able to—"

"Have enough coherent thoughts to commit a murder?" It was Chitti's turn to smile. "I have to agree with that. Chaz doesn't have enough coherent thoughts in one day to do much of anything. But you still would have to prove that Anton knew you were going to Silva's. Or that he knew what John said to you. You see how much of a stretch all of this is?"

"I see what you mean," Sun said, and she meant it. "But I can't shake the feeling that there is something not right about Morvees. Did I tell you what he said when I mentioned that the VHB would be giving him compensation money? He laughed at me, and said that it was too late. That after tonight, he wouldn't need it. Doesn't that suggest that something odd is going on?"

"Are you sure that's what he said?" Chitti drew down her eyebrows as she considered what Sun was saying. "I admit that sounds odd, but he probably just meant he was going gambling tonight. He and John can't keep away from those grimy little gambling rooms on the West End. I gave up trying to get them to stay away from them."

"You think that's all he meant?" Sun bit her lip. "I'm beginning to think I'm not the person to make these assessments. I can't seem to make a decent judgment about these men. The next thing you'll tell me is that Ben Obenlan is a mad dog."

"No," Chitti quickly answered, "but he had a nickname that was something close to that back in the war."

Sun watched Chitti closely but couldn't tell if the woman was serious or if she was just having a bit of fun. She finally decided it must be the latter. She wasn't going to begin believing that Ben, that sweet man who'd found love in the Lazaretto, was a crazy killer.

The idea of someone finding love in the Lazaretto made her smile. Was it presumptuous to think she might have done the same? She hoped not.

63

He was doing it again. Only this time, he was trying something new.

It had occurred to Lepov that if Lilly had been transporting a piece of art for Raley, then she would have had to declare it at Lazaretto Registration. And if Lepov could verify that she had indeed brought in a piece for Raley, then he would know she hadn't been lying. At least that part of her story would be confirmed.

Verifying would be a waste of time. Lepov knew she wasn't lying about her business deal. If anything, she would make sure the paperwork was right to camouflage any of her other activities. That's how Lepov would have done it. And she was as smart as Lepov, if not more so.

There was little for Lepov to do until Pete Landon returned his call. Lepov had never been able to think of a way to get inside the apartment without MacNally's help. He was left with few options.

It hadn't taken long to verify Della Sahdjec's assertion that Bernham was a dead end. There was no trace of the man after he had been exiled in the Lazaretto, save for his name listed as the owner of the apartment. He had found such little evidence of the man, Lepov became convinced that Bernham had either died—in which case the paperwork was never properly completed—or had managed to slip out of the Lazaretto under a false name.

That left him time to check out Lilly's story. He broke into the Entry/Registration databank with the computer equivalence of a hairpin. No one was interested in protecting that kind of information. It was something to think about later. Maybe he'd even mention it to MacNally. After all, if the Lazaretto's goal was to regulate the flow of travelers with contagious pathogens, then they really should take better care of their entry logs. Someone with a little imagination could manipulate the logs to fast-track someone through the quarantine system.

Once inside the system, Lepov had trouble finding what he was looking for. He came to several dead legs in the process and had to back up and start again. Maybe that was why security was lax; the system was so poorly designed, they figured no one could accomplish anything once inside it.

Two more attempts finally brought up the data he needed. But when he read through Special Declarations, he found no listing for Lilly Stewart. He tried several other sub-headings, but her name wasn't anywhere. He repeated the process using Cam Raley's name. The ownership of the piece had to be in his name, so it might have been declared under his name. Raley was not listed.

A careful examination of every sub-heading left him with the conclusion that Lilly had not declared a piece of art upon entry into the Lazaretto; proof that verification wasn't always a waste of time.

She had lied again. At what point was he going to stop looking for excuses and start drawing the obvious conclusions? Damn it. This whole business about Lilly was getting out of hand.

Lepov wiped the screen clean and thought about the pack of cigarettes in the pocket of his coat. That was not the way to deal with this, he scolded himself. Forget the cigarettes, and forget Lilly. She said she would call, and she would have an explanation. The simple truth was that the woman he had partially seen in Morvees apartment was not Lilly. That was the end of it. It was not worth debating anymore. Lilly was not mixed up with Morvees. She never had been and never would be. Not Lilly.

All of this was distracting him from Morvees. The bastard had tried to kill him. *That* was the key point. So how could he learn more about Morvees' intentions?

He was thinking of taking another crack at Della Sahdjec. But he knew that would only end in grief. Lepov didn't have the stomach for forcing information out of people. He could have done it to someone like Morvees. And that might yet have to happen. But the Sahdjec woman was a different matter. If she knew anything, it would not be terribly important. She was right. The man to talk to was Kjarsta Zoltis. If only he could speak with the dead.

So it came down to Anton Morvees. Was that his only option? Should he just tell MacNally to pick the man up and interrogate him? Lazaretto law gave MacNally a great deal of leeway in his pursuit of answers. The planets had abandoned Colony law years ago. As each of the colonies had begun to mirror Earth, they left behind the laws that had been necessary to govern the environs of the wild, wide-open Euxine System. Terran law had brought back a greater respect for civil rights and due process. But not in the Lazaretto. As a government institution, the prevailing law was more in line with military and colony law.

The application of this for MacNally was his freedom to interrogate suspects as he saw fit. And as many of those suspects had discovered, MacNally found violence to be quite fitting.

But Lepov was a former cop from Bukovina who didn't like to abandon civil rights completely. However, he was tempted to let MacNally take a shot at Morvees in this instance; Morvees didn't deserve rights.

Lepov knew he was hesitant to call MacNally because he would have to admit he wouldn't be any help to the man. Well, that wasn't going to be shocking news to the Lieutenant.

MacNally answered right away.

"The only thing I've been able to find out about that apartment is that Kjarsta Zoltis has had that place for a long time. He had the ownership under a few different names, never his own. One of them was a retired nurse. She insists Zoltis had the place."

"That fits," MacNally's response surprised him. "Zoltis was employing Lost Platoon soldiers. MacDenny, Morvees, and Yarmin. There were others. The jobs listed were always vague. A lot of money was moving around."

"Which leaves us with nothing," Lepov said. "Zoltis is dead. He can't tell us anything. And with Reno dead, I doubt anybody knows what was going on except Yarmin and Morvees."

"What does Reno have to do with it?" MacNally asked.

"He and Zoltis were partners. You remember? Hell, you were the one to tell me about it. But I confirmed that connection with some data I found on the Shipping Port. I suspect Reno was working with Zoltis a long time before he became Chief Administrator."

"I hadn't thought about Reno. That's not a bad idea."

"It's not a useful idea. Did you forget that he and I had a bad run-in?" The last time Lepov had seen Reno, he was burning to death in his private car. The fact that Lepov had set the fire was something Lepov tried to forget.

"Do you really think Reno would know something about this?"

"You mean *did* he know about this apartment? Who knows? But he was in deep with Zoltis. I would imagine he knew something. Maybe burning the man to death wasn't one of my better ideas." Lepov had never intended to kill the man. He'd only accidentally set Reno on fire while distracting him in an effort to save Lilly.

"Yeah," MacNally's voice was hard to hear over the connection, "maybe so."

"Sounds like you've got something on your mind, MacNally."

"Well, Russell came up with something a little while ago. Silva MacDenny's mouth was stuffed with the same soil composition that was in the old corpse under the building."

"For God's sake, Mac. We gotta get inside that apartment!"

"I'm starting to agree with you. But there're three things I want to do first. I want to talk to John Yarmin. And I'm gonna have to disclose everything we have to my Captain before I drag Morvees in here and we break down his door."

"That's only two things," Lepov said. "What's the third?"

"I want to talk to Claude Reno."

Lepov laughed. "Sure, why not talk to Kjarsta Zoltis at the same time? They ought to both be sharing a room in hell."

"No," MacNally said without a trace of humor. "Zoltis is dead."

"Reno's dead too. I killed him, remember?"

"Yeah, I remember. Only Claude Reno's not quite as dead as Kjarsta Zoltis."

Lepov swore like a deep-space trader.

The Thief had only to wait for night. Everything was ready. And he had managed to keep the Liar out of his hair. She would never know he had changed the schedule. And she would never catch up. She would know what he had done—would be able to do nothing but curse. He didn't care. Let her curse. He'd be far away by then.

It was a solid plan until he remembered he had vowed to put out those beady little eyes of hers. He had nearly forgotten. That wouldn't do. No, he couldn't leave her here or he'd spend the rest of his days watching his back.

This type of thing would take careful work. She was shrewd. No doubt. She wouldn't walk into just any trap. Not without a great deal of coaxing, anyway. The more complicated the trap, the more likely she was to spot it. He would have to keep it simple.

He called her. Now was the time to keep a cool head. She'd know something was wrong if he didn't control his excitement.

"We need to talk," he said, his voice just above a whisper.

"Can I help you?" She couldn't acknowledge him. She wasn't

alone.

"You can, you can. It's tonight. I changed everything." He whimpered as softly as he could. Why had he just told her what he was going to do? She was a devil, spinning magic to drag the words out of his mouth. "Tonight is the last night before we do it," he weakly added to confuse her.

She did not reply; too shy to speak in front of whomever she was with. But had she detected his lie? Was she so clever? No. She had never been clever.

"Come tonight, but late. Not before midnight." He chose his next lie carefully. "Bring what you need. I've already taken everything I need. We'll stay here through tomorrow, stay out of sight. And then we'll finally have it."

"Okay," she said. The careful tone of her voice confirmed his guess that she was with someone.

"Wait, wait." He drew a deep breath. "Can you go back to my room? I left the razor. You know the one. I'll need it."

Yes, he'd need the razor all right. If he was gonna put out her eyes, he might as well do it right. Razors did more than scrape stubble off a man's throat.

"That's fine," the Liar answered.

"Good, good. Then I'll see you then. You're going to be so pleased." He suppressed his laughter.

The Thief had trouble calming down after that. She was coming. Coming too late. And he'd be ready for her. He had laid his plan. Tonight he would execute it. And when *she* came through the door, his improvisation would close out the deal. And he would walk away, the sole victor.

That little mouthy dish from the Army would not be able to take credit for his good fortune. The Liar with the spying eyes wouldn't be able to take any either. That Engineer with the silly brain had learned the hard way that no one could steal his glory. Even that Fish he'd caught had discovered just how impossible it was to tear away a scrap of another man's glory.

That had always been the fate he could not beat. First it had been the war. There was always the platoon scrabbling to take his glory from him. All of the credit went to the unit as a whole. Even when he did earn serious recognition and was awarded his ring, the Army had to step in and give those other idiots a ring too. But what had they ever done? The Thief's skills as a soldier had been unmatched. Why couldn't anyone see that?

Even after he had come to the Lazaretto, the Shipper was there to take his glory. Who had worked out the plan? Who had put it in motion? No one but the Thief, that's who. What had the Shipper done? He had thought he could buy the glory. But what was money? It meant nothing.

But it was the Strongman who had gone too far. He had broken all the agreements. He had stripped the Thief and his partners of their glory. The Strongman had torn it from their hands and left them to die a slow and inglorious death. The Strongman was to blame. It was time to show the Strongman who was stronger.

Tonight, he would right every wrong. Tonight he would avenge the old and create the new. There was glory to be had, and it was just a fingertip away.

The Thief breathed in deeply and exhaled, trembling. It had been so long. So very, very long. He was tired and the night could not come fast enough.

65

MacNally left the precinct and headed toward the West End — a part of town he hated. The West End had been dying for many years. The only people keeping it alive were the trashy vice dealers who preyed on the bored and lonely Lazars passing through the Lazaretto. Unfortunately, Center City statutes allowed gambling, drinking and whoring, as long as it stayed confined to the West End and out of sight of the few good people who traveled into and out of the Lazaretto.

Without this kind of industry, the West End would long ago have dried up and blown away. Nobody wanted to inhabit a zone this close to the Shipping Port. It was unhealthy, no matter what any government official said. MacNally had seen the evidence. Sickness hovered over that end of town, and not just physical sickness; something always went wrong inside the head of anyone living within its borders.

From what those two women had told him, John Yarmin might be suffering from a screwed-up head. Even so, MacNally intended to question him. If Yarmin were involved in this, MacNally wasn't going to let him play stupid.

Outside Yarmin's building, MacNally climbed the front steps and closed in on the double doors. He stood still for a moment, watching the street behind him. A few people were moving around, but no one paid him any attention. The afternoon was rolling into early evening, and MacNally hoped he hadn't come too late. The red-haired skirt had said Yarmin was a drinker and a gambler. If that were the case, then he might have already headed out for the night.

No, MacNally decided, Yarmin was most likely a night crawler. He would wait until it was completely dark. Guys like Yarmin didn't like to be out in daylight, even when that daylight was as gray and dim as the Lazaretto's.

Four flights up, MacNally came out of the stairwell and looked around the dark hallway. It was filthy. It stank of poverty. The few men who still lived in this kind of place were proud jackasses who should have allowed someone to get them out a long time ago. It wasn't hard for MacNally to feel no sympathy for them. Men like Yarmin had plenty of opportunity to get out of a place like this. The fact that he didn't spoke volumes.

Basically, MacNally instinctively thought, this Yarmin was an honest-to-God rat.

He hit the door with the back of one beefy hand and called Yarmin. There was no reason to be subtle. MacNally hit the door again for emphasis. A dog started barking like an idiot from one of the other apartments.

"What do you want?" A voice that had to be Yarmin's shouted from the other side of the door.

"I want you to open your door. I'm a cop." No use hiding that fact. MacNally had seen Yarmin's fire escape from the street. None of the ladders had enough rungs to help an old man slip away with ease.

"Hang on," Yarmin grunted. MacNally could hardly hear him.

The door scraped and clattered before finally swinging open. Yarmin defiantly eyed MacNally.

"My name's MacNally. Lt. Ed MacNally. I've got some questions for you." That absurd dog wouldn't shut up.

"Show me your badge and then tell me what you want. I've got things to do."

"I'll show you my badge," MacNally forced his way into the room without showing Yarmin the first glimpse of identification, "and I'll show you my desk, my holding cell, my little row of concrete isolation cells, and anything else you're interested in seeing. Later."

"Okay, so you're a cop." Yarmin shoved his door closed and shook his head. "You're arrogant enough to be one, that's for sure."

Yarmin limped to the only chair in the front room and sank into it. The old soldier took a few deep breaths, expelled them with force, and finally studied MacNally with a sideways look.

"So what do you want?" he asked.

"Major Sun Uijong told me you had an interest in knowing what your old buddies from the Lost Platoon were up to. That true?"

"Is that the little thin nag the Army sent out here? Short black hair with tasty legs?" The constant but muffled sound of the barking dog was the only noise in the room for a few moments.

"Major Uijong tells me you want your former comrades investigated." MacNally did not bother with Yarmin's bait.

"Yeah, that must be her. I don't remember names too well anymore." The smile on his face told MacNally Yarmin remembered her name just fine. "What does this have to do with you cops?"

"I want to know about Anton Morvees." Yarmin kept careful control over his facial reaction. If MacNally hadn't known better, he might have believed that Yarmin didn't know Morvees existed. "Your old sergeant is up to something. I'll bet you know what it is."

Yarmin sat back in his chair and let out a slow breath. Some of his cocky defiance came out with it. He ran a hand through his closely cropped hair and smiled wickedly. "You're a dumb bastard, MacNally. I should have known that dumb bitch would do something like this. She don't know what she's done."

MacNally watched the old man laugh nervously. It was obvious something was not funny. "She hasn't done a thing. I caught on to this and I'm here for some answers. She has no idea I'm here."

"Doesn't matter," Yarmin waved MacNally away in the same way he would swat at a fly. "Get out of here. Let's hope he don't know you're here."

"So you know enough about Morvees that he'll come after you if you talk to me, is that it?"

"Don't go promising me protection," Yarmin said with deadly gravity.

"I don't intend to. But I'm here already. So it won't matter if you keep your mouth shut. Will it? You wanted the Major to find out what was going on without getting involved, right? Thought you could stay out of it. Thought you could keep what you know under your hat."

"I don't know enough to talk. You don't get that. I don't know enough to explain it to you. I just knew enough to point the Army in the right direction. I can't help it if the Army sent a woman out here to bungle it all."

"So point me in the right direction." MacNally wanted to come down hard on this old man, but had the uneasy feeling Yarmin was telling the truth. It was possible he didn't know specifics.

"What more do you need? MacDenny's dead, right?"

"How'd you know?"

"I didn't. I just figured that was the next thing to happen."

"Really?" MacNally came closer to Yarmin, with a puzzled look in his eye. Had he been wrong about Yarmin? The precinct had not released information about MacDenny yet. How would Yarmin know about his death? "Were you out on the town last night, John?"

"Don't be stupid." Yarmin pushed himself out of his chair and walked off toward the kitchen. MacNally followed. "You're not thinking right."

"Maybe I've been thinking all wrong," MacNally said. "You ever been to Chettleham Keep?"

"What the hell's that?" Yarmin pulled a stained yellow cup from the back corner of a wall cabinet and twisted a faucet handle over the sink. Water splashed into the cup. He drank it quickly and then looked at MacNally, waiting for an answer.

"When's the last time you saw Silva MacDenny?"

"I haven't seen MacDenny for a long time. Two months, maybe three."

"That when you killed him?" MacNally didn't really think the question made sense, but he was mostly interested in Yarmin's reaction to it.

"Let me help you out, MacNally. He owed me money. That's a solid motive, right? Only it's not. It wouldn't make sense for me to kill him the last time I saw him, because the last time I saw him he told me he was about to make a lot of money. And he wanted me to get in on it too. He said Sarge had a job for him. That's Morvees. Always had a job for us to do. But I gave that up years ago. That's why I live here. I don't do jobs like that anymore."

"Of course you don't, John. Zoltis and Reno are dead, right? No one left to work for." MacNally stopped to think about what Yarmin was saying. "But if that's the case, who had the job? Morvees working on his own now?" He was doing his best to stay with Yarmin. Even though MacNally knew none of the specifics, he knew enough to keep Yarmin talking.

"What do you mean no one's left? They could always work for Raley."

"Raley?"

"Don't tell me you didn't know Raley was part of this?"

"Part of what?"

"MacNally, I said I wasn't going to talk about this. But I will tell you one thing. Morvees ain't working for anyone. Especially not Raley." Yarmin laughed out loud. "You really are a stupid bastard. At least I figured out MacDenny was dead. I hadn't heard from him. It'd been too long. Silva was a dumb bastard too."

"Yarmin—"

"The longer you stay here the more trouble I get in." Yarmin, still holding the stained cup, worked his way over to the door and pulled it open. The dog was still barking.

"I could bring you in and make you talk." MacNally meant it.

"Maybe you could, but it wouldn't be worth the effort." The barking grew louder; the sound of their voices had enraged the dog. Without warning, Yarmin screamed at the dog. The barking stopped.

"Sorry about that," Yarmin said in a more controlled voice.

"You should have done that at the beginning." MacNally walked away.

"Hey, MacNally." Yarmin waited for him to turn around. "Watch out for the daughter." He didn't say any more as he shut the door, leaving MacNally alone in the hall.

MacNally needed to talk to Captain Fisher. It was time to let his boss know what was going on. And then, if Fisher agreed, he'd bring Yarmin in. While he was at it, he'd do the same with Morvees. There was no reason to wait any longer. Maybe if Yarmin and Morvees both knew the other had been picked up, someone would talk.

MacNally hoped so. Because the truth was, they had no idea what was truly going on. And if both officers of the Lost Platoon kept their mouths shut, then he'd have to hope Russell could find enough evidence to prove one of them had killed MacDenny. If not, all they could do was charge Morvees with the attempted murder of Gregor Lepov. And that wasn't much of a satisfactory ending.

Leaving the building, MacNally briefly wondered what Yarmin had meant about a daughter. He'd have to make Yarmin explain after they brought him back to the precinct.

66

Once the idea entered her head, Sun couldn't shake it. By the time she'd finished with two of the assessments, she had convinced herself it was a good idea. It did not take long to close out her assessment documents and bid goodbye to Chitti. She was afraid Chitti might offer to take her to dinner again, but either Chitti had forgotten or was no longer interested. That was fine with Sun.

Her idea was to find Gregor Lepov and take him to dinner. She was having trouble deciding how to implement it. If she called ahead, he might find an excuse to beg off. If she arrived at his office unannounced, however, he might already have plans and she would have to withdraw awkwardly. But if he didn't have plans, then he might be persuaded to join her since she'd already physically be there.

She decided to go to his office. She wanted to ask herself what was the worst that could happen, but that was one of those foolish questions that should never be asked. There were too many possible answers. And most of them weren't good at all.

Before she could change her mind, she grabbed a passing TransitCar and it sped her across the city.

Lepov's door was closed and there was no light shining through its frosted glass. Sun felt foolish. He wasn't there. She'd come to his office and he was gone.

A blue light blinked off and on beside the door handle. If she remembered correctly, it was a signal that the occupant had left a message: an older system, but she had seen them still in use on some military bases. She grasped the door handle, making sure her palm made full contact with the handle's surface.

The blue light stopped blinking, holding a solid blue. After a pause, Sun heard Lepov's voice.

"If you are looking for Gregor Lepov, hang on while this machine calls me. If it finds me, I'll speak with you in a minute."

Sun waited. She was surprised how good it felt to hear his voice. She could tell he had been uncomfortable recording the message. It was nice to know there were some things that made him nervous.

"This is Lepov." This voice was no recording. "Can I help you?"

"Gregor, this is Sun Uijong."

"Sun? You're at my office again? Is something wrong?"

"No. I'm sorry I came without calling. I don't know what I was thinking." Lying seemed preferable to the embarrassment of the truth.

"Well, don't leave," Lepov said, "I'll unlock the office and you can wait for me. I'll only be a few minutes."

Sun heard the door lock slide and opened it with a gentle push. "Are you sure you don't mind?"

"I just had to come back to my place to grab something to eat. I'll be back in a few minutes."

That was bad news. How could she ask him to dinner if he had just eaten something? Sun went into the office and shut the door. Lights came on automatically.

"You don't need to come back on my account," Sun tried to dissuade him. "I can get with you tomorrow. It's really not important."

"Don't give it another thought. I'll get there as soon as I can. Just make yourself comfortable. Okay?" He shut down the connection.

Sun stood in the center of his office alone. She couldn't stop the butterfly feeling in her stomach. She should have been embarrassed at her impulsive interest in this man, but she wasn't.

The first time she'd been in his office, she'd only seen it as the office of a man she could hire for protection. Now, she saw it differently; the office of a man who made her feel safe and secure. There was a world of difference between the two.

The office was plain; the desk big, black, and uglier than an Army transport truck. Lepov must have found it in a junkyard. It had to be older than the Lazaretto. She was surprised to see the deskscreen working and running several scripts. She would have been willing to bet Lepov spent his days investigating with a broken deskscreen. That would have fit him.

A worn couch hunched against one wall. Besides that, there was precious else of distinction in the room. Sun briefly considered sitting in his chair behind the desk but opted instead for a chair in the corner nearest the front door, settling in to wait for his return.

Only a few minutes had passed when she heard the elevator doors open at the end of the hall. He had come back sooner than expected. Her heart beat faster as she realized she did not know what she would say. How would she explain her presence?

Anyone with an ounce of brains would have called ahead to ask if he were busy. Listening to his footsteps down the hall, she decided her dinner idea had been a mistake.

Jumping out the window was an option, but she lacked the courage to leap from the third story to the street below. It was true that broken legs or ankles might be less painful than trying to explain that she'd come by to entice him into a date, but she remained in the chair nonetheless.

The steps in the hallway slowed to a stop just outside the door. It was partially open and Sun waited. He did not come in immediately. He hesitated.

"Gregor?" She paled at the sound of her own voice; she sounded like a little girl. An eager one at that.

The door swung open, but it was not Gregor Lepov standing in the doorway. A woman looked at her. She was strikingly beautiful, with long white hair tied into a pony-tail that seemed to sprout from the top of her head. The woman stared with dark eyes.

"I guess Gregor is not here at the moment," the woman finally said. She took two steps into the office and carefully looked around.

"He's gone home for a few minutes. He'll be back soon." Sun felt a chill as the woman came closer. The high arch of the woman's eyebrows made her look simultaneously amused and angry.

"I'd like to wait for him, if you don't mind." She stood next to one of the chairs that faced Lepov's desk but did not sit.

"That's fine." Sun was silent a while. The woman continued to stand. "I'm Sun Uijong,"

"Lilly Stewart," the woman nodded stiffly. "I wasn't aware Gregor had hired an assistant."

"Oh, no." Sun's eyes flared, realizing what Lilly was saying. "I'm not working with Gregor. I'm just a friend."

The look on Lilly's face compounded Sun's feeling that she had just said something childish. The woman stood like a Duchess or Marquise surveying house servants. But there was more than haughtiness in her eyes; Sun also saw sadness. Put it all together and she was intimidating—Sun was tempted to use the word *frightening*.

"You're a friend? I'm glad to hear it. We have that in common."

Lilly smiled and lowered her head. "I'm afraid I've only known Gregor for about six months or so. Have you known him long?"

"We only just met yesterday, to be honest." Sun could see the relief in the other woman's eyes. "In fact, we're not exactly friends; more or less acquaintances."

"I see."

Lilly was the taller of the two, and it didn't help Sun's lack of confidence that this mysterious woman was standing while Sun remained seated. Sun wished the woman would take a seat.

They waited silently in the muffled atmosphere. By the time the elevator began to whine, announcing it was ascending with another passenger, Sun had begun to panic. If she had not been sure what she would say to Lepov before this woman arrived, she really had no idea what she should say now. It was too late to worry. She could hear him outside the door.

"You in there, Sun?" he called as he pushed open the door. He stopped abruptly at the sight of the woman, shifting his eyes from Lilly to Sun. "There you are. And here's Lilly. This is unexpected."

"Hello, Gregor," Lilly said.

Sun sprang toward the door. "Gregor, I'm sorry about dropping by like this. I'll come back tomorrow."

"Wait a minute," he put a hand out to stop her. "You came all the way over here for a reason and you haven't said what it is yet. Lilly," he turned smiled at Lilly, "I want you to meet Major Sun Uijong from Veterans' Health Benefits"

"We've met." Lilly smiled politely. "But she didn't mention she was a Major."

"Doesn't look like one, does she?" Lepov laughed a little. "Sun, this is Lilly Stewart, an old friend. Now, Lilly, if you don't mind, I'll need a few minutes to speak with Major Uijong."

"No," Sun stopped him. "It's not important. I was just coming to see if you'd eaten. But you have, so I'll call you in the morning."

"There's no need to run off." Lepov sounded angry.

"I think I'd better," Sun's voice faltered. Lilly Stewart hadn't said much since Lepov had come into the office, but Sun was sharp enough to see what was happening. Lilly was more than just an old friend. And the looks that Lepov and Lilly were giving each other—despite the fact that Lepov was doing his best not to pay undue attention to Lilly—told Sun enough of the story. She needed to leave them alone.

"Okay, Sun. I'll call you in the morning."

Sun nodded and said she would. She walked past him, careful not to hesitate as she did. She gave Lilly a quick look. Lilly was watching her with eyes that were not quite as haughty as they had been. Sun even thought she had seen a little kindness in them. She hoped so.

It was hard to choose a restaurant for dinner. Sun had little appetite. Even as she sipped the wine, she still felt the butterflies, only now they were flying for different reasons. She had never considered that there might be another woman in Lepov's life. And if Sun's instincts were right, Lilly Stewart was definitely a part of Lepov's life. Sitting in the restaurant, surrounded by waiters and fellow diners, Sun fought against tears.

She would have to wait for the morning, and hope.

67

We did not see the new man for several days after his arrival. I was sure I heard him in the night, going from his room to the kitchen, but I did not open our door to see. I felt uneasy about him and did not want to interact with him too much.

Calla was growing stronger. She was able to sleep through an entire night without interruption. She was in better spirits. I was able to joke with her. Every smile and wink of the eye told me she felt less pain in her chest each day. She found peace sitting with me in the bed, my arms wrapped around her, her head laid upon my shoulder.

I do not know how a child that age can soldier on through such an ordeal. Do they know that life had detoured them into the cruel world of sickness? Or does such a child think the torment is merely life itself? That they can expect such terrors on a continual basis from one day to the next? I tried to imagine how that might feel. We adults are not used to suffering trials without general expectations. I don't believe I could have endured with the dignity that Calla displayed. Who among us could have?

It was at this time that we crossed a waypoint that was particularly emotional for me. It had seemed that no matter how often I bathed the girl, she would immediately be in need of another cleaning; sweat, spittle, rejected food, there was always a need to clean her again. But there came a time when I bathed her, and she remained fresh and unsoiled for the rest of the day. When I did finally realize this, a fresh round of tears wet my cheeks. I don't think I fully understood how discouraging this aspect of her care had become to me until it had ended.

I no longer watched her with the intent of judging her hygienic state. I found I was able just to enjoy being with her. I could see her for what she was: a small bundle of long hair and chubby cheeks that needed to be held tightly. I had never before understood the link between cleanliness and the warmth of human touch.

Of course she wasn't the only one who was increasingly able to keep clean. My own physical condition improved along with hers. And we were both more willing to cling to each other in light of this.

She was not out of danger. Once or twice the dying virus attempted to reestablish itself within her lungs. But these were brief bouts that did not last more than a day. During such times I could see fear in her eyes and she would withdraw from me, afraid that all of the terror would come back to stay.

I knew what the girl needed. Seclusion was overshadowing her recovery. She needed to get out of that apartment. Beyond that, she also needed to get out of the Lazaretto. She needed a planet where the sun could shine on her round, red cheeks and fill her with energy and warmth.

This would never happen. Kjarsta Zoltis had no intention of sending his daughter away. When I tried to broach the subject with him, he only stared as he always did, and spoke with that same dispassion. "Don't be absurd. She's my daughter. I live in the Lazaretto. So will she."

I wanted to change that. I wanted to get her out. The more she recovered, the more determined I became to get her off that quarantine moon. But I was just a nurse, with no knowledge how to do this one thing beginning to dominate my desires. And the more I realized I would not be able to make good her escape, the more I despaired, the consequence being that the more Calla improved, the more unhappy I became.

Morvees finally spoke to us. And once he did, I wished he had never come out of his hole. My unhappiness for Calla's future switched instantly to fear.

"That's a sweet chitti you got there."

We had been lying in bed, my arms around Calla, never seeing or hearing Morvees open the door. I looked up, shocked to see him inside the room by two or three steps. Bernham had never come into Calla's room. I felt my arms tighten around her.

"What do you want?" I demanded.

"What does everyone want? A little chitti like you've got." Morvees slid a step nearer the bed. His hand was lifted in our direction, a long crooked finger pointing at Calla. "Where can you get one with such pretty hair? That's my question, you know."

I had been through enough with Bernham, and I wasn't going to let this man control me. I was shocked at my own resolve as I let go of Calla and gently laid her back against her pillows. Once assured that she was comfortable, I stood and turned around. Morvees had taken another step closer. He was smiling and looking at Calla.

"Leave this room. Get out!" I put my body between them and advanced against him. No longer able to see Calla, he flinched at my approach and backed away. I kept moving until he backpedaled into the hall.

"I was only saying how pretty she is," he said hastily. "You don't have to shout."

I slammed the door. He continued to defend himself, though I could not make out the muffled words. Eventually the sound faded, and I was left alone with Calla.

I had to get her out. I had to find a way. If these were the kind of men Kjarsta Zoltis hired, I had to get Calla away from them all. She would not be raised in such an environment. I would get her out at any cost.

68

"When you said you'd call me, I hadn't figured you meant that you'd call *on* me." Lepov walked to the door that Sun had left open and pushed it closed. "But I'm glad you did."

"She's very cute," Lilly said.

"Yeah, she's a cute kid. Can I take your coat?" He held out a hand.

"That cute kid seems quite interested in you, Gregor."

Lepov waited, staring Lilly down until she conceded and pulled off her wool coat and handed it to him.

"First of all, Lilly, I hardly know the girl. But if I did, I don't see how it would be any of your business." He didn't want to fight, but he'd be damned if he would let her make an issue out of Sun.

"It's not my business. Only an observation." Lilly approached the large windows facing the street and looked down. "I didn't come here to fight with you, Gregor."

Lepov smiled. "That's funny; I was just thinking the same thing. You want a drink or something?"

"No," she shook her head.

Lepov came close enough to his desk to see the blue icon on the deskscreen. He'd left the MoleRunner open, had meant to shut it down. Had she seen it? Would she know what it was? He needed a few seconds to shut it down but was afraid to draw attention to it. He opted to take off his hat and toss it over the icon.

"Sun and I crossed paths on similar cases." He felt compelled to explain. "We've both sort of helped the other a little. As a matter of fact, we met under funny circumstances. The fact is, we had a misunderstanding. Well, to put it bluntly, I assaulted her."

"That would explain the light in her eyes. We women like it when you get rough, Gregor. It's one of your more refined traits."

The words could have been a simple jest, but Lepov knew they weren't. He felt both ashamed and angry. Yes, he'd been rough with Lilly, but she too had a good deal of explaining to do. What did she expect? Was he just supposed to ignore what was patently obvious?

"I want you to answer a question, Lilly, and I don't want any nonsense. You don't know what's been going on here, but I have a hell of a good reason to demand to know what's going on."

"Okay," Lilly turned and raised an eyebrow. "What's the question?"

"How is it you brought a piece in for Raley but Lazaretto Registration doesn't show any declarations from you during entry?"

Lilly let out a deep breath and headed for the door. Lepov sidestepped to block her exit. He tried to grab her but she shied away.

"Lilly, don't leave. Answer my question."

"You know what the real problem is here, Gregor?"

"What?"

"Both of us are just doing what comes naturally for us. I'm complying with my client's requests, and you're investigating. That's just what we do. I run my business, and you question everything around you."

"That's it?" Lepov suspected she was right. "You couldn't declare it. Whatever it was you brought in for him, he didn't want it declared. Is it stolen?"

"No," she glared. "But if you have to know, the provenance on it is in question. There is a legal battle. Do you want me to give you the entire file? Or can you find that without my help as well?"

Lepov knew that this could only get worse. If she started asking questions about why he was running checks on her, he'd be tempted to tell her about the woman in Morvees' apartment. And once he did, she'd know he had suspected her of ordering his death. That was something he could never let her know. Not if he hoped to preserve their friendship.

"Why did you come up to my office?" It was a safe question to keep her from thinking about the fact he had been digging through Lazaretto Registration records.

"Believe it or not," she chuckled, "I wanted to see if I could fix things between us. I was going to tell you that, after this job, if it meant that much to you, I wouldn't take on jobs like this anymore. I wouldn't put myself in a position where I'd have to lie to you anymore."

For a moment Lepov saw the face of the Lilly he'd met at Comic Joe's; he could see her intelligent amusement that went right to his heart. He'd known that first day that Lilly was a woman who saw the world in ways no other woman could. And *he* liked what *she* saw. She wasn't easily fooled, nor was she controlled by cynicism. If she thought the world was silly and a good deal ironic, that was okay, as long as she handled herself better than those around her.

"You wouldn't have had to do that," Lepov countered. "And you still don't have to lie to me. All you have to do is tell me that you can't tell me the truth from time to time."

"And you'll just let it go?"

"I'd try," he answered firmly.

"Yes, I suppose you would. You'd try." She was standing beside the same chair Sun had been sitting in, and she lowered herself into it. "Gregor, I don't think we're very good for each other."

He ignored that—the kind of line that had little basis in fact, but was hard to combat. After all, that could be said of most friendships. There was always friction of some kind between friends and lovers. The mark of friendship was to work through friction. Hell, sometimes the greatest sign of true friendship was the ability to ignore the friction altogether.

"All I wanted was for you to come back. And when you did, you lied to me. You wouldn't even tell me you were here." So much for ignoring the friction.

"I explained that. See what I mean? This isn't going to improve."

"It can." Lepov wasn't sure he was right. Maybe Lilly was.

"I'm gonna go, Gregor. There's a quadrant closing and I'll be in it."

Just like that, Lepov thought, it was right back to the way it had been all along. He was going to remain in the Lazaretto, and she was going to leave. There should have been something to say that would have brought out a different result. But if so, he didn't know what it was.

"And when you call that girl..." Lilly grabbed her coat and opened the door. "...don't be so rough on her. We women talk tough, but we don't like our men as rough as we say we do."

The door slowly swung shut, stopping a finger's-width from closing. Lepov could hear the heels of her shoes tapping the length of the hallway.

He hadn't even said goodbye. He'd just let her leave. He deserved that. She not only should leave him, but she should never come back. He'd allowed a bent idea to infect his mind until he suspected the woman he loved of trying to kill him. No matter what might happen between them after this, it would never erase that singular sin. It didn't even matter if Lilly ever learned of his transgression. It was something that Lepov would never be able to shake.

After watching Lilly hail a TransitCar, Lepov stepped back from the window. Even now, standing in a room where no one but the walls could hear him, Lepov could not tell Lilly he was sorry. It was an inadequate phrase that ultimately meant nothing.

He pushed his hat away and stabbed a finger at the MoleRunner's blue icon. Once touched, it doubled in size and began displaying the locations in which Lilly's PDT had been documented. Lepov laid his hand on the list, wiping at it in the same way he might brush crumbs from the deskscreen. The list collapsed into a cube.

"I'm sorry, Lilly." He forced out the inadequate phrase and stuck his finger in the middle of the cube. It blinked, then disappeared. He didn't need a computer to tell him that Lilly had never been in Morvees' apartment. He should never have suspected her. Instead, he'd allowed the poison of suspicion to eat into his soul. All he'd managed to do was send away the greatest woman he'd ever met.

69

Lepov wasn't drunk yet. If MacNally had come a half hour later, however, he would have found his friend totally smashed. As it was, Lepov was merely uncooperative.

"Come on, Lepov. We've got to get out of here."

Lepov was sitting at his desk, staring at a blank deskscreen. A bottle of bourbon sat in the middle of the desk.

"Does this mean you're gonna explain what you said about Reno? How he can be not quite as dead as Zoltis?"

"Yeah. All of that. But not here. I'll explain on the way." MacNally, the bigger of the two men, grabbed Lepov by the collar and pulled him out of the chair.

"Tell me now." Lepov shrugged away from MacNally and nearly knocked down the open bottle of bourbon.

"Alright, if that's what will get you to cooperate." MacNally began: "The night Reno's car burned, MedTechs pulled him from the fire. They declared him dead. Only he wasn't. The lead tech found a pulse. He and I were the only ones who knew. I called in a favor from someone at a clinic, and had him brought there. Only me, the MedTech, and Fenelli's brother-in-law—Dr. Duvalls—know Reno is alive. He's badly burned, and will never be able to live outside the clinic. The man is hooked up to more machines than I even knew existed. Considering the crimes he had committed, I thought it was best for the Lazaretto to let everyone think their Chief Administrator had died in that fire."

Lepov swung the back of his hand at MacNally. Catching MacNally off guard, Lepov's shot landed in the soft pocket of the detective's cheek. MacNally jerked away too late.

"You bastard," Lepov looked like he might swing again. "You let me think I burned that man to death. You let *Lilly* think I burned that man to death!"

MacNally was ready for the next swing. He caught Lepov's hand with one of his own and clamped down.

"Dammit, Lepov. I know what I did! But I had to think quick, and I had to make a hard decision. If I had told you Reno was alive, would you have let me leave him there?"

"No, I'd have wanted to see him tried for murder."

"That's why I didn't tell you. And for what it's worth, Lilly's proud of what you did. You saved her life, remember?"

"I don't want to talk about Lilly," he said.

"Have you talked to her?"

"Sure. Turns out all she was doing was bringing some artwork into the Laz for Cam Raley. It's all under the table. Hush, hush."

"Raley?" MacNally's mind went back to Raley's office and the paintings on his wall. "What artwork?"

"Who cares? The point is, I practically accused her of trying to murder me, and she's leaving. I'll never see her again. It's what I deserve."

"Forget about Lilly, right now." MacNally couldn't think of anything he could say to make Lepov feel better. He should never have told Lepov that Lilly was back in the Lazaretto. His best bet was to get Lepov moving, thinking about something else.

They left the office and MacNally drove them to the clinic where Reno was being kept, describing his interview with Yarmin along the way, and the subsequent meeting with Captain Fisher. Lepov was most intrigued by Yarmin's warning about the daughter.

"Who's this daughter?"

"I don't know. You been able to learn more about Zoltis or Reno?"

"No. I'm afraid I haven't been much help to you, Mac."

"That's okay," MacNally set the car down in front of an imposing cinder block building and killed the engine. "That's all I expect from a Private Investigator."

The *Terminal Clinique de Lazaretto* was a private clinic specializing in caring for terminally ill patients with no one to ease them through the last days of their exile. It was the only one of its kind, a rare jewel in the heart of the dark Lazaretto.

A broad-chested security guard met them at the front entrance. He unlocked the door, and let them in. The clinic was not opened to visitors in the evening but MacNally had called ahead and made arrangements with Dr. Duvalls. The guard led them to an elevator and told them to ride it to the fourth floor.

When the doors opened at the fourth floor, they were met by a short woman with dark hair and sad, chocolate eyes. Her shoulder-length hair was tied in a faded blue bandanna, her eyes hidden beneath bangs that stuck out from under it.

"Hello Lt. MacNally, it's been a long time."

"Hello, Maria." MacNally nodded, and removed his hat. There weren't many women who could turn the big detective into a pussycat. But this was one of them. "Maria, this is Gregor Lepov."

"We've never met, Mr. Lepov, but I know who you are. It is a pleasure to meet you." She smiled. "I'm told you've been a good friend to Lt. MacNally. I'm glad. He needs as many friends as possible."

"Arturo Fenelli was Maria's brother," MacNally explained to Lepov. He turned back to Maria and added "you should know I still miss your brother a lot, Maria. Sometimes, too much."

"I'm glad to hear it, Lieutenant." Maria paused and took a slow breath. Perhaps she was offering up a quick prayer for her brother. "Georges asked me to meet you. He meant to be here, but he's been called downstairs. Something urgent. But he asked that I help you. You're here to see John, is that correct?"

MacNally quickly nodded, giving Lepov a warning look. Maria only knew the patient as John Doe. She was not aware that his name was Claude Reno.

"I'm sorry we have to bother him, but it's important. Can he talk?"

"Yes, he can talk." Maria led them away from the elevator and into a small office behind the nurse's station. After shutting the door, she turned and took another slow breath. "Lieutenant, you should know that he talks rather well. You see, I am the only volunteer at the clinic who will care for him. And I am with him for many hours of the day. Georges does not know this, but I am well aware of John's identity."

The two men looked uneasily at each other, unsure of what to say.

"You don't need to worry. John has no desire for this information to come out. As you will see, he has no future. For John, there is always just today. And for him, today is nothing more than one more day hooked up to the machines that keep him alive. He knows it would bring nothing but"—she hesitated, searching for the right word—"but more suffering."

"Why keep him alive?" MacNally asked. "Does he really want these machines to keep him alive? What's the point?"

"Shame on you, Lieutenant," Maria scolded, "I might ask why you didn't leave him to die. Why did you bring him here? But I won't because I know why you did and why we won't. Life is too precious to just snuff it out when it becomes a burden. And no, he doesn't want the machines. He asks me to shut them down daily."

MacNally tried to avoid the question she'd posed, but he couldn't. Why *had* he brought Reno to the clinic? He deserved to die, that was without question. Had it only been instinct? The instinct to save a life, no matter how dreadful it had become? That would have at least been a decent motive. What MacNally feared was another possibility; the ironic justice in keeping him alive. Though Reno had not been the man who beat Fenelli to death, Reno had been that man's employer. Had keeping the man alive in a body that was nothing more than a daily torment for him been MacNally's revenge?

"We want to speak with him alone."

"Okay, I'll take you to him." Maria led them back into the hall. She stopped at a closed door with the number three over it in black. "Ed, please don't push him hard. Please."

MacNally wasn't going to promise anything. But Maria's eyes bore into him. Fenelli had always been the one to keep MacNally from getting out of hand. Now, here was another Fenelli bearing down on his conscience.

"Yes, Ma'am," he said. It was the best he could offer.

Maria opened Reno's door. MacNally was shocked at what he saw. Reno lay in a bed covered with hoses and tubes. The once mighty Chief Administrator was dependent on the surrounding machines for every breath he drew.

The room was warm. Maria made a quick reference to it, telling them it was necessary to encourage the growth of the seeded skin-patch. Reno had suffered burns over ninety per cent of his body, and there was insufficient skin available to develop grafts for him. It might have been possible on Dnepr or Phasis, but not in the Lazaretto. That kind of equipment had never been brought down to the moon's surface. Seeding skin-patches was a measure of last resort. Success rates with synthetic repairs were below comfortable levels for surgeons, who were highly reluctant to use them.

Where Reno's skin was open to the warm room air, MacNally could see that is was not skin at all. A wispy, fibrous film stretched over his muscles. This was the synthetic patch. As it filled in, the fibers spread like cracks in thawing ice. Eventually, it would create a solid layer of skin. The color would never be right—always too pale, translucent—but it would be durable enough.

Reno's face had not escaped the firestorm. His head was scraped clean of hair, and most of the skin. The cranium could still be seen through the diaphanous skin-patch. At the sound of their entry, Reno turned his head to look at them and the gauze-like skullcap slid awkwardly. The former Chief Administrator winced but made no attempt to correct the problem.

Though his gaze seemed to aim straight at the visitors, Maria had warned them that Reno was essentially blind. Despite this, he trained his eyes at them for a count of ten. Then he spoke.

"They're here?" It was the voice of a dead soul from deep inside a tomb. MacNally had never heard a voice speak with such graveled effect.

"Yes, John," Maria used the name with tenderness, despite the fact that it was simply a label, "the men are here to speak with you."

Reno's hand reached up toward his neck but stopped short. He winced as the hand slowly fell back to the bed. The skin-patch over his hands had progressed further along than anywhere else on his body. It looked like he was wearing several layers of cream-colored stockings too big for his hands.

"There are men in hell whose only punishment is an itch that can't be scratched. It is enough to drive a man insane. If I scratch it, I will pull the skin loose on both my neck and my hands. I've done it twice before."

"Your medication is wearing thin. That's why it itches." Maria pulled open a drawer and withdrew a bottle from its depths. "I'll have your next dose ready in just a moment."

"I can't see you," Reno said to the two men standing near the door. "Only shadows. But I know you. Who else would know I was alive? The big, black shadow must be MacNally — my jailer. The shadow beside him — the one in the longer coat is Lepov — my judge *and* executioner."

Neither of the men answered him as Maria administered the painkillers. She gently inserted a thin tube into his mouth.

"This allows him to drink warm liquids when his throat becomes sore," she explained.

For a moment, the sounds from the equipment filled in where words had become useless. Reno swallowed with difficulty, then turned away, the tube slipping from his mouth. Maria caught it in her tiny hand. Her duties fulfilled, she withdrew to the hallway.

MacNally and Lepov were now alone with Claude Reno. Liquids slid through the clear tubes to and from the scarred body. Machines ran with a steady thrum, hijacking the silence and forcing each of them to listen.

"You didn't come to stare. Maria said you have questions. Ask them." His voice and the hardness of his eyes defied them.

"What was the connection between Kjarsta Zoltis and Cam Raley thirty years ago?" MacNally had waded right in. No preamble, no warm-up question. "Why were they hiring soldiers from the Lost Platoon?"

"That's a vague question," Reno rumbled.

"Okay, then what were they doing at Chettleham Keep?" Lepov refined the question.

Reno's rumble was nearly inaudible but MacNally could tell the man was laughing. The guttural sounds rolled to a stop and he sputtered before speaking. "You found the tunnel."

MacNally waited. He wanted Reno to go on. Lepov knew enough to remain quiet. He even encouraged Reno by nodding and lying and saying yes, they had found the tunnel.

"So you want a history lesson? It's no secret anymore. That tunnel's too old for anyone to use now. Kjarsta ran doubles in the quadrants, and I made sure the administration was looking the other way."

"And Raley?" MacNally turned his head to hear more clearly.

"Raley found the clients off-world. He brought them in and Kjarsta put them in the system. You two couldn't figure that out?"

"So Zoltis inserted platoon members legally into a quadrant before it locked down. Then Raley brought in clients just before the quadrant was due to discharge everyone out of the quarantine. Guys like Pan Juarez, right? Only for Juarez, Zoltis had him killed and took the diamonds."

"Juarez?" Reno waved his gauzy hand at MacNally and sputtered again. "Pan Juarez never came through. He double-crossed all of us. Just disappeared with the diamonds. Zoltis didn't get a chance to touch him. Is that what this is about? Juarez?"

"Anton Morvees is using the tunnel again. And we found a body from the old days near the tunnel." MacNally did not flinch from stepping close to Reno's body. "I want to know what's going on there."

"He's running doubles again, I'd guess," Lepov suggested. "That would explain Branithwaite's missing people."

"That kind of stuff doesn't pay any more." Reno tried to shift his position and had to give up. The effort drained him. He closed his lidless eyes and let out a long growl. "Not enough people need to short-cut the quarantine like they used to. It's why we quit."

"You're ignoring my question, Reno. I want to know whose body was in the tunnel. It was either Juarez or the double's. I know that much."

"Do you?" Reno smiled wickedly. "How would I know whose body it was?"

Reno knew exactly whose body was in the tunnel. The man's eyes, behind those cobwebbed eyelids, were laughing at MacNally. He wasn't going to tell them a thing.

"What are you hiding? What else was the tunnel for?"

"That's the wrong question, MacNally." The hoarse whisper rattled with glee. "The tunnel's no good anymore. All it ever did was move people in and out of the quadrants. The Keep was the only exit on the Center City side, besides—"

"—besides what?" MacNally could not make out everything the low voice was saying.

"Besides going to Raley's." The crazy smile was gone from Reno's lips. "I don't want to talk about this anymore. Get out."

MacNally didn't move. "We aren't done."

"Yes, we are." Reno reached up with his loose-skinned hand and scratched the surface of his neck. A patch of skin peeled and caught under his fingernails. He winced as he pulled harder to break the patch free.

Alarms sounded in the room and out in the hall. Maria shoved open the door, brushing past Lepov and MacNally with surprising strength. She surveyed the damage and then spoke calmly to the visitors.

"Leave immediately. The skin has been compromised and there is eminent risk of infection. I'm sorry, he's done this before. We'll sedate him, and restart the patch. I don't think you'll be able to ask him any questions for three or four weeks."

MacNally backed out of the room and motioned for Lepov to join him. It didn't matter that they couldn't ask more questions. Reno might have lived through the fire, but he was clearly insane.

70

The Thief was restless. Night was playing games with him. Darkness had come but he still had to wait. It wasn't true night. Shadows mixed with twilight in the absence of the pale sun, but the solid black of night was still hours away. More importantly, people still went about their miserable lives pretending the darkness was only an aberration that would pass like a shadow across the sun.

There would still be too much hurly-burly. Too many eyes and ears bumping around in the night.

The Thief had no longer been able to stand it. He needed something to do. Idle hands were the devil's workshop, after all.

He crept from his earthen burrow and skittered into the gray night. It might not have been dark enough for the primary objective, but there were enough shadows to provide the cover he needed on this little side trip. There were always shadows you could cling to if you were forced out of your hole.

This side trip would not take long. The Thief had no time to think about what he would do once he arrived. But that meant the Rat would have no warning of his coming.

He had not seen the Rat in ages. It didn't matter. He would be nesting in his hole as always. Once a rat, always a rat. Dress a rat in fancy uniforms, make him a Lieutenant and he was still just a rat.

As he'd suspected, the Rat was in his hole.

"I thought you might show up." The rat tried not to sound surprised but the Thief could see panic in his eyes.

"Unhappy to see me? After all my loyal service at your right hand?" The Thief saw that the Rat's hole was as bare as a winter cupboard.

"Loyal service?" The Rat laughed. "You have to be joking. I was never more nervous than when you were at my right hand. I never feared a fight. Just what you might do to me when I had my back turned to you."

"That's unkind," the Thief watched his former commanding officer warily, "what did I ever do to deserve that kind of abuse?"

"Don't think I never knew what you were up to. And don't think I don't know what you did to all of us."

"What did I do?" The Thief stopped circling the Rat and waited for an answer.

"It was you. You arranged all of this." The Rat waved his arms around in a sweeping motion. "If it hadn't been for you, we all would have gone home, right? I've never been able to prove it, but I knew from the beginning. I just never found the proof."

The Thief nodded. How had the Rat known? Who cared? He couldn't do anything about it now. The Thief had won.

"I did us all a favor," the Thief said proudly, "if I hadn't found a way to keep us here, we all would have gone home to our sad and pathetic lives in the Army. What good would that have done us? At least here we had the opportunity to make something of ourselves."

"Is that what you think you've done?" The Rat was getting bolder. The panic in his eyes had turned to anger. "Look at us! We're nearly all dead. Thirty years stolen from us. You stole those years. I ought to kill you right here. I ought to smother you, the way you smothered my men in this suffocating world."

"Smother me?" The Thief carefully eyed the Rat's hands. "I came to your little rat-hole to tell you I had won. I know what you did. I know you ratted. Tried to stop me. Thought you could still give the orders and I'd have to submit. But I wanted you to know it was all in vain. I've won, and you'll have to sit here in your dismal little hole and think about me for the rest of your dismal little life. But you stand there and dare to say you'll smother me?"

"Yes, that's what I said." The Rat's hands twitched. He might have taken a step toward the Thief. "And I think that's what I'll do. I want to see you beg for air. I want you to join the rest of our dead, where they'll look forward to seeing you. They've been waiting for you. And I'm gonna send you to them."

The Thief smile. He hadn't planned on this, but wouldn't hesitate to kill the Rat. The Rat was coming for him. The Rat would die. And the Thief would leave the Rat in his hole. The Lazaretto wouldn't miss the Rat. There would be other rats willing to creep in and take its place. The Lazaretto was full of them.

71

As soon as Sun walked through the doors of her hotel, she decided to have a drink in the hotel's bar. It was a nice enough lounge. A woman wearing far too much make-up sat on a stool and sang old Terran songs. A viewscreen behind her announced the night's theme: a tribute to Billie Holiday. Sun knew she had been a singer from the twenty-first or twenty-second century, but did not know any of her music.

Settling into a small circular booth in a corner of the room, Sun ordered a drink from a waiter who had to be twice her age. He was fussy but polite, and Sun decided she liked him. He seemed determined to carry himself with dignity.

The music was a nice distraction for Sun. Since leaving Lepov's office, she had felt unsettled; guilty of some sin. She could try to think of something else, but the weight on her spirit refused to leave. The music seemed to lift that weight, if only a little.

She tried to concentrate on the singer, who was obviously Sinopese. There was Terran-Asian blood in her, like Sun, though she was definitely not Korean. The make-up tried to conceal the fact that the woman was beyond her sixtieth birthday. Her red dress was too small and looked like it should have been discarded years ago. Her obvious wig only aged her. Like the waiter, the singer managed a degree of dignity despite her age and tacky costume.

She sang a nice number and Sun found she could hum along with it easily enough. According to the screen, the title was God Bless the Child. For a time, Sun forgot about Lepov.

It wasn't until the next song or the one after that when Sun heard a change in the lyrics. The singer's soft voice spoke of *blood on the leaves*, and *bodies swinging in the southern breeze*. When Sun made out a line about *bulging eyes and the twisted mouth*, she felt unsettled again, as if someone had briefly shaken her like a mixed drink.

She paid for her *Tom Collins* and left the bar.

No one had paid her any attention while she'd been in the lounge. She was glad of that now. Somewhere in the back of her mind she had hoped a man might have shown a little interest. But that had been a foolish idea. She wasn't about to pick up a stranger in a bar. What she had really wanted was to see Gregor Lepov come walking in. She wanted him to come looking for her, to tell her that he was sorry she had left the office. She wanted to hear him say that he had spoken to Lilly for only a short time and sent her away.

Closing her door, Sun pulled off her jacket and dropped it on the floor. She could not believe how like a jealous lover she was acting.

She'd only just met Lepov; there was no reason to expect more from him. And there was absolutely no reason to feel enmity toward Lilly Stewart. If anything, Sun pitied her. If she had read the woman correctly, Lilly was hurt; something had happened between her and Lepov and it was still causing pain.

Sun tried to recall whether Lepov had mentioned Lilly. He had made a brief reference to a failed marriage, but mentioned no names. Was this his ex-wife? Maybe that's all this was about—just an ex-wife with a niggling financial detail to set straight.

Watching herself undress, Sun tried to imagine how she appeared to a man like Lepov. She no longer looked like a teenager. She hoped she didn't, anyway. She had been able to keep off excess weight, but there were small signs her body was beginning to settle. Her hair was beginning to lose its luster; most of the time it went limp shortly after brushing it. But none of these things were serious. If she had wanted, she could have spent the money for necessary corrections.

The problem, as she saw it, was that she appeared tired. She looked fresh out of transport stasis. With each passing year she was beginning to look like that. Is this what Lepov saw? A tired, careworn woman? That wasn't what he needed. He needed a woman who was full of life, who had the energy to pull him out of his dark moods. Someone to whom he could turn when *he* felt worn down.

It was better not to think about that. After one more look in the mirror, she pulled on an old pair of cottons and crawled into bed. It was early, but the *Tom Collins* had been enough to make her want to sleep. And maybe—just maybe—she would wake up in the morning and forget her vain anxieties.

Or maybe Gregor would agree to eat breakfast with her.

…blood on the leaves…the bulging eyes and the twisted mouth…

She'd been nearly asleep when the images paraded across the horizon of her mind. She turned over but it didn't help; she could still hear the singer's doleful cry.

Anton Morvees. Would he really have hurt her? It had felt possible. Even after Chitti assured her he was all bluff. But surely Chitti knew him far better than she ever would.

The bundle of rags dropped close enough to make her flinch. She rolled over, looking around in the dark. She didn't need to start thinking about poor Silva MacDenny. Was the liquor dredging up these images? She wished she could shut them off even as the image of Chaz Grimion and his incessant radio came into focus.

What had John Yarmin been trying to tell her? Why couldn't he just come out and say what needed to be said?

These were self-important dramatics; that's all they could be. Sun decided she would have to talk to John Yarmin again. And this time she would do whatever it took to get the man to explain his cryptic advice. There couldn't be any reason for his reluctance to speak. She'd have to make him see that.

He would see. He would have to see…with *bulging eyes and the twisted mouth…*

72

Sitting at MacNally's desk, Lepov didn't mind telling the others he was confused. Russell and MacNally nodded in agreement. Pete Landon assured them everything was starting to make sense.

"I'm glad you understand what's going on," Russell said. The young detective's face bore his usually pinched expression.

"Let's take it a little at a time."

The four men had gathered in the Homicide office to pool their information. It was after eight o'clock, and there was no one else in the room. Most of the overhead lights had been turned off; only the desk lamps from a few desks lit the meeting. The great pile of filing cabinets and paper files loomed behind them like the shadow of a blacked out city.

"We'll start with what we know has already happened." MacNally was sitting in a chair borrowed from a neighboring desk. He sat back in the chair, his top-heavy frame tilting the chair at an angle that seemed destined to flip it backwards. "We have the body in the landfill that's been buried for decades. Silva MacDenny's been murdered, and Lepov was nearly murdered by Morvees and a woman we have not identified."

Lepov tried not to picture Lilly.

"I might have something on that," Pete Landon jumped in.

"Just hold on to it." MacNally continued. "The missing people Lepov was hired to find are only missing. While they might be dead, we now suspect they were more than likely taken into one of the quadrants through the tunnel. But we can only speculate right now."

"I have something on that as well." Pete sat on the edge of MacNally's desk. He pulled up a white document on the deskscreen.

"Hang on, Pete. Let me finish." MacNally tried to continue, but he was having trouble with his next point. He pulled a cigarette from a nearly empty pack. "Damn it, Pete. I'm too old to be interrupted. I lost my train of thought. Go ahead and say what you wanted to say."

"Sorry," Pete put his palm on the screen, enlarging an image in the document. "This is the guy I said I recognized. Lepov sent me this shot from the recorders inside Chettleham Keep. One of the missing people. It's Silva MacDenny."

"Yeah, that's MacDenny," MacNally nodded.

"Well that makes sense," Russell said. "We know he was in the tunnel. That's what his mouth was packed with, the soil from down in the tunnel. And that's gotta be where the old body was."

"What did MacDenny do?" Lepov examined the image.

"He was the platoon's engineer. Had schooling in that kind of thing." MacNally was having trouble lighting his cigarette.

"Civil Engineering, I would guess," Lepov tried to ignore the smoke as MacNally finally managed to light the cigarette. "Reno said the tunnel was no good. But I'll bet MacDenny was repairing it.

"Then that would mean he had finished it," MacNally said.

"And Morvees killed him once he was done," Russell suggested.

"Yeah. But that was after the other people went through the tunnel. That tells us that either MacDenny was working on one of the tunnels to one of the quadrants, or—"

"—he was working on the tunnel to Cam Raley's building." Lepov could see where MacNally was going. "Pete, you have the shots of the five guys going into the apartment I sent you, right? The dates on those will tell us which quadrants were locked down at each of those times."

"I got it," Pete had already cleared the deskscreen and was attempting to match the dates with the lockdowns. "This won't take long. Wait. Come on. Okay, here. Of the five men who are missing, two of them went to Alpha Quadrant, one to Beta, and the last two went to the remaining quadrants. That means the tunnels were all in working order."

"Except the one to Raley's." MacNally put the cigarette in his mouth and left it there as he rubbed the stubble on his chin. "So Morvees needs to get to Raley's building."

"So then we ask what Morvees meant the night he tried to kill me." Lepov looked up at MacNally. "I know my memory is all screwed up from that night, but I clearly remember Morvees saying he wanted to know if we knew about *the target*."

"Maybe he said the tunnel," Russell suggested.

"No," Lepov shook his head. "He said *target*."

"So what kind of target does Raley have at his place?" Pete asked.

"Lilly's artwork." MacNally was obviously only guessing, but Lepov thought his guess made sense.

"The way she and Raley were acting, I'd say it might be valuable enough as a target." Lepov was sure Lilly had never told him exactly what it was. "I wish we knew what she brought in. That would help."

"Ask Raley." Russell said.

"What?" MacNally asked.

"I said ask Raley," Russell raised his voice.

"You think we should? Sure, we just go in and tell Cam Raley that we've been talking to his dead partner in crime and we think one of the old crew is gonna break into his place and steal something. That'll work."

"I don't think we ought to tell him anything." Lepov had been glad to hear Raley was guilty of running doubles in the Laz, he wasn't about to let anyone help the man. "I say we let Morvees do whatever it is he's gonna do. We grab him after the fact. I don't really give a damn what happens to Raley's art collection."

He knew his opinion of Raley was based more on Raley's relationship with Lilly than on his former crimes. He didn't like seeing Lilly with the man. And the fact that Raley had built an art collection with dirty money was bad enough. But the knowledge that Lilly had assisted him was too much. He hoped Morvees grabbed every last bit of that collection.

"It's not a bad idea," Pete said, "when you consider we don't have much on Morvees other than theories. I suppose we could stick the MacDenny murder on him, but not much more. He did try to kill Lepov, but I think we've all wanted to kill Lepov from time to time."

"Thanks, Pete."

"No problem. So we let him grab some of Raley's art, and we have a better chance to lock him up for the rest of his life."

"But we don't know when he'll do it," Russell pointed out. "He might not do it for another week. Or he could be doing it tonight. So pick him up. A murder charge plus an attempted murder should be enough."

"Doesn't matter when he pulls the job," MacNally stuck the cigarette in an ashtray and discounted the rest of Russell's comment. "I'd guess Morvees will try to use the tunnel to get into a quadrant. Once we know he's hit Raley, we just pass the word to Quadrant Security to detain him."

"Then there's the question of the woman." Lepov sat up and waited for everyone's attention. "If we move on Morvees too early, we may not find out who she is. If we wait, we might still get a break."

"You've got one." Pete smiled. "I tried to tell you this earlier, but Mac was too busy giving his speech."

"Well?" Lepov asked.

"I was doing research for Sun Uijong, just out of curiosity. This Lost Platoon business kind of intrigues me. Anyway, I found something odd. Morvees once listed a daughter and a wife on an application for housing. He never put down any names, and he never listed the wife or daughter again. I'm trying to pull data from everywhere I can think of, but I can't confirm a wife or daughter. This could be a simple lie to get better housing. But I thought it might be worth looking into."

"That might help explain the daughter comment from Yarmin," Lepov said to MacNally. MacNally nodded, but avoided meeting Lepov's gaze. "What's the matter? You had a different idea?"

"I'd rather not say."

Lepov wasn't imagining things. MacNally was making an effort to avoid eye contact. That could only mean one thing. MacNally was thinking about Lilly. Did he know something he wasn't telling?

"Mac, this ain't the time to keep things to yourself." Lepov stared at the big man until he finally turned to face Lepov. "What is it you don't want to tell me?"

Russell and Pete sat, watching silently, waiting for MacNally.

"Okay," MacNally dug in his cigarette pack but it was empty. He wadded it into a ball and threw it at a wastebasket. It hit the lip of the basket and fell to the floor. "When Yarmin said to watch out for the daughter, it reminded me of something. Do you remember Reno telling you and Lilly something about her real father?"

Lepov had to stop and think back to that night he had set Reno on fire. Reno had told them he was going to kill Lilly because of something to do with her real father. He had never understood the remark, and Lilly had told him her real father had died when she was a teenager. Reno had been speaking of someone else, and Lepov and Lilly had decided that Reno was either mistaken or simply crazy.

"After Yarmin mentioned a daughter," MacNally cleared his throat, "I thought it would be best if I did a basic check on Lilly Stewart."

That got Lepov's attention. All of his former suspicions came rushing back in one great wave.

"Who's Lilly?" asked Russell. Pete waved him off with a gesture.

"Who was her father?" Lepov demanded.

"I don't know. The best I can tell, her parents were Edward and Frieda West. But there are contradictions in the records. It looks like somebody falsified either the birth record or one or two of the early medical check-ups. If I had to give a definite answer, I'd say the Wests weren't her biological parents. But hold on. Don't jump to conclusions. There's something else."

"What else could there be?"

"When Reno talked to you the night he tried to kill you guys, you told me he said her real father had just died. Right? I had always believed he meant Zoltis was her father. That was, after all, the night he died. I'm sorry, Gregor, but now I just don't know."

"Wait a minute," Pete interrupted, "do you remember the dates on Lilly's records?"

"Yeah, I do. They were the same year the Lost Platoon showed up. Same year I tracked Pan Juarez in Alpha Quadrant. Probably the same year that corpse was stuffed under the Roth building. That year is getting easy to recognize."

"Well," Pete added, "the application I saw with the daughter listed on it was nearly five years after that."

"I hate to ask this," Lepov looked at the three cops, "but how well are birth records kept in the Lazaretto?"

"I'll find out." Pete slid off the desk and headed for the door.

"So are we doing anything more on this tonight?" Russell asked.

"No," MacNally said, "so go home."

Russell didn't need to be told twice. He shut down his deskscreen, killed his lamp, and followed Pete out of the office.

The room was quiet. Both MacNally and Lepov sat partly in shadow. Only one lamp remained on. The room had shrunk down to one small yellow circle with the two men seated on the edge of it.

"You ought to come back to my place," MacNally finally said. "I hate for you to be alone tonight. My couch is comfortable enough."

"Gee, thanks, Dad." Lepov rose and backed out of the light. "I'll be okay. I'm not gonna jump to conclusions, if that's what's bothering you. I really don't know what to think about her anymore. In the end, this doesn't matter. Lilly's no killer. If she were, the world wouldn't make a whole lotta sense."

"I'm impressed," said MacNally, "it's nice to know you think this world makes any sense at all. I never took you for an optimist."

"Not an optimist," Lepov shook his head. "Just stupid."

He left MacNally and the little desk lamp. Walking home, he took his time getting there. Despite what he'd said to MacNally, Lepov knew he was in for a long, sleepless night; the kind of night it would have been good to have a woman like Sun Uijong in his arms.

True night had taken hold of the Lazaretto; no shades of gray in the streets. Dense cotton cones of light hung from lampposts, the darkness too thick to allow them to spread and touch. This darkness filled each crack and crevice of the Lazaretto like a pall of black smoke, filtering down even into the basement lair of the Thief, hugging the basement walls and spreading over its floor, seeping through the crack under the door to the back room, pouring into the tunnel, dimming the lone bulbs that hung along its length.

The Thief could taste it; a foul breath emanating from this city of the walking dead. He had learned to live with it, but had never found an antidote to its poisonous influence. It could never be suggested that the Lazaretto had corrupted him; that he had once been a man of sound mind and pure spirit. But the Lazaretto had slowly worked away at the Thief's reason until he no longer recognized his own inner rot; until he no longer understood that the words filling the void in his head could be something other than truth. For the Thief, the darkness surrounding him concealed more than a few self-justifying lies; it concealed the truth of his madness.

Standing in the center of a lengthy stretch of the tunnel, the Thief was having trouble breathing. He wanted to cry out, to shout, to tell the world: *I am a genius!*

It had all gone according to plan. He'd been able to slip in unseen. Had moved about with complete freedom, and had struck the Target without raising the slightest alarm. And now, back in the tunnel, the culmination of years of hard work and patient dedication lay on the floor of the tunnel in an aluminum tube that was no more than a meter long and no thicker than the Thief's arm.

She's mine. And she will always be mine. She will make me the man I've always been destined to be.

The Thief was exaggerating, of course. She would not always be his. He would have to sell her. To give her up. But only because it was what he wanted. No one would take her away from him. He would exchange her for a new life outside the Lazaretto. Outside the walls of this diseased prison. She would be the key to his lock. She would free him like no woman ever had. Yes, he would have to give her up, but there would be more women. From now on, there would always be women.

He bent over and snatched the tube from the tunnel's dirt floor. He needed to be ready to move. He would have to make his escape soon. But there was a detail he still needed to clear up.

The Liar would be coming soon. She would be coming to join him. That was a sweet thought; she must be excited at the idea. If only she understood how impossible it would be for her to join him, she'd never come down into that tunnel, she'd never bring him that razor. If she were only as clever as the Thief, she would see how foolish she was being.

The Thief's goal, from the outset, had been to create a new life and leave the old one behind. If that were ever to happen, he would have to sever all ties with the old life. And that meant the Liar must die. She'd have been able to see that if she hadn't been so busy peeking into corners with those meddlesome little eyes.

He felt no regret for his decision; no sympathy for the girl. It was not, after all, a decision. It was only the product of logical deduction.

It disappointed him that she had been unable to work it out. It shamed him to know that she would walk right into the apartment, climb down into the tunnel, and stand idly by while he accepted the razor from her and put out her pathetic eyes. It was enough to make him question her pedigree; to doubt that they shared the same blood. To be blunt, it made it easier for him to erase her from his life. He would never have to regret it. He would never long for her return.

"You're right on time," he said. He had not been able to hear her footsteps in the tunnel but he had felt her approach as she disturbed the darkness around him.

"What are you doing down in the tunnel?" the Liar asked.

"Just waiting for you." He was glad of the dark. The aluminum tube was still in his hand and he did not want her to see it. He slowly reached behind him and gently set the tube against the wall.

A light appeared from her hand. She angled it toward him. "You look flushed. And you're wearing the suit,"

The Thief tried not to look surprised. He'd forgotten he was still wearing the silver-foil suit. He should have taken it off as soon as he was back in the tunnel.

"Just a trial. It restricts my movements. It's tight."

The light spilled over enough for him to see that she was watching him suspiciously. Those damn eyes. What right did she have to distrust him! How dare she?

"Did you bring it? My razor?" This would be the test. This would tell him if she still had any respect for him. Had she done what he'd asked?

"Yes, I have it. It's right here." She dug into her bag and pulled out the razor.

The Thief smiled. She had obeyed him. She had willingly walked into the tunnel and delivered the razor. She still trusted him. She still treated him as a father.

"You're a faithful daughter," the Thief said.

"And you're a good father," the Liar said.

He smiled again, locking his eyes with hers. Those clever, curious trouble-making eyes. He reached out to take the razor. She extended her hand and sliced open his palm.

The Thief shrieked. He clamped his other hand over the wound even as she came at him again. He lifted his arms, blocking her thrusts. The silver suit was no protection against the old blade. He swung his arms like a club and knocked the light from her hand. The light jerked up and then quickly back down, its yellow beam aimed down the center of the tunnel behind her.

She cut him two more times before he hammered her to the floor. Once she fell, he stumbled over her and fled into the tunnel; his shadow bobbing before him like an epileptic marionette.

What had she done? How could she have attacked her own flesh and blood? What kind of daughter could do that to her own loving father? She was out of her mind! And if his ears were not deceiving him, she was following close on his heels.

She still had the light. It bobbed now and then, spraying his shadow in all directions. If she still had the light, she still had the razor too. And she was getting closer. The little bitch had always been speedy, even as a child.

Blood slicked down his arms, soaking the tattered remnants of his silver suit. He felt dizzy; a combination of running and loss of blood. It made running easier. He felt light as a ghost. He hadn't moved this nimbly in years. Maybe he would outrun her. Maybe he would reach the stairway before her. Maybe he could climb up to the room and slam the door on the tunnel. She'd be trapped then. At least long enough for him to stop the bleeding and recover his senses.

But where were the stairs? Had he taken a wrong turn? That was impossible. He knew these tunnels better than anyone; had explored them for years, divining their secrets, mapping them, hatching his plan to escape the Lazaretto with a fortune. He was surely heading straight for the stairs, if only by instinct. He ignored the searing pain in his arms, forcing himself to run harder. He would find the stairs.

The Liar's light bobbed again even as the Thief spied the wooden stairs and shouted in triumph. He was close. Just a few more steps and he would be on them. Just a few seconds and she would be trapped. She would fail. He would win.

His first step on the bottom stair hurt like hell. His back lit on fire. By the time he tried to gain the second step, the fire had spread to the back of his legs. He attempted to pull himself up the stairs, but fell flat, ramming his jaw into the edge of one of the steps.

He saw light, and heard the Liar breathing deeply.

"What are you doing?" he asked, his words barely able to escape his wheezing chest.

"Something you taught me a long time ago; I'm improvising. All I ever needed was an opportunity." She stayed back in the shadows, but even the Thief could tell she was smiling without seeing her face. "But you should know I've always wanted this."

The Thief grunted, struggling to turn his head enough to see her.

"Did you think I would never strike back?" The Liar had regained control of her breathing and there was more power in her words. "If you thought I was foolish enough to believe you were going to take me with you, you're a bigger fool than I ever imagined. You were going to kill me."

"No," he tried to say. It was impossible to know if she heard him.

He had not been able to hear what he said. He tried to reach out a hand in her direction. He needed help. The fire that he'd felt on his back and legs was dripping down between his skin and the silver suit.

"You're a sick old leech who sucked the life out of a poor, dying girl. I never mourned my mother because living with you was a greater hell than death. Go ahead," the Liar said, "try to reach me. Try to beat me one last time. You're finished. And I have no more time to talk."

What did she mean? She wouldn't leave him there? He wasn't on fire. He knew that. He was bleeding to death. Wouldn't she help him? She was his daughter, for God's sake. Where was his little *chitti*? Why didn't she come to her father? If he could only see his *chitti* one last time. Hold her in his arms one more time. Gaze into her beautiful eyes—eyes as beautiful and trusting as her mother's.

He never felt the final blow. He was too lost; far away from that hell of a tunnel. There was only the image of his devoted daughter and her beautiful eyes. It ceased with the last beat of his heart.

Book Three

Improvise

74

I have wasted enough time. I know that my reluctance to tell my tale has allowed me to wander from my purpose. But I will not avoid the truth any longer. I will stop putting off what has been my intention all along.

I will describe what happened on that day.

I awoke, and like any other day, made sure that Calla was cleaned up and fed. Morvees did not appear during the morning. Calla was unusually tired, and was asleep again before lunch. I was working in the kitchen, I had allowed the dishes to pile up and it took a little effort to clean them up.

Before I could finish them Kjarsta Zoltis came through the front door.

I was scrubbing down a countertop when he walked into the kitchen. As always, I felt I had done something wrong. I turned and faced him.

"Well?" he asked. Nothing more. He just asked his one-word question and stood waiting for a reply. I waited too, hoping there was more to the question. There was not.

"Come on, woman. Why did you call me?"

"I did not call for you." I had a feeling something terrible was about to happen.

"I got your message," he barked impatiently. "Don't play games. Is there something wrong with the girl?"

"Mr. Zoltis," I set down the dishrag I'd been holding and dried my hands on a towel that hung beside the sink. I was trying to give myself time to think of what it all meant. Had I asked Morvees to get Mr. Zoltis to come to the apartment? I was certain I hadn't. "I would not play games with you. Incidentally, Calla is fine. However, I don't know why Morvees would say that I wanted to see you."

"Damn it," he marched out of the kitchen, "I don't have time for this."

I followed. He stood in the center of the front room, a rare moment of indecision for him. "Is Morvees in the back?"

I shrugged. I had no idea where the man was.

"Wait here," he pointed at the center of the room.

Why would Morvees have said I wanted to see him? Surely he had to know I would tell Mr. Zoltis the truth, and we would know Morvees had lied. Furthermore, he had to know Mr. Zoltis would never allow one of his men to lie without punishment. It was important to remember Kjarsta Zoltis was not only a violent man, but also capable of making swift, terrible decisions.

It would take Mr. Zoltis no time at all to discern who was lying.

75

Sun rose quickly from bed. She was well motivated. Most of her night had consisted of turning over in bed with moribund images of that song stuck in her head. At times, it had only been the singer's voice, despairingly repeating the words...*bloody leaves...bodies swinging*...while at other times, she could see the blood on the leaves, bulging eyes and twisted mouths. This went on far too long. Getting out of bed had been the only way to escape.

Showered and cleansed of the disturbing images, Sun left the hotel, resolving never to stop in that lounge again. Whether it had been the alcohol or the music, she would not debate. Best to keep away from all of it. The Lazaretto had found yet another way to distort her world — to remind her that she was not living on a sane and safe planet. This quarantine world was a dangerous place where a traveler had to keep her wits about her and a tight control on what she allowed into her psyche.

It would have been prudent for the administrators of the Lazaretto to display a *Traveler Beware* sign where all entrants could read it.

She was able to laugh at that as the glass doors rolled up and out of her way. A weather warning might have been worth displaying as well. Sun was shocked by the cold air hitting her as soon as she stepped onto the street. The biting wind drove away the last fragments of her nightmares and she concentrated on hailing a warm TransitCar and getting out of the direct wind.

The TransitCar's heating system was malfunctioning and Sun had to sit huddled like a child in the corner of the seat, running her hands up and down her exposed legs. For once she wished that the military demanded she wear skirts that reached her ankles. She owned a full-length coat but had not brought it along on this trip. At least she was wearing a warm cap that held her black hair tightly to her ears.

She was surprised to see the office still locked. Chitti had not yet arrived. Was Sun too early? She didn't think so, but she had not been paying attention to the time. She was afraid she would have to wait in the TransitCar but she was pleasantly surprised to find the door lock deactivated once it received a signal from her PDT. That was Chitti, practical in all things.

The office was empty and warm; the climate controller was working. Sun was glad. She stood in the center of the room and soaked up the heat. She was more than just cold. The Lazaretto was sapping her spirit. She knew that. The nightmares and lost sleep had been symptoms of this.

Warm enough, she peeled off her coat, wondering how men like Ben Obenlan and John Yarmin could live in this city without losing their minds. Chaz Grimion had seemed to lose his mind, but maybe this was misleading: had he been the only one to react appropriately to this place?

Even Gregor Lepov would become infected with the Lazaretto to some extent. She could not believe that his state of mind wasn't affected by the atmosphere surrounding him. He was a solid, strong man—both physically and mentally—but was that enough? Would he hold out against the madness after ten years? Twenty? The men of the Lost Platoon had endured this place for thirty years. Sun shook her head and corrected herself. Only a few had been able to endure it for thirty years. Most had succumbed in one way or another throughout that span.

Just as Sun knew that she could not stay much longer, she began to wonder how to convince Lepov that he shouldn't either. She would never forgive herself for leaving him here where he would surely end up defeated by what she was beginning to think of as a sentient and malignant city.

The warm office had melted her chills and Sun began to relax. She fixed coffee. She was not a committed coffee drinker, but she was sure Chitti would want a cup as soon as she came in from the cold. The aroma helped to further clear her mind and soothe her spirit.

Perhaps she had been wrong. Perhaps the Lazaretto was not as sour as she imagined. Chitti Sienté was an example of a woman who could live her whole life on this moon without allowing it to tear her down. Chitti was a lot like Lepov—strong, not given to nonsense, pragmatic from head to toe. She might even have been stronger than Lepov. Chitti was a woman who had stared down the Lazaretto and held her ground, refusing to give in to its despair and decay.

Could Sun? If Lepov insisted on staying, could Sun agree to stay by his side? A chill ran through her. She would be willing to try. But she would try harder to get Lepov to come back with her to Fort Mai Ling. He could easily find clients in Seagen, though that would put him seven hours away. Maybe she could get a transfer. Or maybe leave the Army altogether.

"Let's not get carried away, Sun," she warned aloud. She would have to wait and see what happened after he called. But had he said he would call? Or had she told him she would call? This kind of flightiness would never do. If she'd told Lepov she would call, he would expect her to call. And she had a feeling he'd think her eager and foolish if she did.

The riddle was still bothering her when Chitti entered the office.

"Coffee's hot and waiting for you." Sun put off her decision about contacting Lepov.

"That's just what I need." Chitti did not seem to be affected by the morning's harsh weather. She casually removed her coat and poured a large cup of coffee.

"This tastes good," Chitti moved to Sun's desk and looked down, "I'm beginning to hope you'll never leave. I'm getting used to having you around. When does your boss expect you back?"

"Well, with all the data you were able to put together on the platoon members who have passed on, I'm nearly finished with my reports. I only have a few loose ends to clear up. After that, it's just a matter of getting this information transmitted to my commanding officer, and then he'll set up the funds to be distributed. But that may take a little while. At least for the surviving family members."

"And you'll stay until that's finished?"

"Oh, no. I don't think so. When I say it will take some time, that could mean two or three months before its all sorted out. I could get most of the money distributed to the surviving members. That wouldn't take much. But the family members will just have to be patient."

Chitti turned to walk away.

"Chitti?" Sun's tone softened. "Could I ask a question? You mentioned that your father was in the Lost Platoon. But I couldn't see a Sienté on the enlistment role."

"That was my mother's name: Marta Sienté. She was a mentally impaired young woman who had been stranded here while traveling through the Lazaretto with her parents. She had malaria. Had contracted it while living on Arcobia. Her father was a big shot for one of the Arcobian Corporations. They were fleeing the war. My mother was fifteen, and her parents just left her."

Sun had done it again. She'd left herself open to be hammered by the reality of the Lazaretto. It took an effort to draw in breath and hold back her tears. The Lazaretto never let up, never gave an inch. Sun couldn't help but hate it.

"One of the platoon members took her in for a little while. But all she would ever say was that he was abusive, and she was happy the day he threw her back onto the street.

"Whoever he was, he's dead now." Chitti stared at Sun with no outward appearance of emotion. "I'm not interested in taking money from your department. I hope you understand and don't take offense."

Sun nodded, tried to smile. She had never known a woman like Chitti Sienté, and she likely never would again. A woman who had every reason to hate the men of the Lost Platoon, Chitti had dedicated her life to watching over them. It was a life of love and compassion that Sun could only hope to emulate.

"So you'll be leaving soon?" Chitti asked.

"I haven't decided yet." Sun's thoughts were on Lepov. Should she tell Chitti about him? Sun had a feeling that Chitti would not approve of such impetuosity. It would be best not to speak of her feelings for Lepov.

"Well, I hope you won't need me this morning," Chitti spoke with sudden energy, dropping the subject of her mother. "I have some personal errands to attend to. I may not be back for hours. Did you have plans? Or will you be chained to the desk all morning?"

"I should stay here and compile the last of my reports. I may go out later, but that will most likely be after lunch."

Chitti wasted no time. She spent a few minutes working on her deskscreen, then bid Sun goodbye. Before Sun knew it, she was alone in the large, open office.

Yes, she thought, I ought to finish these reports. But she remembered her determination to speak with John Yarmin again. Would it be too early to knock on his door? She idly poured a cup of coffee as she debated her course of action.

Mostly, she was just waiting to see if Gregor Lepov would call her. And if he did, she'd forget John Yarmin and her reports. She'd gladly forget everything for Gregor Lepov; with him, it would even be possible to forget about this dreadful place for a sweet, brief moment.

76

MacNally wasn't about to admit that Russell had been right. But from the looks of things, the young kid had partially guessed the truth. The night before, Russell had said that for all any of them knew, Morvees would make his move during the night. Of course, he'd also said Morvees might do it two weeks from now, so he had a pretty good chance of being right either way.

Raley had called the police early. Someone had broken into his office and stolen a portion of his collection. Burglary was not MacNally's bailiwick, but Sam Gerbacher, a senior detective from that department, was an old friend of MacNally's, and was happy to bring him along.

"I get the feeling you know more about this than I do," Gerbacher said as they rode the elevator to Raley's office.

"I might. But you do the talking. I'm just gonna listen. Afterwards, I'll tell you what I know."

"Fair enough." Gerbacher had to be twenty years older than MacNally and should have retired ten years ago. He was tall, thin as a laser, and wrinkled like the ancient sands of Dnepr. His hands shook now and then, but the main body was as rigid and strong as the armature of a rocket gantry.

Gerbacher bore a perpetual smile and always seemed ready to laugh. He had once been MacNally's partner, back when MacNally had done an obligatory stretch in Burglary and Theft. During the ride in the elevator, Gerbacher boldly gave Russell a visual examination.

"MacNally treating you alright?" he finally asked Russell.

"About the best MacNally can do," Russell shrugged.

"Just remember MacNally was a rookie once. 'Course that was back when they used winged horses to fly from planet to planet."

"Yeah, you're right, Gerbacher. I was green as they come." MacNally yawned, then added "and you were already an old cadaver back then. Impossible as it seems, you look even worse, now."

Gerbacher took the insult with good humor but continued to address Russell. "Once you get tired of chasing MacNally around, you can come work with us real cops in Burglary. Our cases smell a lot better."

MacNally might have tried to top Gerbacher's crack, but the elevator doors opened and Raley stood waiting.

Introductions were made. MacNally did as he had said he would, staying in the background. He watched as Raley led Gerbacher into his office and pointed out the missing canvases.

"The thieves were choosy," Raley said, sighing at his loss. "He took my ladies. They have my *Femme aux Bras Croises*, one of Picasso's Blue works. I always fancied her. The model was a female inmate from the prison hospital of Saint-Lazare. And Klimt's lady, *Bloch-Bauer*, the first one. Lt. MacNally, you see my *Christina* is gone. But these were all secondary targets. They were mostly after her."

Raley pointed behind them, at the wall facing the front of his desk. A blank space in the center of the wall was well lit with small spotlights. The heavy frame MacNally had seen on his previous visit was on the floor, leaning against the wall. The canvas was gone.

"What was it?" Gerbacher asked.

"You mean who was she?" Raley corrected him. "She was *La Gioconda*."

"You're kidding." Gerbacher's aged eyes lit up.

"No. As you can guess, there is no simple figure to give you as to the value of these paintings." Raley spoke humbly, perhaps speaking more of their personal value. The loss of the paintings seemed to have physically wounded him.

MacNally didn't feel sorry for him in the least. After all, they would easily recover the paintings. Morvees wouldn't get far.

Gerbacher questioned Raley on his security measures. MacNally let them talk. He followed them silently as they crowded into the security office and viewed portions of what the recorders had captured during the night. They could see movement in a few shots, but only with difficulty. The blurred images appeared as a glitch on the recordings.

"Well," Gerbacher had finished with his questions and was preparing to leave, "I'm sure you realize that you have nothing to worry about. Thefts like this always end on a happy note. The thieves have nowhere to go with art this valuable. You'll get them back, I can promise that."

"I am aware of that, detective." Raley was allowing his impatience to show. "My biggest concern is that they might be damaged. These ladies cannot be damaged. It would be a tragedy."

No one argued, and they rode the elevator to the ground floor.

"That's it?" Gerbacher asked MacNally. "You just wanted to watch?"

"No." The elevator opened at the main lobby. MacNally stepped out of the carriage, waving at them to follow. He approached the security chief's desk.

"I need someone here to take us downstairs."

"Which level?" asked one of the two guards.

"I'll let you know after I've looked around."

Gerbacher tried to ask a question, but MacNally stopped him, not wanting a discussion in front of Raley or his employees.

The guard, only too happy to show them how to access the lower levels, left them on their own. MacNally was glad to be rid of him.

"So what are we doing down here?" asked Gerbacher.

"I'm going to show you how it was done." MacNally stood frozen for a moment, reading a floor map mounted on the wall near the stairwell door. "Russell, what do you think?"

"Given the direction of Morvees' apartment, and the layout of nearby SubTransit routes, I'd say about here." Russell stuck his finger on the southwest corner of the map. "Best guess. There are three basement levels here, but I can't think it's that deep. Has to be the first level. It gets more difficult the deeper you dig around here."

Gerbacher paid close attention, but did not ask questions, content to watch and learn.

"You think it's well hidden?" MacNally knew Russell possessed better instincts.

"I doubt it. Probably just broke it through at the last minute. No reason to spend any time disguising it. Morvees probably made a weak attempt to cover it up, so as not to allow anyone to follow him right away, but I'll bet he did a poor job of it. After all, his engineer's dead and can't help him much with that now."

"You want me to help look?"

"Give me five minutes, I bet you dinner I find it," Russell boasted.

"Do I have to eat the dinner with you?" MacNally asked as Russell headed toward the southwest corner of the basement. Russell disappeared without answering.

"He looks like a decent kid," Gerbacher said.

"Better than I expected an Arcobian could be." MacNally pulled out a pack of cigarettes and offered one to Gerbacher. The old man shook his head. MacNally lit one and took a couple of drags before speaking again. "So, you want to tell me about these pictures? I had the idea you recognized these *ladies* he was talking about."

"Oh, sure. Raley's not kidding about their value. These things are probably worth more than the Lazaretto Administration's entire budget for three years. Of course, most of that is in the big one."

"Which one is that?"

Gerbacher gave MacNally a funny look. "What do you mean? *La Gioconda*."

"Oh, I saw it the other day. Heavy woman with a plain face. Not too easy on the eyes." MacNally could not understand why she'd be so valuable. "She really worth all that much?"

"MacNally, are you telling me you didn't recognize her?"

"I guess she looked familiar."

"You're a barbarian, MacNally." The old man rolled his eyes. "You stick to dead people. I'll keep an eye on the artwork. Now, I've been patient. Will you tell me what this is about?"

Russell reappeared with a big grin before MacNally could speak.

"I guess I won't tell you after all." MacNally used the cigarette he'd been smoking to light another one. "I get to show you. Let's take a look."

Russell led them to a small room lined with metal shelves. In a back corner, they saw the entrance to the tunnel. It was no bigger than a man doubled over.

"Like I said," Russell looked pleased with his cleverness, "just some boxes and some old office equipment stacked in front of it."

"You knew this would be here?" Gerbacher asked with disapproval.

"We suspected this was here. There's a difference." MacNally leaned over and peered into the dark hole. "You got the lights?"

Russell pulled two hand lights from a side pocket of his full-length coat. MacNally took one. It came on once he grasped the black rubber handle; the white beam cut deep into the tunnel's opening.

"Let's take a look." MacNally had to drop to his knees to fit his large frame through the hole. "Morvees could have made a bigger hole."

"If he plugs up the hole," Russell said, "we'll cut another hole so we can continue on through the tunnel without him."

"If he plugs up the hole," Gerbacher added, "I'll kick him in the ass until he ain't pluggin' it up anymore."

All speculation aside, MacNally made it through the hole. He kept his head bent to prevent hitting it on the roof of the tunnel. Russell and Gerbacher easily slipped through the hole and joined him.

As they walked, MacNally explained to Gerbacher how they had learned about the tunnel. Russell led the way, his light switching from the floor to the walls, then down the black void in front of them. They moved slowly, listening for any noise that might tell them they were not alone.

It was cold. Not as cold as the wind-swept streets above, but with a wet chill that clung to the tunnel. The walls were slick and clammy. MacNally put his hand on them in several places. There was a great deal of clay mixed with gritty sand. Just as Russell had predicted.

They walked for half an hour. Once, coming to a fork in the tunnel, Russell led in the direction that should take them toward Chettleham Keep. The tunnel continued without change. The farther they walked, the more careful they became, not wanting to alert Morvees to their presence in his labyrinth.

"Hold it." Russell put up a hand, and lowered his light. He knelt on the muddy floor and muttered.

"What did you say?" MacNally leaned in.

"Something's not right." Russell stood, backing against the wall to allow the older men a look. "There's blood on the ground here."

"Yeah, and farther ahead, I think." Gerbacher pointed down the tunnel. "Shine your light along there, young man."

"I'd say he cut himself during the theft, but it should have started back closer to Raley's place." MacNally tried to work out a plausible explanation. "About the only other explanation is a quarrel."

"Morvees killed MacDenny once he was no longer needed. Maybe Morvees did the same to a different partner."

"Makes sense," Gerbacher nodded. "You want to wait for labtechs?"

"Hell no," MacNally brushed past both men and took the lead, his head still bent down. "We've got imminent search rights here. Someone might still be alive who can tell us what's going on and who did this. Let's keep moving."

They walked deeper into the tunnel. The blood was easy to spot, reflecting deep crimson off the white hand lights. Most of the trail was a constant pattern of widely separated drops. Every forty or fifty feet, a larger puddle of blood lay in the clay. Twice Russell pointed out blood smeared on the wall. One smear, starting in the clear shape of a man's hand, continued solidly along the wall for about a meter.

Something made noise in the darkness ahead.

"You hear that?" Gerbacher stopped and looked at Russell.

"What is that?" the younger man asked.

"Rats," said the old-timer.

"There's one." MacNally shone his light down the tunnel. A pair of luminous eyes shone back at them like stars. MacNally moved toward it.

"There's something up there."

At first it was hard to see. A white glow dropping down over shadows. As they drew closer, Russell was the first to recognize it.

"That's the entrance to the apartment." A light shone down from above. "Those must be stairs below the light."

"That don't look like stairs," MacNally pointed out. They slowed down and approached the cone of light one small step at a time. They could see more rats moving around. A few climbed up the stairs; stairs that seemed largely misshapen, as if the stairs had become swollen with large bladders or blisters.

"What is that?" Russell asked from behind.

The rats jerked to attention at the sound of Russell's voice, though they did not run away.

Their next steps brought them close enough to smell what they were seeing. Gerbacher cursed and fought down his gag reflex.

"I hate your cases, Ed. How can you stand this crap?" He held back, allowing the big detective to continue on his own.

MacNally didn't answer. He slowed until he was taking each step with care. The rats still in the tunnel stared, eventually backing away. Those on the swollen stairway stopped, staring boldly back at him.

It was hard to distinguish what he was seeing. Once he recognized what it was, no one could have mistaken what was on the stairs: a body, covered in blood. The rats had ripped at the body's features until there was nothing left to identify. The body lay face down; spread-eagle on the steps, arms hung over both edges of the stairs. Blood had run down the steps from the corpse's multiple wounds. Rats had tracked through the puddles, leaving little red scratches everywhere. The corpse's head was twisted, sightless eyes seemed to stare at the three detectives. The mouth was open enough to reveal the teeth within.

"God save us," Gerbacher muttered as he stepped close enough to see what MacNally had found. "Did you know about this too?"

"No," MacNally was having trouble remembering why they hadn't arrested Morvees last night. "We've got to find Morvees right now. This sick bastard has to be stopped."

"MacNally," Russell had pulled a handheld PDT scanner from his back pocket and now held it toward the bloody scene, "somebody else already has."

"Has what?"

"Stopped him. Look at the PDT signature: that's Anton Morvees."

MacNally closed his eyes and tried to breathe. The air was too rancid to take a deep breath, but he needed air to clear his head. He'd have to explain this to his captain, and he'd have to tell Lepov too. But the first order of business would be to get those damned rats off the body. And from the looks of them, they weren't going without a fight.

77

MacNally woke Lepov with the news. Lepov rolled over in bed and wondered why he felt like he'd contracted the Black Death. His chills were easily explained. His apartment was colder than the deck of that salvage scow in open waters. His furnace was out again. He should be used to that by now. It always broke down when the temperature outside dropped more than fifteen degrees. Now he just had to explain why his head hurt so much.

No, he knew he hadn't spent the night drinking. He had spent the night awake, his mind going over every detail he could remember about Lilly: how they had met, their conversations over coffee, how she had come to him for help with Reno, and the way she had taken care of him after he'd set the man on fire.

And he hadn't stopped there. He had gone over every conversation they'd had after she left the Lazaretto. He worked out the time sequence of when she'd arrived, and what she had lied about. He tried to recall exactly what he had seen in Morvees' apartment, including everything about the woman who had wanted him dead. He tried to fit the pieces of Lilly's past together with the pieces of Morvees' story. He replayed the scene in his office when both Lilly and Sun were waiting for him there.

The pain in his head increased the more he went back over it all. Crossing the room in a pair of cotton shorts, he started the shower, peeled off the shorts, and climbed in. The furnace regulated the hot water temperature, thus the shower was predictably freezing. It hurt more than his head. Lepov stood it as long as he could.

It required incredible effort to get dressed. He was still weak from his dip in the ocean — or did they call it a sea? He didn't know what these people called it. Mostly they never spoke about the water that covered most of the moon. They had found a way to ignore it.

If only he could ignore everything he'd learned about Lilly.

At least MacNally's call had given him a reason not to sit around and devise new ways to spy on her. Dead bodies had a way of arresting your full attention.

He skipped breakfast and grabbed a TransitCar to take him to Chettleham Keep as quickly as possible. When he arrived, the basement hallway was crowded with police, IHS men, nosy tenants, and an angry Branithwaite.

"Mr. Lepov!" He had spotted Lepov as soon as the elevator opened. "I want to speak with you. This is a broken trust. You were not supposed to go to the police without my consent."

"I don't mean to split hairs, Branithwaite, but you weren't too trustworthy yourself. You failed to mention a psychotic killer would cut up Anton Morvees and leave him to drip dry like a gutted rabbit."

"What do you mean?" Branithwaite stopped bobbing about and stared at Lepov as if he'd just accused the landlord of murder. "What is that supposed to mean? I couldn't know this would happen."

"Exactly my point, Mr. Branithwaite. Now why don't you get these tourists out of here? They're not helping the police any."

Lepov didn't wait to see what the landlord would do. He walked away, approaching Morvees' door. An officer blocked the entrance.

"You got orders to keep me out of there, Officer Voshell?" Lepov had to pause to read the young man's badge.

"I guess so, sir. Everyone's been ordered to stay out of there."

"Only I don't fit that description of *everyone*. I'm Gregor Lepov. Lt. Ed MacNally told me to come down here." Lepov's tone softened when he realized the young man did not look well.

"I don't know about that, sir." Voshell put his hand to his mouth and took a slow, deep breath.

"You've been in there, huh? Not a pretty sight from what I hear."

"No, sir." Voshell looked him in the eye. "MacNally really called you down here? I never seen you in uniform, you know? I mostly work night shift. I've been held over to help out."

"Well, I ain't worn the uniform in a long time, Voshell. I don't think it would fit."

"No, sir. I'm sure it would fit just fine." Voshell stood back and allowed Lepov to pass.

The noise and commotion in the hall, combined with the many officers inside the apartment helped to keep Lepov from thinking about the last time he'd been in those rooms. He did not stop moving for fear that he might begin thinking about it again. He saw more uniformed officers in the kitchen, and labtechs waiting in the small room to the left. He caught a glimpse of the Angel painting, looking even more out of place than before. From what MacNally had told him, this was no place for an angel.

The door to the back bedroom was open; the first time Lepov had seen that door unlocked. He stepped through the doorframe and stopped. The room was empty, save for a VTech standing over an open hole in the far corner of the room, MacNally waiting a few steps behind the technician, and Pete Landon to the left of the door, as far from the open hole as possible.

Pete stared at him. MacNally and the VTech had not noticed him enter the room. Lepov quietly moved next to Pete.

"Are they sure it's Morvees?" Lepov asked softly.

Pete nodded, his solemnity disturbing to see.

"Hey," MacNally turned, hearing Lepov's voice. He didn't bother speaking softly. "What took so long? I had to ask my technician to take his time so we could restrict access 'til you got a chance to look at things."

"You want me to look at things?" Lepov asked. He didn't understand why MacNally would want that.

"Don't get a case of false humility, Lepov. Just come take a look."

"I don't need to do this, you know." Lepov came to the edge of the opening and looked over the open door. The view was like looking into the basement of a butcher shop. "Somebody didn't like Morvees. I admit I don't feel the least bit sorry for him."

"Yeah, I had a feeling that would be the case."

"So what am I looking for?" Lepov had never been bothered by scenes like this. They weren't something he enjoyed, but he could stomach them better than most.

"You finished?" MacNally asked the VTech.

The technician nodded, relieved to get out as he grabbed his equipment and made a hasty retreat.

"Pete, close the door." MacNally waited, until the noise from the other rooms had become almost impossible to hear. "This has all gone to hell, Gregor. Morvees was the only suspect we had. Whoever did this is either still moving freely in the Lazaretto, or he's safely in one of the quadrants with the paintings."

"Or she's safely in one of the quadrants." Lepov stared at MacNally but didn't say any more.

"Okay, that's right. Best guess is it's the woman. There's two things I want from you. The first one is to take a good look at that body. Once you've done that, I want you to try and tell me you think Lilly Stewart is capable of doing something like that."

"Are you out of your mind?" The question wasn't rhetorical. "I can't believe what you're saying, MacNally. You want me to believe Lilly is innocent based on the extent of the violence? That's hardly logical."

"I'm serious, Gregor." MacNally moved back a step. "Go ahead. Take a long, hard look. You cannot tell me you think Lilly could do this."

Lepov stepped up to the edge of the steps and stared into the opening. He'd take a good look like MacNally wanted, but he wasn't going to promise anything.

The body was a nightmare. There was little else to be said about it. Lepov stood silently for a few moments, his mind wandering; MacNally had told him they'd been in the tunnel when they found the body. Had they come up on the stairs over the body? No, there would be tracks in the blood. They must have gone all the way back to Raley's and then come over the streets.

"Tell me, Gregor. Tell me she could have done it." MacNally's voice was soft, but insistent. "Lilly could have taken a knife, or a razor, and sliced up Morvees. Say it."

"Mac, back off. I get what you're saying. It's not easy to believe, okay? But don't ask me to ignore everything that's happened this week. And what's your point, anyway? I told you last night I doubt she's involved in this."

"Tell me she cut this man up and left him in his own blood."

Lepov looked away from the body. He refused to look at MacNally.

"She's been lying to me all week. For all we know this is her father."

"Look me in the eye and tell me Lilly did this." Louder now.

"How did Morvees find out about the painting? The new one?" Lepov looked at Pete, avoiding MacNally. "Who knew about the painting besides Lilly."

"Tell me Lilly's psychotic enough to do that." MacNally pointed down into the hole, grabbing Lepov by the arm. Their eyes met. "Tell me she did this!"

"She didn't do it! Is that what you want? What do you care?" Lepov grabbed MacNally by the lapels of his coat and for a moment the two men nearly toppled down onto Morvees. Pete jumped across the room, grabbing them in time.

"What I want," MacNally said calmly, ignoring the fact that Lepov had nearly sent them all down on top of that bloody mess, "is for you to help me find this woman. And you have to forget about Lilly. I need you to concentrate on this woman. You saw her. You heard her voice."

"You think that's gonna matter?" Lepov let go of the big detective and put his hands over his temples. His head had never stopped hurting. "Even if I admit she had nothing to do with this, it won't matter. You want me to say Lilly didn't do this? Fine. She didn't. What do I care? She's a woman who is now just a part of my past. A character from a bad dream. And I can live with that."

It did help to say it. To know that he had nothing left to worry about. And MacNally was right. Now all he had to do was concentrate on this crazy woman.

"I need to get in the other room. That was where I saw her. Not here. I was never in this room." Lepov pushed Pete out of his way.

To say this was all a bad dream was an understatement. If he could have, he would have gone back to the day Branithwaite walked into his office and Lepov would have stayed home. Maybe he would have to go back more than that. He would go back to the day he let Lilly walk out of the Lazaretto alone.

But then again, he wasn't going to think about Lilly any more. He was going to think about that woman. Not that he thought it would do any good. But MacNally had been right about one thing: Lilly could never have done that to Morvees. That had taken an aberrant rage that Lepov knew Lilly could never possess.

78

Like a recording, the images from the tunnel played through the Liar's mind. She didn't object; it felt good to replay the Thief's final moments. She had dreamed of this sort of ending her entire life. She could not believe it had really happened. Replaying the scene and watching those images was a way for her to reaffirm he was dead.

Since childhood, the Liar had never believed he could ever die. She had imagined his death so many times, it had become an impossible fantasy.

She'd known the bastard would double-cross her. Even if she hadn't known him all those years, and watched him betray every man or woman with whom he'd ever come into contact, she would have seen through his lies. Had he intended to kill her from the beginning? She guessed he had come to it by instinct—just following the path that had made the most sense in his lunatic's world.

As a child, she'd listened to his ravings, his warped mind allowing paranoia and delusion to justify heinous acts of betrayal. The Liar still remembered the day she had recognized his madness, and how he would turn on her one day; a sobering, chilling day.

For her, the logical path had been to respond by keeping him happy. She calculated that her best option was to ensure he never turned on her—to satisfy him. It had been a terrible obligation for a small child to carry. She had believed she only needed to be perfect.

The Liar knew, of course, that it had been an impractical solution since she first conceived the idea. The Thief was mad, and nothing she did would ever cure his insanity. He was as likely to kill her for making him happy as for making him unhappy.

Once she had concluded her only hope lay in his death, she had begun to wonder if she could actually kill him. She was not like him. She did not have his capacity for violence. But she did want to survive, and she wanted to escape the Lazaretto.

Getting out was the important part. Killing the Thief was only necessary if she wanted to begin a new life somewhere else; somewhere she could live without the fear of ever seeing him again.

Now, the Liar could not believe that she had been able to pull it off. She had waited for more years than she could count. She had waited until the day when she would not only have an opportunity to kill the Thief, but she would also have the chance to start afresh.

The paintings would give her that chance. All she would have to do was sell them for a fraction of their worth. She wasn't greedy.

But she had needed more than an opportunity to kill the Thief and the means to start over. She had needed a way out of the Lazaretto. The tunnel had been that way out. But she'd been sloppy. She'd expected the tunnel's secret to hold for one more day. She'd only returned to her office to erase her personal information. She had wanted to leave no clues behind; nothing to connect her to the Thief.

More importantly, she had needed to go back to her room and clean up. Killing the Thief had been far messier than she had imagined. Even now, she wondered at how it had all happened. She had intended to incapacitate him with the Para-Lazar. Once she had him down, she only had to suffocate him. He would be helpless to stop her. Her plan had been well developed.

The one thing she had not counted on was her own emotion. It had overwhelmed her at the critical moment. When he asked for his razor, all she had needed to do was reach into her bag and pull out the Para-Lazar. But she hadn't been able to do it. The thought of the razor was surprisingly exciting. The impulse to make him fear her as he'd made her mother fear him was too strong. And once she'd drawn blood, she had lost all semblance of control.

The Liar watched the scene in her mind. Yes, she had *enjoyed* it. She had been elated as her attack drew blood. She'd caught a glimpse of his eyes during his frantic attempts to deflect the razor's cutting bite. This was not fear based on paranoia. It was the kind of fear that overwhelmed the senses. It shut down the mind and saturated the soul. She had seen it in his eyes and it had only driven her to attack with more intensity.

She did not want to reexamine the last moments on the stairs. She had given herself over to something that had been too frightening to acknowledge. Whatever she had done, her mind was already building walls around that memory to prevent her from ever staring at it — from ever experiencing it as long as she lived.

The Liar forced herself to stop thinking about what had happened and she tried to decide what she would do next. With the tunnel compromised, she would have to find another way out. At least she hadn't hidden the paintings in the tunnel. That would have been a disaster.

She would find a way out. There was no question that she could find a way through the quarantine. But there were a few details left. The first was to eliminate anything that might tie her to the Thief. And that meant she would have to silence the Old Soldier. He was the only one who knew that she and the Thief were related.

Once she silenced the Old Soldier, she would concentrate on getting out of the Lazaretto. It wouldn't be difficult. And she already had an idea that should work. It would take a little effort, but her idea was sound.

79

To Sun's disappointment, Gregor never called. It was more than disappointing; she was confused. Had she messed up? Was she supposed to have called him? Or did he just not want to speak to her? Had she been too assertive?

No, she decided, that wasn't possible. Lepov seemed like the kind of man who couldn't be intimidated by women.

She was in no mood to sit at her desk and compile her reports. What else could she do to take her mind off of Gregor Lepov?

John Yarmin. That was the answer. She would try to speak with him one more time. She might find a way to get him to explain why he'd started this whole business. After all, if it hadn't been for him, she never would have come to the Lazaretto.

And she would never have met Gregor Lepov.

Before she could ask why he had never called again, she grabbed her coat and braved the cold of the street. She had considered walking to the nearest SubTransit station, but her legs started to hurt as soon as the air hit them. She warmed herself with thoughts of sheltering in Gregor's arms until a TransitCar driver saw her waving and she climbed into his back seat. Thankfully, the heater was working in this one.

The cold weather only magnified the desolate look of John Yarmin's neighborhood. No one was on the street. The harsh light of the cold morning made the run-down storefronts look pale and sickly.

She thanked the driver and hurried to the entrance of Yarmin's building. The door swung open with a startling shriek, the hinges must have been objecting to the low temperatures. Her shoes echoed loudly in the stairwell as she ascended to his floor. She tried to walk more softly in the hallway as she approached his door.

She knocked.

There was no reply.

It was too early for him to have gone anywhere. Was he still out from last night? Maybe he'd gotten drunk and ended up in jail.

She knocked harder. More than likely he was just sleeping off a long night of drinking. She'd had a brother like that. He would come home and sleep the whole day. He was always as mean as a cornered cat when he woke. Sun had learned the hard way never to wake him on days like that. Would John Yarmin be the same way?

Maybe it would be best to leave. No, that's what she had done before. She'd left without learning what John Yarmin had meant. She wasn't going to make the same mistake twice. If she had to, she would wait as long as necessary.

Why she tried the door she could never say. She expected it to be locked. It should have been locked. Whether he was at home or not, the door should have been locked. As soon as the door opened, she knew something was wrong. Her first thought was to call Gregor. Or maybe his friend the cop. Calling Chitti was another option. But no matter who she called, she would have to wait. And she was too concerned about John Yarmin's health to stand around waiting for someone else to go through that door.

Dread filled her, and yet she could not stay in the hallway. She inched the door open, taking some small comfort in the certainty that something was wrong. At least she knew that whatever had happened was done, and she would not be asked to try and stop it. All she could do was discover it.

Her worst fear was quickly confirmed. John Yarmin was sitting in the lone chair in his front room; his face frozen in suffering. Thankfully, the eyes were closed. His position in the chair suggested that he had struggled in his last moments. Perhaps he had suffered a massive heart attack and fought for life. It was hard to tell.

She left the door open—an avenue of quick escape—it was silly, but she left it open all the same. Reluctantly, she stepped toward his body. She saw that his fists were clenched.

It wasn't until she was standing within reach of the body that she could see the purple bruises on his neck. They were barely discernible, looking much like extensions of his shirt collar.

Was it possible he hadn't suffered a heart attack? She knew the answer. It wasn't only possible; it was improbable that this was natural. It would be too coincidental that Silva MacDenny and John Yarmin would die within days of each other.

What did it mean? Was she the cause? It made no sense. She'd been lured to the Lazaretto to investigate something, but whatever it was, she had been unable to do anything while two men died. Had they been murdered? Murdered because of her? Sun felt sick.

The room closed in and she became aware of the smell of the dead man's body. Too late, Sun raised a hand to cover her nose and mouth. She felt flushed and dizzy. Her eyes searched the room and she saw the kitchen and stumbled toward its sink.

The events of the past few days had finally caught up with her; the tragic demise of the Lost Platoon, Silva MacDenny's broken body, and now John Yarmin's death. She felt her stomach rebel against it all; rebel against the Lazaretto itself.

...Blood on the leaves...the bulging eyes and the twisted mouth...

Sun gagged and fought for control of her stomach. She drew in quick, short breaths but they weren't enough to stop her body from purging her already empty stomach.

She ran water in the sink, and sipped it from her cupped hand. Hard, bitter water. Just what she should have expected from the Lazaretto. She spit it out and had to settle for using the water to wash her lips and chin. Unable even to rinse out her mouth, she backed away from the soiled sink, shaking uncontrollably.

"Sun?"

She jumped at the sound. Chitti stood just inside the door, staring at John Yarmin.

"What happened?"

"I don't know," Sun shook her head, unable to say more.

Chitti smiled strangely. Sun could see a grim satisfaction mixed with that smile. She began to feel that certainty again; a certainty that something was terribly wrong.

"He did this." Chitti looked at the body in the chair. There was admiration in her tone. "That crazy bastard choked him to death."

"What?" Sun leaned forward, despite her queasiness. "Who are you talking about?"

"It doesn't matter," Chitti turned away from Yarmin. "Sun, I need your PDT."

"My PDT?" Sun was confused. What could Chitti want with her identity tag? Sun touched her neck and felt the pendant hanging there. "Shouldn't we call the police? Do you really think he was strangled? Is this happening because of me. Do you think? Did Mr. MacDenny and Mr. Yarmin die because I came to the Lazaretto?"

"Don't load yourself down with guilt, Sun. It's unhealthy, and a bit egocentric of you. You take too much of what's going on to heart. You better learn some things just happen and you can't do anything about them." Chitti held out her hand. "Now, give me your PDT."

Sun took a step back. "Why do you need my tag?"

"As sweet as you are, Sun, you ask too many questions. In fact, you talk too much." Chitti reached into her bag and pulled out the Para-Lazer.

Despite Sun's shock, she wasn't so far gone that she couldn't recognize her danger. She had nowhere to run. The room was bare;

nothing could be used as a shield or weapon. Her only option was to spring forward and attempt to gain control of the Para-Lazer. Maybe Chitti would be hit by her own weapon.

The sooner the better. Sun lurched forward. Chitti could not have anticipated that Sun would come at her immediately. She would never be ready to fire right away.

But Sun was wrong. The shock from the Para-Lazer's blast might as well have been a cannon. Her outstretched hand took the brunt of the shot. Sun felt the impact as the concussion blew up and through her arm. She was painfully aware that her body had been flipped backwards, jumping off the floor.

The power of the stars blazed through her, culminating in a brief explosion at the tip of every nerve. Her overloaded sensors mercifully shut down. She knew she'd fallen to the floor because she could still see what was happening. But she felt nothing even as she remained conscious.

Chitti was kneeling beside her. She must have been looking for Sun's PDT. It was a curious sensation, watching Chitti search her body and not being able to feel her doing it.

Once Chitti discovered the chain around her neck, she jerked, breaking it free from Sun's neck.

"A dragonfly pendant," Chitti said, in mockery of the trinket. The voice was muffled; Sun seemed to hear it coming from another room. "I should have known. It's so cute."

Sun could see the pendant, and watched Chitti snap open the case to reveal the PDT. What was she doing? Why was this happening?

"Don't worry. We'll make an even trade." Chitti fiddled with the pendant before closing it and dropping it on the floor.

Sun watched as Chitti dragged John Yarmin's body from the chair. She couldn't see what Chitti was doing with the body once she moved out of Sun's line of sight, but it took some time. She could hear Chitti sighing and grunting, wrestling with the man's body. Again, the noise was muffled, leaving Sun with a feeling of detachment. Was she still alive? Surely this wasn't how death felt. The shot had only paralyzed her. That's how Para-Lazars were supposed to work.

Muted footsteps told Sun that Chitti was coming back. To her horror, she saw the room begin to move. Chitti was pulling her. Where? Where was she taking her?

She wasn't moving toward the front door. She was going deeper into the apartment. Panic blurred her vision. What was going on? What was Chitti doing?

And then her view began to change. She was in the small bathroom. Chitti bent down. She wasn't smiling, she wasn't angry;

she just looked at Sun with a blank expression. Did she know Sun could see her and hear her? Chitti grabbed Sun by the shoulders.

Sun could see that she was being lifted up. She caught a brief, bizarre glimpse of both herself and Chitti in a mirror before her line of sight rotated to a porcelain bathtub. John Yarmin lay in the tub on his back. Chitti was dumping her in the tub with his body. Sun watched as she fell into the tub. Her view was immediately blocked by Yarmin's face. Their faces touched nose to nose.

God, no! Don't leave me like this! Sun could not feel it, but she could hear herself hyperventilating. She would have screamed if it were possible. Instead, she lay on top of Yarmin and frantically tried to move any part of her body. Nothing. As far as she knew, she couldn't even cry.

"This should work," she heard Chitti say. What would work? What had she done?

From a great distance, Sun heard a door shut.

Unable to close her eyes, she was forced to stare at John Yarmin's face a breath away from her own. A voice drifted through her head.

...the bulging eyes and the twisted mouth...

80

We were still standing in the front room when we heard the mechanical lock on the door to the back room. I felt a chill when I saw who came down the hall. It was the little man, Fortunado. Bernham's judge and executioner. What did this mean?

"What are you doing here?" Mr. Zoltis nearly shouted.

"I wanted to talk with you."

"You?" His eyes narrowed. This time, he did not shout. Instead, he spoke with a chillingly-soft voice. "What could you want to talk about?"

I worriedly saw Fortunado glance in my direction. Was he going to tell about Bernham? I had no idea if the man would tell the truth. I suddenly didn't like the idea of this man telling Mr. Zoltis how my attacker died. So much did it bother me that I was tempted to tell the story before he could. But I was too afraid.

"The package is almost here," Fortunado said, "and it's time we discussed our arrangement."

"Arrangement?" Calla's father drew up to his full height, enormous beside this little man. "Is that what you think this is? A renegotiation?" To my astonishment, Mr. Zoltis began to laugh.

Fortunado didn't laugh. Neither did he look intimidated by the bigger man's mockery. He simply waited until his employer had finished.

"Yes, that's just what this is. Your package is an extremely valuable package. And it won't do for him to get stuck here. We both know Pan

Juarez needs to be in Arcobia within the week. He'll never make it now unless he comes in as planned and takes my place."

"I know that, you jackass!" Mr. Zoltis was close to attacking the little man. "That's why you're being paid for this job. Why you're getting more than twice your usual rate. Don't you dare come in here and demand more money."

"There's a young security officer who keeps following me around. He smells a rat. It wouldn't take much for this cop to figure out what's going on."

"You don't understand how this works, Fortunado. So let me explain it to you. You think you've got leverage right now. That you can threaten to turn yourself in. But you've got it backwards. I have the leverage. Not you."

I knew what Mr. Zoltis meant. It was obvious Fortunado did not.

"I'll explain this just one time." Mr. Zoltis had calmed down though his face was as hard as ever. "If Pan Juarez does not get through the Lazaretto, you will take the blame. The switch has already been arranged. Everything that has been done to this point is in your hands. If you interfere now, you are a dead man. No one involved in this will back you up. Too much time and money has been invested. Your life is the leverage now. All of us stand to lose a great deal of money if you shoot this down. But you're the only one who will lose his life."

Fortunado should have been able to understand the danger he was in. All he had to do was go back and complete his job. But he didn't. He just stood there smiling.

"You won't kill me, Zoltis," Fortunado said. "And my life is not the leverage. There's no gun pointed at my head. It's pointed at the girl's head."

A cold pain shot through my heart.

"What girl?" Zoltis asked.

"Your girl. Your daughter."

"No!" I cried. Calla's father spun toward me.

"Shut up, woman."

Spurred by MacNally's insistence, Lepov made new attempts to find information on the woman in Morvees' apartment, but he was only trying to mollify his friend. Lepov didn't care about her anymore; she was just a reminder of how he had screwed up his relationship with Lilly. But for MacNally's sake, he went back over the recordings in Chettleham Keep's security office.

He spent an hour pulling up images and cursing the electrical interference that ruined most of the recordings. The only detail he had found on the woman was that she wore a hooded coat. But in the

Lazaretto, this wasn't rare. It certainly wasn't rare enough to run a check throughout Center City.

Lepov sat at the console facing the wall of monitors. This was getting him nowhere. They knew nothing about this woman, save that she might be Morvees' daughter. That was the best lead they had, and Pete Landon was doing his best to dig up anything from that angle. Lepov had nothing to offer in the form of help.

His work had served a purpose; he'd been able to help MacNally tie the old corpse to Anton Morvees' apartment. There was still no evidence that Morvees was involved in the death of the old corpse, but evidence might come once the tunnel was examined.

Maybe he was just tired. Or maybe he was feeling sorry for himself. Either way, Lepov was beginning to think he'd do everyone a favor by jettisoning the case. Branithwaite was angry and no longer wanted Lepov on his payroll. Who would care if he just went back to his office and forgot the whole thing?

Lilly might have talked him out of quitting, but he wasn't about to go looking for comfort from her. He doubted she'd even agree to talk with him again. No, Lepov was on his own.

He shut down the recording archive and the wall monitors. There wasn't any point in pretending any longer. He wasn't interested in finding Morvees' daughter—or whoever she was. He just wanted to let it go.

He left the security office and crossed the open lobby. He was almost to the glass doors when he heard someone call his name.

He turned and saw the boy, leaning against the half-wall entrance to the sunken chat room.

"Hello, Josh." Lepov backtracked through the lobby and held out his hand. As before, Josh did not hesitate to take it. "I believe I owe you a great big thank you. My cop friend says you saved my life."

"Yeah," Josh shrugged, "I just did like you said and stayed out of sight. But I had to keep an eye on you. No one else was gonna do it."

Lepov sat on the steps and reached into the outside pocket of his coat. "This is the first installment."

"Installment?" Josh's eyes lit up when he saw the green box of chewing gum.

"On paying back my debt. That sound fair to you?"

"Sure," the boy nodded eagerly. He stuck a piece of the gum in his mouth and began to chew it even as he asked Lepov a question. "They really find that old man dead *under* his apartment?"

"Sort of," Lepov said. "You still need to keep away from there, you understand me? I don't want to hear about you hanging around down there. I'd hate to have to come back down here and smack you around."

"Ain't you gonna be around anymore?"

"No, I don't think so. I've done what Mr. Branithwaite hired me to do. I'll have other clients and I doubt you'll see me here anymore."

"You gonna see your lady friend again?"

Lepov squinted. "What lady friend is that?"

"Well, you know, the one you met here."

"Which one did I meet?"

"I don't know. The one you carried over your shoulder."

"Josh," Lepov couldn't help but smile, "you were watching me again, weren't you? That was just a misunderstanding I had with a woman. Her name is Sun, if you have to know."

"Yeah, that's the one. She's kind of pretty, I guess. You plan on seeing her again?"

"I don't know. Why?"

"Well, you met her here, and if you see her again, that means you got no excuse not to see me again either." His eyes widened at Lepov, waiting for a response.

"You think so? I'll have to think about that. But, I think you're missing an important point, Josh."

"I am?"

"I only said I wouldn't be coming back around here. But I also said I had a debt that I intended to pay back. Now what that means is, you're gonna have to come around to my office now and then to get your installments. You think you can do that?"

"Yeah, I can do that." Josh was visibly relieved.

"Okay then." Lepov pushed to his feet. "Now, you gotta stay out of trouble. I can't send you chewing gum if you get in trouble with your mother. Can you promise to stay out of trouble?"

"Yeah," Josh nodded.

"Then I got to head out. And you remember what I said—you stay away from that apartment."

Lepov was glad the kid had showed up. It felt good to talk to a young man with a pure heart; both rare qualities in the Lazaretto.

But not impossible to find. Sun Uijong also fit that description. She was still young and from what he had seen, she still had a pure heart. If she spent much more time at her job that would change. But for now, she was free of cynicism and bitterness.

All that talk of Sun had reminded him that he was supposed to call her that morning. MacNally's wakeup call had driven the thought straight out of his mind.

He paid the extra fee for a TransitCar and made it back to his office as soon as possible. He did not think Sun would be at her hotel—she would be off saving the world one veteran at a time—but he called to check on her anyway. The manager at the front desk surprised him with the news that she was in her room.

"Would you please connect me?" Lepov asked.

"Certainly, sir."

Lepov waited until the manager's voice came back on the line.

"I'm sorry, sir. She does not answer. Perhaps she is sleeping."

Lepov thanked the man, and closed the connection.

Sleeping? Not this late in the morning. That was too unlikely. Could it be she did not want to talk? That she was avoiding him? Maybe. It was possible she had picked up enough bad vibes from Lilly to know she needed to stay out of the way.

That was about right. He'd ruined a friendship with Lilly Stewart; why even start one with Sun Uijong? Better to leave her alone. There was no reason for a girl like that to get mixed up with an old man like him.

What a waste, Lepov thought. She was cute.

One of Lepov's questions had stuck in MacNally's head. It was a pretty good question, and one that ought to be answered. Had anyone other than Lilly and Reno known about the painting she had brought in?

To get the answer, MacNally did the exact opposite of what he had told Lepov to do: he was going to find Lilly Stewart. But he wasn't going to tell Lepov. That wouldn't turn out well at all. He wanted Lepov to quit thinking about her. And MacNally would have done the same if Lepov hadn't posed his question.

Lilly had already left Center City and taken a room in Alpha Quadrant. It would lockdown tomorrow at noon. Subsequently, the place was a madhouse.

MacNally had not needed to enter Alpha Quadrant for many years. He probably had not been inside that sector more than four or five times since he'd been a young security officer assigned to it. He saw right away that some things never change.

A great many of the people in Alpha were not preparing to settle in for the forty-day quarantine. Instead, many of them were clearing out, heading back into Center City. These were the servicemen, vendors, and entertainers who moved from quadrant to quadrant before each lockdown. Inveterate nomads who worked the circuit from Alpha to Delta and back around again. They stayed as long as possible before lockdown, and then took a few days off before the next sector opened.

On this last day before lockdown, the streets of Alpha appeared to be full of refugees, fleeing an invading horde. Travelers loaded with luggage and supplies wandered from one street to the next looking for their living quarters, many simply taking the rooms assigned to them. Some paid for slightly more comfortable quarters. A few paid a stiff price for penthouses. But for all of them, time was running out.

MacNally had to push his way through the crowds to reach Lilly's hotel. It wasn't deep inside the quadrant but it had taken half an hour just to reach its entrance. The reception desk was even more chaotic. Ignoring the main check-in counter, he circled to a back entrance for employees. His PDT gave him access to the manager's office, one of the benefits that came with the badge.

"What do you want?" a surly bald man in a white button-down shirt asked. His pants had no chance of getting around his grossly oversized waist. A pair of greasy suspenders held them precariously in place.

"I'm here to see one of your customers." MacNally offered his badge. "I just need her room number and I'll get out of your hair."

"You're a real comedian," the man grumbled, rubbing his bald head, "what's her name?"

"Lilly Stewart."

"Room 7403. If you arrest her, I still charge for the room. She don't get a refund."

MacNally walked out and had to bull his way onto an elevator. If he had been gentle, he might have had to wait for an elevator all night. Shouldering his way off he walked the full length of the seventh floor's hallway in search of Lilly's room.

She opened the door, obviously recognizing him, but saying nothing. He entered and shut the door quietly behind him.

"You don't look surprised to see me," he said by way of a greeting.

"To tell you the truth, Ed, I am. I expected *him* to come and find me. Not send a surrogate." She wore black synthetic pants that fit tight as a glove, a long-sleeved white shirt of the same fabric, and nothing on her feet. She sat on a small sofa, curling her bare feet under her.

MacNally understood why Lepov couldn't get her out of his system. Lilly was cool, hard, and graceful; a woman impossible to ignore. She looked good, forever slim, her skin milky white. Her white pony-tail, as always, sprouted almost directly from the top of her head.

"He doesn't know I'm here, Lilly. And this doesn't have anything to do with him."

Lilly smirked. "He told you about the job I did for Raley, didn't he? You plan to take me in for smuggling or something like that?"

"Mind if I smoke?" MacNally didn't wait for a reply. He pulled out a cigarette and lit it as she watched. Once it was lit, she rose and took the pack. Withdrawing her own cigarette, she allowed him to light it with his.

"So what do you want?" She inhaled deeply and returned to the sofa.

"I want to know about this painting you brought Raley." He saw her lips compress. "Not for the reason you think. I don't care about your part in this. I'm sure you've covered yourself legally. You're too smart not to. But I want to know who was involved in this. You *did* hear what happened last night, didn't you?"

"Yes, I heard." She let out a long sigh. "I told Cam he was being careless. I guess next you'll ask if I'm the one who took it."

"Well, I understand the ownership of the painting was in question. It's not impossible that you stole it back for the other side. A chance to double your money. Did you take it?" MacNally wasn't shy about such things. Besides, unlike Lepov, he wasn't trying to protect a friendship.

"No," she answered without taking offence.

"Well, it's my job to ask." He settled into a straight-backed chair.

"Like Gregor," she added. This time he detected a note of sarcasm. "And now is it your job to search my suite?"

"Nope. You wouldn't keep it here if you had it, would you?"

"I hope I wouldn't be so stupid."

"You wouldn't." MacNally watched the smoke curl up from what was left of his cigarette. "Hell, Lilly, you wouldn't even be stupid enough to steal from Raley, would you?"

Blowing smoke from her pursed lips, she slowly shook her head.

"So who knew about this painting besides Raley?"

"Nobody that I know of. Raley wouldn't allow me to tell anyone, and he didn't tell anyone either. I know. When I showed up at his office they were shocked to see me. The receptionist did not even have me on her list. I had to argue with her that Cam was expecting me."

"Somebody had to know, Lilly."

"I wish you would believe me. I don't think anyone knew." For once, her eyes were pleading, a rare moment of vulnerability. "I've thought about this all morning. I know this doesn't help you. But no one else knew. Ed, I didn't do this."

"I know, Lilly. A man named Anton Morvees did it. But he's dead. His partner still has the paintings. We're looking for his daughter." MacNally stubbed out his cigarette in a wooden ashtray and gave Lilly an encouraging smile. "I didn't come here to accuse you. I just hoped you'd know something I didn't."

Jason Phillip Reeser

He could see the relief in her eyes. She was still as cold as ice; he'd only caught a glimpse of her warmth, but it was enough for him to see the source of Lepov's fascination with her. It would make his next job easier.

"That's the end of my official visit." He stayed in the chair. "The rest of this is just a conversation between acquaintances."

She cocked her head—her ponytail slid down her shoulder— "the rest of what?"

"I have a feeling Lepov didn't tell you what happened the other night. The night he almost died."

Lilly had been sitting with her legs still tucked under her, but now she let them slip out as she leaned back against the sofa pillows. He'd guessed right. She didn't know.

He gave her the details. His years as a cop had taught him to speak without emotion or opinion. He made sure she understood that Lepov had received a blow to the head, and that under stress he had seen her, Lilly, standing over his makeshift coffin, ordering that he be drowned.

Her hand shook. The cigarette shook with it, scattering ash onto one pant leg.

"When did this happen?" She nervously wiped at the ash.

"Three nights ago."

"What is he doing walking around?" She was angry now, but not with Lepov. "Why isn't he in a hospital?"

"He should be, I guess. But he won't sit still. You know him."

"I know you. You needed his help, didn't you?"

"Lilly," he snapped, "I'm telling you this for a reason. You need to know that he's been in a bad spot. And he got some bad ideas stuck in his head, like a corrupted recording. I'm trying to tell you that he's not to blame for his behavior lately."

"I thought we agreed I'm not stupid, Ed." She sat forward enough to touch his knee, her hand and cigarette no longer shaking. "I get it, okay? And you're a good man to try and help."

"I'm just saying it matters. It matters that you two work things out."

"Maybe so." She withdrew her hand, dropped the cigarette in a square ashtray, and crossed her arms. "And maybe not."

83

Sun was going mad. She could not close her eyes, nor could she sleep. She lay on top of John Yarmin's body staring into his twisted face, unable to move her eyes to the left or right; her view numbingly static.

She had never spent much time wondering about the existence of God, being an agnostic who neither put faith in a greater being nor insisted that such a being did not exist. Yet now, as measureless time dragged her into panic, she did not hesitate to call out to *Him*. It was her only option. She called out to Lepov, as well. She called again. She called so many times that she began to hear cries even when not consciously calling. It did not matter. No one would hear.

Not John Yarmin, his face as immobile as her own.

She was alone, and she felt it. Felt it like an ice-cold hand slowly drawing her down. Maybe it was Yarmin's hands, clinging to her in an embrace from one dead body to another. Cold, creeping cold, clawed at her from below.

Could Yarmin feel it too? No. No, he was dead. Wasn't he? Sun couldn't remember. Odd, she should forget. They were as close as they would ever be, staring face to face. But despite this, she could not remember if he was dead.

The biting cold reached her heart. Of course he was dead. She could see as much. He was like a synthetic replica that will never rust or decay. A statue which cannot be worn down. He would forever dominate Sun's view. A lifeless, empty visage of despair.

For a time, she could see Gregor Lepov. He too was dead, his face distorted with pain. She wanted to cry. She might be crying, for all she knew. Not because Gregor was dead, but because he would not look at her. He would not touch her; speak to her, offer a hint of love. Why must he be so cold? What kind of man could be filled with such ice?

The cold was growing.

But the face before her was not Gregor's. It was Yarmin's. And Yarmin was not dead. He was moving. He was slowly turning from her.

No, he wasn't moving. He was rising. His whole body was pushing her out of the way, rotating her upward. Finally, she understood what was happening. And when she did, she silently cried out again.

Oh, God! We're floating! The cold she'd felt was water. Chitti had turned on the water. The tub was slowly filling. The buoyancy of Sun's body aided in righting her, leaving her now with a view of the ceiling. But she did not stop there. She continued gradually turning, the view shifting as her body began to turn from lying on its back to lying on its other side.

Sun could see herself slipping along this arc. She wanted to kick at the tub, to claw at the water surrounding her. Turning ever more, she would end up face down in the water. God and Lepov drew farther and farther away.

At least she wouldn't feel herself drown. That was something in which she could take comfort. She wouldn't feel any of it.

But how could she feel the cold? Was this just a trick of her mind? Or had her body played a trick on her, giving her one last sensation before her life would be smothered in cold, bitter waters?

Sun watched helplessly as her view continued to shift left.

84

The Liar had been right; the Major's clothes fit her well enough. She could easily be mistaken for the Major while in uniform. All she had to do was keep her hair covered. The Major's black hair was about the same length—a little longer, maybe—and the military cap was sufficient to hide the difference. When she passed by the front desk, it would have to look like the Major had left on her own. It would not do to seed the concierge with suspicion.

She was still in the Major's hotel room. There was no reason to leave in a hurry. Surely the Major was dead by now. It had been silly of the Liar to balk at killing her. But she had been afraid to make the same mess she'd made with the Thief. Drowning her seemed the best alternative.

Once it was dark, the Liar would pass through the front entrance. There would be enough lights casting distracting glares off the windows to keep anyone from noticing that she was not the Major. And once she left the hotel, she would retrieve the paintings and enter Alpha Quadrant. It was easy. The Liar felt a tremor of impatience. Just a few hours.

The phone began to ring. It was the second time someone had called since the Liar had come into the room. She read the caller's PDT signature. The Liar did not recognize it. Could it be an interplanetary call from the Major's office? No, this had to be a Lazaretto number.

A chill ran down the Liar's neck. Who would be calling the Major? As far as the Liar knew, the Major had not met anyone in the Lazaretto since her arrival. Did this caller know the Major? If the Liar tried to impersonate the Major, would they know something was not right?

The hotel knew she was there. They must have a PDT reader that picked up the Major's PDT signal. If this caller remained persistent they might become worried when she failed to answer. Maybe they already knew that she was impersonating the Major. Maybe it was the police, trying to trick her into answering. Were they in fact standing in the hall waiting for her?

How many could she immobilize with the Para-Lazer? Not all of them. They'd get her. In the end, they'd get her and she'd be imprisoned on this rock forever.

No. The Liar cleared her head. She was beginning to sound like the Thief. She had heard that kind of paranoia before. She wasn't about to lose her mind as he had. She closed her eyes and took four deep breaths.

The caller gave up.

Now what? Should she stay? Wait until dark? Or should she get out immediately? She could leave the back way, though that would ruin any plans she had of witnesses confirming that the Major had left the hotel.

Who was this caller? Whoever it was, the call was forcing her to change her plans.

She would have to leave. If they hadn't already, they would eventually send someone to check on her. She couldn't risk that. She must not interact with the hotel staff. They undoubtedly knew the Major; enough to know that she was an imposter.

Stay or go?

She had little choice.

85

For Lepov, it was no longer about checking on Sun's safety. He'd spent the better part of the morning and early afternoon looking for her. She wasn't answering at her hotel; she wasn't at the *Society's* office. He had even gone back to Chettleham Keep to make sure she hadn't gone to Morvees' apartment.

Now, back in his office, he searched for any trace of her; the hotel had her listed on their PDT reader for most of the morning, but there was no answer in her room. Lepov had become convinced their reader was malfunctioning.

MacNally had not heard from her. Could she be taking the day off, needing to get away? Was she wandering around Terran Park or losing herself in the shopping district on Masthead Avenue? That might be the most logical assumption. Women were always finding comfort in shopping, weren't they?

On a hunch, he made a call to the IHS office. Just maybe, she was there digging up records on the Lost Platoon. He hoped so. He was starting to get annoyed. She shouldn't have been so hard to find.

"Interplanetary Health Services," the woman's voice was a balance of civility mixed with institutionalized tedium, "Records Division."

"I was hoping you could tell me if an officer from the military has come through your office today looking for death certificates and the like on the Lost Platoon. She's a Major, short black hair."

"I'm sorry, sir, we don't allow access to our records." Her tone suggested Lepov should know the rules.

"Well I thought you might have made an exception for her, being a representative of the government." He was exaggerating. He hadn't expected any such thing. This was only a shot in the dark.

"I'm sorry, sir. No one has been allowed into the record room all day. And before you ask, let me add that no one has even asked for access."

When Lepov cut the connection, he saw Lilly through his office door's glass pane. She knocked on the door before opening it.

He tried to think of something to say, but discarded everything that came to mind. He was most worried that he would say something that would anger her. When she came into the room, he saw right away it was too late. He read anger in her eyes.

"You should be sitting down," she said. Her words surprised him and he did not know how to respond. Unable to think of what to say, and unable to think of a reason not to, he sat down.

"You should tell me why I'm sitting down."

"Why haven't you told me what's really going on?"

"And what would that be?" Lepov asked.

"How bad is it?" Her tone softened, and she stepped close. "You know, you take the prize. I was going to leave, and you were never going to say a word."

Lilly gently touched the side of his head, turning it so as to get a better look. Lepov winced as she brushed back some of his hair.

"I take it someone's been talking about my recent interest in diving."

"Ed came to see me. You're an idiot, you know, running all over when you should be in bed."

"I'm fine," he said, pulling back. "Just a few bruises."

She shouldn't have come back. Whatever MacNally had told her, it didn't matter. They weren't about to start hearing soft music as they kissed. Things were only going to get worse. Lilly had been right: they weren't good for each other.

Besides, he was too worried about Sun to deal with Lilly.

"There's more than just bruises, Ed told me about *her*."

"He shouldn't have," Lepov grumbled. It was none of MacNally's business. He made a mental note to kill his friend the next time they met.

"Why did I have to hear this from Ed?" Lilly asked. "And don't tell me you didn't want sympathy. You thrive on sympathy, Gregor Lepov. You just don't like us knowing that."

"Maybe I like it when you think I'm just being a jerk. It's an image I've carefully cultivated." What was he supposed to tell her? That he had become convinced she was a killer? That she was in league with someone like Anton Morvees?

"You're trying to make me leave again." Lilly wasn't making a joke, and she wasn't being dramatic. But Lepov could see she was hurt. She must know that he was keeping his distance — pushing her away — for a reason he would never explain.

And he never would explain it because he didn't understand it well enough himself. He couldn't tell her his suspicions because it would hurt her to the point they could never have the kind of relationship Lepov wanted. But if he kept pushing her away to hide the truth, they would never have that relationship. For all practical purposes, their chance to be together had passed.

And by the look in Lilly's eyes, she suspected the same. The hell of it was, this all was coming out of a case that was essentially about some lousy, stolen paintings.

"I'm not going to." Lilly crossed to a chair and sat. "You're not going to make me leave."

A small red flash drew Lepov's attention to his deskscreen. He had started a data-mine in the hopes of finding Sun. The flashing red headline reported her in the process of checking out of her hotel. Lepov leaned forward and read the information under the headline. Checking out?

"Lilly, give me a minute, will you?" Lepov grabbed the data-mine report and backtracked the data until he was convinced it was accurate. Sun had informed the hotel of her intention just minutes before. She must still be in the room.

"I need to make a call." He didn't bother to look at Lilly as he made the connection with the hotel. "I'd like to speak with Sun Uijong, please."

Lilly did not say or do anything to indicate that she had heard him, concentrating instead on the office windows. By all appearances, she wasn't paying attention. But he knew better.

As before, the concierge told him Sun was not answering.

This was getting him nowhere. He needed to see her. Make sure she was okay. Of course, he was worrying for selfish reasons. Was she angry or hurt after meeting Lilly? Was that why she had never called? Lilly had been right. It was obvious Sun was interested in him. It wasn't hard to explain. She was impressed with an older man, despite his shortcomings; father-figure, nothing more. But he was surprised by his response. Sure, he felt flattered. It was nice to know a younger woman could still be attracted to him. But he was more than flattered. At the thought of Sun leaving, Lepov found he was eager to find her, to stop her. Even more so than when Lilly had left.

No. That wasn't true. But knowing that things with Lilly were impossible, Lepov needed to know he had a chance to be happy with someone like Sun. He didn't want to be alone for the rest of his life because he'd let yet another woman walk out.

"You look worried."

Lilly's words broke his train of thought. At the same time, they reminded him that Lilly hadn't truly walked out on him. Not yet.

"Something's wrong." Lepov tapped on his deskscreen. "The girl you met yesterday, Sun, won't answer my calls."

"You didn't assault her again, did you?"

"I haven't seen her since she left last night. Haven't heard from her either. Now, the hotel says she's checking out. The last thing I knew, she wasn't planning on leaving. She still has work to finish."

"Then I'd better go, Gregor, so you can go stop her."

"You don't need to go, Lilly." He didn't want her to leave while he was distracted with Sun. "Let me get this script running. Once I can be sure nothing's wrong, we can finish talking."

"What's the script?"

"A MoleRunner," Lepov answered before he realized what he was doing. The last thing he wanted was for Lilly to find out how he'd been tracking her.

"What does it do?"

"It tracks down a person's PDT—any purchases, anywhere there's a reader that will pick up the signal. If you walk past a police vehicle, for instance, the police PDT readers usually pick up all signals within a quarter-block radius. Or maybe you step into a building where readers are recording who enters and who exits. The MoleRunner compiles all of these hits so that I can see where a person has been and what they've been up to."

"You can get hits from the police readers?" Lilly leaned over the desk and scanned the MoleRunner data.

"Sure, they don't mind. They don't know about it, either. And I don't intend to tell them." Lepov was glad he'd shut down the MoleRunner's search for Lilly. He had the irrational fear that the MoleRunner would suddenly display the results of its search with her name on it.

"So this is how you find someone you're looking for, huh?" Lepov wasn't sure, but Lilly's expression suggested she knew what he had been up to.

There was nothing to do but set up the search and try to steer the conversation to a different subject.

"So why were you talking with MacNally?" Lepov raised a hand. "Let me guess: he questioned you about the paintings, right?"

"Yes, he did." Lilly leaned forward and continued to read.

"He asked you who knew about the painting you brought in."

"Yes, he did that, too." She stood up straight and turned her attention away from the MoleRunner and looked at Lepov. "Nobody knew about it but Cam and me. And no, I didn't steal it."

"I never said you did. I'm pretty sure we know who did."

"That's what MacNally said. If you want my opinion, I think the guy who did this just got lucky. He couldn't have known the Mona Lisa was going to be there."

"He didn't exactly get lucky." Lepov's mind flashed back to the figure on the tunnel stairs.

"How long will your little mole take?" she asked.

"Not long. I'm only having it check her movements this morning and into the afternoon. I'm just trying to establish that nothing out of the ordinary happened with her."

"This is how you found me at the hotel."

"Yeah," Lepov answered before he realized what he was saying. So much for changing the subject. "I'm sorry."

"No reason to be sorry, Gregor."

"Okay," he nodded, not knowing what else to say. Did she mean what she'd said? There had been no sarcasm in her words. Yet, he wasn't ready to believe she could simply ignore everything that had happened. Yes, she might have some sympathy for him regarding his injuries, but that wouldn't erase the hurt she would feel once she learned that he had believed her capable of murder.

"I can make a pot of coffee while we wait," she offered.

"You're going to wait?"

"I want to know if the girl is okay. I'll stay if you don't mind."

"I won't mind, not if you make coffee."

She smiled, and for a moment he started to feel as if things could be right between them. But could they? He had little faith in it happening. She might try to forgive him, but Lepov knew how deep his suspicions of her went; just how much he had bought into the lie his injured brain had conjured.

A cup of coffee wouldn't make it all go away. Lepov knew this. But was it possible a cup of coffee could introduce hope into a hopeless situation? He wasn't sure it could, but neither was he sure it couldn't.

86

"So that's it? That's your leverage?" Mr. Zoltis stood towering over Fortunado. I took a sharp breath and held it, knowing that Calla's father was about to teach Fortunado the dangers of threatening a man's family; especially a man like Kjarsta Zoltis. "Well? You'll do what, hurt her? Kill

her?"

"No," Fortunado took a step back, "I'm not so stupid. I'm not about to give you an excuse to kill me. But I will tell them about her. IHS. They'll know she's been sick. And she'll never leave the Lazaretto."

I let out the breath I'd been holding and moaned. Mr. Zoltis glared. I couldn't help but plea: "No, no, leave her alone." We had worked so hard. I had done so much to bring her through so that she might get out of the Lazaretto. It couldn't end like this.

And it wouldn't. Calla's father wouldn't let it. He was about to show his true character. I was about to see how dangerous this man really was. I had always seen glimpses of his treachery, but now I knew I would finally see the real Kjarsta Zoltis.

He started to laugh. I thought at first he was beginning to growl, to bellow in rage. But no, what had started as a low, rumbling howl grew into a full-bodied cackle. It was worse than an angry howl; it chilled me spiritually. There was no rage in that noise, no terrifying signal of imminent violence; there was only straightforward, genuine amusement. Mr. Zoltis sounded like a drunk who had decided the world was a colossal joke.

Fortunado was as disturbed by the laughter as much as I was. It dawned on both of us that Kjarsta Zoltis was not in the least worried what happened to his daughter.

"This is all you've got?" Zoltis managed to ask between his giddy wheezes. "You're threatening to expose my daughter's sickness to the IHS? I'm supposed to lose all composure and capitulate to your pathetic blackmail by throwing money at you? Fortunado, you're not only a bastard, but you're a complete incompetent. Good God, how did a fool like you ever make it through combat in one piece?"

My chest felt ready to burst. Was it possible I misunderstood what was going on? I hardly thought it was possible. Fortunado had the same incredulous look on his face. Could Kjarsta Zoltis be this callous a man? Surely he was bluffing.

"Are you trying to call my bluff?" Fortunado set his jaw and leaned forward, no longer willing to back away from the man he had just threatened. "Don't underestimate me. And don't bother threatening me either. You need me."

"Underestimate you?" Zoltis bent his head to look at Fortunado. "Threaten you? You must be out of your mind. Do whatever you have to do about the girl. I don't give a damn where she spends the rest of her life. Just make sure you stay out of trouble until I tell you to move aside for Pan Juarez. Do you understand?"

I don't know if Fortunado understood, but I did. I understood so well tears fell from my eyes as I saw everything that we had done for that sweet little girl fall to pieces.

Somewhere out there was a woman capable of terrifying violence. MacNally had seen violence before; his partner's death had been particularly violent. But that had been at the hands of a killer only trying to disguise murder as something else. But this violence—displayed on those steps in the tunnel—was something that could only have been scraped off the bottom of a black soul. When MacNally considered that the murderess was most likely the victim's daughter, he felt unclean.

This had happened right under MacNally's nose. He'd had an opportunity to stop it before it ever started, but had chosen to wait. The decision had made sense at the time, but now came the season of doubt and speculation.

Worse, the killer was still unknown. They had nowhere to begin. To think she was in Alpha Quadrant would be logical, it was just closing. But thinking that way would be a mistake. The killer had been down in the tunnel, where she could have gone to any of the quadrants. Delta was the closest to raising its lockdown. And once that happened, this woman would take a transport out of the Lazaretto and never be seen again.

"Menya, you were right. Weren't you the one who suggested we arrest Morvees right away?"

"I don't remember," Russell murmured. He was young, but not so young that he didn't recognize the importance of discretion. "It doesn't matter, anyway. She might have killed him before we were done talking. We don't have the results back on the Visuals yet."

MacNally had already discussed their options with Captain Jenkins, including the possibility of a full-scale search of every quadrant, but the logistics were impossible. Even ignoring the lack of manpower available, the quadrants would have to be compromised for each to be searched properly. The quadrant security forces were not large enough to make more than a perfunctory search. And no one on God's Green Earth, or any of the other planets for that matter, would authorize the contamination of all four quadrants.

All of which meant the killer would be gone long before they ever figured out who she was.

"You know what, Russell?" MacNally pulled out a fresh cigarette but threw it away before lighting it. "I think it's time I retire. By the time you figure out who this woman is, I'll be buried out there on that rocky slope. I deserve as much."

"Oh, stop whining."

"What?" MacNally had heard the words, but wasn't sure he had heard them correctly. Russell was getting brave. He turned to see

Pete Landon come into the office. "What did you just say to me?"

"You heard me. Your ears aren't that bad yet." Puzzle Pete was grinning, his mane of hair flowing behind him like a king's train. "Where would you street cops be without us desk jockeys, huh?"

"You got something?" MacNally asked in a hushed voice, afraid that he had misunderstood.

"I got something. You and Lepov told me to find out how reliable birth records are in the Lazaretto. Remember?"

"Yeah, I remember. So?"

"Well it was just like Lepov suspected — birth records here are less reliable than death records."

MacNally stroked his bushy mustache and cleared his throat. "You didn't come up here to tell us that, Pete. Now quit the theatrics and tell us what you got."

"Okay, okay. Birth records are pathetic, because IHS doesn't care much about the health of any babies born here. If they are the offspring of someone who has been exiled here, then they have no chance of getting out, right? So there are only good records of the children with a reasonable chance of getting out. If Morvees had a daughter, he would have made no effort to get her documented. Okay, so that means we don't have her listed for her birth."

MacNally made a motion for Pete to speed up his presentation.

"Just hold on. You'll want to hear this. I thought about what you said about Lilly Stewart and Kjarsta Zoltis. So while I had access to birth records, I looked this guy up. He did have a daughter. She was born a few years before all this happened. But she died the same year this all went down. His daughter was a plague victim. Lilly was not his daughter."

"And Morvees? You had to find something out, right?" MacNally was getting angry. "If you went through all of that to say Lilly was not connected to Zoltis, I'm gonna pull you into little pieces and give us all a better reason to call you Puzzle Pete."

"Morvees was willing to admit he had a daughter to get housing upgrades, right?" Pete paid no attention to MacNally's bluster. "So I started thinking. It occurred to me that Morvees would do what he had to, for money. Not for any other reason. He wouldn't have bothered to send the child to a doctor unless it had been absolutely necessary. And then, if he did, he wouldn't pay one fraction of her bill. No way. Not if money were so important. So I ran a check on all medical records. That's an extensive check, mind you. That's why it's taken this long."

MacNally had not seen Pete this excited and talkative since he had come to Anton Morvees' crime scene. In fact, Pete's reaction to the bloody scene had been bad enough that MacNally had suggested he get some professional help. But here was the old Pete, grandstanding as he talked his way through yet another investigative puzzle. Research had been just the thing Pete needed to rid himself of those horrific images. MacNally was envious.

"But just an hour ago, I hit the jackpot. I know who his daughter is."

"Well?"

"Well, it's a little anti-climactic. Morvees was sued by a dentist over a bill regarding a young girl who needed to have a wisdom tooth pulled. He admitted the girl was his daughter, but was able to prove in court that she was not under his legal care because the mother had been raising the child on her own. They had never been legally married, either. But the daughter turns out to be someone we never heard of. She's some charity worker on the east end of Center City. Her name is Chitti Sienté."

MacNally stared at Pete as though his mane were on fire. "What?"

"You need ear surgery, MacNally. I said her name was —"

"I heard her name, Pete. But what did you mean she was someone we'd never heard of?" MacNally thought Pete was just playing games.

"You recognize her name?" Pete asked.

"Don't you? She's the woman that's been helping Sun Uijong. Don't tell me *you* forgot." That was impossible. Pete would never miss such an obvious connection.

"The MacDenny report." Pete's face paled at the realization. "She's the other woman. You think she's the one who did *that*?"

"I'm not gonna jump to conclusions," MacNally stood and grabbed his coat, "but I'm not gonna start believing in coincidences. Chitti Sienté better start thinking of an alibi."

Russell and Pete were right on MacNally's heels. For the first time since this case started, MacNally felt he might actually accomplish something. Even if they couldn't find this girl right away, at least they knew what she looked like.

"We'll start at her office. She won't be there, but maybe we'll find something to tell us where she's going."

Pete cursed as they stopped at the elevator. MacNally and Russell swung around and stared, shocked by his uncharacteristic language.

"What's the matter?" MacNally asked.

"Sun. She's been working alone with this woman. If Sienté could kill Anton Morvees the way she did, you think she might have done something similar to Sun?"

Neither MacNally nor Russell had an answer for him.

"We gotta hurry, dammit." Pete jammed the elevator call button repeatedly. "How could I have been so stupid? How did I not recognize that name? I should have figured all of this out this morning. I've been too damn slow."

"Take it easy, Pete. We're going to be there in no time. She's probably just fine. Morvees' daughter had no reason to hurt Sun. In fact, given the ferocity of her attack on her father, I'd say she was so focused on killing Morvees that she's probably no threat to anyone else."

Pete nodded, but it was easy to see he didn't believe it. Well, that was no surprise. MacNally didn't believe it either.

88

The first problem had been getting the paintings into Alpha Quadrant. The Liar had known they would be bulky — rolled in their aluminum cylinder — but she had expected to bring them into Delta Quadrant through the tunnel. Now, forced to go into Alpha Quadrant legally, she had to think of a simple explanation. No one would look closely at what she was carrying, but it wouldn't do to have no explanation as to what she was carrying.

Lazaretto Quadrant closings were chaotic affairs, with few restrictions on what travelers could bring as they moved into a quadrant. But she was certain the police would be watching for the paintings.

The next problem had been the Para-Lazer. Should she take it along? Or was it too much of a liability? As the prissy little Major had pointed out, weapons were illegal in the Lazaretto, and she did not want to draw any unnecessary attention upon entering.

But the weapon made her feel safe. To be without it was unthinkable. No, she hadn't kept the razor. That had been an easy decision. She had no desire ever to go back to that kind of experience. When she realized she still had it with her at John Yarmin's apartment, she had no trouble leaving it behind.

The Para-Lazer would stay with her. She could slip it inside the cylinder with the canvases. There was enough room, and as long as she could keep the authorities from examining the cylinder, she'd be fine.

She was half way to Alpha Quadrant when she finally realized how to make it work. The answer was simple. A quick trip back to the office would be sufficient.

Once she entered the office, she quickly powered up her desksystem and started searching for the necessary document. It was not available to the public, but the government system safeguards were substandard. And as she had suspected, the office of Veterans' Health Benefits made practically no attempt at encrypting their document storage.

Once in the system, the Liar forged an official set of travel papers with the VHB letterhead. Though not wanting to waste time, she worded the travel order with precision. Despite her rush, it had to bear examination.

The falsified papers were simple enough. She just had to give Major Sun Uijong authority to travel through the Lazaretto with classified documents that must remain sealed in their cylinder. It didn't make much sense, but the Army was famous for its lack of logic.

Along with the travel documents, the Liar printed a VHB label and affixed it to the cylinder.

Finished and ready to leave, the Liar had to admit she was impressed with her own cleverness. The Thief never would have thought of this. She would make it out, and when she did, she would be able to get far, far away from that man. She began to feel the same euphoria she'd felt in the pit of her stomach when she had first realized he was dead. She had done it. No one was going to be able to stop her now.

A last glance around the office and the Liar walked out, her arms wrapped around the aluminum cylinder. She deserved this. For the first time in her life, she was doing something for herself; not for the homeless and hopeless men of the Lazaretto, and not for her psychotic father.

Even a cold wind could not shake her joy. She had won. She had kicked fate squarely in the teeth. It was good to be alive.

How long had it been? Sun no longer had any idea. All she knew for certain was that by some miracle, she had not drowned. Her body had stopped rolling to the left, and instead, had rolled back to center. She was now facing up. Perhaps a part of her body had caught on Yarmin's below her. She didn't like to think about that. She had been trying not to think about John Yarmin.

He was under her, and had to be completely submerged. Her view of the spotted and mildewed ceiling told her she was floating every now and then. At least that was the best explanation as to why the ceiling rocked back and forth once in a while. For a time, she became convinced John Yarmin was still alive, his struggle to break free of the water the reason she was rocking. She fought to keep that image from her mind; that twisted face grimacing and screaming to get out of the water, his legs kicking spastically as he grappled at her body for something to pull up on. The thought drove her insane.

...the bulging eyes...

No, he was dead. No, he was dead! She sought comfort in the mantra that John Yarmin had been strangled to death. The thought had not started out as comforting, but now she clung to it like the gentle words of a lover; a prayer on a dark night.

To her astonishment, tired of staring at the ceiling, she was actually able to close her eyes. She had never thought such a simple act would bring such welcome relief. At the same time, she knew she was finally able to cry; she could feel tears pooling at the corners of her eyes. She still could not feel them run down her cheek, but it was enough to know she was able to make tears; warm tears that proved she was alive.

But the tears were all that could be considered warm. She had ceased long ago to feel anything other than ice. It had to be the water; the same cold, foul water she'd tasted in Yarmin's sink. She was beginning to believe she had always been this cold. It was getting hard to remember warmth. Eventually, she knew, she might not even remember warmth had ever existed. By then, her tears might even begin to flow from her chilled heart as burning drops of ice.

But that time had not yet come. They were still warm, weren't they? Sun became desperate to know if her tears were still warm; if they flowed from a heart that had not yet turned to ice. She wanted to wipe them away, wanted to feel them with her own hands. She moved her arm.

It really had moved. She didn't see it move, but she felt it move. Its movement disturbed the water. Sun's view shook as if someone had grabbed her by the shoulders and twisted her from side to side.

Yarmin's image tried to insinuate itself into her mind. She forced it out. The poor man was dead, and could not grab her shoulders. Merely her juvenile imagination. She pushed the image harder, shoving until it no longer threatened her focus. She had to remember something important.

She had moved her arm! That was impossible. The shock from the Para-Lazer should have kept her immobile for more than twenty hours. Had she been in the water that long? Maybe. She didn't know. Maybe it had been the way she'd been hit. She had, after all, taken the shot in her palm. Did that matter? For the first time since being tossed face down on John Yarmin's corpse, she was beginning to hope. And hope was warmer than all her tears combined.

She concentrated, and moved her arm again. This time, she must have hit it against the side of the tub because she saw that she had slid over to the left—not by much—but enough to know she was regaining some of her strength.

But to her shock, she saw that once her body settled into its new position, she again began to roll right. And if she were too far from the edge of the tub, she would probably roll all the way over until she was face down in the water.

No! Not now! Not like this! Sun tried to shout, to make other parts of her body move. *Wait!* Rolling slowly, she began picking up speed. John Yarmin had finally grabbed her shoulders. He was dragging her under the water. He was determined not to drown alone. He demanded that she suffer with him. He would join them as one.

A sharp pain shot up her hand and along her arm. She must have struck her hand against the tub. Her body had almost stopped rolling. She was facing the walls of the bathroom now and could barely see the side of the tub. Her mouth must nearly be in the water. She had to do something now, or she'd drown with or without the dead man's help.

Had she known a proper prayer, she would have uttered it a thousand times. But she had never learned her prayers as a child. A cry to God was all she could manage; one long, soundless call on a God whom she had never bothered to speak to during the whole of her wonderful, happy life.

As if propelled by massive transport engines, her arm struggled to break free from its liquid grave. And just as the ugly but reliable transports slowly broke free from the grip of a gravity well, so too did Sun's arm break free of the water. She could see her arm as it punched into the air.

Her joy shattered as she saw scarlet water streaming down from her hand and arm. In one exultant moment, she understood what she was seeing. Chitti's parting words were instantly clear. *That should do it.* It hadn't been the water she'd been talking about. Chitti had cut Sun open; she had left nothing to chance. If the water didn't kill her, then she would bleed to death. And she'd been bleeding for a long time. How bad was the cut? She might never know.

The creeping cold had been more than the water. As the cold water slowly began to cover her, a different cold crept over her from the inside out. She had been bleeding to death.

Sun now knew she was never going to get out alive. She had enough use of her arm now to keep herself from drowning, but it was wasted effort. Perhaps the best thing she could do was let go. There was little reason left to fight what was surely inevitable. Holding on could only mean hours and hours of more pain and terror.

Sun closed her eyes, and imagined that the man beneath her was Gregor Lepov as she allowed him to reach out and pull her into his

313

arms.

90

The afternoon glare from a steel colored sky scored the office walls with pale, horizontal streaks. Lilly sat on the sofa, her head turned away from the windows and resting against the wall. She might have been asleep. Lepov wasn't sure. The pattern of streaks covered her body as well. She appeared to have been painted into the scene; beautiful, though merely a ghost.

That was Lilly's contradiction. She was more spirit than flesh. Her presence—once she entered a room—could be felt. She was a shade, passing through the realms of the living; a chill that both alarmed and excited Lepov. A woman wasn't supposed to do that. Women were warm, they burned with life. But Lilly's cold intensity burned just as fiercely.

Sun was everything a woman ought to be; a tangible presence impossible to ignore. She made Lepov feel like a young man again. Like he could take her by the hand and conquer the world. The idea was more wearying than thrilling. He wasn't sure he wanted to conquer the world any more. Not this world or any other.

Lilly wasn't interested in conquering the world either. They had both seen enough to realize it wasn't worth it; the only thing you could hope for was a small enough portion of the world to stay out of everyone's way, while still finding room to breathe.

Maybe that was the problem. Maybe they had both built up the walls around their little worlds and they were too suspicious ever to allow anyone else to come all the way in.

Lilly stirred. She opened her eyes and saw that Lepov was watching her. As it was too late to look away, he continued to watch. She yawned.

"Any luck yet?"

"No," Lepov said. "I should get a detailed report in another ten minutes or so. There's still some coffee."

"No thanks, I had too much already."

She crossed over to the desk and looked down at the deskscreen. The MoleRunner was in the center, conducting its search with a minimal visual display. Lepov tried to see Lilly's expression. She seemed to regard the MoleRunner with bemusement rather than irritation.

"We should talk about this," she said, not looking at him.

"If you need to." Lepov was resigned to whatever consequences came his way.

"I don't need to, but you do." Now she was looking at him, and she was smiling. "I finally understand what's happening here. You think you've offended me in some unforgivable manner, isn't that right? But we ought to talk this through. You might find that I'm a lot more understanding than you've been expecting."

"Okay," Lepov shrugged, "so you understand. That's all that needs to be said. I'm glad. It's good news."

He poured another cup of coffee and sipped. It had gone lukewarm, but he didn't care. After taking a deeper drink from the cup, he lowered it and looked at Lilly. She was staring at him without a smile.

"You're going to be difficult, now, aren't you?" she asked.

"No, that's not true." He shook his head with solemnity. "I've always been difficult. This is just more of the same."

Her response was interrupted by a chime from the MoleRunner. They both turned their attention to the report.

"Sun left her hotel early this morning," Lepov read, "and paid for a TransitCar that dropped her off at the *Lazaretto Benevolence Society*—that's where she's been working on this Lost Platoon business. But she left there, and another TransitCar dropped her off somewhere out on the West End. That's a bad neighborhood."

"What's out there?" Lilly asked.

"My guess is that's where one of the old soldiers lives. I went with her to visit all of them except the officer, a Lieutenant. I don't remember his name. But he might live out there. She was there for a while, but she took a SubTransit back to her hotel. That's funny—"

"The SubTransit?"

"Yeah, I've only seen her use TransitCars. Her department pays for them."

"She's used it twice more. See, back to the area of the office, and then from there to Alpha station."

"And she's just entered Alpha Quadrant." Lepov pulled up the last log entry and looked at the details. "What…? She just entered through the departures entrance."

"She's leaving." Lilly looked at Lepov. He knew she must be able to see how much it upset him. There wasn't time to hide the fact.

"She still had work to do, as far as I know." He made a call to her hotel, where the front desk manager confirmed what he had suspected.

"Well?" Lilly asked.

"He said she checked out." Lepov sat back in his chair. He couldn't believe she'd left. Just like that. Gone. What would make her do that? Surely meeting Lilly the night before hadn't been enough to make her want to get out.

Lilly was silent, sitting on the edge of the desk and watching him.

"I don't understand why she'd do that." When had Lepov ever understood a woman? When his wife left him and what he had thought was a good marriage, Lepov had never understood. He was still trying to figure out why Lilly had never come back, or why she had come back now. And here was Sun running off without saying goodbye.

"I don't think she would have," Lilly said.

"But she did."

"Gregor, the woman I saw last night was not the kind of woman who would just leave without talking to you. I could see that in the way she looked at you when you came into the office. The way she reacted to seeing me there. The way she looked when you said you would call. Trust me, she wouldn't leave without talking to you."

"Well, it looks like you're wrong." He pushed the report to a corner of the deskscreen where it shrank to half its original size and faded until it could only be seen as a ghostly image.

"She hasn't left yet. She might come back before the lockdown. Or maybe she's about to call and ask you to leave with her. Why do you always do this?" Lilly asked sharply.

"Do what?"

"Give up at the first sign of trouble. You did the same thing when I first met you. You're always looking for a reason to run."

"I don't get it." If Lepov understood her correctly, she was telling him to go after Sun. "You want me to go find this girl?"

"No, as a matter of fact. I don't." She chuckled at her own selfishness. "I wish this girl *would* leave. But then I'd have to nurse you through months of self-pity. The best thing would be for you to go and talk to her. You'll find out that this has nothing to do with you. Maybe she wasn't being honest with you; maybe she has a fiancé back on her world. Who knows why she wants to leave? Maybe she finds you attractive but knows you'd depress her to the end of time."

"Watch it, Lilly. You're starting to make me cry."

"See what I mean? You're a real pain. I'm trying to help here. So why aren't you putting on your coat?"

And just like that, Lilly was taking care of him again. She had a way with him; he'd never been bullied like this by anyone else in his life. It was this very thing that made him crazy about her.

"So I go down there with my hat in my hand and ask why she's leaving?"

"Don't be ridiculous, Gregor. That's not what you did with me. Now, go down there and tell her you accidentally ran into her while following a lead. She won't believe you, but neither did I."

"Lilly," Lepov said as he put his hat on his head, "you'd better come with me and feed me lines. I don't know what I'm gonna say."

"You better believe I'm coming. I won't leave you alone with her. She's liable to drag you off to mom and dad. I won't let that happen."

Lepov shut the door to his office and followed Lilly to the elevator. He felt the shockhammer that was still in the outside pocket of his coat and smiled. If Sun gave him any trouble he could always hit her with it and drag her back to her hotel. Then again, he might have to use it on Lilly if she and Sun got into a fight.

91

They made no attempt to conceal their approach. Two police cruisers were running ahead of MacNally. They weren't using lights and sirens, but they were running in a lane above normal traffic patterns, hitting speeds difficult to maintain. Twice they had to make right turns, along with a left, and each time they nearly hit buildings, in one case nearly running into each other. The police rarely got a chance to drive like maniacs.

"I can see why this kind of thing is discouraged," Russell said, holding tightly to his restraints as MacNally spun the steering wheel. Both detectives, along with Pete Landon, tried to roll with the car as it bent around the corner of an intersection.

"Don't slow down," Pete said from the back seat. "Or I can drive!"

"I got it, Pete." MacNally accelerated but had to ramp down immediately to avoid hitting a TransitCar. "I want that guy's name, dammit! This is an emergency lane!"

"We'll get it later, Mac." Pete glanced back before leaning forward into the front of the cabin. "This is it. Up ahead."

"I see it." The two cruisers had already dropped to street level and settled down an equal distance from the front door of the *Lazaretto Benevolence Society*. There was enough room for MacNally to set his down between them.

"Just hold on, Pete," MacNally stopped Pete from jumping out onto the street. "Let the uniforms do their job, okay?"

"We got guys in the back alley," Russell said as he climbed out of the front door. He pulled a service weapon from his jacket and checked to make sure it was loaded.

Two officers in uniform had already forced their way into the office. A third and fourth uniform stood outside the door with short-barreled RiotTamers.

"Stay behind Russell, Pete. He may be new at this job, but he's a heck of a field man." MacNally was content to stay behind Russell as well. There was no reason not to send the young guy in first. This was the sort of work young guys like Russell loved. MacNally had been a part of far too many shoot-outs to ever want to be in one again.

The office was empty, just as they had expected it to be. Chitti Sienté was nowhere to be found. Pete was agitated to find Sun gone as well, but Russell suggested that might be good news.

"At least we didn't find her carved up like Morvees," the Arcobian commented.

Pete did not find Russell's comment helpful. "Let's not make jokes, huh?"

"I wasn't joking," Russell added.

"What are you guys saying?" MacNally was off to one side of the office, looking at a deskscreen. "I can't understand a word you two are saying."

"Sun's not here," Pete nearly shouted from the other side of the office. "We need to find her."

"Pete," MacNally paged through the files on the deskscreen's archive, "we have to find Chitti Sienté. There is nothing here to suggest Sun Uijong is in trouble. She's probably having dinner with Gregor Lepov."

MacNally realized he'd made a mistake when Pete asked: "Why?"

"Well," MacNally shrugged, doing his best to sound disinterested, "they've been doing a little work together, that's all."

"Well, you two can look for Sienté. I'm gonna find Sun." Pete turned to the nearest desk and started working quickly.

"Pete, wait." MacNally stopped his own work and moved over to watch Pete's attempts to link his deskscreen with the police computer system. "Pete, hold it. Listen to me. I understand you're worried about the Major. But we need to find Chitti Sienté now. Not later. And you're the man who can find her. I promise you, as soon as we find Morvees' daughter, I'll help you find Uijong. Okay?"

Pete's fingers stopped above the deskscreen as he stared at MacNally. It was easy to see he wanted to ignore MacNally, but Pete was a good man who understood priorities, whatever his personal misgivings.

"Fine, I'll find your killer." Pete wiped the deskscreen clean and started over. He had an idea how he could find Sienté. And if he was right, it wouldn't take much time at all. "Russell, while I'm doing this, I want you to start going through that other desksystem. Find anything that's been accessed today and get ready to match any addresses that come through. I'll only be a second."

Russell, service weapon still in hand, crossed to the other desk and did as Pete had asked.

"Pulling up her PDT?" MacNally asked as he watched Pete work.

"She'd be crazy to still be using it. But I think we might get lucky if there is something here that gets us going in the right direction. I'm working on TransitCar records right now. I'll pull up SubTransit records as well. This place is pretty isolated. There's nothing in this neighborhood but run-down apartments full of people who want to be left alone. This girl had to go somewhere. And from what I'm seeing here, she was here today. There should be a record of her leaving the area."

MacNally found a chair and dropped into it. He was content to let Pete and Russell work this. There was little left to do. Sienté could be anywhere. They weren't going to find her unless they caught a break.

That gave MacNally time to think about what he had told Pete. Yes, Lepov might be having dinner with Uijong. But he hoped not. He hoped Lepov had gone after Lilly. He was going to put a bullet through Lepov's foot if he was stubborn enough to let Lilly leave without trying to make things right.

92

He knew I was staring at him. Kjarsta Zoltis kept his eyes fastened on Fortunado and never looked in my direction. It might have been the best thing. If he had looked at me with that cruel indifference masking his face, I might have been tempted to scratch at him like a mother protecting her child. And that's what I was. I was the mother in that room. He was no father. He had no attachment to the child. She might as well have been the child of an enemy. He cared nothing for her.

"Was there anything else?" he asked Fortunado. Kjarsta Zoltis seemed able to ignore the fact that Fortunado had attempted to renegotiate his fee.

I could see that Fortunado did not know what to do next. He had failed to force more money from his boss. And now, he had no choice but to continue as before. But I could see he was still trying to decide how to proceed with regard to Calla. Once or twice he cast a glance at me.

Maybe he would leave her. Maybe, now that he had failed, he would slink off and Calla and I would never see him again.

"No," Fortunado lowered his head, "there's nothing else."

He was going to have to make an extra effort to behave if he wanted to come out of this with his job intact—maybe even if he hoped to come out of it with his life intact.

"Good, get back down that hole." Zoltis did not waste words or time. He moved in on Fortunado with his large bulk and almost pushed him back down the hallway. He never said another word until the little man disappeared into that back room and the door swung shut, the lock clicking loudly into place.

Jason Phillip Reeser

"Don't give him another thought, woman. Do you understand me?"
This time he did look at me. His penetrating stare made me uncomfortable.

"Is that it? Did you stand up to him because you knew he would never
do what he threatened?" I felt better as I asked him the question. Surely he
could never allow harm to come to Calla.

"Don't make the same mistake he did, Della." I was shocked to hear
him call me by my name. "Don't ever assume I would allow my feelings to
interfere with my business. The one had nothing to do with the other. I do
not allow the weakness of kindness and concern to weigh down my work.
Do you understand?"

"No," I shook my head. "No, I don't understand. And I hope I never
do."

He seemed to find something amusing in what I said. His smile was
dangerous. "You're too attached to that girl. Don't you know what happens
when you get too attached to something or someone? Nothing good ever
comes of that. You've got to learn to spurn attachments, woman. The more
you care about something the more chance there is you'll both lose it and be
hurt by its loss."

He had never spoken this much to me at one time before. I wished he
would quit. I didn't like to hear him say such things.

"So, go back and keep her safe. You've got a fifty-fifty chance that
Fortunado will leave her alone. At any rate, he won't do anything before his
part of the job is done. After that, he'll keep the threat a possibility to
prevent me from taking revenge for his impertinence. We'll be at something
of an impasse, and the girl will be fine."

I hoped he was right. I had been shocked how disturbed I'd become as
Fortunado stood threatening my little girl. I had discovered I was willing to
do anything to save that little girl. I didn't like the feeling.

93

Instinct fought despair, and as more of Sun's body began to
respond, the more she fought to live. She had turned over, her arms
hooking the curled edge of the tub. Her head rested on the edge as
well. She'd been there a long time. It had taken great effort just to
turn over and pull herself into that position.

She was probably kneeling on Yarmin, though there was still not
enough feeling in her legs to be sure. Still numb over so much of her
body, it was impossible to get out of the tub completely. She had tried
two separate times to pull her entire body out of the water. She
hadn't made it far either time and the effort had exhausted her.

But she knew that she could not hold on much longer. She was
still bleeding, and she was getting weaker. If she did not do
something soon, she would slip down under the water.

She had to use her knees; she was never going to be able to do this without them. She wondered why she had recovered so much control and feeling in her body but had not regained the feeling and control of her legs.

It took a great amount of time, hanging on to the tub's edge, before she came up with a plausible answer. Was it possible she actually had regained control and feeling? If so, then she could not feel her legs because she was simply numb from the icy water.

That meant she ought to be able to move them; she just wouldn't know they were moving. She would have to take that on faith. But if she could push her body out of the water with her legs, she ought to be able to pull herself the rest of the way over the lip. It was worth a try.

As she pushed and pulled, Sun backed away from her body and watched with breathless anxiety. The woman in the tub was getting frantic. She was scratching and clawing at the lip of the tub like it was her path to Heaven. And maybe it was. If only she could get a little more of her torso over the edge.

And she did. Somehow she managed to get more than half of her body over the side. Incredulously, she watched as the woman's body, soaked in bloody water, slid over the edge like a stillborn baby from the womb. So desperate had she been to escape the water that she was able to ignore her head smacking the tiled floor.

Fueled by adrenaline, Sun kept moving, sliding around in the ankle deep water as she twisted and turned into a near-sitting position against a wall. From this vantage point, she could see that her legs were indeed able to move and that she was bleeding as suspected.

There were three cuts on the back of her arm, near her right triceps. Her uniform jacket was still on, but the sleeve was cut, as was her blouse. If she turned her head enough, she could see the incisions. They were deep and as long as her fingers. She must have lost a lot of blood. The thought scared her—more than the thought of drowning—a primitive terror. But seeing the cuts on her arm was a scientific terror. She had time to consider what would happen as the blood poured out of her body. She began to expect her heart would fail at any moment.

The fact that her heart was still beating both perplexed and encouraged her. Surely there was still time. There had to be time to stop the bleeding. Only, she was far too tired to think how. The cold water had aided her, slowing her pulse, but she was now out of the water and she had to come up with a plan quickly.

Lepov would already know what to do. She had an idea that he was never at a loss for proactive measures. His instincts were most likely always the right instincts. She liked that about him. He did not hesitate when decisions were needed. He wasn't one to waste time.

Like that first time they'd met. He had not hesitated to hit her, to knock her over and pick her up like a ragdoll. It was something normal people didn't do. But he had, because he had seen no other way to detain her. She should have been angry with him for it. But she couldn't be. There was no cruelty in his heart. Just a willingness to act. She should learn from him, and not waste time worrying over details.

That's what she was doing. Wasting time. She reluctantly stopped thinking about Lepov and tried to work out a plan. She needed to stanch the blood flow. She had to improvise and find a tourniquet. That would be hard. Her hands still did not act like hands; more like clubs on the ends of her arms, blunt hammers that could not grip anything.

The tub had overflowed, water soaked the floor. For the moment, however, it had stopped; her body was no longer in the tub, and the water level had dropped below the lip. Her blood had mixed with the water, a terrifying amount of bloody water was left covering the floor of the little bathroom. She knew it was an illusion; knew that there was far less blood than there appeared. But it was distracting all the same. She had trouble concentrating on what she wanted to do.

Her jacket could be used as a tourniquet. But it would be difficult to remove; she was not sure she could get her shoulders out of it. She would have to sit up, and that was something that seemed impossible. She didn't think she would be able to sit up for weeks. Lying down was exhausting enough. It would be easier to remove her skirt. But before she could begin to try, she realized her skirt was useless. She was too weak to tear it in two, and as it was, the skirt was not long enough to knot.

She would have to get out of her jacket.

It was too much to consider. She was beginning to feel her arms; she was shivering now, or had she been shivering all along? Her right arm burned where she bled, the rest of it tingling as if it had been hammered into jelly.

She'd never get her jacket off. She hurt too much.

What did you want? To hurt too little? Lepov's voice startled her. She didn't need his heckling, but it helped to know he was watching.

She reached forward and hooked her sleeve on a water valve at floor level. It was heavily rusted and she wasn't sure it would hold up under her weight. But it would have to do. She was in no shape to pull her arm out of the sleeve the conventional way. By hooking the sleeve on the valve, she could pull her arm out as she rolled away from the valve.

That worked until her elbow caught in the sleeve at an awkward angle. It had nowhere to go. The arm and shoulder were in the way, and both hurt more than before. Sun did her best to ignore the pain, but it wouldn't go away. The more she tried to pull out of the sleeve, the more she cried in pain.

But her legs were beginning to respond better. At least she could tell where they were. And she was able to retract one until her foot jammed against something solid. She had leverage now, but did she have the strength to use it? She tried to kick, at the same time she renewed her efforts to pull free from the sleeve.

Her leg was too weak to kick, but it was enough to make a difference. Her arm slipped free as she rolled over; her body splashing in the chilly water, her shoulder nearly ripped from its socket. She would have lost consciousness had her face not hit the bloody water. She gasped, sucking in water; choking, coughing, and vomiting in one breath.

When her breathing was finally under control, she was kneeling in the water, leaning on her hands. Her jacket hung down from one arm. She couldn't believe it. She had never actually believed she could do it.

Don't pat yourself on the back yet, lady. You're still bleeding to death and you look like hell. Lepov was such a pessimistic bastard.

She wished she could pat herself on the back. It was better than crying. Unfortunately, crying was the easiest thing to do right then. Especially when she thought about what she had to do next. Lepov might be a pessimist, but he was right.

You might have been able to take off a jacket, but do you honestly think you can use that jacket to tie a knot?

No, she didn't. But what choice did she have? It had to work.

94

They had said few words while sitting in the TransitCar. Now, as they walked through the Alpha Entry Lounge, Lepov wished he had said something—anything. He'd been glib with her when she told him she understood what he had been going through. He shouldn't have done that. He should have looked her in the eye and told her the truth; told her that he was afraid he had ruined any chance of happiness that they might have had together.

And he should have told her that no matter what Sun said, she was not the woman who could convince him to leave the Lazaretto. Only Lilly could do that. All she had to do was ask.

Lepov knew he would never say that. He'd accept her offer only if it were her own idea. He wasn't going to influence her.

"We should find her easily enough," Lilly glanced around the

Jason Phillip Reeser

crowded lounge. She tried to smile but the smile never reached her eyes and Lepov knew it was forced.

"She's already in the quadrant. She won't be out here." Lepov couldn't think of a way to add that none of this was important. He wouldn't have gone looking for Sun except that Lilly had insisted. And yet there Lilly stood, worry written all over her. He wanted to take her by the hand and tell her to forget Sun. He should have. Instead, he led Lilly toward the Entry Lounge exit. The glass doors rolled back and they entered Alpha Quadrant.

Alpha Quadrant was a mess. It reminded Lepov of a vacation his family had taken once, back on Bukovina, to a resort town on the shores of the Chaylon Sea. Lesbos was a full throttle resort that had something for everyone—and *everyone* was there. The streets of Lesbos were packed with people day and night. The crowds were absent only during the morning. That was the best time to take the family out for a walk through the shops and parks. But once midday hit, the rowdy crowds began to descend onto the streets, and Lepov and his brother had made sure to get the kids safely back to their hotel, despite protests from their wives.

Looking at the crowded streets of Alpha Quadrant, Lepov was glad he wasn't trying to shepherd a flock of kids around. It was going to be hard enough to keep from losing Lilly. He took her hand and forced his way into the mass of people.

"Where are we going?" she asked, nearly shouting to be heard.

"There's an information desk just on the other side of this concourse. Hang on." He pushed forward as he felt Lilly grip him more tightly.

Most of the crowd was headed into the quadrant, but part of it moved in the opposite direction. Lepov and Lilly were trying to cut across this flow and counter flow. It made for slow going.

With only a few steps to go, Lepov felt Lilly's hand slip out of his, and he spun around. He lost her. Just like that she was nowhere to be seen, with little chance of finding her in that throng, he decided his best chance lay in getting to the other side and finding a higher vantage point from which to look for her. With applied force, he knocked two people out of his way and reached the edge of the concourse.

Out of the flow, he was able to stand still and look for something to climb. The base of a light stanchion was all he could find. It was sufficient to get up high enough to be more than a head taller than the tallest travelers in the crowd. From there it did not take him long to see Lilly's white ponytail. She was not far from where she had lost him, but only holding her own and not able to make any headway. Lepov called out, but there was no way of telling if she could hear him.

He hopped down from the stanchion base and cut back into the shifting throng, aiming to her right. He would have to overshoot her position to compensate for the heavy flow moving to his right. It only took a few moments before he could reach out and grab her shoulder. She jerked her head round and smiled at the sight of him.

They made it back to the base of the light stanchion and paused to catch their breaths. Lepov was struck by how quickly he had begun to see Lilly as he had before all the trouble had started. Just losing her for such a short time had threatened to make him panic. Just catching sight of her again had filled him with peace.

How had he ever suspected her of wanting to kill him?

She was giving him an odd look. "You okay, Gregor?"

"I'm feeling better all the time," he said, gently grabbing her by the back of one arm. "Let's go this way."

They made it to the information desk without further problems and asked the desk clerk for Sun Uijong's quadrant address.

"She has private quarters in Harbor Gardens," the clerk said after pulling up Sun's name on his display.

They followed the clerk's directions and were soon standing at the doors of Harbor Gardens. There were no harbors in any of the quadrants, and as far as Lepov could see, there was no garden at this hotel either. But that didn't matter. The patrons of Harbor Gardens were paying too much money to stay in a place without a fancy name. They weren't about to tell family and friends that they were staying at the Quarantine Inn.

"Didn't you say the Army was picking up her tab?" Lilly asked. "They're terribly generous."

"Only the best for officers, I suppose." Lepov frowned, reluctant to admit Lilly had a valid point. This kind of place was too pricy, even for officers. Maybe Sun had family money she didn't like to mention.

"Should I stay here in the lobby?" Lilly asked.

"If you don't mind. I won't be long. "

The lobby was a central atrium whose glass ceiling and steel frames created a spider's web design. The three main towers of suites rose up around the glass dome. The center of this atrium was dominated by a large, shallow pool. Fountains sprayed complex designs as miniature, automated boats rushed from one end of the pool to the other, simulating a busy harbor on a resort lake.

"Enjoy the harbor," he said with a wry smile.

"I'll be a good girl and wait right here." Lilly picked out a plush chair and sat down. "You be a good boy and say whatever you need to say. Just don't be unkind if she says anything that hurts your ego.

Okay?"

"Okay. Does that mean I shouldn't assault her for old time's sake?"

"Keep your hands to yourself," she demanded.

The elevator was the nicest he'd seen in the Lazaretto. He was afraid to lean against its textured walls. If he'd known he was going to visit a swanky little shack like Harbor Gardens, he would have combed his thinning hair and worn clean socks. He began to wonder what he had ever been thinking. Sun Uijong must be too far up the social ladder for Gregor Lepov. It wasn't going to be hard to understand why she was leaving. She'd had her share of slumming and was ready to return to real life.

At least there wouldn't be much of a scene. Just a quick *sorry to see you go*, and a *hope you have a good life*. There wouldn't be much need for anything else. It wouldn't take long at all.

It was taking longer, in fact, for Sun to answer her door. Lepov hit the bell — a real, honest-to-goodness bell — two or three more times. No one came to the door.

He was beginning to get irritated. A simple search for a lady he hardly knew had turned into an all-day affair, and he still had not seen her or spoken to her since the night before. He might not be in her league, but that was no reason to go this far out of her way to avoid him.

Lilly might have ordered him to behave, but he wasn't about to walk away without ever talking to the girl. Not after tracking her down this far.

The lock on the door was little more than a nuisance. He worked it open and pushed. Inside, he could see that for all the fancy decorations, the main room was empty. He crossed to the bedroom where he saw that the bed was undisturbed and the closet empty. Even the bathroom contained no personal items.

Now what did this mean? Lepov searched the suite two more times before coming to a stop in the middle of the main room.

The MoleRunner had indicated this room as her last location. That had only been an hour ago. Had Lilly been right? Had Sun intended all along to go back into Center City and show up at his office one last time? He was beginning to think they were both wrong; beginning to think Sun didn't exist. He had the feeling he was chasing a ghost.

He saw the door to the front closet was slightly ajar. He was sure it had been closed when he first entered the suite, so certain that he moved to the closet and carefully put his hand on the door's ornate handle. Someone was playing games with him. He was in no mood for games. He was officially annoyed.

Yanking the door open, he bulled his large frame into the closet, hoping to overpower whoever was hiding there. It was empty, of course, and he had it backwards. Someone had been in the closet, but had slipped away while he was searching the bedroom.

Lepov didn't bother to check out the rest of the suite. Whoever it was had gone. He located a phone—too garish for his tastes—and called down to the front desk.

"Concierge," a fussy voice answered.

"Yes, I'm calling from room 1203. My wife checked us in over an hour ago, but I can't find her up here. Did she leave any messages for me?" He wandered over to a window and stared down at the glass dome of the lobby. He could see the water sparkle as the tiny boats raced around like water bugs.

"Your wife? I was unaware Major Uijong had a husband. I'm sorry, sir."

"Well, she wasn't sure I'd make it in before the quadrant closed. If there wasn't a message, maybe you could tell me where she went."

"I'm not sure where she went, Mr. Uijong. She stopped here at the desk to ask about our house safe. She did not seem to think it was safe enough for the military package she was carrying. I'm afraid she felt she needed to find a more secure location. I mentioned the name of a nearby bank where she could use private security boxes."

Lepov thanked the man and hung up. Military package? That was news to him. He was beginning to believe that he didn't know anything about Sun Uijong beyond the fact that she was an attractive woman.

Well, he decided, maybe it was best that way. He had all that he could handle with Lilly Stewart. And he didn't have to go looking all over the Lazaretto for her. She was waiting for him in the lobby, and he wasn't going to make her wait any longer. She was probably already worried about Sun stealing him away. He would have to make sure she knew she wasn't that lucky. Lilly was going to be stuck with him for a long time.

95

"This is taking too long," Pete Landon smacked the deskscreen in front of him and cursed again. He was quickly developing a bad habit. "Lazaretto reliability."

"What?" MacNally thought Pete had muttered something about Lazaretto *Itty-Bitty*.

"Transit system data cache is all screwed up." Pete flipped a document around and enlarged it to twice its original size to read a small banner at the bottom. "Security shut down the system when it detected an attack. It does that when someone runs a data mine on it. Or a MoleRunner. Could just be a false alarm. But what it means is that I can't get the Transit records from this location. Not for a while, anyway."

"So we go back to this desksystem," Russell said, already scanning pages from the other desk. "Looks like this was Major Uijong's desk. At least she was using it. Lots of Lost Platoon data."

Pete wanted see that, but he tried not to show it. Instead, he gleaned what he could from the desk in front of him. "I don't get this."

"What?" MacNally asked. He stood and tried to read Pete's screen from too far away. "Find something?"

"No. I can't find anything. This thing is empty. If I didn't know any better, I'd say it was wiped clean. This girl Chitti knew we'd be coming. She dumped everything."

"Can you get it back?"

"Sure," Pete nodded, "in about seven or eight hours."

"We don't have that kind of time," MacNally growled.

"Don't you think I know that?" Pete kept opening datacells and VS cabinets. He kept at it, even after MacNally grew tired of watching. Ten minutes passed before Pete stopped digging.

"Well?"

"I don't know. This might be something."

Pete flipped over an envelope on the deskscreen so MacNally could see it. "That's from Sun's desk. Or it should be. I haven't seen one document or file from Sun Uijong on this desksystem, Russell should have them all over on his. But this one is recent. *Very* recent. It's not even the actual file. Just a ghost that shouldn't be there. Something from a default report. Looks like a label. For travel authorization. Classified materials. I can't open the original. It's been dumped."

"I don't get it," MacNally cocked his head to one side and stared at the label.

"Neither do I," Pete closed his eyes and tried to work out the puzzle in his mind. "No address on the itinerary. Just a *bearer authorization*."

"The paintings." Russell said from across the room. "She has to get them out somehow. With that label, she might get them into a quadrant."

"No she can't," Pete pushed the envelope to one side and opened a document link to his system back at the station. "Because she can't leave."

"Sure as hell can't," MacNally agreed, "we won't let her."

"No, I don't mean that." Pete found what he was looking for.

"Right here, you see it? She can't get out because she was labeled *Nullus Exitus* when she was a kid. I saw the symbol by her name when she first came up on my system, but I didn't pay much attention to it. Chitti Sienté is not going anywhere."

"So what, then?" Russell asked. "Does Uijong have the paintings?"

"No, Sun's not in—it's about time!" Pete shouted. He cleared his screen. "Transit system back up. And we already have something."

"And?"

"Chitti was here this morning, but she left. Her last stop was out on the West End. Russell, check those addresses. I need something relevant out on the West End."

"Well, Morvees' is in that direction, but Yarmin's place is closer."

"I don't see any movement after that." Pete bounced at the desk with anxiety. "Maybe she's hiding at Yarmin's. Maybe they're working together."

"Or she met Uijong there."

Pete glowered at Russell. "What do you mean by that?"

"You forgot to put Uijong in your Transit search. It seems they both met at Yarmin's. In fact, by the data I see, it looks like Uijong left not long after they met at Yarmin's. Either Sienté is still there, or she walked out of the West End."

"Okay," Pete read through Russell's results. "And I see that Sun came back to this office."

"Same time as the classified label," MacNally noted. He pulled out a cigarette but waited before lighting it. "Maybe Uijong does have the paintings now. Maybe she is tangled up in this thing. We don't have any reason to think she isn't."

"And no reason to think she is," Pete said softly, lacking conviction.

"Well, reason or not, Sun Uijong was dropped off at the Alpha Quadrant entrance." Russell was still checking through the Transit report.

"And Chitti Sienté is most likely still at John Yarmin's," Pete added.

"We go after Uijong," Russell said. Pete nodded in agreement.

"Hold on," MacNally, his cigarette now lit, held out a hand. "Think this through. If Uijong checked into Alpha, then she's in plain sight, and we can have Alpha security grab her whenever we want. But Chitti Sienté is a violent threat. It doesn't matter which one has the paintings. We'll get them when we sort this out. Right now, Chitti Sienté is the real threat."

"But we can get to Uijong before Alpha locks down," Pete argued. "After that, we can find Sienté."

"I say we concentrate on Morvees' daughter." MacNally stopped and thought for a moment. "I'll call Lepov and see if he can get over to Alpha. I'll have Alpha Security meet him and he can help them find the Major."

"She's not involved in this," Pete said quietly.

"Fine. Then we definitely go after Sienté."

MacNally yanked open the door, not waiting for Pete to follow. He understood the man's reluctance to suspect the woman of doing anything illegal. But at this point it didn't matter. He just wanted to grab Chitti Sienté and Sun Uijong and then they'd figure out what was going on.

And maybe they'd catch a killer. And just maybe they'd recover the paintings. Was that asking too much? MacNally was well aware that in the Lazaretto, it just might be.

The police cruisers rose up and over the street like birds of prey hunting new victims. MacNally engaged his engines and followed them. Cold Lazaretto air made for easy maneuvering; the colder the better. Yarmin's apartment was far enough away that they decided to ascend above the buildings for a straight run to the West End. It would cut their time in half, and they wouldn't have to look out for stray TransitCars. Only police engines were capable of climbing out of the street canyons.

96

The Liar felt secure enough to sit down to a proper meal. The package was safely tucked away. No one would ever challenge her authority to keep its contents sealed. She had only to enjoy her meal and prepare for forty days of leisure until she could finally slip the bonds of this prison moon.

Her waiter was a young man, with soft eyes and softer hair. His unassuming manner caught her attention. He made no bold suggestions off the menu, neither did he comment when she chose the Phasian Chicken Marsala. Most waiters would have at least made a face—Phasian Chicken was known to be tough—but this one only smiled modestly.

The Liar would have dismissed him had she still been the woman overshadowed by the Thief. But that shadow was gone, and she could carve out a new role. She was, after all, someone new. Both inside and outside. The scene in the tunnel had empowered her like nothing else. And assuming Sun's identity wasn't a bad way to start her transformation.

She still wore the Major's uniform. It had a powerful effect on the young waiter. She could see him appraising her when he thought she wasn't paying attention. It felt good to know he was looking. She tried to sit as straight as possible, like any good officer, during her meal.

She had never known the love of a man; had only ever known one man's hate. She wasn't inexperienced with young men like the waiter. But the few times she had allowed a young man to take advantage of her, she had crawled away with bitter regret. All men, eventually, became merely an image of the Thief and all that he embodied.

But that would change. It had to. The Thief was dead. The Liar had liberated herself through a blood-ritual guaranteeing her freedom. Now, with all things new, she had a chance to find a man's love. And there was no reason for her to look beyond this waiter.

He served her a small dessert plate of fruit and thick cream. She hadn't ordered it, but he had shyly set it on the table. Perhaps he, too, could sense that she was ready for him.

"You're too kind," the Liar said. She had never tried to speak like that to a man. She slowed her words and dropped her voice. "I should repay you."

"You don't have to," he stammered before fleeing the dining room.

The Liar raised her fork and stared at the gleaming tines, filled with the unfamiliar sensation of lust. The young man excited her and she would not let him get away. She stabbed a strawberry and watched its red juice stream onto the dessert plate.

An image of the Thief flickered across her mindscape, frantically waving his bloodied hand.

The Liar did not flinch. Instead, she smiled. Free to build a life beyond the Thief's shadow, free to love and be loved; she would start with the waiter. He was clean and pure; untainted by hate. She would partake of his innocence and beauty.

He returned to her table as she stood to leave.

"What is your name?" she asked.

"Chance."

"That's perfect." She reached out and touched his arm. "Have you eaten?"

"No Ma'am. I'm still working."

"I think we can fix that, don't you? Would you like me to fix that?"

"Maybe later."

"No, not later. You won't want to wait until later," purred the Liar.

More bloody images flickered across her vision. What did it matter? The Thief was gone; the Liar now free to enjoy any opportunities that arose. And for now, her opportunity had soft eyes and softer hair. He was exactly what she needed.

She reached into her purse to pay for the meal. It took her a moment to remember the dragonfly pendant around her neck. The only thing in her purse was the Para-Lazer. The Thief's razor was gone. She'd thrown it away.

Minutes later, they left the restaurant, the cold Lazaretto air buffeting them as darkness enveloped the quadrant. An orange glow clung to the western horizon. The young man tightened his coat but the Liar held her head high, ignoring the biting wind.

"Chance, you don't shave yet, do you?" She ran her hand along his smooth, youthful cheek.

"No, not much," he shrugged.

"I didn't think so."

She tucked her arm into his and they pushed through the crowded streets of Alpha Quadrant.

For the Liar, the night held so much promise: of love, of companionship, of empowerment. It was going to be a long, lovely, forty-day quarantine. Why had she never thought of this before?

97

A great waterfall of blood poured from on high, threatening to drown Sun in her prison pool. She needed to get out, but the sides were too steep and she was doomed to swim until her legs and arms grew too weary. Then, she would drown. How long before she gave in? Before she allowed the blood to encompass her?

The illusion was growing stronger. Each time, it lasted a little longer. The waterfall wasn't real. She knew it was only water running out of the tub and onto the tiled floor; pink water stained with her blood.

The bleeding had stopped. Somehow — she was having trouble remembering this part — she had tied her jacket sleeves around her arm. It had been enough to stop the bleeding. But had it been soon enough? She was weak. So weak.

The imaginary sides of her pool — those too steep to escape — were the walls of the bathroom. She couldn't even remember anymore why she was in a bathroom. There was something dreadful in the bathtub, from where the water kept running. But what the dreadful thing was, she could not remember. Her ability to recollect the past had faded.

But she did know something about the present: her need to get out of the bathroom. It was important. She couldn't say why. But getting out was the only thing on which she could focus.

She thought of nothing else. Of no one else. Not even the man in the dark hat who occasionally stepped into the bathroom to make wry jokes about her pathetic condition.

That's no way to mop the floor, woman. I like a woman who puts blood, sweat, and tears into her work, but you've got an imbalance. Too much blood.

He was always saying things like that. At first they were funny. She wanted to laugh at them; wanted him to know she liked his little jokes. But as time wore on, they began to be in poor taste. She was dying, after all. He could have eased her through her last hours with something kinder than jokes.

That skirt's gonna stain with all that blood. If you'd like, I'll help you out of it.

What a charmer. She'd have to slap him the next time he came in.

But that had been in the past. He hadn't come through the door in a long time. And Sun couldn't even remember who he was. Some guy with a smart mouth. Too bad. She had a crazy idea she had loved him once.

Get out of the room. That was her focus. But how? It's true she was now sitting up. It made her head spin, but she managed to stay upright. One of her legs was bent beneath her; cold and numb in the water. The other leg was as straight as a flagpole but she couldn't feel it either. She couldn't stand up and walk out. She would have to be clever.

The door was a problem. It was closed. She needed to get near enough to grab the door handle. But once she did that, the door would need to swing inward, and she would be in its way. She would have to find a way to turn the handle while not blocking the door.

There was a seat near the door. A large, white, porcelain seat that might be what she needed. If she could climb onto it, she might be able to reach the door. From there, she could pull it open and not be in its way.

It was her only option. And time was running out. She wiped the bloody water from her hands—they were excessively slippery in that water—and tried pulling herself into a kneeling position. If she could do that, she could lean forward and grab the seat. From there, she would have to find a way to climb onto it.

It proved easier than expected. Amazingly, she made it to her knees without much effort. Hope surged through her and she used this momentum to half pull—half push her body up and off the floor.

She was now bent over the seat. Water ran down her legs as it drained back to the floor. She held on, catching her breath; her right arm throbbing with pain where the tourniquet twisted tight. She was forgetting something. Something about blood poisoning, but it would have to wait. She had to keep moving. Had to drag more of her body onto the seat.

If only the man would come back to make one of his wise-cracks. She'd stop him. Plead with him to leave the door open. It was the least he could do after cutting her so many times with his sharp tongue.

With both hands she grasped the sides of the seat and pushed. She could not remember ever feeling so heavy. Had the Lazaretto's gravity shifted?

If she could get high enough, she might be able to slip a knee up on the seat. It was all she needed. From there, she'd make it. She'd be able to reach that door.

The man wasn't coming. It was up to her. Everyone was counting on her. All of those poor, old soldiers depended on her. They had died before she could get them help. She wouldn't let them down again. Not this time.

If she was lifting her knee, she couldn't tell. She had lost all feeling in her knees — how long ago had it been? An hour? A year? Did it matter?

Her head was throbbing as much as her arm now. She was dizzy. There was a specific reason for this, but it eluded her. Something to do with blood pressure and all the blood staining the bathroom.

She had to focus. On what? Getting onto the seat, of course. But that made no sense. She was already on the seat. When had that happened? Who cared? As long as she could reach that door. All she would have to do was grab the handle, twist it, and pull.

She wanted to laugh. She couldn't. She tried again. It was no good. She could clearly see her face and it was not laughing. It was crying. How could she see her face? That was nonsense. She was up on the seat, staring down at the woman sprawled on the tile floor, half covered in a puddle of faded pink water.

No. Sun put out her hands, to stop the woman from crying. *No, don't cry. We did it! We made it off the floor! We won't drown!*

But that was nonsense. Clearly, the woman had never made it off the floor. Clearly, she would never reach the door. The only thing to do was lie down and cry with the woman. She shouldn't cry alone.

But she wasn't alone, Sun knew. The man was there, still hiding in the water, afraid to surface and speak. He was, after all, dead, and had no reason to come out. It was his simple duty to remain submerged and watch the room slowly fill until they could both sleep beneath the water.

She wrapped her arms around the woman and they became one. Sleep would come soon. Sun was glad of that. She was tired. There was no fight left in her; just the peace in knowing she had done all she could. And with peace, sleep would follow.

98

The last light in the sky faded from the black horizon as MacNally sped diagonally above the city rooftops. He stayed tucked in behind the cruisers as they banked around a few of the tallest buildings that rose up from the city like colossal black missiles, poised for an attack.

MacNally steered with one hand as he punched in a call to Gregor Lepov. Maybe Lepov could get to Alpha Quadrant in time.

"You want me to do that while you're driving?" Russell clearly didn't trust MacNally's one-handed driving.

"No, I got it," MacNally shook his head. The vehicle shook as his hand followed the shake of his head. Russell jammed a hand against the side door and held on tight.

"Lepov?"

"What do you want, MacNally?"

It was hard to know where to begin, so MacNally skipped the details that could be explained later. "Can you get over to Alpha Quadrant? We think Sun Uijong is trying to leave the Lazaretto. Stop her!"

"MacNally, what are you talking about?" Lepov raised his voice. "I'm in Alpha right now. I'm looking for Sun right now."

It was MacNally's turn to ask Lepov to explain. "Didn't Lilly come looking for you? She should be at your office."

"She was. She's with me now. We think something's wrong. We haven't heard from Sun all day."

"Lepov," MacNally nearly ran into a cruiser when it braked hard without warning, "there's a chance Uijong has the paintings. She might be trying to get them out through Alpha."

Lepov didn't respond. Pete Landon did, however. Reaching out from the back seat, he smacked MacNally's shoulder. "Tell Lepov there's no proof of that! She's not a fugitive. You know we don't have proof she's involved in this at all."

MacNally waved Pete off. "Lepov, did you hear me?"

"I heard," Lepov answered.

"Okay, Alpha Security has been informed. They're expecting you."

"MacNally!" Pete grabbed his shoulder. "Tell him Uijong could be in trouble for all we know!"

"I hear him," Lepov's voice came through loud enough for Pete to hear him too.

MacNally had to kill the connection as the cruisers began to descend. He grabbed the steering column with both hands and

335

followed them in. From their entry point, MacNally decided they could land on the roof of the building. It was only an eight-story building, and Yarmin's apartment was on the fourth floor. The uniforms would seal off the exits at street level. They could come down to Yarmin's apartment faster than they could climb up to it.

"Let Russell go first," MacNally warned Pete again. They were on the stairs and dropping down to the fourth floor as fast as they could. Russell pulled ahead and reached the door leading to the fourth floor. He glanced back at MacNally.

"You got a reading?"

MacNally shook his PDT reader. "Not yet. Too many other tenants. Let's get out of this stairwell."

Russell gently opened the door and bobbed his head, checking the hall in each direction. It was empty. He stepped through the door, Pete and MacNally right behind him. As before, a dog started barking furiously.

They were halfway down the hall before MacNally picked up a weak signal. Two people were in Yarmin's apartment.

"Is it Sienté?" Russell asked.

"Can't tell," MacNally tried to adjust the strength.

"Give me that," Pete said. He snatched it from MacNally's hand and started punching buttons. He stopped long enough to read the screen, nodded and handed it back to MacNally. "Okay, she's there with Yarmin. Reading is perfectly clear."

"I got her," Russell put his hand on the door.

"Wait for the uniforms, Menya." MacNally wasn't about to throw caution to the wind because they finally had this woman trapped. She was extremely violent, and he saw no reason to hurry.

"What? I can't hear you," Russell whispered, winking. Service weapon at the ready, he rammed open the feeble wooden door and lunged into the room. Pete was right behind him.

"My God, what is it?" Pete was staring at the floor.

"Move," MacNally snarled, shoving Pete aside. He rushed in the darkened room and saw the wet floor, glistening in the hallway's light. Russell found a switch and hit it; a red sheen covered the wooden floor.

"It's blood," Pete said. His voice shook as he backed away from the crimson stain.

"Mostly water, I'd say." Russell splashed across the room. He pointed toward a door by the kitchen. "Coming out of there."

MacNally followed. They stood outside the door and listened. They heard running water. A soft glow came from under the door.

"Ready?" MacNally grabbed the handle. The younger detective cradled his service weapon with both hands and nodded. MacNally twisted the handle and shoved. The door swung inward and Russell forced his way in.

The scene was impossible to take in all at once. From behind Russell, MacNally could see blood spattered walls, and blood soaked water as it ran down the sides of the tub. A body lay at the bottom of the tub, magnified and distorted by the water. A woman lay on the floor, her blouse and skirt soaked in bloody water. Where the blood did not stain her skin, she was as white as the porcelain sink above her. Her short, black hair was smashed against her head with dark crimson stains running from it.

Her eyes were open.

"Damn," Russell said, standing in the flow of running water. "I think it's safe to say Chitti Sienté's dead."

"No she isn't," Pete squeezed passed MacNally, crowding in next to Russell, "this isn't Chitti Sienté."

MacNally looked at Russell, whose only response was a shrug.

"Get the MedTechs up here—now!" Pete shoved Russell out of the way and dropped to his knees, splashing cold water on the detectives. "Do it, MacNally! This is Sun, dammit! Hurry!"

MacNally, energized by the cold water sloshing over his shoes, shouted for MedTechs. He couldn't tell if Pete was right. And even if he was, it looked like it wouldn't matter. Whether it was Uijong or Sienté, the fact remained that the woman was obviously dead.

He and Russell stood back as two MedTechs entered. One of them pulled Pete out of the bathroom as the other one knelt and began to scan the woman's body.

"You know what this means, don't you?" Russell asked MacNally.

"What?"

"Lepov's looking for Uijong, but if Pete is right, then he won't find her. He'll find Sienté instead."

"Let's hope he does." MacNally pulled out his phone and tossed it to Russell. "Here, call him."

MacNally walked over to Pete, who was standing at one of the windows, staring into the darkness.

"We wasted so much time. We could have been here hours ago." Pete's voice was still shaky. "I wasted too much time."

"You don't know that, Pete."

"Do you understand what happened in there? Did you see how much she struggled to get out?"

"Yeah, I saw." MacNally didn't know what to say.

"I could have figured this out this morning. It was kids' stuff. I wasn't trying hard enough."

"We all did the best we could, Pete." MacNally knew it was

inadequate. But there was little else to say.

"Who's the guy in the tub?" Pete asked.

"Yarmin, I'd guess."

"MacNally?" Pete was still staring out the window into the Lazaretto's black streets.

"What?"

"You ever get sick of this place?"

"Sure." Who didn't?

"I don't even remember how I got here, do you?" Pete bowed his head; his great mane of hair fell over his face.

"I don't worry too much about how any of us got here." MacNally pulled out a cigarette and stared at it but did not light it. "All that matters is what we've done since we got here."

"That's not the best news I've heard all day." Pete lifted his head and looked toward the bathroom. "We didn't do a whole lot today."

"That's true," MacNally nodded. "But it was the best we could, with what we had."

"Does that make you feel any better, Lieutenant?"

"No." MacNally broke the cigarette in half and threw it into the bloody puddle at their feet. "No, it sure as hell don't."

99

They were still sitting in the luxurious lobby of Harbor Gardens. Lepov watched the boats circle each other. Small crafts and larger yachts managed to move in random patterns without ever colliding. They were mesmerizing, an easy distraction, something to do instead of brooding over what came next.

The officer from Alpha Security had contacted him, and for now, Lilly and Lepov had only to wait while the security team did their best to find Sun. Lepov tried not to think about what MacNally had said. He did not want to believe that Sun was involved. That kind of suspicion would be too much to take. First Lilly, and now Sun?

No, he wasn't going to consider it. Some mistakes should never be repeated. The worst part was the fact that Lilly had heard MacNally's words. Now, she could see he was not jumping to conclusions; a courtesy he had not extended to Lilly.

"After they find her," Lilly said hesitantly, "what will you do?"

"About what?"

"Do you plan to keep living here, in the Lazaretto?"

Lepov could see the question was hard for her. Maybe she was afraid to hear his answer.

"I haven't given that much thought, Lilly. I suppose I'll stay." He waited for her to argue, to protest.

"Yes, I suppose you will."

He went back to watching the boats. A little one darted between two yachts and shot into the center, where spray from one of the fountains drenched it. It turned hard in the rough water and managed to break free of the fountain's reach.

Well, if Lilly wasn't going to attempt to make him leave the Lazaretto, there was no reason to go. If he did, he'd most likely annoy her more than anything. And if he were going to be alone, the Lazaretto was as good a place as any.

Out of the corner of his eye, Lepov caught sight of a woman in an Army uniform crossing the lobby. It wasn't Sun, though there was some resemblance. That was the trouble with memory. One could always find a way to blend memories, until you couldn't trust them anymore. During his short-lived marriage, Lepov had begun to notice how many women reminded him of his wife. But once she was gone, and he was able to get over the fact that she was, few women resembled his wife. Happiness wreaked havoc with memory just as much as bitterness.

The Sun look-a-like only matched her general size and shape. The hair was as short, but lighter—might even have had a tinge of red. Mostly Lepov noticed the woman did not walk like Sun; she had a more masculine walk, as if stalking prey. Sun had always looked more like someone who was being hunted, not the other way around.

The woman, with a companion, disappeared into an elevator.

Lilly watched him; had seen him eyeing the woman in uniform.

"That wasn't Sun," Lepov said.

"I know. Maybe I should go back to my hotel. You could come see me once you find her."

"I'd rather you waited a while longer, I don't like sitting here alone." That wasn't much excuse for her to stay but he wasn't feeling the desire to be clever. He didn't want her to go and she knew it.

"Okay, I'll wait with you."

When the call came through, it wasn't what Lepov had been expecting. Menya Russell had alarming news.

"Lepov, MacNally wanted me to call. We didn't find Chitti Sienté. We found her PDT, but it was Sun Uijong's body, not the Sienté woman's."

"What do you mean it was Sun's body?" Lepov nearly shouted into the phone. "*What* was Sun's body?"

"Oh, sorry. We found a woman at Yarmin's apartment. It's hard to explain, but Sun Uijong is dead. Well, the MedTechs are in with her now, but I don't think she's alive."

"What are you talking about?"

"I don't know what happened yet. And frankly, if you were here, you wouldn't know either. This will take time to figure out. But the reason I'm calling is that you're not looking for Sun Uijong anymore. You're looking—"

"—for Chitti Sienté." Lepov looked around the lobby as he tried to order his thoughts. Sun was dead? How had that happened? "Give me a description of Sienté."

"Thin build, short, with short red hair." Russell paused. "I can get you specifics in a minute."

"Not now." Lepov looked toward the front desk.

Lilly put out her hand and tried to get Lepov's attention, but he brushed her away, dashing across the lobby.

"Hey!" he smacked the front desk's countertop. "You, come here!"

A man in a silver vest looked up from the far end of the counter. He stopped fiddling with a deskscreen when he heard Lepov's tone.

"May I help you?" he asked measuredly.

"I want the PDT signatures of everyone coming into the hotel in the last ten minutes."

"Sir, I hardly doubt—"

Lepov was way ahead. He had expected the man to protest and there was no time. He side-slipped the end of the counter to jump a short swinging door. The man tried to stop him but Lepov pushed him over as if he were made of collapsible plastic.

At the deskscreen, Lepov made several attempts to find the list he needed. He put his finger on the list and pulled it through the names until he stopped on one in particular. *Sun Uijong*. She had entered four minutes ago.

It had been *her*. The woman in uniform was Chitti Sienté. Surely she wasn't going back to the same room. She must have been the one that was in the closet. By now, she would have a different room. Pulling up more records, he tried to find her new room; *Uijong* was not on the list, and no *Sienté*. There were too many guests. He'd have to search through eight hundred names. But not if he got lucky, and for once, luck held out. *Morvees*. The use of that name took some nerve. Despite having to change rooms, she must have been feeling cocky.

The room was a floor below the first room: 1103. Lepov ran over the concierge as he tried to stand up again.

The elevator felt much too slow but it was faster than trying to sprint up eleven flights of stairs. Halfway there, he realized he'd rushed off without telling Lilly what was going on. She'd have to get the details later.

Sun dead? There had to be a catch. Russell had to be wrong.

The elevator doors split and Lepov stormed into the hall. He had no plan. He wouldn't wait for the security team. He wanted to finish this. Since that first day Branithwaite had come into his office, he'd had more grief than he could take. Now, the woman who had tried to kill him, the woman who had killed Sun, and the woman he'd mistaken for Lilly was within his reach. He wasn't going to stop until she was dead or locked in prison.

Approaching the door, he heard a man yell. Someone was angry, and in a lot of pain. Lepov didn't bother with the lock. He simply rammed the full weight of his body against the door. It nearly snapped in half as it broke inward. Lepov stumbled into the suite.

The same young man he'd seen in the lobby stood in the bedroom doorway. His shirt was off, and he held a hand to his face. He saw Lepov and started shouting.

"That lunatic bit me!" He pulled the hand away from his face to prove his point. Blood spilled from a gash in his cheek.

Lepov scanned the room but didn't see Chitti. He squared his shoulders on the boy and asked "Where'd she go?"

"In there," he pointed into the bedroom. "Who are you?"

Lepov pushed the kid aside. The young man grabbed his shoulder.

"I said who are you? Her father or something?"

Lepov didn't have time to argue. From his coat pocket, he jerked out the shockhammer, swung backhanded and punched the boy in his stomach. The shockhammer's distinctive bass chord rang out as the boy shot backwards onto the floor.

Lepov stood in the doorway and looked around the bedroom. He had just decided Chitti must be in the bathroom when she ran at him from the closet. She was silent, like a darting, red-haired panther. Lepov caught a glint from the Para-Lazer in her hand and fell back, rolling to one side as she fired, its blue laser just missing his legs. Scrambling away, he became entangled with the boy's body.

Sienté made no noise except her heavy breathing. Her pupils were dilated and Lepov saw blood on her lips. The Para-Lazer had a few shots left before recharge. She hesitated. She wasn't sure if she had hit him.

Lepov didn't wait. He grabbed a small side table and pulled himself off the floor, regained his feet, and slung the table back in her direction. He knew it wouldn't hit her, but it would keep her off balance. He grabbed anything he could throw. A lamp came next. He hurled it and kept moving. She dodged, raising the Para-Lazer for a second shot. He yanked a buffet table from the wall, knocking it over, and diving behind it as the shot surged through the wood. Lepov smelled smoke and burnt wood.

Lepov had had enough. If she hit him, she'd have to make sure she hit him dead on. The damn thing was already low on power, and its last shot wouldn't completely stop him. He only needed a few seconds.

For the first time, Chitti cried out. Lepov grabbed the buffet and launched himself from behind it. Only, Chitti wasn't where he expected. Instead, Lilly was standing there, the broken lamp in her hand. She must have tried to hit Chitti. But Chitti was still standing, backing away from both of them.

"Get down, Lilly!" Lepov ordered, hoping to gain Chitti's attention, and succeeding. The wild-eyed red head swung her arm and fired. Lepov felt the surge hit him in the shoulder and ram him backwards. He slammed against a wall and heard it crack. Bits of glass rained down as he realized he hadn't slammed into a wall but had hit a window. Off balance, he slid down the cracked glass. Once on the floor, he rolled to one side even as the window gave way and dropped to the atrium dome below.

Lepov felt cold air. With the window gone, his shoulder no longer had anything against which to rest, and one shoulder, arm and everything, from the neck up, tried to drop off the edge with the falling glass.

Lilly screamed his name.

Opening his eyes, Lepov saw the atrium dome as the broken panes sliced into it. A sparkling explosion filled his view. He could see the little boats zipping back and forth as broken glass fell into the mock sea.

100

The Liar had to deal with the woman first. She was coming toward her with a broken lamp in hand. The Para-Lazer was dead. But the Liar wasn't helpless. She just had to get the man's shockhammer. He was down, nearly out the window, and not going anywhere. The Para-Lazer hadn't been enough to paralyze him, but it had been enough to shut him down momentarily.

Dropping her weapon on the broken glass, she bent down and tore the shockhammer from his hand. It was a heavy weapon, and useless except in close combat. She advanced toward the white-haired woman, eye on the lamp.

The fight was over almost before it started. The woman swung the already-damaged lamp and it crumbled in her hands. The Liar stepped in and swung the shockhammer in a high/low arc that struck the woman's head. The boom of the blow told the Liar there was plenty of charge left in the shockhammer. The woman with the white pony-tail dropped soundlessly to the floor.

It was sad to see her young man lying on the floor. He would have been fun. But his violent reaction to her had been irritating. She would have had to finish him off far too soon. A shame.

But now she had to deal with the man at the window. He was vaguely familiar, but she couldn't be sure where she'd seen him before. Whoever he was, he had ruined everything. He must have been the one who had come in the room earlier in the day. He was no cop. But he was up to no good, all the same.

The Liar was angry with him. The man had no right to interfere. Whoever he was, he had to be punished. It was only right.

And it did not escape her notice that he was lying on broken glass. Great shards of glass lay all around him. She liked that. It was poetic.

He stirred. The Para-Lazer had been too weak. But what did that matter? He would die, all the same. She knelt beside him, and dropped the shockhammer beside the Para-Lazer. A shard of glass lay across his chest; big enough to fit in her hand. She closed her fingers over it and looked into the man's eyes.

She'd start at his neck. It was the most exposed; his head hung off the floor into the open air. But she wouldn't stop there. She would have to make sure he was dead; the same way she had ensured the Thief was dead.

The man's head snapped up and his hand reached out, the Liar's hand shooting out at the same time. She grabbed the shockhammer before he could and smiled.

"No, no. This one's mine now," she purred.

"You can have it," he said with his own odd smile. "You've got the wrong one."

The Liar swung the shockhammer with all her rage.

101

Lepov pulled the trigger on the Para-Lazer and prayed he'd guessed right. There had to be just enough juice left to knock this crazy hellion down. If not, he had no way to stop her.

A jolt of blue energy hit her below the arm. It raised her off her knee even as she continued to swing. Her momentum tipped her forward and she hammered down on thin air centimeters from his head. There was nothing to stop her from pitching forward. She scraped at Lepov with the glass still in her hand. He felt it rake his shoulder as she fell.

Lepov rolled, and inched his way back from the edge. He didn't need to look. He knew what had happened. Eleven floors below them, Chitti Sienté had fallen through what was left of the glass atrium dome. And in a small mock sea, boats and larger yachts made random passes through a harbor momentarily disturbed by a falling sky and a body that would come to rest on the bottom of that sea.

102

The hum of an air system was the only sound Lepov could hear. He sat in a small uncomfortable chair, his legs stretched in front of him. The room was lit by one small lamp on a corner table. A bed stood in the middle of the room. A woman lay in the bed with hoses connected to her throat and her nose. Several smaller ones were attached to her arm. The only movement Lepov observed was her chest rising and falling each time she took in a long, slow breath.

He'd been there all night. He'd taken off his jacket. His shoulder hurt, the repair would take a week to heal. Until then it would feel like someone was stepping on him. All of that was minor when he considered the woman in the bed. She had a long way to go.

He still felt a chill from the Para-Lazer shot. He couldn't believe he'd been hit. During all his years as a cop he'd never been hit by one. Yet here he was, not even in the Lazaretto one year, and nearly shot from an eleventh-floor window by a psychotic little girl with a nearly depleted Para-Lazer.

Well, at least he'd won that argument.

A door opened slowly, and a short man with a neat beard came into the room.

"Dr. Duvalls, good morning." Lepov stood up, speaking softly.

"Good morning, Mr. Lepov." The doctor spoke with a French accent and made no effort to speak quietly. "I think you'll be happy to know why I'm here. We feel it is safe to remove the artificial respiration today. She won't be needing them anymore."

A nurse had followed him and she turned on overhead lights. Lepov closed his eyes until he could adjust to the bright lights.

He watched as they gently untaped and removed the tubes. The woman showed no sign she was aware of the activity.

"Will she wake soon?" Lepov frowned, impatient.

"I think so." Dr. Duvalls nodded, studying his patient. "We will have to wait and see. But I am hopeful. You look tired, Mr. Lepov. Isn't it time for your friend to come and relieve you?"

"Any minute, now." Lepov grabbed the jacket lying across the foot of the bed and worked into it.

"The shoulder?" Dr. Duvalls watched as he wrestled with the jacket. "It still hurts a great deal?"

"Not as much, no." Lepov knew it was pointless to lie to a doctor, but couldn't help himself. "I'll be fine."

Lepov stood beside the bed, watching the woman breathe. He rubbed the stubble on his chin, wishing he could ask the Doctor for a guarantee that she would pull through. He was afraid, however, that the Doctor would deny him this one, simple wish. He settled for an easier question. "She's tough, isn't she?"

"Tougher than I thought possible."

"Tough enough, I hope." Pete Landon stepped into the room and nodded at the two men.

"Your relief," the Doctor smiled. "Go home, sleep, and don't worry."

"Hey, we can see her face now," Pete closed on the bed and bent to look at her. "She looks better every day."

"I wish I could say the same about me," Lepov dead-panned. "But the doc here would only fix my shoulder. He wouldn't do anything with my face."

"I wouldn't let him." This comment came from out in the hall.

Lepov turned to see Lilly near the door. She was still bruised where the shockhammer had slammed into her temple. But beyond that, she appeared to be fine. Lepov put out a hand and touched the covers at the foot of the woman's bed.

"Pete's here to watch over you now, Sun. If ever you were gonna wake up, do it while he's here. He's a lot better sight to behold than I am. And he's been spending more time watching over you than the rest of us combined."

"Be sure he rests," Dr. Duvalls said to Lilly. She nodded, assuring him she would.

"So," Lepov followed Lilly down the hall, "you wouldn't let him work on my face, huh? That's sweet of you. Unexpected, but sweet."

"You're assuming I meant he couldn't improve it. I only meant it would have cost too much money. It would have been an extensive procedure."

"Now that," Lepov said, "I expected. Where are we going now, off to bed?"

"You're going off to your bed. I'm staying far away from it."

"Yeah, I expected that too."

103

She wasn't sure what she was seeing. The walls were cream, but that couldn't be right. They should have been crimson. No, that was wrong too. The blood had been gone a long time. That had been a long time ago.

She'd heard people talking. That man again, the one in the hat, the man who'd pestered her so mercilessly in the little bloody room.

He had been there. So had a smaller man with a French accent. And there had been others. Sometimes one at a time, at other times three and four voices crowded into the room.

The man with the hat had been there many times. But another had been there far more, always sitting in a chair in one of the corners, never saying anything.

He was doing it right then. Alone. She could see him with one leg crossed over the other, his head bowed. He was working on something in his hands.

She wanted to thank him for his faithfulness. She knew he'd been the most faithful watcher. She only wished she knew his name. She should have known it, but it eluded her. She wanted to ask him, but she could not find her voice. She had to be patient and wait until she could think of it.

When it came, she realized that his great head of hair should have been a clue. She was afraid to speak his name aloud, not certain she had the correct one.

Peter Landon.

"Peter."

He sat up straight.

"Sun?"

"Peter." She said it again. She liked the sound.

"I'll get the doctor," he jumped to his feet.

"No," she whispered, "wait."

"Take it easy now, you've been through a lot."

"I'm hungry," she said.

"Okay, we'll get you something. I'll go get someone."

"Wait." It hurt to speak—made her dizzy. "How long?"

He nodded. "Three days."

"But my report?" The remark made no sense; she was urgently worried about her job. She knew it was absurd, but had to ask.

"I sort of broke into your files. There was only a little bit left to finish. I've finished it for you. I hope you don't mind. It's why I had to miss most of your first day after... I was at your office."

Sun felt a wave of panic and she physically tried to push it away. Pete took her hands and tried to calm her down.

"You're okay."

"No, wait. They need to know. Chitti—" she had to tell them. They had to know.

"We know," Pete nodded as he spoke, "we know all about her."

Sun felt the panic subside. They knew. It was good to hear. She couldn't think why it mattered. In truth, she couldn't remember what it was they should know about Chitti.

"I'm tired," she admitted, "and my arm hurts. What happened?"

Pete hesitated before answering. "You don't remember?"

"I'm trying...why?"

"Well," Pete realized that he was still holding her hand. He set it carefully on the bed and backed away, "It's a good thing you can't remember. For now, take my advice and try not to change that. Over time, you'll remember far more than you'll want."

She nodded. Not knowing what had happened was unsettling, but Pete Landon's solid presence helped.

"Now, let me get a nurse to bring you something to eat."

"Thank you," Sun whispered. She closed her eyes and felt as if she might fall asleep. She should have asked about Gregor Lepov.

104

The morning had started with rare sunshine—a tiny break in the clouds; an auspicious beginning. Lepov showered, doing his best not to irritate the shoulder repair. He toweled off, dressed, and felt good enough to walk to his office.

By the time he entered his building and climbed the stairs, the sunshine had gone. At his office windows, he watched people on the street scurry for cover as thunder rattled the panes. Yes, sunshine did make it down into this crazy world every once in a while, but never for long. The rain always returned with a vengeance.

He had made coffee and settled into his desk chair moments before a tap at his door. She was on time.

"Come in," he said.

The door opened and Sandella Sahdjec entered, carrying a small bundle in her hands. Her face lit with a smile.

"Good morning, Mr. Lepov." She shuffled into the room. He waited patiently while she sat. She set the bundle on his desk.

"I made coffee."

"I'd like that," she said. She drew a deep breath and added, "I can smell it."

He poured a cup and replaced the decanter, then leaned against a corner of the desk and raised his eyebrows. "Well, I'm not exactly open for business today. But I got your message and I have to admit I'm a little curious what it means."

"I appreciate you seeing me, Mr. Lepov. I suppose it could have waited, but I'm getting old, and time is not on my side anymore."

Lepov nodded. Though not as old, he already had an idea of how right she was. He had once imagined that all the time in the world was his to exploit. He had also once believed in Santa Claus.

"I've been thinking about that day you came to see me," Miss Sahdjec paused, "are you still interested in the apartment?"

"My investigation is finished, Miss Sahdjec. There's no need for you to worry anymore."

"I'm glad to hear that. And I wish you were right. But—" she stopped and took a deep breath. He could tell something was bothering her. "I didn't think it would be this hard, you know? I've wanted this a long time, but I never knew how to go about it. When you came the other day, I finally saw a way to make it happen."

Lepov said nothing. This was something she was working through on her own and it was best to let her talk.

"Mr. Lepov, I would like to give you something. That little stack of paper there on your desk," she pointed to the bundle, "I'm giving that to you. I know paper is old fashioned, but I didn't want to use a desksystem to write it down. It's too personal for that."

"What is it?" he asked, turning to look at the bundle without picking it up.

"You should know that I lied to you the other day when you asked me about Chettleham Keep. I don't like to lie. Not any more. It's time I stopped lying and started telling the truth. And I think you're the man I can trust with the truth."

"And this is the truth?" He picked up the little bundle.

"Yes, Mr. Lepov. Be careful with it. There's someone who will be greatly affected by what I've written down; someone who is important to both of us. I suppose I should have destroyed it, but you'll have to excuse an old woman's superstitions. Over the years I've come to believe in something greater than life, something that demands more from us than just the least we can do."

"You're talking about God?"

"Yes, Mr. Lepov. I don't suppose you can understand how someone can find God in this rotten world. There was a time I wouldn't have believed such a thing possible."

"And He wants the truth to be told, is that it?"

"Maybe He does, Mr. Lepov. Or at the very least, he wants me to tell the truth. It doesn't matter how many people hear it. You'll be enough, if that's what you decide."

"You intrigue me, Miss Sahdjec. If I didn't know better, I'd say you were acting like someone with a guilty conscience. That hardly seems necessary in your case."

She only nodded in response. It took her a moment, but she finally pushed herself out of the chair and stood facing Lepov. She wanted to say more, but never did. She nodded one last time and left.

Lepov was still leaning on the corner of his desk, the bundle of papers in his hand. They were bound with black ribbon. He pulled on a loose end of ribbon and the knot came undone. The papers were folded twice over. He smoothed them out.

Moving to the sofa against the wall, he sat. The script on the page was hand-written; a flowing script with graceful curves and soft angles. Lepov had meant to pour a cup of coffee but he soon forgot the coffee as he read Sandella Sahdjec's story:

By the time I had heard of the Lost Platoon, everyone had heard of them. Of course, it was no surprise I was one of the last. I wasn't anybody important. I wasn't even unimportant. To those around me, I didn't exist. I was, more or less, an appliance. I had a job to do and I did it. That was all that mattered. What I thought, what I believed, who I was; these things had no meaning. Not to my employer. He only cared about what I did. He only cared that I nurse his child, my sole purpose to care for the girl. And to the best of my abilities, that is what I did...

105

MacNally arrived in front of Chettleham Keep and saw Lepov standing at the rim of the open pit that had once been the Roth Building. It was raining and MacNally pulled his hat down and cinched the belt on his coat after getting out of his car. Lepov better have a damned good reason for wanting to meet him like this.

"We couldn't meet at your office?" MacNally shouted once they were within earshot. Lepov stood gazing into the pit. MacNally joined him.

"I'm about to meet Lilly in Alpha Lounge. The grace period has almost closed. Raley's paying her fee to get her in, before she gets stuck again."

"So what are we doing here?"

"I wanted to know what you were gonna do about that body you found." Lepov looked over at MacNally. Rain collected on the brim of his hat and dribbled down his shoulder.

"I'll keep looking for an answer. I'm close. The best guess I have is that Zoltis killed the Pan Juarez double. According to Pete, one of the only Lost Platoon members missing is a guy by the name of Fortunado. Why do you care?"

"Why do *you*?" Lepov asked in return. "Why not just let it go?"

MacNally had a feeling this was far more than simple curiosity for Lepov. Something had changed.

"Well, I'm a cop. I'm suppose to uphold the law. I like to see people pay for their crimes."

"That doesn't make sense, Mac. If you think Zoltis or Morvees did it, they can't pay for their crimes anymore."

"That's true." MacNally had a different explanation, but he was hesitant to tell Lepov. "Look, I know you and Lilly are still close friends. And she's working for Raley."

"You think Raley did it?" Lepov looked surprised.

"To be honest, no. But I keep hoping I can find that he was involved in some way. He was as dirty as Reno and Zoltis. I just haven't been able to get anything that will pin him to my wall. Maybe I'm a romantic, but I'd like to think I'll get him one day."

"This isn't the way to do that," Lepov said.

"Okay, I'll ask you again. Why do you care?"

"Can I have a cigarette?"

"Lilly won't let you smoke."

Lepov stared at him until MacNally finally fished out a cigarette. Lepov stuck it in his mouth and MacNally leaned in to light it. Lepov had to shield the flame with both hands.

"I'll tell you why I care," Lepov said, the cigarette still in his mouth. He withdrew a folded stack of papers from inside his coat. With the cigarette, he patiently lit one end of the papers. After a few attempts, the edges began to burn. Smoke curled up through folds and roiled out the top. "This is an eye-witness account of what happened in that apartment thirty years ago. Your murderer's name is in here. As well as who put the body in the tunnel walls." The flames began to lick higher up on the paper, and Lepov turned it sideways to keep his fingers from burning.

MacNally watched the paper burn; made no attempt to stop it.

"You'll have to take my word for it, Raley's got nothing to do with it. And furthermore, you'll have to believe me when I tell you it doesn't matter who killed Fortunado." The paper was almost completely engulfed now. Lepov let it drop to the ground where it sizzled on the wet pavement but continued to blacken the handwritten pages.

"It was Fortunado then?"

"Yes, it was."

"How did he get the ring? And whose was it?" MacNally wasn't going to press Lepov for the killer's name, but details like the ring would bother him for a long time.

"I don't know, there was no mention of the ring. Maybe he won Morvees' ring in a poker game. Maybe he bought MacDenny's or stole Yarmin's. None of those guys had their rings."

"And none of them lived to tell the tale." MacNally looked at the eye-witness account. It was nothing more than black flakes now. "I guess I'll also never find out how the body ended up in Magtite."

"Do you care?"

"No. Russell will. But he'll get over it. You know, I was never gonna get enough evidence to pin this on Raley anyway. It takes a lot of evidence to bring down someone like him. The kind of evidence I'm too lazy to go get."

"So you'll let it go?"

"Are you ever gonna tell me who wrote that confession?"

"You wouldn't know the name." Lepov pulled the cigarette from his mouth and flicked it into the open pit.

"You're an ass, Lepov."

"You gonna let the name of a murderer come between us?"

"I don't care who killed this guy. Good Lord, that was thirty years ago. But I hate to see you waste one of my cigarettes like that."

"I gotta go." Lepov began to walk away.

"Lepov," MacNally called after him, "you're an idiot if you let her leave without you again. You know that, right? A genuine idiot."

"Sure I know it," Lepov turned and looked back as he spoke. "Don't try to tell me you never thought I was an idiot."

"That's a good point, Lepov. A damned good point."

He watched Lepov cross the street and head back in the direction of Alpha Quadrant. If he had the authority, he'd have kicked Lepov out of the Lazaretto and forced him to go with Lilly. But some people never knew what was best for them. MacNally had to admit that he sure didn't. In fact, it was becoming more and more clear every day that there was little he did know. And that included who had killed the rotten little corpse that had been dug out of the basement of the Lazaretto.

As far as MacNally knew, he'd only been right about one thing: it had been one helluva week in the Lazaretto.

106

As soon as Kjarsta Zoltis left, I heard the back room's lock click open. I was still in the front room, and too far away from Calla to protect her. I panicked and rushed down the hallway. I saw the door opening as I hurried into Calla's room and tried to slam it shut. I was too late. Fortunado blocked it before I could get it completely closed.

"Stay away!" I shouted at him.

"Calm down, lady. I'm not gonna hurt the girl." He was panting on the other side of the door, I was bigger, but he was stronger. He was inching the door open.

"What do you want?"

"To talk to you."

"About what?" As if I didn't know.

"I want to know what the girl was sick with." He had the door open enough to lean into the room. I gave up trying to stop him and backed up to the bed. He did not come into the room.

"What do you need to know that for?" His question terrified me.

351

"What was she sick with?" he asked again.

"I won't tell you. Why do you need to know?"

"Because Kjarsta Zoltis is a greedy bastard who has to learn he can't treat men like this. I won't let him. He asks too much and gives too little. It's time he learned I can make him pay in other ways."

"By doing what?" I asked.

"I'm going to turn the girl over to the IHS. I don't need the details if you refuse to tell me. They'll check her out and find out. Then Kjarsta Zoltis will know that he's not untouchable."

"Don't you get it?" I pleaded with him. "Don't you see how he is? He doesn't care about the girl. He doesn't care what happens to her!"

"That's too bad, isn't it?" Fortunado looked over at Calla. "But I think he's bluffing. I think he cares a great deal."

Fortunado backed into the hallway. I was stunned. How could this have happened? After everything I had done to save Calla? Was she to be doomed to a life of exile because of two proud men locked in a test of wills?

I rushed into the hall and saw Fortunado opening the door to the back room. He turned warily toward me. I didn't wait for him to speak, I didn't wait for him to slip into the room and lock the door. I ran straight at him.

At the last moment he raised his hand to ward off my attack. It was indeed an attack, though I was just as surprised as he. I grabbed him by his shirt and shoved him into the room. He must have been as shocked as I was because he did not fight back. Instead, he stumbled backwards toward what appeared to be a door sticking up sideways from the floor in the corner of the room. The door was held in place by a rope that ran through a pulley with a counterweight at its end. The counterweight was similar in size and shape to a large loaf of bread.

I can describe all of this now, though I hardly saw much of this at the time. I only knew that he was falling back toward a hole in the floor and I saw that he was attempting to escape my attack. I couldn't let him get away. He was going to tell them about Calla. He was going to ruin everything we had done to save her. I would not let him do it.

He made a dash for the steps, but I caught him before he ducked down into the hole. I had him by his hair and yanked him back. He began swinging at me but I had him from behind and he was unable to reach me. I shoved him against the open door. It began to fall shut but the counterweight pulled it back open. I saw the counterweight swinging there above his head and I grabbed it.

I wish I could say that I did not know what I was doing. I wish I could say that I could only see the angelic face of Calla. But that would not be the truth, and I want to tell the truth. I am not looking to justify what I have done. But I still wish I could say I didn't know what I was doing.

He should have been able to stop me. He was, after all, stronger. But I was a mother bear fighting for her cub. I was enraged at the man who was threatening my girl. It is the only explanation I can think of; the only reason

I was able to do it.

The details of his death are not important. Allow me this mercy. I have relived my sin too many times to count. Suffice to say, I was able to swing the counterweight around and choke him with the rope.

It was not an easy murder.

There is little left of my story after that. Mr. Zoltis came back after his man Morvees found Fortunado. I confessed what I had done. Mr. Zoltis did not appear to care. It seems he had just discovered that Pan Juarez was not coming as they had expected. He had disappeared with the diamonds, just as historians have believed.

Morvees buried Fortunado in the tunnel.

I was able to do one last thing for the child. I begged Mr. Zoltis to send her out of the Lazaretto, and he did. She took Fortunado's place in the quadrant, and left a week later. Mr. Zoltis allowed it under one condition; I was to stay behind, and never see her again.

I used to think it was because he was envious of what I had done; what he should have done. I don't know. He might have done it simply because he could; to show he was in control. I know now that I had to stay—to pay my debt. After thirty years in the Lazaretto, my debt is paid in full.

The girl made it safely out of quarantine. She boarded a shuttle under the name of Pan Juarez but discarded it as soon as she landed on her new home planet. There, as arranged by Mr. Zoltis, she was taken in by a family who raised her with a great deal of love; far more than Kjarsta Zoltis could have ever given her. Not more than I could have, but it was sufficient.

They did not call her Calla. I never knew what name she was raised with, until one night shortly before Kjarsta Zoltis died. I was one of the nurses caring for him, and he finally admitted to me that he had kept an eye on her. I was surprised to hear it. I was under the impression that he had never given her another thought.

He said her name was Lilly Stewart, and that she frequently came to the Lazaretto for business reasons.

Since that time, I have found out a thing or two about her. I have a few contacts left over from when I worked for Kjarsta Zoltis. I am aware that Lilly Stewart is a friend of yours, Mr. Lepov. And I know that you will make the right choice as to what should be done with my story.

Epilogue

Lilly was waiting for him at a table in the Alpha Entry Lounge. The lounge was nearly empty. A man in an outdated suit sat at a corner table with four empty glasses in front of him. He was drunk. If Lepov had to guess, he would have said the man had gambled away his grace period money.

"I was beginning to think you wouldn't come." Lilly rose and pulled him into her arms.

"Aren't you afraid I'll give you a disease or something?" He pulled back and eyed her suspiciously.

"I'm willing to take the chance. You look like you need some attention." She pushed him down onto a chair and chose a chair close to his. "Are you still worrying about us?"

"No," he shook his head. She was wearing a white sweater with a knee length skirt. A long white coat lay across the back of the chair on the other side of the table. "I was just taking care of some business with MacNally. But that's over now."

"Are you sure that's all? You don't look well. Is it Sun?"

"No. And you were gonna stop asking about her. We decided to be friends and that's it. You're the one who said you could detect a mutual attraction between Sun and Pete Landon. You're just looking for a fight. That's not the only thing we know how to do, you know."

"I'm not looking for a fight, Gregor. I'm trying to make sure you're going to be okay when I walk through that gate."

"Don't worry about me, okay?" He tried to smile, but he was sure she could see through it.

If he were honest with himself, which he never was, Lepov would have had to admit he was worried about Lilly. She was doing her best to be cheerful, but he could see she was upset.

Was she right? Were they truly better off staying away from each other? That question had been bothering him since she'd put it in his mind. If she were right, then he wasn't an idiot for letting her leave without him. MacNally was wrong. But if she were wrong, and his life would be better with Lilly, then MacNally would be absolutely right. He would have to been a complete idiot to let her go.

But maybe, just maybe, they were both right. After all, wasn't it possible that they weren't good for each other, and that they were destined to cause each other trouble for the rest of their lives and despite all of that they'd never be happy unless they were together? If that were the case, then yes, she'd be right, and so would MacNally.

Lepov had decided not to tell Lilly about her real father. There was no reason for her to discover that her father was a heartless criminal who cared nothing for her. Or that a woman she would never remember had sacrificed her life so that Lilly might escape the Lazaretto for a life of freedom. The same was true for MacNally. It didn't matter that he wanted to know who killed the little weasel Fortunado. Nobody had to know. There was enough going on in the Lazaretto that made looking into the past a fruitless gesture. And in the end, why should an old woman be punished for a rash, violent act of love that had taken place thirty years in the past?

"Gregor?" Lilly touched his hand. "I'm going to have to go."

"Yes, you are. This is no place for a lady." He stood up and took her by the hand.

"I wish you'd come with me. I don't like being alone anymore."

"I thought you were the strong independent type." He walked her toward the entrance gate.

"I am, but it doesn't mean I like being alone." She approached the gate counter and smiled at an attendant in a blue blazer. "My name is Lilly Stewart."

"One moment, Miss Stewart." The attendant pulled up the list on his screen. "Yes, I have you right here."

"Well, this is gonna happen too fast, I guess." Lilly's troubled smile only made her that much more beautiful.

"Hold it a minute, will you?" Lepov pulled her close and kissed her. She let him, and briefly, they were no longer in the middle of a world that shunned physical contact. They were someplace where affection was a thing to bring comfort and not to be feared.

"Gregor," she pulled away and he saw tears in her eyes. "Don't."

He brushed gently at a tear that rolled down her cheek.

"Maybe I should stay."

He shook his head. "This place is no good for you."

"Who are we to say what's good for either one of us?"

A metallic screech broke their concentration. The man behind the desk unfastened a clasp on the quadrant gates.

"I'll have to close the doors, ma'am," he said softly.

"Don't act like you can't ever come back." Lepov took her by the shoulders. He wanted to pull her back. To keep her away from those gates. But if a woman had been able to set Calla Zoltis free in exchange for a self-imposed exile, there was no reason to believe Lepov couldn't do it as well. He gently pushed her into Alpha quadrant. "Get out of here."

"No," she pushed against him. "I'm staying. You aren't getting rid of me this time."

"You aren't staying." Lepov knew he would have to be quick. He grabbed the clerk by his sleeve. "How fast can you get me a ticket on this train?"

"Excuse me?" The man jerked his arm away, alarmed by the physical contact and confused by the question.

"Gregor, don't."

"Oh hell, Lilly, Raley's paying for you, he might as well pay for me. Remember Raley's finder's fee I snagged for locating his paintings? It ought to about cover my ticket."

Lilly stood by as Lepov handed his PDT to the clerk.

"You know," Lepov caught her eye as he put the PDT into an inner pocket, "you don't have to look so darned cheerful about this.

I'm compromising just to keep you out of this hellhole."

"And I get to hear you complain for forty more days."

"For that, I'm sorry." Lepov put an arm around her waist and led them through the gates.

"I'm not," said Lilly.

The End

About the Author:

Jason Phillip Reeser, having the spent the first half of his life traversing state lines in a nomadic life that covered ground from the snow-covered forests of Michigan to the sun-bleached sands of Florida, now lives and writes in Westlake, Louisiana. His ghost story anthology, *Cities of the Dead,* which Louisiana Poet Laureate Julie Kane called "a twist of Louisiana Gothic," is set in the cemeteries of New Orleans. he recently published *Room With Paris View*, a travel memoir with his wife, poet Jennifer Reeser. He is currently writing the third book in his *Lazaretto* trilogy. His short stories have appeared in such publications as *The Louisiana Review*, *Bewildering Stories*, and *Danse Macabre*. If you would like to contact him, send email to editor@rocketfirebooks.com. He welcomes comments and questions of any kind.

Visit his FaceBook page at:
FaceBook.com/Jason-Phillip-Reeser
Jason's blog, *Room With No View*, can be read at:
roomwithnoview.blogspot.com

Rocket Fire Books is a small publishing company. If you enjoyed this book, we would appreciate your willingness to mention it to friends who might also enjoy it. If you are active online, at sites like Facebook, Goodreads, Amazon, Shelfari, or similar sites, we ask that you remember us when reviewing and recommending titles. Look for us at rocketfirebooks.com, as well as our Facebook page:

Facebook.com/TheLazaretto.
Thank you in advance for your kindness.
RFB

**In New Orleans, Louisiana,
the dead refuse to be buried.**

Turn the page for news on current and forthcoming
books from Rocket Fire Books.

Look for Book One in The Lazaretto Trilogy

Rocket Fire Books Proudly Presents:
Jason Phillip Reeser's
The Lazaretto

The Lazaretto: A central quarantine system built in response to the rampant interplanetary epidemics that once ravaged the colony worlds of the Euxine System. Its simple design is centered on one premise: survive the forty day quarantine without contracting an infectious disease. If you are lucky, you will be free to leave the quarantine moon, otherwise, you will not be allowed to leave the Lazaretto. Ever. Gregor Lepov arrives to discover just how paranoid and dangerous such a world can be. Hired to find a woman's missing son, he must carefully pick his way through a depressing healthcare system populated with dubious government bureaucrats and overzealous cops even as it becomes evident that there is a violent killer loose in the city.

Available at online bookstores and eBook retailers.

Ask for it at your local bookseller.

Non-Fiction from Jason Phillip Reeser and Jennifer Reeser:

Saint James Infirmary Books Presents the travel memoir *Room With Paris View*

"The detail, the curious footfalls of the Reesers are a joy to follow, even when they are regularly lost. There are many confused steps, but none are wasted. You see, this really is a guide book for those who want good ideas, but certainly don't want guiding." – author Richard Bunning

Jason and Jennifer Reeser arrived in Paris on a windy day in April. For the next two weeks, as rain fell every day, they explored the city of Eiffel, Rodin, Picasso, the Louvre, Notre Dame Cathedral, Sacré Cœur, Saint-Sulpice, and Père Lachaise Cemetery. Choosing to steer clear of hotels and canned tours, they rented an apartment on the top floor of a six-floor walk-up. Despite the cold and the rain, despite their lack of traveling experience, they were determined to see all they could of the city that inspired the likes of Vincent Van Gogh, Claude Monet, Charles Baudelaire, Victor Hugo, Oscar Wilde, Emile Zola, and Earnest Hemingway.

For anyone who has ever thought that a trip to Paris would be full of rude waiters, bad food, and insufferable crowds, this will set the record straight.

Full of advice for first-time travelers, literary and historical notes, as well as an entertaining account of their views on art, culture, cuisine, and the people of Paris (both the locals and the tourists), *Room With Paris View* will certainly give the reader a new perspective on the City of Light.

www.ingramcontent.com/pod-product-compliance
Lightning Source LLC
Chambersburg PA
CBHW032132190626
46814CB00005BA/1667